To So Few

Frustration

Books by Cap Parlier:

Anod series
The Phoenix Seduction (1995)
Anod's Seduction (2004) [reprint of The Phoenix Seduction]
Anod's Redemption (2004)

Sacrifice (2000)
The Clarity of Hindsight (2016)

To So Few series
To So Few – In the Beginning (2014)
To So Few – The Prelude (2014)
To So Few – Explosion (2015)
To So Few – The Trial (2016)
To So Few – The Verdict (2017)
To So Few – Frustration (2018)

---

and with **Kevin E. Ready:**
TWA 800 - Accident or Incident? (1998)

Coming soon from Cap Parlier, **To So Few – Defliction**, the sixth book of the series novel of flight and a warrior's life.

These and other great books available from Saint Gaudens Press
Post Office Box 405
Solvang, CA 93463-0405
URL: http://www.SaintGaudensPress.com
Visit Cap Parlier's Web Site at: http://www.Parlier.com

To So Few

Frustration

by
Cap Parlier

SAINT GAUDENS PRESS
Phoenix, Arizona & Santa Barbara, California

Saint Gaudens Press
Post Office Box 405
Solvang, CA 93464-0405

Http://www.SaintGaudensPress.com

Saint Gaudens, Saint Gaudens Press
and the Winged Liberty colophon
are trademarks of Saint Gaudens Press

Print edition ISBN: 978-0-943039-45-9

Library of Congress Catalog Number - 2018907670

Printed in the United States of America

Dedication

—

This volume of the To So Few series
is dedicated all those patriots
who have stood watch at the gates
to keep the barbarians at bay
in defense of freedom.

Acknowledgments

—

Words cannot express my gratitude to John Richard and Peter Gipson for their critical and constructive review of the manuscript. Their care for and interest in this story have made it better in multitudinous ways. Thank you so much for giving so generously of your time.

I would be remiss if I did not convey my sincerest appreciation for the courage of the staff at Saint Gaudens Press for their continuing encouragement and support. They are truly a blessing.

Most importantly, I must publicly thank my wife Jeanne for tolerating my dedication to this story and taking such good care of me. She is a saint.

Prologue

—

Events during the late spring and summer of 1940 radically changed Europe and arguably the world. *Reichskanzler* Adolf Hitler had taken Germany to war when he ordered the *Wehrmacht* – Germany's armed forces – to invade Poland in the pre-dawn hours of Friday, 1.September 1939. In less than a year, the Germans had defeated and occupied Poland, Denmark, Norway, Holland, Belgium and France. With their Italian ally, they controlled Europe from the River Bug in the East to the Atlantic Ocean, as well as much of North Africa.

Great Britain stood alone against the indomitable wave of German aggression. Since Friday, 10.May.1940, with the Battle of France raging, Prime Minister Winston Leonard Spencer Churchill, CH, TD, Member of Parliament for Epping, assumed the charge of King George VI to form a coalition government. In a matter of days, Churchill deftly and quickly formed a coalition unity government led by a small, compact, War Cabinet. He also held the additional positions of First Lord of Treasury and Minister of Defense.

The Miracle of Dunkirk (Operation DYNAMO) concluded on Tuesday, 4.June.1940, and successfully evacuated nearly the entire British Expeditionary Force (BEF) and allied soldiers of the Northern Army – a third of a million men. A month after the fall and subjugation of France, the Germans began their aerial assault on Great Britain in their attempt to establish air superiority over Southern England, as a prerequisite for the apparently inevitable invasion [*Unternehmen Seelöwe* (Operation Sealion)]. The epic aerial combat became known as the Battle of Britain.

All through the battle, the intelligence evidence mounted rapidly that the *Wehrmacht* was preparing for the cross-Channel invasion. The grossly outnumbered Royal Air Force Fighter Command came frighteningly close to collapse until Hitler made a fatal mistake. On Saturday, 7.September.1940, Hitler diverted the attention of the *Luftwaffe* from the domination of Fighter Command and the air superiority objective, to carry out massive reprisal bombing raids on London – the beginning of what would become known as The Blitz. From that point, the condition of Fighter Command would never again be as weak, fragile and tenuous, and the Germans would be denied their necessary air superiority they sought.

From a time before Churchill returned as First Lord of the Admiralty and eventually became Prime Minister, he had carefully nurtured a communications relationship with President of the United States Franklin Delano Roosevelt.

Churchill made several impassioned pleas to Roosevelt for American intervention in an effort to keep France in the fight against Germany. Once France fell, Churchill amended his pleas; by this time, the requests were for U.S. material support to refit the troops rescued from Dunkirk and bolster the Home Forces against the looming German invasion. Roosevelt hesitated with more than a little uncertainty regarding the capability of the British to stop the Germans. At the same troubled time, the President faced a historic decision to stand for an unprecedented third consecutive term as the commander-in-chief. The President was reluctant to commit critical U.S. military assets, if they were at risk of being overrun by the Germans, along with the concomitant at least implied provocation of Germany. Using an obscure surplus weapons provision of a 1920 appropriations act, the U.S. Government walked a fine line to circumvent the restrictions of the Neutrality Act, by declaring arms as surplus. The first shipload of rifles, machine guns, artillery and associated ammunition departed the army docks at Raritan Arsenal, New Jersey, on 13.June.1940, in the cargo holds of SS *Eastern Prince* – the first trickle of what would eventually become a flood of war and sustenance supplies bound for Great Britain. With the plight of the British people, now standing alone against Hitler's aggression and tyranny, the pacifist neutrality of Congress waned swiftly. Congress passed and the President signed into law two massive rearmament bills (19.July.1940 and 9.September.1940). The President and Prime Minister Churchill also concluded a clever barter scheme trading 50 'surplus' World War I vintage destroyers, for the long-term use of British military facilities in Canada, Bermuda, Bahamas and Caribbean. The first transfer began on Friday, 6.September.1940, when eight, fully provisioned warships of U.S. Navy Destroyer Division 67 entered Halifax Harbor, Nova Scotia, Canada. The Royal Navy crews were waiting and ready for the transfer.

By the end of October, the intelligence indicated the Germans had abandoned their invasion plans . . . at least until the following spring. However, The Blitz would continue virtually unabated through the fall, the entire winter and into the spring of the following year.

———

Beyond the political and military leaders, their strategic decisions, and the nation-states and armies in conflict, individual citizens stood to serve a greater purpose, lived their lives as best they could in the circumstances around them, and collectively carried the weight of the conflict. It is through their eyes that history comes alive for future generations.

Pilot Officer Brian Arthur 'Hunter' Drummond, DFC, of Wichita, Kansas, turned 19 years old in April of 1940, three days after the Germans invaded Denmark and Norway. Brian Drummond stood out physically among his brethren, standing 6 feet, 2 inches, with an athletic, 185-pound body, a distinctively chiseled, unblemished face, light brown, wavy hair, blue-gray eyes, and a fair complexion. He looked older than he was. His aerial victories had come with a price. Four aircraft had been shot out from around him; the last one on Friday, 27.September.1940, had nearly killed him and left him on extended recuperative leave.

Charlotte Grace Palmer née Tamerlin had saved Brian's life once, when she risked her own life to pull the unconscious pilot from her farm pond and out from under the tangle of the sinking parachute. King George VI awarded her the George Cross – the highest civilian award for heroic action – at the same ceremony where Brian had received his DFC from the King. Charlotte was a strikingly attractive, 27-year-old, relatively tall woman with porcelain skin, prematurely gray hair, blue-gray eyes, and distinctive features. She was a strong, independent and confident person, who ran the 190-acre, Hampshire, Standing Oak Farm that had been in the Tamerlin family for more than two centuries. Charlotte was also a widow, having lost her Royal Navy lieutenant husband with the sinking of the aircraft carrier HMS *Glorious* the previous June, during the evacuation of Norway. The relationship between Charlotte and Brian beyond his rescue did not start off well. The brash, young, American volunteer, fighter pilot made too many assumptions and moved too fast for Charlotte. For reasons not even they understood, their tenuous relationship began to take root by the time Brian was wounded the last time, and she volunteered to care for him during his recuperation.

Newly promoted Flying Officer Jonathan Andrew Xavier 'Harness' Kensington of Newcastle had been Brian's classmate during their flight training and fortuitously gained assignment to the same squadron, seven weeks after Brian. The two pilots became more than brothers-in-arms. Jonathan cut quite the figure of virile British manhood – curly blond hair, ice blue eyes, and half a foot shorter and 20 pounds lighter than his buddy, but also an accomplished Spitfire pilot. Jonathan was also chosen as one of a few 'line' fighter pilots to fly captured enemy aircraft with the exploitation team at the Royal Aeronautical Establishment, Farnborough.

The fighter squadron to which Brian and Jonathan remained assigned – No.609 (West Riding of Yorkshire) Squadron – had been whittled down in combat to a mere skeleton of what the unit had once been. Numerous pilots had been killed in combat over the past three months, and the surviving Czech and American pilots had been transferred to newly formed units of their countrymen. Fresh replacement pilots from operational training had just begun to arrive.

Brian's benefactor and protector in the Royal Air Force – Air Commodore John Henry Randolph Spencer, CMG, DFC – had been squadron mates with the Great War, American volunteer, fighter and ace Malcolm Bainbridge, who had been Brian's flight instructor since the young man had been 9 years old. John was now 42 years old, of moderate stature – 5 feet 9 inches tall and 155 pounds at his last check – green eyes, and dark brown hair, speckled with gray, now limited to a laurel band just above his ears. He luckily managed to marry the beautiful and out-going Mary Elizabeth Ann Spencer née Armstrong 15 years ago. His commitment, energy and expertise garnered him the promotion and assignment as Chief Controller, No.11 Group, at Uxbridge, the air defenders of Southeast England, who had borne the brunt of the German air assault of the last three months. Although he did not and never would brandish his family connection, John Spencer was also a nephew of Prime Minister Churchill, to whom he had introduced Brian before the war and after the American's arrival in England.

Squadron Leader Lord Jeremy Robert Kenneth 'Mud' Morrison, now commanding officer of No.32 Squadron and the younger brother of the 8th Duke of Cottingstone, had been Brian Drummond's first RAF flight instructor and had become friends.

Trevor Thomas Andersen graduated from Cambridge University with a degree in European history in 1926, and he already had a job. During his college years, he attracted the attention of an influential man, Director of Naval Intelligence Vice Admiral Sir Geoffrey Ian 'Jumper' Pike, KCB, DSC. Trevor's frankly rather ordinary appearance, long-ish light brown hair, blue eyes and medium build attracted little notice. Trevor's fluency in French, German and Polish, along with the unusual ability to quickly switch to one of several dialects, made him nearly ideal for intelligence fieldwork. After several apprenticeship missions, Trevor was given a code name – Diamond. He also picked up several alias persona, including that of Robert Henry Stone Johnston, a leather goods salesman. After the formation of the Special Operations Executive (SOE) – tasked by Churchill to set German-occupied Europe ablaze – Andersen transferred from the Admiralty to the SOE.

And so, here begins our story.

—

Chapter 1

Genius, all over the world, stands hand in hand, and
one shock of recognition runs the whole circle round.

- Herman Melville

Sunday, 3.November.1940
Headquarters, No.11 Group
Uxbridge, Middlesex, England
United Kingdom
02:15 hours

John Spencer stared into the ink black night sky, as he stood alone on the roof balcony of the commandeered manor house that served as their headquarters building. The effectiveness of the wartime blackout on London and its suburbs never ceased to amaze him. The clear, chilly, night air and the waxing, near quarter moon illuminated the nearby barrage balloons anchored by their retention cables. Not one source of light could be detected—no errant curtain, no headlight suppression slit, not even a candle or match. The wartime blackout was absolute. There were no beams of searchlights stabbing the darkness. There were no muzzle flashes of the anti-aircraft cannons, or bomb explosions. There were no fires. There were no sounds of any sort. The night devoid of the pulsating drone of unsynchronized engines of the German bombers was the most dramatic.

"Where are they?" John said aloud to no one beyond himself.

This is the first night since that fateful night of the 7th of September that no German bombers visited their destruction on Mother England. Thank you, Lord, even if this is but one night's respite.

John heard the roof access door open behind him. Not one sliver of light escaped into the night. He turned toward the sound. The moonlight illuminated the door, but was insufficient to help him identify the intruder.

"I suppose you are wondering the same thing as me," came the distinct New Zealand accented voice of his immediate superior—Air Vice Marshal Keith Rodney Park, MC+Bar, DFC, Air Officer Commander-in-Chief, No.11 Group.

"Indeed sir."

Park stopped next to John. "I cannot imagine they are done with their vile deeds. I suspect they took a break to rest and replenish."

"They have been at it for two months . . . every single night. Why stop now? What are they up to?"

"I have no answers and I suspect we will not know the answers until history examines these events when this dreadful affair is done, quite like that unexplainable halt of the enemy's armor advance on Dunkirk last spring."

The two senior Air Force officers stared into the darkness for several quiet minutes. Neither man moved.

John was the first to speak. "We've not seen them in the daylight since the 29th last month," he stated matter of factly.

"Quite so. On that, I think we have won the daylight. When they shifted their targeting from our aerodromes and fighter assets to the cities, we quickly regained strength and bloodied them quite well. I imagine they saw little benefit for their mounting losses." Park paused, perhaps to consider his words. "I doubt we have comparably won the night, however."

"Will we ever?"

"If you are asking my professional opinion, yes, I think we will. We are still fighting in our sky . . . not theirs. Our night intercept capability is increasing and improving by the day. While we are a long way from mastering the night as we have the daylight hours, the trend lines are positive, especially for the night fighter aeroplanes. I am guardedly optimistic the electronic wizards will solve the gun-laying predictor problem in the not too distant future, but even the manual guns are realizing improvement in their success rate."

"Indeed. I've seen the reports."

"I am certain the Germans feel our mounting strength. They can only ignore our improvement at their peril. I suspect we will have to endure The Blitz, as the newsies are calling it, for some time to come. The next key milestone will be spring weather, when we will see if they wish to renew their invasion attempt."

"I hope not."

Park chuckled softly. "You are not alone, I'm sure. However, as defenders of this precious green isle, we cannot rest on hope."

"I wasn't . . ."

"Don't take it so personally, John." Keith paused, again. "All I was going to say is, we have four to five months at most to be as prepared and strengthened as we can possibly be, if they do decide to renew their invasion effort."

"We will be."

"It is our task and I trust we will be. Now, despite the calm and solitude of our moment, the night chill is approaching my threshold, and I surmise yours as well. It is time to retire."

"Yes sir." They turned together and walked toward the barely visible roof access door. "If I may be so bold, sir, what of your future?"

Park stopped and faced his operations officer. John could see enough to recognize his commander's stern expression.

"I shall answer your query, but this is the last I want to hear of it." Park paused for John's acknowledgment.

"As you wish."

"I believe my time at this post is finite . . . always was, always will be. I have had the honor of leading Eleven Group through what history may record as the greatest air battle of all time. His Majesty's Government, including your uncle, has determined that the time for a change of leadership within the Air Ministry and specifically Fighter Command has arrived. I do not know what my future holds in store for me, but I am fairly certain my time in this command is drawing to a close . . . and sooner rather than later . . . a matter of weeks, I do believe."

"I did not mean to offend, sir."

"No offense, John . . . just a sensitive topic. I shall not confide my opinion on these changes. However, I am and will remain confident Fighter Command and Eleven Group will be in good and capable hands. You have been privy to some of these machinations, so I am certain you can arrive at the proper assessment. Rest assured, I do not think your position is at risk in all this by any measure, however, you well recognize such decisions belong entirely to the new commander whomever that may be."

"Thank you, sir. I am sorry this Big Wing nonsense has been so detrimental."

"It's not nonsense. It is the natural course of military tactical evolution. I had my say. Your days of such debate are still ahead. Learn from this."

"I shall do my best."

"Of that I am certain. Now, let us return to the warmth."

"Yes sir. Thank you for your tolerance."

Park waved his hand dismissively, and then opened the door. No detectable light was observed. John knew the blackout curtain surrounding the platform was there, although he could not see it. Park stepped in and waited for John to join him and close the door before pulling the blackout curtain aside. Fortunately, the dim stairwell light did not hurt their eyes as they adjusted to the light. They descend the stairs. Another day of duty was nearly done.

———

Monday, 4.November.1940
RAF Middle Wallop
Middle Wallop, Hampshire, England
United Kingdom
14:00 hours

Brian presented himself at the appointed time, date and place for his examination and assessment to return to flight duty. In fact, he had been antsy all morning with anticipation. He insisted they leave early. Charlotte handled it all quite well with quiet understanding and surprising empathy. They arrived nearly an hour early, even with a short stop at a small country public house for lunch on their drive up to the fighter base.

"Mister Drummond," the nurse called out.

"Here," Brian answered. He stood, stabilized himself on his crutches, and followed the nurse to the examination room.

"If you would be so kind, Mister Drummond please remove your clothes down to your underwear and be seated on the examination table. The doctor has ordered your cast removed, so he can properly examine your leg. I will take your vital signs first, and then I will remove your leg cast."

Brian did as he was instructed.

The nurse took his temperature, blood pressure, heart rate, and noted her findings in his folder. She retrieved a small cutter from a cabinet drawer. The tool in her expert hands made quick work of the plaster binding on his leg. Soon, the skin of his leg felt the cool air for the first time in five weeks.

Brian wiggled his toes, and then flexed his ankle. No pain . . . a good sign. His muscles were weak, but no pain.

"Please remain still until the doctor examines your leg," the nurse commanded, as she left the room. Several minutes later, she returned with the same doctor from last week.

"Good afternoon, Mister Drummond."

"And, to you, sir."

"I know you are anxious to see how your leg is doing."

"Yes sir."

The doctor first felt all parts of his freed leg and pressed progressively harder on the site of his break. Brian felt the pressure, but no pain. He then manually flexed Brian's ankle to check range of motion, muscle tension and whether Brian experienced any pain. Brian still felt no pain.

"Well, I would say you have healed quite well, Mister Drummond. Let me take one last look at your whole body." The doctor methodically stepped through his examination of Brian from top to bottom, and each of his extremities. "I will pronounce you healed. However, I must caution you that your leg will need exercise to return to full performance. We will trade your crutches for a cane that you can use as necessary to support your leg. I will notify the Air Ministry that you can return to flight duty on Friday the eighth."

"My girlfriend will not be pleased."

"Most are not, from my experience. Good luck, Mister Drummond. I am sure we both would prefer that I do not see you again in this capacity."

"Quite so," Brian responded.

"Very well, then. Have a great day. Make amends with your girlfriend. We will give you a slipper to get you home," he said, nodding to the nurse. She withdrew a one-size-fits-all footwear from another cabinet drawer and handed it to Brian. He adjusted it to his foot. "Be safe. Fly well. Kill Germans."

Brian laughed, partly from relief and partly from anticipation. "Thank you, sir."

The doctor and nurse left the room. Brian dressed. He looked in the wall mirror to make sure everything was in place and took a deep breath. "What am I going to say to Charlotte?" Brian said aloud to himself. He took another deep breath and headed to the lobby.

As he passed through the lobby door, he saw Charlotte's anticipatory face and captured her eyes. She waited. Brian smiled and nodded his head, and then Brian looked at the silly slipper he had on his foot. Eventually, Charlotte smiled back at Brian.

"Are you returned to duty?"

"Yes. The doctor said this coming Friday – the eighth."

"So, you don't need me anymore."

"Charlotte . . . ," Brian protested, but stopped when she held up her hand.

Charlotte walked swiftly to her automobile. Brian moved as quickly as he could behind her, hobbling along on his marginally functional foot. She was in the car with the door closed by the time he reached the vehicle.

"Would you mind if we drive the flight line before we leave?" Brian asked.

"As you wish, my lord and master."

"Charlotte . . . ," again he protested, and again he stopped when she held up her hand. She knew the way.

A new Spitfire squadron and two new Hurricane squadrons returned to their pre-battle flight lines, almost in defiance of the Germans' attacks of the previous four months. He liked the symbolism. Then, as they approached the No.604 Squadron flight line, Brian noticed a new aircraft among the Blenheims with their peculiar antennae and protuberances of the night fighters.

"Would you mind if we stopped to take a look at the new aircraft?" asked Brian.

"No, I would not mind at all," she answered. "I like these machines, too."

Charlotte found a parking spot out of the way. To Brian's surprise, Charlotte got out of the automobile and joined Brian. They walked together to the new aircraft. Brian's leg felt pretty good – no pain, but his foot and ankle control felt awkward. He still used the cane for reassurance more than necessity.

The two aircraft were similar in size, appearance and purpose. Both were twin, radial-engined aircraft with tail wheels and conventional tails. The newer aircraft had a more streamlined appearance and larger radial engines gave the Beaufighter the image of being faster. The most notable external characteristic was the armament. The Blenheim had 30 caliber (7.69 mm) machine guns similar to the current versions of the Spitfire and Hurricane. The Beaufighter sported four 20 mm cannons – much greater punch.

"Great to see you back on your feet, Hunter," a familiar voice came from behind them.

They both turned. Brian saw John 'Cat's Eyes' Cunningham approaching, now with the sleeve stripes of a squadron leader on his uniform tunic. Brian saluted the senior officer.

"Congratulations, sir," Brian said, pointing to Cunningham's sleeve stripes.

"Thank you, Hunter," Cunningham responded.

"Sir, may I introduce Charlotte Palmer. Charlotte, this is Squadron Leader John Cunningham. We call him Cat's Eyes, but he doesn't like that name."

John took Charlotte's proffered right hand, kissed it, and said, "An honor to meet you, Mrs. Palmer – the holder of the George Cross, as I recall."

"A pleasure to meet you, Mister Cunningham. If I may ask, why do they call you Cat's Eyes?"

"Because these blokes," he answered, motioning over his shoulder, "do not respect my wishes."

"Don't let him fool you, Charlotte," Brian interjected. "He is the best night fighter pilot in the Air Force."

"I will make no such claim."

"You are almost a night ace, sir. No one else is."

"Lucky. Well short of your 19, I must say Hunter."

"None of mine are at night." Brian turned to Charlotte. "He flies these," he said, swinging his arm to the flight line of twin engine, night fighters. Charlotte nodded her head and smiled at John.

"So, you stopped by to admire our new Bristol Beaufighter."

"She looks faster . . . and you gotta love those cannons."

John glanced at Charlotte, probably not wanting to get too deep into the technical details. "She does have some punch, bigger engines and much faster. We also have the latest night intercept equipment. Both aircraft were designed and produced by the Bristol Aeroplane Company, so there are many similarities, but you touched on the key features we like – speed and firepower."

Charlotte looked at her watch. "We have our afternoon milking, Brian. I'm afraid we must be on our way."

"Yes, certainly."

"Thank you for showing us your new machine, Mister Cunningham," she said.

"The pleasure was mine." John turned to Brian. "When do you return to flight status?"

"Friday, the doctor said."

"Welcome back. Be safe on your drive home."

"Yes sir."

They all shook hands. Cunningham remained at the Beaufighter. Charlotte and Brian headed to the automobile and departed for the farm. Charlotte chose not to talk, and Brian did not want to press her.

—

Monday, 4. November. 1940
Standing Oak Farm
Winchester, Hampshire, England
United Kingdom
19:30 hours

The drive had been uneventful and faster than the last several journeys. Horace Morgan and Lionel Bridges, Standing Oak Farm's long-term hands, had nearly finished the afternoon milking and processing by the time Charlotte and Brian arrived. Satisfied the afternoon chores were essentially done, Charlotte jumped into preparing an unusually sumptuous meal given wartime rationing and shortages for the three men in her current life, with nearly all of the ingredients grown on her farm or bartered from neighboring farms. Horace and Lionel left for the night. Brian helped Charlotte complete the clean up, all without words. She motioned toward the plush chairs by the fireplace and modest fire.

"Thank you for respecting my silence," Charlotte began. Brian nodded his acknowledgment. "I have wanted to avoid the topic . . . to push out the inevitable as long as possible."

"Charlotte . . . ," Brian interjected and stopped when she shook her head.

"Brian, please don't. I must ask you to allow me to say what I must say for my emotional stability and hopefully our relationship. I know how you feel. You have nothing to explain. You have been very plain, direct and clear. I will also say you have been resolute in your resistance to my womanly wiles. I have no doubt whatsoever that you appreciate my concerns and apprehension. One of many attributes that attracted me to you and that I love in you is your passion for flight. You have confidence, dedication, commitment and loyalty that amplify and complement your passion. I love that in you, as I truly love you as no other. I am proud to be carrying our child, my first child, in my womb. Conversely, I believe I have been frank and honest with you regarding my serious concern for my mental and emotional health. I have no intention and shall not belabor my frailties, as you are well aware. Now, with that said, I will say this as plainly as I possibly can. I love you. I want to spend the rest of my life with you, just as I believe you do with me." Brian opened his mouth to speak, but stopped again when Charlotte shook her head. "I have learned to love that you love aeroplanes and flying. I respect your passion, Brian. I truly do. We have a few days together before you must leave me. I want to enjoy every day. We leave tomorrow morning for London and your award ceremony. I want to make this trip a little holiday."

"In the middle of the Blitz?"

Charlotte laughed and Brian joined her.

"I suppose that does seem a bit odd. Two or three days will be consumed by your ceremony. In fact, now that I think of it, you should really depart for the North Country from London. It does not make sense coming all the way back here for you just to turn around head back to London to reach Catterick by your reporting time."

"Good point. Then, we shall find a way to celebrate in London. It will give us another night together. I must report by noon on Friday."

"Agreed."

"Then, we have a plan."

"Yes, apparently we do. I shall do my best to make these last few days memorable. I want you to leave me with joy in your heart. I want you to return to me when this dreadful war is over. I can make no promises for what the future may hold for either of us. Yet, I know what my heart tells me."

"You are a most amazing woman, Charlotte Palmer. I love you . . . more than I have loved anyone in my life. I share your sentiments. I shall do my level best to survive this war and return to you in one piece."

Charlotte smiled broadly at Brian, stood, extended her right hand to him, and said, "Now, I need you to take me to bed and make me a happy woman."

Brian leapt to his feet with a grin so big it hurt his cheeks. He took her and led her to the bedroom for the first time without his cast, crutches or even his cane. He needed no further encouragement.

—

Tuesday, 5.November.1940
RAF Lympne
Lympne, Kent, England
United Kingdom
13:30 hours

For fighter pilots, waiting was never easy. No.609 Squadron had begun the day's mission before dawn, a few minutes after the beginning of morning twilight, when they took to the air for repositioning to Lympne, near the Channel coast of Kent. Their part of the mission entailed serving as back-up fighter cover for a squadron of Blenheim light attack aircraft along with their escort of Hurricane fighters. The primary target was a large railway-switching yard at Amiens. Fighter Command apparently anticipated the Germans would be none too happy about the strike and might well be chasing the attackers back across the Channel. No.609 Squadron was positioned and being held in reserve to scrub off any chasers. The mission plan called for them to go to Standby in 15 minutes, when they would mount up and prepare their Spitfire fighters for flight, just short of hitting the engine start button. They expected to launch ten minutes after going to Standby and pre-position as an airborne reaction force in case they were needed to provide assistance.

Every pilot had donned their flight gear in anticipation of the approaching transition from Available to Standby, despite the warmth of the Dispersal hut interior provided by the old-fashioned, wood-burning stove. Surprisingly, there was no talking on any topic. Everyone was apparently lost in their own thoughts.

The hut telephone ring snapped all heads and eyes toward their acting operations clerk, a rather young corporal. "Six Oh . . . ." He did not finish his programmed greeting. "Scramble the squadron."

The pilots sprang to their feet, made it out the single door and ran toward their assigned fighters. Several engines had already begun the start sequence, as the crew chiefs turned over the engines to get them as much warming time as possible before take off. *Something has not gone to plan*, Jonathan thought as he ran to his PR-K Spitfire. The senior aircraftman assigned to his fighter had his engine running smoothly and was extricating himself from the cockpit. Jonathan waited at mid-span of the left wing, outside the propeller wash and engine exhaust. The aircraftman came to him and leaned to Jonathan's left ear. Jonathan raised the left flap of his headgear along with his left earphone.

The aircraftman shouted, "She's runnin' smoothly, sir. All switches are on."

Jonathan nodded his head in acknowledgment, jumped onto the left wing root and into the cockpit. The crew chief brought both parachute harness straps over Jonathan's shoulders. As Jonathan fastened his leg and shoulder straps, his seat shoulder straps were waiting for him. While Jonathan fastened his seat harness, the crew chief connected his earphone and microphone cable, and his oxygen mask hose to the aircraft. *I'll check everything on the way out.* Jonathan depressed the wheel brakes and signaled for the wheel chocks to be removed. The crewmen held up both chocks and saluted. Jonathan returned the salute and looked over to his left. Squadron Leader Jason Billings 'Stack' Long-Roberts' aircraft had already started moving. He looked to his right. Both his wingmen held up their left thumbs. Jonathan waited his turn in sequence, and then released the brakes and advanced the throttle. He knew his wingmen would follow accordingly.

The entire squadron was airborne in less than two minutes.

"Short Jack, this is Sorbo calling."

"Sorbo, Short Jack, go ahead."

"Short Jack, Sorbo passing angels one, climbing, heading one eight zero."

"Roger Sorbo. Adjust vector one four seven, angels eight should do." Stack turned slightly to the left, and the Biggin Hill controller continued his instruction, "Your CIRCUS customers are in a tussle mid-Channel. Escort is near bingo and need help breaking free of bandits."

At the Prime Minister's insistence, the Air Ministry began planning and executing offensive operations against German forces occupying Belgium and Northern France, once the enemy's daylight bombing operations ended. One of those operation types was code-named CIRCUS— daytime bomber or fighter-bomber attacks with fighter escorts. The primary purpose was to occupy enemy fighters and keep them in an area of concern. If managed to inflict damage of any form on the enemy, it was a mission bonus.

"Roger, Short Jack. Vector one four seven, angels eight."

Stack leveled them off at 8,000 feet and kept their power up to get to the fight as quickly as possible. The squadron spread out a little more than usual, since they had very little power margin for formation station keeping.

A few minutes later, Jonathan spotted their objective. "Tally ho, eleven o'clock low." He counted only ten Blenheims running as fast as they could to the north at wavetop height. The tangle of fighters was just behind and above them, and the Germans sought to engage the more vulnerable bombers while holding off the Hurricanes.

Stack held his course and power to gain the best sun line he could. "Let's get to it, lads. Here we go." He rolled his Spitfire to the left and into a shallow dive. The rest of the squadron followed their leader.

Jonathan rechecked his armament switches were in the proper positions for combat. He instinctively moved his right thumb to rest on the gun-firing button on the control spade. His left hand moved the throttle slightly to maintain position in the formation. Jonathan's eyes scanned the ball of fighters ahead of them. The grays and greens of enemy and friendly fighter became easily discernible.

The Germans recognized their precarious situation. Several 109's turned to face the diving swarm of Spitfires. Their leader must have assessed their situation as less than acceptable. Suddenly, all the gray fighters turned away and dove for the wave tops.

Stack adjusted to pursue the Germans. The Hurricanes quickly disappeared behind them. Stack bumped his nose up slightly and puffs of smoke burst from his wings, attempting a rather distant lob shot to keep their attention, but with no detectable effect. They were not closing on the running bandits. Stack pressed the pursuit for another few minutes, once he determined the Germans were not going to engage, and they had achieved sufficient separation to protect the Blenheims and Hurricanes low on fuel.

"Sorbo, break it off, RTB. Keep your eyes open for possible trailers."

Jonathan and his section turned slowly 180 degrees for their return to base . . . *well, at least their refueling aerodrome.* He continued his constant scan of the sky around them for the dots that might manifest as enemy fighters. The sky remained clear. The distinctive coastline of Southeast England grew in detail as Stack initiated a gradual descent and adjusted their heading for landing back at RAF Lympne. The operation plan indicated that they were part of this particular CIRCUS mission. The Blenheim and Hurricane squadrons in the primary strike unit were expected to be on the ground at Lympne. The intelligence lads would debrief them upon landing. Perhaps, they would have a short time to chat with the strike lads to learn how the mission played out. They would probably be released in the afternoon for the return flight back to their currently assigned home base at RAF Catterick in North Yorkshire.

The landing back at Lympne was smooth, easy and uneventful. As they taxied to their temporary assembly area on the busy aerodrome, Jonathan took note of the 'ZK' Blenheims of No.25 Squadron and the 'GZ' Hurricanes of No.32 Squadron—Mud Morrison's squadron. They were indeed all on the same airfield, at least for a time. These lads were a growing number of RAF Fighter Command pilots flying missions into German occupied France and Belgium. Their turn would come soon enough, until then, he wanted to gleen as much experience as he could from those pilots who had actually done it. *I'll try to track down Lord Morrison, if I can*, Jonathan thought to himself and turned his attention to the immediate task of parking his Spitfire and securing the aircraft for refueling.

———

Tuesday, 5.November.1940
Springwood Estate
4097 Albany Post Road
Hyde Park, Dutchess County, New York
United States of America
14:15 hours

"Mister President, the Secretary of State has arrived," announced Harry Lloyd Hopkins – Franklin Roosevelt's friend, confidante, advisor and all-around 'Mister Fix-It.' Hopkins had held a series of governmental positions in the Roosevelt administration, the most recent being Secretary of Commerce. During the election campaign, the President relied upon him more and more, so much so he moved into a family quarters guest bedroom of the White House. He was destined to play a vital role as Roosevelt's unofficial emissary and was arguably one of the most influential individuals in the Roosevelt administration.

President Roosevelt nodded his head to acknowledge Harry's announcement and to signal his readiness for their scheduled meeting. Franklin wheeled himself to his usual spot in front of his desk between the couches as Hopkins showed Secretary of State Cordell Hull of Tennessee, a Democrat, who had served as the U.S. chief diplomat since 1933, into the Oval Office and closed the door.

"Good afternoon, Mister President."

"Good afternoon to you, Cordell. I trust you both cast your precious votes today."

Both men appeared a little puzzled. They knew the president understood voting requirements.

"I voted early this morning, first thing," responded Hopkins, "at my local precinct, before coming up here."

Hull seemed a little annoyed that he was odd man out. "I have not switched my residence from Tennessee, plus my residence is in the District. I took the train up last night. So, I'm afraid I was not able to vote in this election."

"I did not intend to make you uncomfortable, Cordell. I'm sure your heart was in the correct place. So, we shall wait for the judgment of the voters."

"Yes sir," answered Hopkins. "We are confident of your victory."

As he had done on previous elections, Franklin Roosevelt returned to his New York estate to vote at his local precinct and face the will of the voters. On this day, the national election featured the President's run for an unprecedented third term as President of the United States. No candidate from George Washington on had sought a third consecutive term as president. His adversaries pointed to his cousin, Theodore, who passed on nomination for re-election in the 1908 campaign, because in his mind he had served two terms, having ascended to the presidency by succession six months into President McKinley's second term, and then being elected in his own right in 1904. Disappointed and perhaps a little angry after Taft's first term, Cousin 'Teddy' ran as a third party candidate in the election of 1912; he argued that it was not a consecutive term. Franklin offered no such subtlety of interpretation. He had accepted the Democratic Party nomination by radio address from the White House on the 19th of July. Franklin had run a somewhat subdued campaign against the Republican candidate Wendell Lewis Willkie of New York and his vice presidential running mate Senator Charles Linza McNary of Oregon.

Today was Election Day. Now, they waited for the judgment of the citizens to be tallied and recorded.

"No sense wasting time fretting about what is out of our control," Roosevelt said softly. "I understand you have a recommendation to replace Joe Kennedy?" . . . the former U.S. ambassador to Great Britain.

"Yes sir, we have. Governor Winant will be an ideal choice. He is well respected by both parties, and he is nearly the opposite of Joe Kennedy."

Governor John Gilbert 'Gil' Winant of New Hampshire was an accomplished Republican politician, highly regarded by President Roosevelt.

Roosevelt chuckled, "That is an intriguing and attractive attribute, I must say. We need an ambassador who will help us help the British without raising a ruckus."

"Gil Winant should fit that bill in spades."

"How soon can we present his nomination to the Senate? What is your assessment of passage?"

"Based on our preliminary, unofficial, ground work, and with our priority request, we should gain rapid confirmation, say a month, two at the most. Our legislative team has seen no obstacles or even resistance from either party."

"Excellent. Then let's get his nomination to the Hill today and press for swift confirmation." Hull nodded his agreement. Roosevelt looked over his shoulder to Hopkins usual position. "Harry, when do we expect results?"

"If we are lucky . . . by early morning. If not, perhaps by noon or later tomorrow afternoon."

"The sooner this is decided the better. The uncertainty has to be a major worry for Churchill. He doesn't know who he's going to be dealing with and more importantly whether he will have a sympathetic administration in this country."

"He will have to wait along with the rest of us."

"He is fighting a war. We are not."

"Quite so, Mister President. Yet, we wait, nonetheless."

Roosevelt turned back to Secretary Hull. "The election may not be in our hands, but the ambassador's confirmation is."

"More or less."

"Are you both trying to make me feel like an impotent eunuch?"

They all laughed. Hull wiggled in a nervous manner, as if he was suddenly uncomfortable.

Roosevelt chuckled, again. "Don't worry, Cordell. I've not gone over the edge, just yet."

"Yes sir. I am relieved."

"Very well, then. Let's get Gil confirmed and in place as soon as humanly possible. We need to settle things down with the British quickly. Winston has been most indulgent of the exigencies of our democratic processes, and he deserves better. We must keep the British in this fight at least until we can mobilize. We are starting from such a low point and have such a long way to go before we are ready."

"Yes sir."

"Once your congressional liaison team feel his confirmation is assured, please schedule us to sit down for a little chat with me. I want him to have a clear view of my expectations."

"Yes sir."

"Anything else we need to discuss this afternoon?"

"I'm not sure if you have been informed as yet. The British have moved troops from Egypt to reinforce Greece."

"Secretary Stimson and General Marshall briefed me yesterday – ballsy move for Winston. They do not have overwhelming force in Egypt. While they have the Italians on the run, they have not beaten them, just yet."

Secretary of War Henry Lewis Stimson of New York was a conservative Republican politician, with a wealth of governmental service experience, including Army service in France during the Great War, attaining the rank of colonel. As Secretary of War, he was the civilian leader of the Army.

Chief of Staff of the Army General George Catlett Marshall, Jr., USA [VMI 1901] was the highly regarded, senior Army officer and had been the Chief of Staff since September 1939.

"A calculated move . . . according to Lord Lothian."

Lord Lothian had been the British Ambassador to the United States since June 1939. He was highly respected, well known and liked on both sides of the Atlantic Ocean. He was born Philip Henry Kerr and became the 11th Marquess of Lothian on the passing of his cousin in 1930. He also held Kt, CH, PC, and DL honors.

"Hope it pays off for them."

"Indeed. Also, before I left Foggy Bottom for our meeting, reports were coming in about a major engagement by the German pocket battleship *Admiral Sheer* with an eastbound British Convoy HX-84 We have no details, as yet. I'm sure Frank Knox and Admiral Stark will brief you when they have sufficient information. The escorts, including one of our transferred destroyers, were seriously out-gunned, so this may not turn out well."

Secretary of the Navy William Franklin 'Frank' Knox of Michigan was a conservative Republican; an Army artillery officer during the War to End All Wars in France, attaining the rank of major; and he was the 1936 Republican vice presidential candidate with Alf Landon, standing against the Democratic Roosevelt-Nance ticket.

President Roosevelt had asked both Stimson and Knox to serve in key positions in his Cabinet with the clouds of war darkening every day. The President had nominated both men and the Senate confirmed them in less than a month. Both men had been sworn into office the previous July.

Chief of Naval Operations Admiral Harold Rainsford 'Betty' Stark, USN [USNA 1899] had been the senior naval officer since August 1939.

"I imagine they are carrying food stuffs from this country. Do you know if there was an arms shipment from us in that convoy?"

"No sir. I do not. I will see if we can find out. Lord Lothian may be of assistance in answering that question."

"Yes, certainly, he knows our sensitivity – my sensitivity – about antagonizing the Germans as our involvement in supporting the British becomes more publicly known."

"Yes sir. I will let you know what we can find out."

"Thank you, Cordell. Also, I don't need to say that we must keep our support of the British as quiet as we can. The last thing we need now is some America Firster isolationist to get a hold of such information."

"I clearly understand that and I will continue to ensure the sensitivity of our staff folks."

"Try to keep the fewest people involved in all of our support work."

"Yes sir. We have been and will continue to do so."

"Excellent. Anything else?"

"No sir."

"Very well, then. Thank you for stopping by. Please keep us posted on Gil's confirmation."

"Of course, Mister President."

—

Chapter 2

Even forms and substances are circumfused
by that transparent veil with light divine.
And, through the turnings intricate of verse,
present themselves as objects recognized,
in flashes, and with glory not their own.

- William Wordsworth

Wednesday, 6.November.1940
Cabinet War Rooms
New Public Offices
Whitehall, London, England
United Kingdom
11:00 hours

Secretary to the War Cabinet Sir Edward Ettingdene Bridges, KCB, MC, FRS, convened the morning War Cabinet meeting spot on time.

"I suppose the first item of business not on the agenda is the American election. We received a message from Lord Lothian a short time ago. It appears President Roosevelt has soundly won re-election to a third term. The results will not be official, of course, until mid-December, when their Electoral College meets to tally the state votes."

"Good news, indeed," proclaimed Churchill. "Perhaps, now, we can move onto the next stage, and get on with winning this war together."

"That might be a shade premature," observed Edward Frederick Lindley Wood, KG, GCSI, GCMG, GCIE, TD, PC, 3rd Viscount Halifax of Monk Bretton – Secretary of State for Foreign Affairs; Conservative Party member and Peer in the House of Lords, and popularly known as Lord Halifax. "We need to see what Congress looks like. All members of the House of Representatives and one third of the Senate faced re-election."

"The President has stretched his authority quite far already . . . without Congress."

"True. He is walking a fine line without Congress. While the public mood in the United States may be shifting in our favor, the movement is certainly not as fast as we would like."

"You are quite correct, Ed. Nonetheless, we must see this as a positive sign."

"Yes, indeed . . . quite positive."

"Anything else on the American election results?" asked Sir Edward. Hearing or seeing none, he said, "Now, to the agenda. I do believe the Admiralty has the floor."

The First Lord of the Admiralty, the Right Honorable Albert Victor 'A.V.' Alexander, PC, Member of Parliament for Sheffield, Hillsborough, member of the Labor Party, successor to Churchill as First Lord, and ministerial leader of the Royal Navy, cleared his throat. "Regrettably, I must inform the War Cabinet that eastbound convoy HX Eighty-Four was engaged late yesterday afternoon by the pocket battleship *Admiral Sheer*. The convoy was one day short of the mid-Atlantic rendezvous hand off to the eastern escort and was only covered by the armed merchant cruiser HMS *Jervis Bay*. Captain Edward Fegen ordered his convoy to scatter, to make the *Sheer*'s task more difficult, and turned his ship directly to engage the German battleship," Alexander caught himself, swallowed hard, and took a deep breath to gain control. "Her six-inch guns were no match for the *Sheer*'s eleven-inch guns. Fegen and his crew managed to occupy the *Sheer* for a sufficient time for his convoy to scatter and make it to nightfall, before they fell. Fegen's swift action enabled all but six of the 38 ships in the fast convoy to survive the initial engagement yesterday afternoon and make it to the cover of darkness. We will not know if the *Sheer* can re-engage or whether U-boats will take a further toll. The eastern escort is attempting to deploy between the *Sheer* and the dispersed transports. The surviving ships of that convoy will be out there for another week or possibly a fortnight. Weather in the North Atlantic has been particularly nasty, so we will not know until all of the surviving vessels arrive under the protection of Liverpool Roads."

Halifax interjected, "I might add the initial report went out implying the convoy had a full escort, including at least one of the transferred American destroyers."

"Yes," the First Lord responded. "There was some confusion about where they were relative to the eastern escort. The situation was clarified during the night. They had not reached the rendezvous point. The *Jervis Bay* was alone against the *Sheer*, yesterday. We have issued a correction to the Americans."

"Can we do anything to help the survivors?" asked the Right Honorable Clement Richard Attlee, Member of Parliament for Limehouse – Lord Privy Seal and Leader of the Labor Party.

"We are doing everything we can," Alexander replied. "They are still beyond the reach of Coastal Command aircraft. We are trying to free up two more destroyers to give them some coverage. Yet, the reality is, they dispersed to disappear from the Germans, and they will remain invisible to us until they get close enough for aircraft to find them. They are under strict orders to maintain radio silence to avoid radio direction-finding by the Germans. I suspect it is fairly certain the German Condors will be looking for them as well. They had a big success yesterday. History tells us they will do their best to advance their victory."

"Captain Fegen undoubtedly saved many more ships and scores of men, and our precious supplies," observed Churchill. "Once the Admiralty has completed its analysis, I pray let me review your report. Likewise, if the actions of Captain Fegen to save his convoy hold up under scrutiny, an appropriate award is warranted. Such heroism will save us all."

"Yes sir."

"What are we doing to find and neutralize the Sheer?"

"We have deployed a heavy cruiser squadron along with the aircraft carriers *Formidable* and *Hermes* as well as their destroyers to find her and deal with the surface raider. We suspect she will make for the Norwegian coast to refuel and resupply."

"I am certain you will do all you can to avenge Fegen and *Jervis Bay*."

"Yes, of course."

"Where are we on the additional destroyers from the United States?" the Prime Minister asked.

"We just took delivery of the fifth group, which brings our total to 32. The sixth and final group is scheduled for acceptance on the 21st of this month. I must inform the War Cabinet, as I am certain the Prime Minister knows quite well, these antique destroyers from the Great War, are hardly ready for modern combat. They can barely be called warships."

"Yes, well, would you rather have none?" offered Churchill, somewhat rhetorically.

"No, they are better than nothing. They can shoot, drop depth charges and fire torpedoes, but they do not possess the necessary search equipment for contemporary anti-submarine operations. We have nearly a dozen of the American destroyers in retrofit, installing the equipment, and getting them to an operational level."

"Press on. Anything else, A.V.?"

"That should be enough from Admiralty, I do believe."

"Very well," interjected Sir Edward. "The next item on the agenda is Greece . . . first the Foreign Office, and then the War Office."

Lord Halifax leaned forward. "The War Office has the bulk of the news. I will only say the Greek government, just this morning, reinforced their request for air support and armor-infantry forces. We have not yet responded and we are working with the War Office to prepare a response."

The Secretary of State for War, the Right Honorable Robert Anthony Eden, MC, PC, Member of Parliament for Warwick and Leamington, Deputy

Leader of the Conservative Party, and ministerial leader of the British Army, picked up the lance. "The War Office received the same, or at least similar, request for support as the Foreign Office. As a reminder, the Italians attacked across the northern frontier from Albania. They met limited resistance, mostly from border guard units for several days. The Greeks began their general counter-attack early this morning and frankly are making surprisingly good progress pushing the Italians back. We took the risk to deploy a mechanized brigade, more as a defensive or symbolic force to protect the light and medium bomber squadrons we moved from Egypt to Crete. We also have conflicting information regarding the German units deployed on the Balkan frontier. We expect them to engage, especially if the Greeks continue to have success. The Germans cannot allow the Italians to be defeated or expelled from Albania."

"We must support the Greeks. Like the Germans, we cannot allow the Greeks to be defeated," pronounced Churchill.

"We have been through this. In principle, we all agree. Where we disagree is the risk to Egypt, the Suez, North Africa and the Middle East. We are spreading our limited forces very thin."

"We are not going to debate our order of battle assessment," Churchill said. "I understand and genuinely appreciate the generals seeking overwhelming force for the situations they face. We simply do not have those forces. We cannot diminish the Home Forces, since the threat of invasion may have subsided during the winter months, yet it has not been removed for the potential of a spring offensive against us. General Wavell has expressed his perspective thoroughly and completely."

General Sir Archibald Percival Wavell, KCB, CMG, MC, PC, had been General Officer Commanding-in-Chief, Middle East Command, since July 1939, and was advanced to Commander-in-Chief Middle East in February 1940, with responsibility for East Africa, Middle East, Greece and the Balkans.

"Yet, the War Cabinet does not, never has, and never will have the luxury of focusing on one region, one command," Churchill continued. "We must find the winning balance to fulfill our commitments and obligations. Until the Americans join us on the journey to victory, we will continue to be forced to shift our resources to deal with the exigencies of the moment. Wavell has the Italians on the run in the desert. We must support Greece without sacrificing any of our friends."

"Winston, there is no argument on those general points," Clement said. "However, I think Anthony's point is the judgment of that balance and assessing the risk. Everything cannot be the number one priority."

"How do we say no to our friends?" Churchill mused.

"Your loyalty is laudable," answered Attlee, even though no answer was sought. "Anthony offers a valid point. General Wavell is the soldier in the field whom we have charged with defending that portion of the empire under his shield."

"And, our generals and admirals take their orders from the War Cabinet," Churchill said, lowering his forehead, as if he was about to charge. "Let us not diminish our place in this process. We must take the much larger, strategic decisions that we believe will lead to victory. We cannot abandon Greece."

"No one is suggesting we abandon Greece," replied Attlee. "I am only saying we cannot jeopardize Egypt in an attempt to save Greece. For years, Greece refused our assistance. Now, when they are under physical attack, they demand our support. We have agreed to provide what forces we can, but we must not ignore the expert advice of our field commanders. I simply urge caution and deliberation in these decisions. We did the best we could in Norway, and we were not successful. We face precisely the same conundrum now in Greece."

Churchill grunted heavily – a common response to a worthy opposing argument. "Very well, then, we shall carry out the current orders and closely monitor the situation."

When no further words were offered, Sir Edward said, "Very well. I believe we are adjourned. I remind the War Cabinet that we reconvene at sixteen hours this afternoon."

The ministers and small staff shuffled out of the comparatively small cabinet conference room. The Prime Minister headed to his office farther back in the underground bunker. An armed Army sergeant stood outside his office door, and came to attention and saluted as the Prime Minister approached. It was the tan-colored, rectangular case manacled to his left wrist that attracted Churchill's attention. The 'Buff Box,' as they called it, was a hardened, secure, watertight, fire-resistant, rectangular container with a beige-colored leather covering. The case looked like a lawyer's case. Only a few men on the planet knew what the 'Buff Box' contained. Once it was locked at Broadway House or at Bletchley Park, it could only be opened by a secure key upon return, or by a single key held on the person of the Prime Minister.

"What have you for me, sergeant?"

"Good morning, sir. I have an urgent message from 'C.'"

"Very well, then, let us see what you have, so you can return to your duties."

The sergeant followed the Prime Minister into the office and closed the door. He placed the case on the desk and turned away, as he has been instructed to do.

Churchill retrieved the key from a chain around his neck by opening a couple of buttons on his shirt and unlocked the case. There was only one piece of paper in a red folder inside the case.

MOST SECRET - ULTRA

```
SECRET
DATE: 5 NOVEMBER 1940
TO: ALL 16TH ARMY UNITS
FROM: 16TH ARMY HQ
BEGIN
RETURN ASSIGNED BARGES TO STORES BREAK PROCEED
TO DISPERSAL BIVOUAC LOCATIONS AND STANDBY FOR
REDEPLOYMENT ORDERS BREAK
HAIL HITLER
END
SECRET
```

MOST SECRET - ULTRA

Churchill smiled, returned the paper to the folder and locked the case. He recognized the significance of the simple message—one more confirmation the Germans has postponed their invasion attempt . . . at least until next spring. Winston considered whether he should take any action.

"Thank you, sergeant. Please inform 'C,' no further action required."

"Yes sir." The sergeant checked the case lock to ensure it was properly latched and departed.

The yield from ULTRA—the deciphering of encoded German Enigma messages—over the last month has provided a surprisingly clear view of German intentions and strongly suggested they had defended their sacred isle . . . at least for now.

Wednesday, 6. November. 1940
Springwood Estate
4097 Albany Post Road
Hyde Park, Dutchess County, New York
United States of America
09:05 hours

The duty chief of presidential Secret Service detail pushed President Roosevelt's wheel chair into the mansion's study that served as his office at the country estate. Harry Hopkins was already waiting for the President's arrival.

"Good morning, Mister President," Hopkins said.

"Good morning to you, Harry. You must have important news to be here ahead of me."

"Yes sir. I think this news qualifies. The election results accumulated overnight are quite positive. I think it is safe to say congratulations on your election to a third term."

Franklin motioned for position between the couches, so that Hopkins could sit. The Secret Service supervising special agent placed the wheelchair as indicated, departed the office and closed the door. Roosevelt gestured for Hopkins to sit on the couch to his right. "Don't you think your congratulations are a bit premature?" he asked.

"To be honest, no, the counting is not complete, but the reported results so far have you several million votes ahead of Willkie with more than 80 percent of the vote counted. Even better, this distribution across the states indicate you will fare better in the Electoral College vote next month. Our count so far looks like you will be over 400 votes in the Electoral College."

"Thank you for that, Harry. More than required, but I will wait for the official results. Now, the process of governance goes on. "Have not talked to Henry or his staff?"

In a highly controversial and contentious move, Roosevelt had chosen the more liberal Henry Agard Wallace of Iowa, his former Secretary of Agriculture, to be his running mate, replacing his two-term, Vice President John Nance 'Cactus Jack' Garner III of Texas, on the 1940 ticket.

"No, but I will tend to that as soon as we are done here."

"Thank you, Harry. Now, what is on the calendar for today?"

"First, there is more good news." Franklin gestured somewhat impatiently for the information. "We have received Joe Kennedy's signed resignation letter this morning."

Roosevelt chuckled more to himself. "Perhaps he knew the jig was up for him as the election results were coming in."

"Perhaps."

"Make sure Cordell is informed as soon as possible. I want Cordell to hold his resignation letter personally and securely, and make sure he clearly understands we will not accept his resignation until we are assured of Winant's confirmation by the Senate. We'll let Joe hang in limbo for a month or so. If there are any inquiries on the status of his resignation, our response should be we are considering it. We need to get Winant vetted, nominated, confirmed and in place as soon as possible . . . too much going on in England."

"Indeed. I'll talk to Secretary Hull to see if he needs any assistance. He headed back to Washington after your meeting yesterday."

"Oh, certainly. It can wait until we return to Washington as well."

"As you wish. Now, the only event we have on the calendar today is a ceremony to lay the cornerstone for the new Hyde Park Post Office, approved in this year's budget. We are scheduled to leave before midnight on your overnight train to Washington. We will arrive back at the White House tomorrow, a little before mid-morning."

"Very well. Since there is nothing urgent this morning, I think I will do a little reading."

"I'll come get you when it is time to depart for the scheduled ceremony."

"Thank you."

Hopkins departed the study, leaving Franklin alone. The President retrieved his bookmarked and personally autographed copy of Mahatma Gandhi's "*The Story of My Experiments with Truth*," which he had nearly finished. A good hour or two reading should finish it off—an interesting book. Gandhi's autobiography would keep his mind off of the election and challenges of a wartime world.

—

Wednesday, 6.November.1940
Cabinet War Rooms
New Public Offices
Whitehall, London, England
United Kingdom
15:45 hours

Bomb damage seemed to be everywhere, even in Whitehall and Westminster – the heart of London. The beautiful city had been deeply scarred by The Blitz and the nightly attacks continued. While some of the bomb damage was quite recent, most of the streets had been cleared to allow vehicular traffic, although pedestrian movement had become more tortuous and circuitous. Fortunately, on this trip at least, an Air Ministry automobile and driver had been offered, so that the Underground or taxis could be avoided.

Air Commodore John Spencer stood at the northwest corner of the New Public Offices building when the Air Ministry automobile stopped on Horse Guard Road. The driver opened the passenger door. Mrs. Charlotte Palmer stepped out of the car, followed by Pilot Officer Brian Drummond in his new Royal Air Force uniform. Spencer approached them with a broad smile.

"Great to see you, again, Mrs. Palmer, and of course, you as well Mister Drummond," Spencer said.

Brian saluted the senior officer crisply. "Good afternoon, sir," Brian said.

Air Commodore Spencer returned the salute and extended his hand to Brian, and then to Charlotte. He gently took her hand and bowed to kiss the top of her hand in his before he released Charlotte's hand.

"The Prime Minister has asked to meet with you," John said to Brian, "with us, before the War Cabinet meeting. We will meet with him in his office in the War Rooms."

"The War Rooms?" asked Brian.

John Spencer smiled. "A rather visionary anticipatory response to what has come to pass in our fair capital city. The governmental offices have been moved underground to ensure the continuity of government while under threat of bombing."

Brian looked around. He saw nothing that even remotely indicated an underground facility.

Air Commodore Spencer laughed. "The entrance is over there," he said, pointing to what appeared to be a wall of sandbags between the stone of the building and the stone of the stairway leading to the northwest entrance. "I have made the arrangements for all of us to enter. Security is rather stringent, as you can imagine."

"Yes sir."

Air Commodore Spencer led them to the wall of sandbags. The armed guards, protecting the entrance, checked the credentials of all three of them against their list. Apparently satisfied, the corporal of the guard gestured for them to proceed inside. They walked through the zigzagged entrance, intended to prevent a direct line of sight to the interior, entered into the interior, and went down a set of stairs to a landing, where another set of armed guards. Two serious looking, heavily armed soldiers stood ready for action on either side of the sergeant of the guard seated behind a modest desk, and a lieutenant standing behind the sergeant. Again, they checked their credentials against what Brian presumed had to be a pre-arranged access list. Once satisfied, the sergeant used a desk telephone to announce their arrival. Another lieutenant appeared on the landing.

"Air Commodore Spencer, Pilot Officer Drummond, Madame Palmer, if you would be so kind to follow me, the Prime Minister is expecting you."

The army officer led them down another, longer stairway, through a large, open, heavy door that was most likely part of the security system for the offices. They passed a door labeled conference room, another labeled map room, and turned left down a long, well-lighted corridor. The beehive of activity and the hum of work filled all available space on either side of the central corridor. A man appeared and stood in the corridor, clearly waiting for them.

"Great to see you again, Air Commodore Spencer."

"A pleasure to see you, again, Jock."

"May I present Mrs. Charlotte Palmer and Pilot Officer Brian Drummond."

"Charlotte, Brian, this is 'Jock' Colville, Private Secretary to the Prime Minister."

John Rupert 'Jock' Colville had been one of several assistant private secretaries since Churchill had become Prime Minister last May.

Colville shook hands with them. "The Prime Minister is expecting you." He knocked twice on a nondescript door on the right side of the corridor, opposite his desk. "Sir, Air Commodore Spencer, Pilot Officer Drummond and Mrs. Charlotte Palmer have arrived."

"Please show them in, Jock," came the distinctive voice of Winston Churchill from inside.

Prime Minister Churchill stood beside his desk, with his small bed and nightstand behind him. "Great to see you, again, John."

"Thank you Uncle Winston."

"Great to see you as well, Brian."

"Thank you sir.

Churchill turned to Charlotte. "And, it is an honor to finally meet you, Mrs. Palmer. There are not many holders of the George Cross . . . from the King, no less."

"Thank you, Mister Churchill. It is an honor to meet you. Your speeches have always meant so much to me, Mister Prime Minister."

"Thank you, my dear." Churchill motioned to the chairs around the table in front of his desk. "We do not have much time before our scheduled War Cabinet meeting." He looked to Brian. "I asked John for a private word with you before the meeting and the presentation of your award. John also informs me, you have been cleared by the doctor to return to duty."

"Yes sir . . . Friday."

"John also informs me that you wish to remain with your original unit . . . Six Oh Nine Squadron is it?

"Yes, that is correct. They are the only mates I have ever known. They are my brothers."

"Your loyalty is quite laudable, Brian. Yet, I asked John if I could make an attempt to convince you to transfer to Seventy-One Squadron with your countrymen."

"Excuse me, sir?"

"Brian, my boy, you undoubtedly have no comprehension, or perhaps very little, of your importance in the regrettable but noble affair in which we are currently engaged. If I had my choice, I would take you out of your Spitfire cockpit and return you to the United States, to help convince your citizens to join us in the present conflict, in the defense of freedom for us all. However, I know your sense of brotherhood quite well. I still, to this day, see myself as a member of the 4th Queen's Own Hussars, with whom I served in India before the turn of the century. So, I shall not ask you to sacrifice your passion. That aside, I must ask you, and I do sincerely mean ask, to move to the new Eagle Squadron. You were the first American to cross the Atlantic Ocean and join our cause . . . even before the war began. That makes you a very special young man." Churchill looked at Charlotte. "He is special in many ways, Mrs. Palmer, as you are special to all of us."

"Thank you, sir. Yes, I know he is special, which is why I love him, and . . . I am proud to carry his child."

All three men dropped their jaws in surprise. Churchill was the first to recover. "Well, then, Charlotte, may I call you Charlotte?"

"Yes sir, you may."

"Congratulations, my dear." He cleared his throat. "Well, that presumes this is what you both want."

"Yes sir, it is," Charlotte answered. "This is not a mistake for either of us, if that is what you are implying."

"I meant no such implication, Charlotte. I am an old man. I am a product of the Victorian era. I am not so wise in the ways of the world, I'm afraid."

"Prime Minister, please excuse me, if I am too blunt here. I am a widow. Brian and I are not married. That fact is not because Brian has not tried mightily to convince me to marry him and make me an honest woman, before I give birth to our child out of wedlock. However, as he well knows, I cannot marry him as long as he remains at risk in this war. I have lost too much already."

"I did not mean to pry, Mrs. Palmer. I can only say His Majesty's Government is extraordinarily grateful for the sacrifices of your family in defense of the realm."

"Thank you, sir, but I would rather have my family."

A knock at the door stopped the conversation. Jock Colville opened the door and partially entered. "Prime Minister, the War Cabinet has assembled."

"Thank you, Jock. We will be there shortly." He looked back to Charlotte. "Quite understandable, my dear. I cannot undo what has been done."

"I am terribly sorry to have commandeered your meeting with Brian. He deserves much better than I have given him. My grief must not distract him from his service. I am immensely grateful for your interest in my man-friend," she stopped to look at Brian. She smiled at him. "And, the father of our baby and my future husband, when this dreadful war is done."

"You did not commandeer anything, Charlotte. You said what had to be said." Churchill turned to Brian. "I trust you will consider my suggestion, Brian."

"Yes sir. I hope you are correct. I shall do as you requested."

"No request, Brian. No order, either, although I certainly have the power to do so. You must do this of your own free will."

"Yes sir. I will do my best to serve."

"We all know you will. Now, we really need to not keep the War Cabinet waiting. However, before we tend to the official business of this afternoon, Mrs. Churchill and I would be honored to have the pleasure of your company in our humble temporary dwelling above ground tonight." He looked to John. "I trust Mary will be able to join us."

"Yes, Uncle Winston. She will join us."

"Excellent. Also, I am honored to inform you, on behalf of his Majesty, the King and Queen have requested the presence of both of you at the Palace tomorrow at fourteen hours."

"Oh dear!" exclaimed Charlotte. "I did not bring an appropriate dress for an audience with the King and Queen."

"You have both met the King. He is quite understanding, as regents go. This is to be an informal social visit, at his Majesty's request, not a formal audience. What you have on today will be appropriate."

"Thank you, sir," said Brian.

"Now, we have kept my fellow ministers and the chief of air staff waiting long enough."

Prime Minister Churchill stood. Brian, John and Charlotte stood as well, and followed the Winston down the corridor and into the conference room.

"My apologies, gentlemen," said Churchill. "I kept our guests too long in my office. May I introduce to you our guests of honor Pilot Officer Brian Drummond, presently of Six Oh Nine Squadron, and George Cross holder Mrs. Charlotte Palmer, and their Air Ministry escort Air Commodore John Spencer."

The full War Cabinet was present. Each member as well as the Secretariat staff were introduced, including the two invitees: Secretary of State for Air the Right Honorable Sir Archibald Henry Macdonald 'Archie' Sinclair, Bart, PC, CMG, Member of Parliament for Caithness and Sutherland, 4th Baronet of Ulster, Leader of the Liberal Party, and ministerial leader of the Royal Air Force (RAF); and Chief of the Air Staff Air Chief Marshal Sir Charles Frederick Algernon Portal, KCB, DSO & Bar, MC, former Air Officer Commanding-in-Chief Bomber Command.

Sir Edward began, "Gentlemen . . . and lady, if you please, our first order of business is Mister Drummond's recognition. Sir Charles would you please do the honors."

The Chief of the Air Staff stood. "Pilot Officer Brian Drummond . . . front and center."

Brian stood, marched as sharply as he could, halted and saluted. Sir Charles returned the salute and turned to face the Prime Minister at the head of the U-shaped table.

"Attention to orders," said Sir Charles. Everyone in the conference room stood. "First, Pilot Officer Brian Arthur Drummond, Six Zero Nine Squadron, Fighter Command, Royal Air Force, is hereby promoted to the rank of flying officer, effective this day. Second, Flying Officer Drummond is to be awarded the Military Cross for conspicuous gallantry and devotion to duty when engaging hostile aircraft in aerial combat. The citation reads, on the 13th of August 1940, enemy dive-bombers carried out a surprise attack on his aerodrome. With total disregard for his safety, he managed to get his Spitfire fighter airborne amid bombs exploding throughout the alighting area and taking serious damage to his aeroplane. Alone, he engaged and single-handedly shot down two enemy aircraft and damaged three others. His valiant actions saved precious aircraft and fellow airmen. He displayed the highest courage and the finest fighting spirit."

The gathered ministers applauded. Sir Charles pinned the Military Cross – a silver cross with a white ribbon and large center purple stripe – on Brian's tunic above his wings. Sir Charles shook Brian's hand. Brian saluted. Sir Charles returned the salute.

"I must add to Mister Drummond's citation," Sir Charles continued. "His actions alone that day deserve this decoration. However, when the citation says total disregard, I should translate that for you. He responded so quickly to the threat to his aerodrome that he did not take even another second to don his parachute or even buckle his seat harness. He was so focused on his mission that day, he did not recognize his mistake until the engagement was over. I have known many warriors in all services during my career. There are very few, truly very few, who stand up to the mark as Brian did that afternoon in August last. I should also inform you, for those who don't already know, Brian has been credited with nineteen aerial victories, an ace three times over, and also the holder of the

Distinguished Flying Cross. Lastly, and what's more, Mister Drummond is an American volunteer pilot, who left his home just after his eighteenth birthday to join our little band of merry men. He is here with us not because he has to be, but because he wants to be." Again, the ministers applauded.

For the first time since the ceremony began, Brian noticed Charlotte had been crying and was still crying. She disguised her tears well. He felt enormous sympathy for her being reminded of the risks he took in flying.

"I would also like to acknowledge the contributions of Air Commodore John Spencer. John and his brother-in-flight, the late Malcolm Bainbridge, both serving with the Royal Flying Corps during the Great War, found, nurtured and supported Brian. We are immensely grateful."

"His Majesty's Government is immensely grateful," Prime Minister Churchill added.

The various ministers rose to shake Brian's hand. Churchill was the last.

Churchill shook Brian's hand as well and whispered to him, "Keep doing what you do so well. Stay safe, my son." Churchill patted him on the back.

Charlotte, John and Brian left the cabinet conference room and the War Rooms bunker. It was already dark outside, made even darker by the nightly blackout. The air was crisp and dry, and the little breeze offered a welcome refreshing sensation.

"Congratulations, Brian," John said to Brian, and then turned to Charlotte. "I am sorry you had to endure that, Charlotte."

"I am very proud of him," she said, "perhaps too proud."

"Charlotte . . . ," Brian stopped when she held up her hand. *This gesture from her seems to be happening a lot these days.*

"Well, let me get you two to your hotel, so you can freshen up before dinner with the Prime Minister." He motioned for the automobile. "Where are you staying?"

"The Dorchester, sir."

"Very well. That is on my way. I'll have the driver drop you at the hotel, and then take me home to retrieve Mary. We'll pick you up at half seven. That should give us plenty of time to return to the Annex."

"That should work, sir."

They entered the vehicle. Brian took the forward jump seat, while Charlotte sat next to John Spencer. They made it to the hotel in 20 minutes, surprisingly swift considering the bomb debris in the streets, the darkened streetlights and building, mere slits over the headlights, and the other traffic continuing life in the bomb damaged city.

—

Wednesday, 6. November. 1940
No. 10 Annex
New Public Offices
Whitehall, London, England
United Kingdom
20:00 hours

Air Commodore and Mrs. Spencer along with Pilot Officer Drummond and Mrs. Charlotte Palmer arrived at The Annex ten minutes early to make it through the security provisions for the dinner with the Prime Minister and his wife Clementine Ogilvy Spencer-Churchill née Hozier.

No. 10 Annex was a constructed, reinforced, protected, modest apartment on the first floor of the New Public Offices building, above the Cabinet War Rooms. Neither Winston nor Clementine liked the accommodations of The Annex and only begrudgingly used the facility. Bomb damage to No. 10 and Whitehall government buildings pushed the Churchill's out of the traditional residence into the bunkered facility.

The ladies wore various colors of elegant, evening dresses. John and Brian were in their respective RAF uniforms. Prime Minister Churchill wore the uniform of an RAF air commodore similar to John's attire with different ribbons and no wings.

After introductions and a social evening cocktail, they moved to and filled the small dining room. The Churchills voiced their dislike for The Annex and apologized for not entertaining their guests at No. 10 or Chequers. Everyone understood and accepted the realities of wartime London.

"In deference to our ladies, we shall curtail our war talk, gentlemen," declared Winston.

"Thank you, Winnie," responded Clementine. "Charlotte, I understand you were awarded the George Cross for saving young Brian's life back in July."

"Yes ma'am," Charlotte answered.

"Please, Charlotte, we are friends here. I prefer Clementine, or even Clemmie as Winnie calls me."

"As you wish, Clementine."

"So it seems, your selfless act of heroism initiated your relationship."

Brian glanced at Mary Spencer, who quickly connected with his eyes, winked at him, and returned her eyes to Mrs. Churchill.

"Yes, I think we can say that," Charlotte said.

"A love story . . . even in wartime."

"So it would seem. But, I must be candid here, I truly wish he was a farmer rather than a fighter pilot in His Majesty's service."

"Quite understandable, my dear. I remember quite vividly when Winnie decided on his very own to run off to join the Grenadier Guards in France during the Great War, after he was cashiered as First Lord."

"That is rather harsh, Clemmie," protested Winston.

"I think it safe to say, Winston, the ladies at this table share a common revulsion of war and the silly sense of duty that takes our men off to war."

"Hear, hear," added Mary Spencer.

"I thought I said at the outset, and I acceded to your wishes, my dear Clementine, that we were not going to have war talk."

"Yes, but I felt the duty to speak for the ladies."

"Well said."

Clementine quickly changed the subject. She turned to look at Mary. "How far along are you, my dear?"

"Four months, Aunt Clemmie. I'm due next April."

"Again, congratulations to you and John. This is your first, is it not?"

"Yes . . . our first . . . and I must add, hopefully not our last."

"Well done, John," Winston said.

John looked at Brian and winked at him, as well. "Thank you, Uncle Winston."

Dear God above, what have I done? I have impregnated two of the three women in this room. Even my mentor knows.

"And," said Winston, "Mary is not alone in that category."

"Really?" exclaimed Clementine as she looked to Charlotte. "And you, my dear?"

"Yes . . . two months for me."

"So, you are due in June?"

"Yes."

"And, to avoid any awkwardness, our young Brian is the father of their child," Winston interjected.

"Congratulations to both of you . . . to all of you," said Clementine Churchill.

They finished their exquisite meal despite the rudimentary preparation facilities in The Annex.

Winston said, "Please excuse us, ladies. We have been gentlemen long enough."

The men stood and followed Churchill into what served as a living room, parlor, study or gathering place. The ladies shifted positions to sit on either side of Clementine Churchill in the dining room.

"Brandy, gentlemen," Churchill offered. All three men accepted a small snifter of brandy. Only Winston and John took cigars from the cabinet humidor.

"Now that we have you alone, young Brian," Winston said, "we can double-team you. Have you considered my earlier suggestion?"

"Yes sir. I shall request a transfer as soon as I report for duty."

"I'll take care of it tomorrow," offered John. "It will take a day or two to process the paperwork." He looked to Brian. "You should report to Catterick as expected. Someone will notify Squadron Leader Long-Roberts of your impending transfer."

"Thank you, sir."

"What are your concerns about flying with the other American volunteers in Seventy-One Squadron?" asked Winston.

"No concern, sir. I can fly anything, anywhere. It is just my best friend remains in Six Oh Nine Squadron."

"Flying Officer Jonathan Kensington," interjected John. "He is one of the few selected exploitation pilots. Mister Kensington has flown the captured and refurbished German aircraft we have at Farnborough."

"Most impressive, Brian. I must say it remains a genuine thrill to follow your exploits, as I have continued to follow my nephew," Winston said, nodding his head to John, and then turned back to Brian. "Now, I must ask, are you concerned about your audience with the King tomorrow?"

"No sir. Should I be?"

Churchill laughed. "You Americans are so innocent and free of noble birth. No, you should not be concerned. There are certain protocols . . . rules . . . but, the stewards will ensure you are mindful of those. He is a good man, although I thought the same of his brother, until Edward's affinity for the present Germanic mania became apparent to all of us. I understand you have already met the King."

King George VI pinned Brian's Distinguish Flying Cross on his uniform tunic during the same ceremony the King awarded the George Cross to Charlotte. "I don't think I would claim 'met,' sir. He gave me my DFC in late August."

The muffled thuds of distant bombs exploding stopped and perked up Churchill's ear.

"So, the nightly insult and abuse has begun," observed Churchill.

"The night fighters are rapidly improving their techniques," John offered, "in using the new Mark IV airborne intercept RDF kit, and the equipment is also improving swiftly."

"So I have been informed by the Air Ministry. Unfortunately, as on this night, there are many more bombers each night than we have night fighters to intercept them, and perhaps even worse, the anti-aircraft artillery fire one hundred plus shells to achieve each success – not the best of efficiency, I must say."

"We have heard the same in Fighter Command. We have also been told that Watson-Watt's Research Establishment is near completion on an RDF-assisted, fire control system for the guns to achieve significantly higher efficiency for Anti-Aircraft Command."

"That makes sense. We need such equipment tonight." As the thuds of bomb explosions gradually came closer, Churchill raised his finger, as if to emphasize his point. The sound of the guns firing was discernible but less intense than the bombs.

"Is it safe here?" asked Brian.

John and Winston laughed. Churchill answered, "Here, yes. Although I must confess, I have been known to observe the Hun's malevolent work from the roof of this building. Detective-Inspector Thompson does not look kindly upon my curiosity."

Detective-Inspector Walter Henry Thompson had been assigned as Churchill's bodyguard since 1921. He was technically on loan from the Special Branch, Metropolitan Police Service, more popularly known as Scotland Yard – a rather tall man who was always armed and quite serious regarding his assignment.

Winston continued, "Yet, it is imperative I share the pain our people endure in these nightly insults, and my little gesture brings that pain to me. Regardless, I shall not subject either of you to my bravado. If past performance is any measure, the Germans should finish this night's rendition in another hour or so. Until then, all of you must endure my yammering, and you are safer here than anywhere outside the Underground."

Shortly before midnight, the thuds stopped and they could hear the muffled siren wail of the 'all clear' signal. Thirty minutes later, their driver and automobile arrived. The Churchill's evening guests conveyed their appreciation and gratitude before departing.

John and Mary deposited Brian and Charlotte at the Dorchester Hotel that thankfully remained undamaged in The Blitz bombing so far. Brian and Charlotte were both tired, did little talking, and went directly to bed. Tomorrow would be slightly slower paced, yet perhaps, even more exciting. Charlotte had been deeply impressed by Clementine and Winston, as well as Mary and John. The ladies made her more comfortable with tomorrow's meeting. Sleep quickly claimed them both.

—

Thursday, 7.November.1940
Buckingham Palace
Westminster, London, England
United Kingdom
14:00 hours

Charlotte and Brian traded glances and facial expressions of wonderment and awe as the vehicle approached the Palace. Neither one of them could believe this was happening. Yet, each step of the progression added to their confirmation . . . *yes, this is actually happening.* Charlotte was impressed. Brian was impressed as well, perhaps not quite as deeply as Charlotte – a British citizen who grew up amid the societal hierarchy that placed the king at the pinnacle.

They were met and greeted by one of the palace stewards whose name did not register with Brian. The grandeur of the interior proved nearly incomprehensible to Brian. He had never seen anything like it – the history, the elegance, and the sheer magnitude of the building. The steward briefed them on what was expected during the meeting. He confirmed this was a private meeting with the King and Queen, and expected to last 30 minutes. He also explained proper conduct in the presence of the monarch. Following the short briefing, Brian and Charlotte were shown into an exquisitely decorated hall. Everything seemed to be gold in the room. They were left standing near opposing couches on either side of the fireplace with a modest fire warming the room.

"Can you believe this?" Brian whispered.

Charlotte leaned toward him and said softly, "I am very proud of you, Brian."

"Thank you. I am proud of you."

"I don't know what for, but thank you, nonetheless."

The far door opened. King George and Queen Elizabeth, along with their oldest daughter, 14-year-old Princess Elizabeth, entered, followed by two royal stewards. The King wore a simple dark blue business suit, while the Queen and Princess wore nice day-dresses. Charlotte curtsied and Brian saluted. The steward who had shown them into the palace made introductions. They all shook hands. The King motioned to the couches and offered tea or something more substantive. The stewards stood ready to serve, but no one wanted anything. The King sat on one couch with the Queen and Princess on either side of him. Charlotte waited until all three royals were seated, and then she sat, with Brian following and next to her.

"Mister Drummond, it is an honor to meet you, again," began King George VI, "and, you as well Mrs. Palmer."

"Thank you, your Majesty," answered Charlotte and Brian in unison.

"Have you recovered from your combat injuries?"

"I believe I have, although I still have a bit of a limp. I am ready, sir."

"Our oldest, Princess Elizabeth," he continued, nodding to his daughter, who was smiling broadly, "asked to join us at our meeting. I hope you don't mind. She has been fascinated by the pilots who fly above us and protect us every day." The Princess nodded her concurrence. "I have several reasons for wanting a private meeting, not least of which is to thank you personally for your extraordinary efforts in defense of the realm and of freedom itself. We are very proud of you, both. I understand from what I believe are reliable sources that since our meeting August last to award Mrs. Palmer's much deserved George Cross and your Distinguished Flying Cross, the two of you have embarked upon a relationship."

Brian looked to Charlotte, wanting her to respond. "Yes, your Majesty, I think it safe to say Brian and I have become close."

"But, not yet married, I understand."

"No, your Majesty . . . my apprehension, I'm afraid. I have lost too much to war already, and I deeply fear losing another. Somehow, I feel not being married will somehow lessen the pain, if something was to happen to Brian."

"You have sacrificed far too much already, my dear," the Queen added.

"Thank you, ma'am."

"The Prime Minister informs me, my War Cabinet awarded you the Military Cross yesterday for your astounding exploits on the 16th of August, I do believe."

"Yes sir."

"And, you are due to report for duty on Friday."

"Yes sir."

"Are you certain you are ready?"

"Yes sir. I miss flying . . . much to Charlotte's chagrin."

"We understand the trepidation, my dear," the Queen said to Charlotte, who nodded her acknowledgment.

"If the Prime Minister informs me properly, you are going to return to Seventy-One Squadron, the new American volunteer unit the Press has dubbed the Eagle Squadron."

"Prime Minister Churchill convinced me to transfer to Seventy-One, which I believe is in work, but I will report to my original unit – Six Zero Nine Squadron – on Friday . . . at least until the transfer arrives."

The King chuckled modestly. "Yes, Mister Churchill can be quite persuasive, can't he?"

"Yes sir. He has always been most generous with me, as has his nephew Air Commodore Spencer."

"John has served the Crown well, and he has much more to offer before he is done."

"Would you be so kind to describe what it feels like for you to fly Spitfires?"

"I am not sure words are adequate, your Majesty. It is the most magnificent machine I have ever flown. She is fast, agile . . . and she has a helluva bite." Brian caught himself. "Excuse me, I did not mean to curse."

"Think nothing of it," the King responded. "A spontaneous expression of what I believe to be the truth. It is hard for us non-aviators to appreciate the extraordinary strain you must have faced during the worst of the battle. What was it like up there . . . against those odds?"

Brian looked to Charlotte. She avoided Brian's eyes and lowered her head, as if she wanted to stare at her knees. Brian waited for her, but she did not move. "Your Majesty," Brian looking back to the King, and then took a quick glance at the Queen and Princess, and back to the King, "I would be happy to answer your query. I know my answer will not be something Charlotte would like to hear, and I am not certain my answer would be appropriate for ladies."

"Quite so. Perhaps another time."

"I would like to hear what happened," Princess Elizabeth said.

"Your Majesty, perhaps you will excuse me," Charlotte interjected. "I do not want to be the wet blanket here."

"Mrs. Palmer, we do not want to cause you discomfort."

"Your Majesty, Brian loves talking about his flying. I know he would tell you as much as you want to know." Charlotte stood. The King and Brian stood. "I will wait outside until you are done."

"Thank you, Mrs. Palmer."

Queen Elizabeth stood and declared, "I shall keep our guest company."

King George waited for the stewards to close the doors and sat down.

Brian sat down as well. "Thank you for your understanding, sir. My profession is very difficult for her. She has lost so much in her life. She is a very good woman, who took great care of me during my recovery. Not to get too personal, I love her very much."

"We understand, Brian. We truly do."

"Thank you, sir. I will attempt to answer your question without getting too graphic."

Brian began his dissertation with his genuine pleasure in flying the Supermarine Spitfire – the speed, the agility, the power, the sounds and even the smells. He recalled for the King and Princess the intensity of aerial combat; the mind-numbing fatigue of multiple, combat sorties, day after day; and the debilitation of removing rest periods. Brian offered several examples of the consequences of pilots falling asleep in the cockpit, in the mess at lunch or dinner, and the Pavlovian response to telephone rings and the scramble bell. The King and Princess asked surprisingly pointed questions about the descriptions provided by Brian. Both appeared to be genuinely empathetic and impressed. Brian was impressed by first their depth of knowledge about combat flying and about what had just happened over the last four months.

"Never in the course of human conflict have so many owed so much to so few," King George quoted Prime Minister Churchill's eloquent words. "You shall forever be counted among The Few who stopped the German invasion of our ancient and noble realm."

"I am honored to have been a part of it, Your Majesty, and I have more to offer . . . although Charlotte wishes I was done."

"The honor is ours young man . . . just to be in your presence."

Brian kept hidden his internal shock at such a statement from the King of England and simply nodded his acknowledgment for the King's gracious statement.

"Now, I have a rather unusual surprise for you that not even the Prime Minister knows about, just yet, but he will in short order." The King turned to his stewards. "Please ask the Queen and Mrs. Palmer to rejoin us, and the Lord Chamberlain should be ready." The King noticed Brian's curious expression. "This shall not take long and is an honor richly deserved."

The Queen and Charlotte entered first. The King and Brian stood and waited for the ladies to be seated, and then joined them.

An elderly man dressed in a fine tuxedo with a large purple sash entered, followed by two smallish, armed, oriental guards in green ceremonial uniforms, and then two Yeomen of the Guard dressed in the distinctive royal red uniforms with red stocking and black shoes, squat black hats with red and white hat bands, and each of them carrying a long, fancy lance. A Gurkha orderly officer stood at attention on either side of the closed doors and a Yeoman stood beside them beyond the door. One of the stewards placed a short, red cushioned, kneeling bar in the middle of the room. The man Brian presumed to be the Lord Chamberlain stood at attention beside the kneeling bar to signal his readiness for what was about to happen.

"Before carrying out this investiture, I must tell you, Brian, I decided to bestow this honor in a private ceremony rather than in our usual formal investiture ceremony." Charlotte reached for and squeezed Brian's hand. "For now, the pomp and circumstance of a formal ceremony shall have to wait until the United States and your countrymen join us in our march to victory over the fascist regimes. I see no purpose in antagonizing the sensitivities of your countrymen. Yet, I also see no need to wait to recognize and honor your contributions to the valiant defense of the realm. Further, I know, understand and respect your country's reluctance to accept such honors from a regent, especially one your forefathers broke with 164 years ago. None of this alters the appropriateness of this honor for you. This afternoon, in our private little ceremony, before these witnesses, and properly recorded in the Central Chancery records, I shall bestow upon you the honor of Commander, Most Excellent Order of the British Empire. Now, if you would, please stand at attention to the left of the bar. I shall join you to the right. Charlotte stood when Brian rose. The Queen and Princess moved to stand behind and to either side of the King. Charlotte stood two yards back off Brian's right shoulder. The King came to crisp attention. The national anthem – "*God Save the King*" – played from an unseen source.

When the music ended, the Lord Chamberlain spoke in a clear, distinct, crisp voice. "Flying Officer Brian Arthur Drummond kneel before the Sovereign." Brian did as he was instructed. "King George VI, By the Grace of God, of Great Britain, Ireland and the British Dominions beyond the Seas King, Defender of the Faith, Emperor of India, does hereby bestow upon Flying Officer Brian Arthur Drummond the honor of Commander, Most Excellent Order of the British Empire, for services to the Crown far beyond and above the call of duty as a pilot in Fighter Command, Royal Air Force. Flying Officer Drummond, please stand."

Brian stood at attention, his heart racing a bit more than expected. The Lord Chamberlain stepped forward, holding a purple cushion with a single-ribboned medal in the center of the cushion. The King took the medal and pinned it to Brian's uniform tunic above his wings and the Military Cross medal still on his uniform. Brian saluted and the King returned his salute even though he was not in uniform. The King extended his right hand to Brian. They shook hands.

"Congratulations, Brian . . . justly deserved, and I suspect the first of more to come for you. Thank you, truly and deeply, from the bottom of my heart, for everything you have done and will do for our little country and for freedom itself."

"Thank you, your Majesty."

"Now, if you will excuse us, we must return to our other duties." He turned to Charlotte. "An honor to see you, again, Mrs. Palmer. I trust this shall not be our last meeting. Take good care of yourself and our young Brian here."

"Yes, your Majesty," she answered and curtsied.

The royals departed followed by the Lord Chamberlain, the Ghurkas, the Yeomen, and all but one of the stewards.

The remaining steward said, "If you would be so kind to follow me, sir."

Brian and Charlotte followed a few steps behind the steward. Charlotte was beaming like he had never seen her smile before. She grasped his hand, squeezed it tightly and pulled it to her chest. "I am so proud of you," she whispered.

"Thank you, but I am the same man I was before all this."

"Indeed, just as I am the same woman with the same fears and the same doubts. Let us just enjoy the moment."

"Yes, my darling."

The steward led them down several progressively narrower corridors, and ushered them into a rather small, non-descript office where the Lord Chamberlain was waiting for them. He shook hands with Brian and Charlotte.

"I am the Earl of Clarendon, Lord Chamberlain of the Royal Household. You both did quite well, especially considering my office did not have sufficient time to prepare for the ceremony, or prepare you, since His Majesty wished the honor to be a surprise. Nonetheless, I wish to inform you that the Central Chancery will properly inform the Prime Minister's office and the Royal Air Force of this private investiture. You are entitled to the post-nominal CBE in recognition of the King's honor to you. Since you are an American and not likely to be aware, the CBE is one step short of knighthood and an exceptional honor, especially for a young American. Do you have any questions that I may answer for you?"

"No sir," answered Brian.

"Mrs. Palmer?"

"No, Lord Chamberlain."

"Very well, then. I do believe your automobile is waiting to take you back to your hotel or wherever you wish to go. If you ever have any questions or concerns, please do not hesitate to call my office. Again, congratulations, Mister Drummond, and thank you for your service to the Crown."

"Thank you, sir."

The Lord Chamberlain motioned to the door, which miraculously opened. The steward, who had delivered them, escorted them to their waiting vehicle. What a day . . . and it was not yet done.

Brian and Charlotte returned to the hotel. They had time for a celebratory dinner, one last episode of pleasure that would have to hold them for an unknown period, and then Brian would take an overnight train north to report by noon the next day for duty. Charlotte planned to spend the night in London – The Blitz permitting – and return to Winchester in the morning.

—

Friday, 8.November.1940
RAF Catterick
Catterick, North Yorkshire, England
United Kingdom
12:00 hours

The rail journey had been surprisingly smooth and uneventful. Brian slept through most of the trip. He was deposited at Northallerton Station shortly before nine in the morning. He managed to find an RAF truck at the station to pick up a parts shipment. The leading aircraftman had been quite willing to give Brian a lift to the aerodrome and have the company for the ride. Brian had the driver drop him off at the Officer's Mess, so he could check in, clean himself up from the overnight travel, grab a bite to eat, and then make his way to No.609 Squadron.

The few remaining original squadron mates greeted him enthusiastically, marveled at the two new medals still on his uniform, since he had not had time to replace them with conventional ribbons. There were more new faces than there were old ones. Introductions were completed in due course. Jonathan and Victor Clegg had launched on a mission and were due back in 30 minutes.

Squadron Leader Jason Billings 'Stack' Long-Roberts, the current commander of No.609 Squadron, appeared at his office door and motioned with his head for Brian to join him. He closed the door once Brian entered.

"Flying Officer Drummond reporting for duty."

The senior officer extended his hand to Brian. They shook hands. "I'm Jason Long-Roberts. Nice to finally meet you, Hunter."

"Thank you, sir. It's great to be back."

Stack motioned for Brian to be seated. "Congratulations on your awards and honors. I was informed this morning that Chief of the Air Staff Portal pinned the Military Cross on your chest, and just yesterday, King George himself honored you with a CBE . . . most impressive, and even more so for a young American volunteer to receive such recognition. "

"Yes sir. It was quite a surprise."

"I can only imagine. I am also informed you are to be transferred to Seventy-One Squadron at Church Fenton."

"Yes sir, although I was not told when."

"Well, then, I can inform you the effective date is today. Your replacement aircraft has been waiting for your return. Seventy-One Squadron is flying Brewster Buffalos for God's sake, so I figured you might appreciate what may be your last flight in a Spit for a while. When Harness returns with his Green Section, we will turn him around, so you can go stretch your legs. I am sorry we shall not have the benefit of your experience to help the newbies learn the ropes, but we all move eventually. You are due to report to your new squadron on Tuesday. When we are finished with you, I am to release you for another few days. I presume you will return to Winchester."

"Yes sir. I expected to be there for those few days, so I have no idea what the rail schedules are like up here."

"Corporal Warren can help you with that."

"Thank you, sir," responded Brian.

Squadron Operations Clerk Corporal Jennifer Warren, Women's Auxiliary Air Force, had been with the squadron at least as long as Brian had.

"The Air Ministry also informs me the flight surgeons have returned you to full flight status and duty. Are you ready to fly, again?"

"Yes sir, absolutely. I've missed my Spit. Thank you for allowing me one last flight, for now. I hope it is not my last forever, but yes, I am quite ready to run the legs out."

"Since you lost your kit in the crash, we need to refit you. So, let's get that done, so you are ready when Harness returns. We shall at least have a few hours at full strength."

"I wish I could stay, but I have been told I need to move on."

"Quite understandable, I should think."

Brian found the supply building and received his new issue of helmet, goggles, oxygen mask, flotation vest and flight gloves. He returned to the Dispersal Hut, found a wall peg with his name above it, stowed his flight equipment on the assigned peg, and found an open chair to wait for Jonathan's return. Brian removed the two new medals on his uniform tunic and put them in his pocket. No one needed those things flopping around in flight. He leaned back against the wall and closed his eyes.

"Excuse me, sir."

Brian opened his eyes to see a boy-ish looking flight sergeant standing before him. He shrugged his shoulders, as if to say, well, what do you want?

"You must be Flying Officer Drummond"

"Indeed, I am."

"I heard from my family and my brother that you visited our farm a fortnight ago."

"Carrwood?"

"Yes sir ... Flying Sergeant George Carrwood," he said, extending his hand.

Brian settled his chair, shook hands with Carrwood, and patted the open chair next to him. "I met your family last month. Your Brother Peter saved my life, when I crashed on your farmland at the end of September."

"That was you?"

"Yep. I was very lucky to have your brother and his farmhands close by that day."

The two men shared their versions of the story. The impressions of the Carrwood family as told to their middle son proved quite insightful, especially having met the family and seen the site first hand.

The distinct sound of two Merlin engines on approach captured Brian's attention. He raised his hand, stood and looked out the window. Two Spitfires approached for landing from the east. Brian could not see the tail designator letters, so he was not certain. Their landing was flawless and taxied to the 609 flight line. Their gun port tapes were still intact – no fight. As they turned to their parking spots, Brian saw 'PR-K' and 'PR-S' – Jonathan and his right wing, which had to be Victor Clegg. Brian excused himself and went outside. The canopy came back, the access door flung open, and Jonathan hopped out and walked briskly toward Brian. The two men embraced like long-lost brothers.

"Great to have you back, Brian."

"Great to be back and even greater to see you again. How was the sortie?"

"Boring . . . convoy patrol. They don't send squadrons anymore . . . just a light section these days."

Jonathan's right wingman joined them. "Brian, this is Victor Clegg – right wing." Brian shook hands with Clegg. "Victor, this is THE Brian Drummond – fighter pilot *extraordinaire*."

"Great to meet you finally. Flying Officer Kensington has told me so much about you."

Brian looked back to Jonathan. "Flying officer . . . really?"

"Hey, we must maintain proper military comportment, after all we are a Royal Air Force combat squadron."

"Nonsense, we all die just as easy, my friend."

"Now, you don't need to be the damper here, Hunter. Are you ready to go fly?"

"Absolutely."

"As soon as they get our birds turned around, we'll take you up for a work out."

"Excellent."

"Skipper told me this morning you are being transferred to Seventy-One when we are done this afternoon."

"Yes. The Prime Minister did not order me to move, but he sure made it clear he thought I should join the other Americans. I guess they are calling Seventy-One the Eagle Squadron."

"So I hear. The Prime Minister, ay . . . do tell."

"You met Prime Minister Churchill?" interjected Clegg.

"Victor, what did I tell you? A wingman is to be seen and not heard."

Brian quickly recounted the events of the last few days. Questions from both men filled in any blanks in Brian's story. Brian pulled out the two medals to show his brethren.

"I'll be damned!" Jonathan exclaimed. "Congratulations all around, my brother."

"Congratulations, Mister Drummond."

"Brian or Hunter, Victor. I am not much on pretense or hierarchy." Clegg nodded his head.

A senior aircraftman Brian did not recognize walked up to inform Jonathan their aircraft were ready.

"Shall we cut the cords that hold us to this earth, my brother??"

"If you insist, let's do it."

Jonathan looked over his shoulder and gave the launch hand signal. Brian looked back to the rest of the squadron, including Corporal Warren and Squadron Leader Long-Roberts, standing outside the Dispersal Hut to observe the launch of the finally complete Green Section.

Brian smiled when he saw the 'PR-F' letters on the tail, either side of the roundel, on what appeared to be a brand new Supermarine Spitfire Mark IA fighter. His crew chief was another new man, who assisted Brian in donning his parachute harness, tightening the straps, and then attaching himself to the machine. *Damn, it feels good to be back in harness, again.* Brian made the necessary connections – microphone, headphones, oxygen. He quickly stepped through the pre-start checks and settings, and then looked past Clegg's 'PR-S' Spitfire to wait for Jonathan's start hand signal. Brian smiled broadly when the big Merlin engine sputtered to life, came to a nice fast idle, and he switched everything on. The vibration and hum of the engine combined with the prop wash swirling through his cockpit made Brian feel like he was home, again. *I'm going to truly miss this beautiful machine.* Jonathan called for their taxi permission. The westerly breeze made them taxi to the far end of the field. They would be taking off just past their Dispersal Hut. Jonathan allowed Brian the extra time for him to complete the added first-flight-of-the-day checks to ensure everything was in proper working order.

Jonathan called for a section takeoff to the west. Brian took his assigned position off Jonathan's left wing. Jonathan nodded his head forward signaling their takeoff. Brian advanced the throttle to match Jonathan's acceleration across the field. He felt the tail rise. The aircraft got light on the landing gear as their speed rapidly increased, bounced a few times, and in a blink, they were airborne. Brian retracted his undercarriage with Jonathan and adjusted his controls to maintain position off and below Jonathan's left wing. Jonathan kept all three aircraft low and at full power, presumably to give their squadron colleagues a good show. He entered a full power climb and turned left 180 degrees. Jonathan signaled for their frequency change.

Brian heard "Two," and then broadcast, "Three," telling their leader they were on frequency.

"Echo, this is Sorbo Green calling."

"Sorbo Green, Echo, go ahead."

"Sorbo Green with three climbing zero nine zero. We need a training area. We are armed and available, if you need us."

"Roger, Sorbo Green. You can take angels one five. There are no aircraft in your area. We should have a quiet afternoon. Welcome back, Hunter. Give him a good workout Sorbo Green."

"Wilco," responded Jonathan. "The sky is yours, Hunter. We'll stand off for now."

"Roger Sorbo Green Leader," Brian answered.

Brian banked his machine hard left and pulled firmly back on the control spade. He felt the g's pull on his body. He continued around until he re-acquired the other two Spitfires that were in a shallow right turn. Brian rolled his aircraft right through a full roll, and than rolled left through a full roll. He lowered the nose to build-up speed, and then pulled hard into a loop. As he approached the inverted position, Brian looked down. It took him several second to find the two Spitfires. He continued to pull through the first loop and into a second. Again, he searched to re-acquire his brethren. This time through, as the nose dropped below the horizon, Brian rolled the aircraft smartly to the upright position. He was not quite with the sun behind his tail but close enough. Brian had the two Spitfires centered up in his gunsight. His speed was increasing rapidly toward red line. He pulled through several hard S-turns to control his speed as he closed with his prey.

"Tack-a-tack-a-tack-a," Brian broadcast, as he dove past them.

"Green break. So, you are ready to play are you?"

Brian did not respond but immediately pulled into another loop to gain height and perch for a re-engagement. He re-acquired both Spitfires; they were in climbing turns coming after him. Brian turned out of his loop to pick his 'target' for a head-on pass. The two fighters quickly closed at their combined opposing speeds. Brian saw the other Spit quickly adjust his flight path to assist his comrade, but he was not close enough.

"Tack-a-tack-a-tack-a," Brian broadcast his pretend shots, and then rolled hard left to pick up the wingman closing to engage. Neither of them got a shot as they passed canopy to canopy. Brian rolled back hard right and pulled his nose up. He pushed on his throttle to feel the resistance of the emergency gate wire. There was no need to press the engine in a training exercise. The wingman had done the same thing and quickly realized he was not going to gain position on Brian, so he rolled hard right and dove away. Brian rolled to chase at least to maintain his superior position, as he strained his neck looking for the other Spit. This time, he was not so lucky. The other one was turning ahead of him. He had the superior position. Brian rolled and dove to pass underneath his attacker, hopefully before he attained a firing solution. It worked.

The three aircraft continued their aerial dance for several more minutes. None of them knew whether Brian's two shots would have eliminated their intended 'target.' The best he could do was to keep either adversary from gaining a firing solution on him.

They flew several more mock engagements with Brian starting in an inferior position. He was able to defend himself. They had been airborne over an hour, which made them less useful for any potential enemy action.

"Have you had enough, Sorbo Green Three?"

"Are you giving up?" Brian broadcast.

"No, but I do not want to wear you out on your first day back."

"Thank you for your thoughtfulness. Let me do a couple of stalls and a spin, and then we can call it a day."

"As you wish. Enjoy."

Brian pulled his throttle back to idle to allow his aircraft to decelerate. He maintained his altitude. The aircraft slowed past 90 miles per hour until he felt the characteristic wing shudder and the nose dropped. He recovered. Then, he configured the aircraft for landing, lowering the undercarriage and flaps. He maintained level flight at approach speed for a few seconds, and then throttled back, entered a shallow left turn and raised the nose slightly to allow the airspeed to decay. This time the wing shudder was followed by a snap roll. Brian centered his controls, let the airspeed build and returned to smooth level flight. He cleaned up the aircraft, checked his altitude, kept his throttle back at idle, and as he entered another stall, he added rudder, which snapped the aircraft over and into a spiral. Brian allowed the spin to stabilize for a half dozen turns, and then centered his control. The spin rate slowed. Brian applied slight opposite rudder and aileron. The spin slowly stopped with the nose below the horizon. Airspeed increased rapidly. Brian looked over his shoulders – Spitfires on both wings matching his speed and descent rate. As they passed 300 miles per hour, Brian slowly pulled the nose up to the horizon and pushed his throttle forward to stabilize their airspeed and altitude. With the heads of the two pilots trailing him covered by their helmets, goggles and oxygen masks, identification took a little more time to recognize Jonathan was on his left wing. Brian pulled up smoothly and barrel-rolled left over the top of Jonathan's aircraft. He quickly settled into his proper position on Jonathan's left wing.

Jonathan checked out with Usworth Sector Control. They switched to Catterick Tower. Jonathan requested a high speed, low pass, followed by a left break for landing. Brian knew what that meant and shifted his position behind and below Clegg's right wing. Jonathan throttled up to not quite full power to leave Victor and Brian maneuvering power to maintain position, and descended to 200 feet height above the trees to allow Brian sufficient ground clearance. As they crossed the airfield boundary, Jonathan dropped a little lower. Brian felt like his propeller was cutting the grass. They were at nearly full throttle and probably doing better than 350 miles per hour. When they approached the far end of the field, Jonathan, Victor and Brian pulled up smoothly. In sequence at three second intervals, they rolled left. Brian pulled his throttle back to idle, allowed his speed to decrease, adjusted his flight path to follow his comrades, and when his aircraft slowed sufficiently, he reconfigured the machine for landing. They landed nicely, taxied to their respective parking spots and shutdown.

Brian sat in the Spitfire cockpit to relish the moment – it would have to last him. He unstrapped, unplugged and extricated himself from the confines of the small cockpit.

Again, the entire squadron was outside. Squadron Leader Long-Roberts nodded his approval and retired to his office. The Green Section pilots recounted the afternoon's event . . . well, mostly Clegg regaled in Brian's skill against two comparable adversaries. Brian did not talk much – rarely did. The informal debriefing transitioned to war stories from the previous months of battle.

While they were flying, Corporal Warren called to check on available trains south, through London, to Winchester, from any of the nearby stations. There was nothing until early tomorrow morning, which would place him at Standing Oak Farm by mid-afternoon, if he was lucky. Jonathan offered to take him to Carlingon Castle. Brian considered the offer and declined, not that he did not thoroughly enjoy the Kensington family home and Jonathan's parents, but he wanted to spend what time he had left with his few remaining mates. They would have dinner at the Mess, and then they would visit a favored local public house in Catterick village.

The sun disappeared in an hour and they were well into twilight when the squadron was released. Brian had his orders endorsed. Dinner was served at the Mess by the time the pilots arrived. No.609 Squadron was the last of the Catterick squadrons to be released. Brian called Charlotte to inform her of his plan and schedule. She had an uneventful journey back to home and had arrived just after noon.

The night at the pub became a celebration of Brian's service in the squadron. They enjoyed plenty of drink, with the veterans – 'Sparky,' 'Waggle,' Harness, 'Boxer' and 'Fog' – offering their favorite stories about Hunter. They also dragged information out of Brian about his visit with the King, Prime Minister Churchill and the War Cabinet.

Most of the pilots including Jonathan and Brian returned to the Mess before midnight. The two friends would leave at 04:30, since they would have to travel to Darlington for a 06:00 train south to King's Cross Terminal in London. Jonathan would depart 45 minutes later for Newcastle and his family home for the weekend.

—

Friday, 8.November.1940
Ditchley Park
Enstone, Oxfordshire, England
United Kingdom
18:45 hours

"Welcome to Ditchley Park," announced the handsome, smartly dressed, middle-aged man with an attractive, elegantly dressed woman standing next to him, as Clementine and Winston Churchill stepped out of the Prime Minister's black limousine.

Arthur Ronald Lambert Field 'Ron' Tree, Member of Parliament for Harborough and Conservative Party politician and his wife Nancy Keene Tree née Perkins, a celebrated interior decorator in her own right, purchased the country manor house and 730 acres of gardens, farm and woodlands from the estate of the 17th Viscount Dillon on his passing.

"Thank you for your hospitality and generous offer of refuge," answered Churchill. "Detective-Inspector Thompson," he said, nodding to his bodyguard behind him, "and the War Cabinet fret about my staying at Chequers near the time of the full moon. We closed Chartwell at the end of the Phony War because of the bombing threat. Now, they deny me relaxation at Chequers, all because of these damnable Hun bombers. We shall do our best to avoid drawing attention to your manor house."

"Quite understandable, Prime Minister. We are happy to be of service and are not concerned in the least." Nancy Tree smiled, as if to emphasize her husband's statement. "Since both you and Clementine have been our guests before, I do not believe you need a tour, unless you or Clemmie would care for a refresher."

Winston looked to Clementine, who shook her head. "I suspect our memory should be sufficient."

"Very well, then, shall we," Ronald said, motioning toward the front entrance. As they walked, Tree continued, "Dinner will be served at eight, if you would care to freshen up from your journey and perhaps imbibe a cocktail before supper."

"Most generous of you, Ron. We shall join you, shortly."

Drinks before dinner and the sumptuous meal were most enjoyable with idle chitchat about the weather, productivity of the farmlands, and the beauty of surrounding forest. The manor offered lodging for visitors to the royal hunting ground of Wychwood Forest. They retired to the library for after-dinner drinks and conversation. Approaching 22:00 hours, the Tree's butler announced the arrival of Colonel Menzies to see the Prime Minister on urgent business. No one other than the Churchill's and Ron Tree knew the colonel was none other than Director-General, Secret Intelligence Service (MI6), Colonel Stewart Graham Menzies, DSO, MC, known as 'C' for his position.

"Do you have a private room I may use, Ron?"

"Yes sir."

Churchill waited in a small office at the end of the corridor. 'C' joined him and closed the door behind him.

"Judging from the hour of your arrival and the distance you had to travel, I suspect you are not the bearer of good news," Churchill observed.

"I wanted to discuss this with you personally and privately. We decoded three messages today that I have with me in the Buff Box, if you wish to review them. Taken in combination, I am left with the suspicion the Germans may be wary of the integrity of Enigma."

Churchill dropped his lower jaw, remained speechless, and the shocked expression conveyed his emotions. He carefully read each of the three decrypted messages. After reading the messages, he quickly scanned each message, again. "I see the basis of your assessment. I agree; however, they seem to be fishing for others who might be suspicious. Have they changed their encryption processes?"

"Not yet."

"Dear God above, we cannot lose ULTRA."

"The Germans were trying to understand why we were so successful in stopping their air superiority campaign during the summer and their perception of achieving less than desired success in hitting targets during their current night bombing operations. Our successes at sea have increased in the last two months as well."

"We must be more careful and deliberative with our use of ULTRA material. Where is the list of those who have access to the ULTRA product."

"In the Buff Box, sir."

Menzies placed the manacled case on the small desk beside the Prime Minister. Churchill retrieved the only key that could open the box, outside the Secret Intelligence Service. He found the single sheet of paper in the 'Top of the Box' folder.

MOST SECRET -- ULTRA

SECRETARIAT
Winston Churchill
Sir Edward Bridges
Major General Sir Hastings Ismay
FOREIGN OFFICE
Lord Halifax
Sir Robert Vansittart
Sir Alexander Cadogan
Sir Orme Sargent
Colonel Stewart Menzies
NAVY
A. V. Alexander
Admiral of the Fleet Sir Dudley Pound
Vice Admiral Sir Thomas Phillips
Director of Naval Intelligence
ARMY
Anthony Eden
General Sir John Dill
General Sir Robert Haining
Director of Military Intelligence
AIR FORCE
Sir Archibald Sinclair
Air Chief Marshal Sir Charles Portal

```
Air Chief Marshal Sir Wilfrid Freeman
Director of Air Intelligence
     WAR CABINET
Sir John Anderson
Clement Attlee
Arthur Greenwood
Lord Beaverbrook
Ernest Bevin
Sir Kingsley Wood
Sir Alexander Hardinge (for the King)
Secretary of the Joint Intelligence Committee
   (Colonel Denis Capel-Dunn)
Officer in charge of 'Secret Records'
Duty Officer at the Central War Room
Professor Noel Hall, Ministry of Economic
Warfare
```

MOST SECRET -- ULTRA

Churchill studied the list for several minutes, clearly thinking about each name on the access list. "Very good. I presume you have included Commander Denniston and his Station 'X' analysts and staff."

Commander Alastair Ignatius Denniston, CMG, CBE, had been instrumental in forming Room 40 within the Admiralty in 1914, to break enemy codes and analyze their secret communications. After the Great War, the Room 40 operation was renamed the Government Code and Cypher School (GC&CS) in 1920, and transferred from the Navy to the Foreign Office under the Secret Intelligence Service (MI6). Denniston had been the director of GC&CS since its inception. Before the war, GC&CS moved to Bletchley Park, which was often referred to as Station 'X' in association with Station 'Y', which was the radio interception network that fed GC&CS with coded message traffic.

"Yes sir. Denniston keeps things fairly well compartmented. He has perhaps a dozen individuals who would see enough of the decrypts to know the significance of what they have before them, and perhaps another score of technical experts that see portions of the material and could deduce the importance of what they see."

"Do you think Denniston has sufficient control of his people?"

"Yes sir. He has and continues to put the fear of God into his people. They are also fairly cloistered at Bletchley Park and they are watched by a healthy contingent of MI5 agents."

Churchill was satisfied with the answer. "What about these unspecified personnel at the bottom?"

"They are a handful of specially selected clerks to maintain the files and paperwork. Secret Records is our internal sub-section of the administrative group that deals with special intelligence material only. The War Room is your Map Room in the bunker."

"I presume the unspecified service intelligence directors have other individuals within their directorates who might have access."

"We have tried to respect their positions within the intelligence system."

"So, if we total up every single individual who has any knowledge of what ULTRA is, or even might guess what ULTRA is, we are talking about double this list of 31 individuals."

"Yes sir."

"No one outside His Majesty's Government?"

"No sir."

"I do not like these unnamed individuals having access. We are not granting access to incalculably priceless intelligence to a position. We are only granting access to a specific named individual. I want every single individual with ULTRA access to know precisely that their name appears on this list, and we know who they are. Also, for now, I shall retain the sole authority to add or subtract from this access list. We cannot tolerate even the slightest risk to our golden egg."

"Yes sir. I understand. I will coordinate with Sir Edward and General Ismay to specify Secretariat staff with access, and with the service intelligence directors to specify their individuals. Certainly, I will take care of the MI6 and Station X personnel."

Major General Sir Hastings Lionel 'Pug' Ismay, KCB, DSO, served the Prime Minister in several positions – Principal Assistant to the Minister of Defense (Churchill), Secretary of the Imperial Defense Chiefs of Staff Committee, Deputy Secretary of the War Cabinet, and otherwise the principal conduit between Minister of Defense, and the Chiefs of Staff and the military service branches.

"Pray give me the revised list next week, the sooner the better. Also, please focus on the German suspicions. If their worries are substantive, pray use every tool you have to determine why? We must know if we have a leak. If we do . . . well, let us just say that man will never see the sun again."

"Yes sir. It shall be done."

Menzies retrieved the paper, returned it to the proper folder, closed and latched the Buff Box. "If there is nothing else, Prime Minister, I shall be off."

"It is late, Stewart. Perhaps you and your driver should spend the night. I am certain we can find something for both of you to eat as well."

"Thank you, Winston, but no. I must decline. My driver and guards are the night shift crew. I will probably sleep a little on the return journey. I really must get back to Broadway House. We have analysts working around the clock on this German concern."

"Hopefully, this is just routine suspicion and not the product of a leak on our part."

"An understatement, I am certain. We are leaving no stone unturned."

"Thank you, Stewart. Then, safe journey."

Menzies departed. Churchill's mind churned over what they might be facing. They had only recently become more proficient in deciphering the German Enigma-encoded messages, and even that was spotty as the daily wheel settings changed or they changed the plug board configuration. It could take days or weeks to break. Bletchley Park – Station 'X' – improved their techniques, but there were always setbacks. On a good day, they could read messages in near real time, and then the yield would go dark for a day or more. Even with the intermittent performance of decryption, the messages they did see were of incalculable value. Those deciphered messages saved lives and precious supplies. They simply had to make absolutely certain there were no leaks.

Churchill returned to the others. He remained pensive and unusually quiet. The others did not question him or try to engage him in the conversation, and he was thankful for their understanding.

—

Chapter 3

As soon as questions of will or decision or
reason or choice of action arise,
human science is at a loss.

- Noam Chomsky

Saturday, 9.November.1940
Standing Oak Farm
Winchester, Hampshire, England
United Kingdom
14:30 hours

Charlotte stood outside her front door as Brian's taxi came to a stop in the driveway. The air was on the chilly side, but at least it was dry and bright. Brian paid the driver and thanked him for his service – Great War, infantry, Western Front.

"Welcome home," Charlotte said, when the car door closed and the taxi drove away. "A pleasant and most welcome surprise, I must say. Thank you for your telephone call last evening."

"Thanks. Likewise. Things just happened that way."

"How long do I have you for this time?"

"A couple of days. I have to report to RAF Church Fenton by noon on Tuesday. I'll need to at least get to London by Monday night and probably take the overnight train to York."

"Did your squadron move again?"

"No. My transfer to Seventy-One Squadron came in earlier than expected."

Brian carried his bag in one hand and held Charlotte's hand in the other hand as they moved to the warm interior. He dropped his bag inside and released Charlotte's hand to remove his uniform cap and tunic, and placed them on a chair near the door.

"How was your journey?"

"Quiet and on schedule. Squadron Leader Long-Roberts allowed me one last flight in a Spitfire for some playtime with Jonathan and one of their new replacement pilots."

"I'm certain you enjoyed yourself."

"Without question. I will miss Spits. I am told Seventy-One is flying American Brewster Buffalos."

Charlotte chuckled. "I have no idea what that is."

"Let it suffice to say, Buffalos are a long way from Spitfires."

"Why would they do that to you?"

"Charlotte, my dear, they are not doing it to me. It is just the way things are."

"Then, why would Churchill ask you to go to a squadron with a less capable aeroplane?"

They sat at the kitchen table. Charlotte poured a cup of tea for each of them. She had a small plate of crackers and cheese slices on the table rather than her favored fresh-baked cookies.

Brian answered, "I doubt Churchill was even aware of what aircraft the American volunteer squadron is flying. I suspect he is far more concerned with the imagery, the politics, of me being elsewhere."

"Are you OK with that?"

"I trust Mister Churchill. I am doing what he needs me to do, for whatever reason. I will make do. After all, flying is flying."

"Well then . . . as long as you are happy."

Brian held her eyes, did not blink, and waited several minutes. "Charlotte, I will not be happy until this war is done, we are married, and we are living together ever after with our children. I was an only child. You say you want children. I do not want our child to be an only child."

"On that we are agreed."

"As some Chinese philosopher said many years ago, 'Long journeys begin with a single step.' We shall take this journey together."

This time Charlotte looked into Brian's eyes. "Do you feel up for a walk?"

"My leg is fine, but it is a bit on the chilly side, don't you think?"

"Perhaps, but we can dress for it, and the fresh air will feel good."

Charlotte retrieved a heavy overcoat and gloves for Brian, and a headscarf and an ample overcoat for herself. They walked past the lake toward the stand of elm, birch and conifer trees that ran along the eastern boundary of her land.

Charlotte was the first to speak and said matter-of-factly, "I wanted to thank you for allowing me into your life."

Brian stopped, turned to face and placed his hands on her shoulders. "You say that like you are telling me we are over."

She shook her head. "No. I am just trying to convey my gratitude. You are a special man. You deserve a younger, more tolerant, accepting and supportive woman."

"Nonsense!" Brian said on the verge of shouting.

"You can have anyone you choose. I am eight years older than you. I will be an old woman while you are still young and virile."

"Is that what this is all about?"

"I'm serious, Brian."

"As am I. Do you really think I am too young to love you properly?"

"That is not it at all. I just worry." She turned from his embrace and continued their walk. "Our trip to London was very overwhelming. I kept my emotions to myself as best I could because I knew it was your moment and I did not want to spoil it for you. Portal's recounting of your exploits scared me, disturbed me . . . thinking you had come so close." She walked in silence for several yards and Brian did not want to disturb her thoughts. "That was my first time to London since The Blitz began in September. The destruction staggered me. I mean I have read about it in the newspaper, but to see it first hand and up close . . . well . . . it brought home why you are doing what you do. The bunker for the government, where we met Prime Minister Churchill . . . I would not have believed it if I had not seen it for myself. The thought of German oppression on our precious land is beyond comprehensible. Meeting Churchill, the King, the Queen, even Princess Elizabeth . . . I never in my wildest dreams would have imagined doing such things, and they were all so very nice, gracious and . . . well . . . human."

"They are no different from you and me."

Charlotte laughed as they walked. "Yes, they are, Brian. They are quite different. They were born to high station."

"I do not see them that way."

"You are blessed with that perspective."

"You have met them, shaken their hands and listened to their words."

Charlotte did not respond. She remained pensive for a dozen yards. Birds were chirping and singing in the trees. The earthy smell of the land and the scents of the forest complemented the air. Brian wanted to speak, to ask questions, to convey his feelings, but he knew better than to intrude on her thoughts. *Whatever she is dealing with I have to let her get it out.*

"I owe you my candor, Brian." This time she stopped to face him. Brian did not let go of her hand. "I was embarrassed to be introduced as Mrs. Palmer, not that I am ashamed of my marriage to Ian. I think of myself as Mrs. Drummond. I want to be Mrs. Drummond."

"We can fix that today."

"Brian, don't! I am trying to be honest and forthright with you. You know how I feel. You know how vulnerable I am; how raw my emotions are."

"Yes, I do. What can I do to help?"

"Just listen." Charlotte turned and walked on. "Let's head back. I am taking on a bit of a chill."

Brian put his arm around her as they walked. By the time they reached the house, it was nearly time for the afternoon milking. They tended their afternoon chores with Lionel and Horace. Charlotte fed the men after the animals were taken care of for the night. After supper, Lionel and Horace departed. Brian helped Charlotte with the cleanup. Charlotte blew out the candles. Brian saw her expression, her eyes, and knew what she was telling him. She switched off the lights. They readied themselves for bed. They both needed the intimacy of lovers and neither of them was disappointed with their shared pleasure. Eventually, they gave into sleep and would remain intertwined for most of the night.

———

Sunday, 10.November.1940
Standing Oak Farm
Winchester, Hampshire, England
United Kingdom
12:00 hours

"Thank you for lunch," Brian offered.

"You are most welcome, always,"

"What would you like to do this afternoon?"

"Talk."

Brian chuckled, more to himself. "That seems to be all we do."

"Perhaps so, but we do not have much time together, and there is much to discuss."

"Very well, then. What would you like to discuss?"

Charlotte did not answer and simply led Brian into the living room. She wanted to sit opposite Brian, presumably so she could see his face and eyes. Brian studied her face. *Where is this going to go?*

"Where to start?" Charlotte mused aloud.

"At the beginning might be appropriate."

She smiled. "Oh you cheeky rogue." Brian returned her smile. "I want nothing between us."

"Likewise."

Charlotte lowered her head breaking eye contact with Brian. "I have not mentioned my mother before now." Brian waited, giving her all the time she needed. "I knew my mother took my father's passing rather hard, but I did not know how hard." Charlotte swallowed hard several times and wiped tears from her eyes. "I was not quite four years old when my father and uncle were both killed within days of each other during the Battle of Passchendaele in Flanders, Belgium, in September 1917. That was bad enough, but I was barely old enough to understand what had occurred. My mother worked very hard to shield me from that pain, from her pain. It all came home to me when

I turned 18 years old. At first, I was confused by her wild emotional swings between deep, withdrawn depression and frenetic almost manic efforts with lawyers." She paused, swallowed hard and stared down at nothing on the table. "I remember vividly last year, in August, at our award ceremony with the King at Middle Wallop, telling you that my mother died in a ferry accident."

"Yes, I remember," Brian said softly. All of his senses remained riveted on Charlotte, but he could not divert his attention.

Charlotte did not move. Brian noticed the first round spots appear on the table – tears. She was silently crying, no sobbing, no sounds, just tears descending her cheeks and dropping to the table. Charlotte raised her head and eyes to capture Brian's eyes. Streams of tears sparkled on her cheeks. "That was not the truth, Brian, and I cannot live with anything hidden or false between us."

Brian swallowed hard. *This cannot be good. What could possibly be bothering her this much?* He nodded his head in recognition, or perhaps his emotion was agreement.

"Three months after my 18th birthday, she committed suicide."

Holy shit! No wonder this is affecting her so much. I wonder how she did it? Did she see her Mom after . . . ?

"She left me a long letter explaining that she would have ended her life the day she was notified by the Army of my father's death, if it had not been for me. She lived to get me to my age of majority, and then chose to join my father in heaven."

"Charlotte . . . Charlotte . . . I am so sorry. I had no idea."

"Because I did not want you to know. I did not want to remember. I was embarrassed. I did not want to admit, or perhaps the proper word is confess, the tragedy of my family. I am grateful Mum did not follow her banal instincts, and that she gave me the few years she did, but her selfish action put a terrible, terrible stamp on my father's death." Brian did not move, did not blink, and did not say a word. He wanted to reach out to her, to embrace her, but knew he could not. "I have no siblings. Both my parents and all my grandparents are gone. I am all that is left of my family. I went through a crazy phase, perhaps to compensate for my mother's actions . . . to blot out the pain I felt. I slept with anyone who could walk and showed the slightest, ever so slight, interest. It did not matter who, just that they were willing. I have absolutely no idea how many, and alcohol probably erased portions of my memory of those years. That phase lasted through my college years. I am still amazed I managed to complete my studies and examinations, to obtain my degree. It was Ian who saved me from that destructiveness. I did not love him, at least not at first, but I was grateful, oh so grateful, that he loved me enough to give me stability, to marry me despite what he knew I had done." Again, she stopped, probably to consider her words. Brian gave her space and time. "Ian was a good man. I am still close to his parents, to his family. His mother, father and younger brother still live in a delightfully idyllic cottage in Devon near Plymouth, on the edge of Dartmoor Forest. Ian's father is a very successful shipping merchant, although the war has hurt his business as well. Ian's family virtually adopted me as their daughter. This is a bit awkward, yet I feel the necessity to introduce you to Ian's family . . . before I begin to show. I want them to know you and hopefully to accept you in my life and theirs."

"That does not leave us much time."

"No, it does not."

"It might take some coordination since I am back at duty. I would recommend you contact the Palmers to at least alert them, and make them aware of my constraints."

"Quite so. I will contact them next week. Let us try to make the visit before Christmas."

"I shall do my best."

"I know you will, and thank you for accommodating the peculiarities of my life, Brian. Do you have any questions?"

"Wow! I probably have plenty, but I have not organized my thoughts. Is this the only opportunity I will have to ask questions? I am curious, but I do not want to offend your generosity and openness."

Charlotte smiled and giggled softly. "No, you can ask anything you wish whenever you wish to know."

"Thank you. Then, in the spirit of your openness, I owe you the same candor." She nodded her acceptance. "As I told you before, Malcolm Bainbridge taught me to fly, largely without my parents' knowledge or consent. He died in a plane crash in March of this year. It was Malcolm and John Spencer who helped me travel to Canada, to join the RAF, and they protected me from extradition. I actually have a presidential pardon for my violation of U.S. law. My parents gave up trying to get me to leave and return home. I miss them. I must say you have far more experience than me. I had no idea how people were supposed to learn about sex, other than masturbation, which I figured out on my own, my first experience was with my first girlfriend in high school."

Brian continued his confession about his relationship with Rebecca Seward and her dumping him when she went off to college and he went off to join the RAF before the war in Europe sparked to full blaze. He also told her about Jeremy Morrison and his introduction to Anne Booth. He was not bashful with Charlotte about Anne's teaching him properly about matters of pleasure, or about his love for her. Brian told Charlotte about the arrest and execution of Anne and Virginia, and he recounted his questioning by MI5 and the Metropolitan Police. Charlotte had already met Rosemary Kensington, Jonathan's younger sister, and the two women had shared their experience and love for Brian, so he did not feel the need to expand on his feelings for Rosemary. Brian found it most difficult to tell Charlotte about his relationship with Mary Spencer, because she was married to his RAF mentor, and she was pregnant by her insistence and Brian's contribution. Charlotte kept her emotions and questions contained, not wanting to interfere with Brian's thoughts. His long pause and vigilant gaze convinced her he was done with his exposé.

"Thank you for sharing all that Brian. I know that had to be difficult, especially your involvement with Mary and her pregnancy. When is she due, if I may ask?"

"In April, I do believe."

"Does John know?"

"If he does, he has kept his knowledge to himself and very well hidden. Both of them were very gracious last Wednesday."

"Yes, they were. Mary gave me no hint of her intimacy with you, and certainly John offered no clues regarding any knowledge or even suspicion. Do you love her?"

"Mary?"

"Yes, Mary. We have already discussed your feelings for Rosemary and hers for you."

"Yes, in a way, I would say so, but certainly nothing like my love for you. She has been very kind and generous, set aside persistent, with me. I respect her as I respect her husband."

"You don't need to qualify it, Brian. It is quite all right . . . normal, in fact. For being of the Victorian era, my parents were surprisingly liberal and open. They taught me to have a far more expansive view of human relationships. I feel your love, Brian; I truly do. There is no need to convince me. It is the love we share and the relationship we have that matters to me, not who you have or may be intimate with in the future. Just love me, and I shall love you. That is all that matters."

"You are an incredible woman, Charlotte Tamerlin."

Charlotte smiled, stood, leaned forward across the small table and kissed Brian. "You remembered my family name."

"Yes. I try to remember everything about you. I have never loved anyone as much as I love you, and every new leaf I turn over makes me love you even more."

"Do you think Mary will ever tell John?"

"I don't know. That is her decision alone. I will have to deal with the consequences no matter what she decides to do or when. If she does tell him, I hope she also helps him understand and appreciate her persistence and my resistance. I did not seek intimacy with her, but she is a very persuasive woman."

"I gather that much from talking to her when you were in the hospital and when we talked after dinner the other night. You know, Brian, I may have had my wild years, but you have seen and done so much more than me. Except for a family holiday to France before the Great War that I can barely remember, I have never been outside England, and rarely outside Southwest England. I dare say, you have been to London more than me, and you are not even British."

Brian changed the subject. "Like you want me to meet the Palmers, your surrogate parents, I really want you to meet my parents someday, sooner rather than later . . . and hopefully, Mrs. Bainbridge, Malcolm's widow."

"I would be honored, Brian."

"Someday."

"Indeed, someday."

"I had not been outside Kansas, except when I was flying with Malcolm, and until I left for Canada. Sometimes, I do not believe I am here, doing what I am doing, but then it becomes all too real."

"You are a most fortunate man, Brian Drummond."

"To know you, yes I am."

They laughed together. Charlotte sat across his lap. They embraced and kissed passionately, this time. Brian felt better, much better, now that nothing remained hidden. He liked the special intimacy of their sharing. He felt it brought them closer together. Brian so wanted to marry Charlotte, but he knew he could not ask her again until he was convinced she was receptive and ready. He would not press her one step farther. Whatever the next steps would be would come entirely from her control and wishes. Brian was fine with that . . . at least until the war was over and her conditions were met.

—

Tuesday, 12.November.1940
RAF Church Fenton
Tadcaster, North Yorkshire, England
United Kingdom
10:30 hours

"Flying Officer Drummond reporting as ordered, sir."

Squadron Leader Walter Myers 'Baggy' Churchill, DSO, DFC, was an accomplished fighter pilot and had been the commanding officer of No.71

Squadron since its formation in September. Brian had been forewarned the Skipper did not appreciate being asked about his name or whether he is a relation of the prime minister, at least none anyone was prepared to inform him, and he certainly was not going to ask.

"We have been waiting for you, Mister Drummond. You are the last American volunteer fighter pilot in duty status to join our new, little band of merry men. Please close the door." Brian did as he was commanded.

Churchill gestured for Brian to be seated.

"You hold a unique place in the squadron in many ways," Baggy said. Brian must have displaced a confused expression. "Humility is an admirable trait, but facts are undeniable. I will add my congratulations to those of others for your CBE and Military Cross – richly deserved from what I know."

"Thank you, sir."

"It was my understanding you resisted the transfer to Seventy-One."

"Yes sir, that is true. Since I joined the RAF in June of last year and completed my prescribed training, Six Zero Nine was the only squadron I have known. Most of my mates were killed during the Battle, but they are still my mates."

"Quite understandable. Your loyalty is laudable. I am not sure what or who changed your mind, but I would rather not have you here, if you do not want to be here with us."

Do I tell him, it was none other than Prime Minister Winston Churchill who changed my mind? No, best let that remain private. "No sir. I am honored to be here."

"Very well. As you join this squadron, you remain the youngest pilot on our tote board. You are also the highest scoring ace in our squadron and nearly the whole of Fighter Command. You have also been shot down more times than all the other squadron pilots combined."

"Not a particularly admirable reality, I'm afraid."

"My point is, you have a wealth of experience and more of that experience than any of us, including me. This squadron still has a way to go before being declared operational, and that day may not come for several months, judging how these lads fly together at present. You are a key to helping these pilots become a fighting combat squadron."

"I've not taught anyone before."

"Just answer their questions. Be patient with them. And, most importantly, show them how to fly the bloody hell out of these aeroplanes."

"Yes sir."

"Now, a couple of administrative items. I notice that you have not tended to your sleeve stripes. You were promoted to Flying Officer last week, were you not?"

"Yes sir."

"Then, get your sleeve stripes taken care of soon. You will also need to add these patches," he said and tossed two blue and white patches across the desk to Brian, "to the top of your tunic sleeves. They designate you as an American volunteer pilot." The patch had an eagle quite like the eagle on the Great Seal of the United States along with the initials E. S. that stood for Eagle Squadron. "Pilot Officer Langford has been holding your flight position temporarily. You will be Green Section Leader. Langford will be your right wing, and Pilot Officer Tolly will be your left wing. As you probably noted on your way in this morning, we are in transition. Blue and Red Sections have transitioned to Mark I Hurris. They are comparatively old, beat up, heavily repaired, but still functional. Green and Yellow Sections are flying Brewster Buffalos – a far cry from the Spits we flew – but, they will do. On the positive side of the ledger, they are in pretty good shape, having not seen much combat, as the Hurris have, and they have more bite, being armed with four Browning M2, 50-caliber, heavy machine guns." Brian nodded his head in acknowledgment. "As you are the most experienced, you will be the last of our pilots to transition to the Hurricane. I want you to show these blokes that an inferior machine in the hands of a skilled pilot can be a formidable instrument."

"Yes sir."

"Langford saw action in France, and flew with 'Billy' Fiske in Six Oh One during the Battle – a pretty solid soul, it seems to me. Tolly arrived a few weeks ago from OTU7. He barely has a hundred hours in the air. He's seen no combat time, fired his guns a couple of times in training, and seems to have an over-inflated opinion of himself and his skills, such as they are. You can help Langford polish his skills, but you can save Tolly's life. He will not last long in combat, if he does not settle down quickly."

"As I said earlier, sir, I am not a teacher, but I will do my best. I agree with you explicitly, humility is an honorable trait. Truth be told, I do not take kindly to irrational arrogant exuberance."

"Yes, well, teach him quickly."

"Yes sir.

"If I am properly informed, the flight surgeons have returned you to full flight status, correct?"

"Yes sir. Squadron Leader Long-Roberts let me take one last flight in the Spit on Friday."

"I hope you enjoyed it. Chances are, we shall not see Spits for a while. The last of your replacement Hurris is not scheduled to arrive until mid to late December. Have you flown the Buffalo before?"

"No sir."

"Do you need or want a check ride?"

"I think I can handle it. Give me a couple of flights to get the feel of her, I'll be ready."

"Very well, then. After lunch, take a training flight or two this afternoon. I do believe you have been assigned the 'George' machine, which should be fueled and fully loaded. Corporal Harris, our ops clerk, will provide your flight map. Take a few days to get comfortable and let me know when you are ready. Then, take up your section to work them the way you want them. I would like to get a squadron training exercise in next week."

"That should be no problem, Skipper."

"Do you have any questions?"

"No sir."

"Alrighty then, let us introduce you to your new squadron mates."

Brian followed Churchill into the main room of the Dispersal Hut.

"Hunter, you old son of a bitch," shouted 'Red' Burns. "I thought that was you."

Churchill held up his hand for quiet. "Gentlemen, some of you clearly know our newest member. It is my honor to introduce Flying Officer Brian 'Hunter' Drummond, now holder of the CBE, the Military Cross and the Distinguished Flying Cross for gallantry in combat action. He is currently credited with nineteen victories in aerial combat. As soon as he is ready, he will be Green Section Leader. We shall welcome him properly tonight at Mess." Brian knew what that meant. *At least I will have a reason to change my sleeve stripes, since I will have to get my uniform cleaned.*

Introductions were made.

-- Blue Section, Right Wing, Pilot Officer Peter Bruce 'Horse' Harrow from Cheyenne, Wyoming.

-- Blue Section, Left Wing, Pilot Officer Andrew Adam 'Rocket' Downing from St. Louis, Missouri.

-- Green Section, Right Wing, Pilot Officer Paul James 'Dusty' Langford from Los Angeles, California.

-- Green Section, Left Wing, Pilot Officer Edward Jonas 'Bulldog' Tolly from Baltimore, Maryland.

-- Red Section Leader, Flight Lieutenant Charles Gordon 'Whitey' Whittington from Bristol, and the only remaining British officer until an American was promoted to replace him.

-- Red Section, Right Wing, Pilot Officer Frank Oscar 'Red' Burns from Dayton, Ohio, and Brian's only surviving American mate from No.609 Squadron.

-- Red Section, Left Wing, Pilot Officer Arnold Samuel 'Salt' Morton from Oakland, California.

-- Yellow Section Leader, Flying Officer Charles 'Rusty' Batemen from Dallas, Texas.

-- Yellow Section, Left Wing, Pilot Officer Robert Charles 'Sweet' Sweeny, Jr., an ex-patriot American from London.

-- Corporal James 'Jimmy' Harris, squadron operations clerk.

According to Churchill, the Air Ministry expected to fill the yellow section, right wing position within a fortnight, with another American volunteer completing the newly reinstated training regimen.

Sweeny . . . where do I know that name? His familial name sounds quite familiar, but an ex-patriot American? What is his story I wonder?

"Corporal Harris, please report us Available in 30 Minutes. Lunch time."

The pilots, who needed to, hung up their flight equipment. They departed together and walked to the Mess. Corporal Harris closed the door behind him. Lunch was simple, as was so common within Fighter Command. Red was over-the-top in regaling to their comrades in his version of stories about Hunter. Brian was not sure if Frank was speaking to elevate his own importance or tout Brian's accomplishments. Brian chose not to participate.

After lunch and the squadron's return to Available status, Brian took the Pilot's Notes for the Brewster B-339E Buffalo Mark I to absorb the features, characteristics and procedures for operating the aircraft. The export version was equivalent to the F2A-2 fighter in service with the United States Navy and Marine Corps. The propulsive power came from a three-bladed, 9-foot diameter, variable pitch propeller, or airscrew as the Brits say, driven by a 1,100 shaft horsepower, supercharged, air-cooled, single bank, 9-cylinder, Wright R-1820-G105A radial engine that was the main contributor to the aircraft's fat, stubby appearance. The engine had the same power as the Merlin III engine in the Spitfire Mark IA, but the Buffalo was nearly a 100 miles an hour slower than the sleek Spitfire. The Buffalo sat on a rather odd looking W-shaped, retractable, main landing gear, or undercarriage in Brit parlance, with a castering, partially retractable, tail wheel. The British Buffalos did not have the tail hook installed like the U.S. naval aviation variants. Once Brian completed his study of the Pilot's Notes, he grabbed his flight kit and went to his 'XR-G' aircraft.

Brian introduced himself to his new ground crew.

-- Crew Chief Corporal Henry Joyce Jacobs from Birmingham,

-- Leading Aircraftman Stephen Hawking from Sheffield – the crew rigger or mechanic, and

-- Aircraftman Stanley George Easton from Blackburn, north of Liverpool – the crew armorer, who maintained the big Browning machine guns.

All three had combat experience with other Fighter Command squadrons in recent months. The ground crew knew the accomplishments of their new pilot and did not have to ask.

Brian walked around the aircraft with Jacobs' knowledgeable assistance to ensure he had a good image of the machine. He then sat in the cockpit to make sure he knew where all the controls and switches were. Brian also closed his eyes and reached for all of the primary controls numerous times to create muscle memory, if things ever got dicey in the air. The aircraft had a simple straight stick for elevator and ailerons, rather than the circular 'spade' he was used to in the Spitfire. The instrument layout was also different and would take some adjustment. Brian rehearsed the procedures several times, until he considered himself ready.

"OK, Corporal Jacobs, let's see if I can start this beast," Brian said.

Jacobs jumped off the wing and went to stand in front of and to the left of the propeller arc. Brian had switched on battery power, cracked the throttle open a quarter of an inch, and primed the intake manifold with fuel. When Corporal Jacobs gave him the start hand signal, Brian shouted, "Clear!" to warn anyone close by that the propeller was going to move and stand clear of the propeller arc. Brian mashed down the starter button. The whir of the starter coincided with the slow rotation of the propeller. He counted the passage of three blades through the 12-o'clock position and switched the magnetos to BOTH. The engine sputtered and coughed to life. Brian adjusted the throttle position to produce a stabilized, fast idle of 1200 RPM. He had normal oil pressure. Brian stepped through the post-start procedures to make sure the generator was ON and producing proper electrical power, before he began switching on his radio, gunsight and other equipment. He called for taxi and signaled for the wheel chocks to be removed. Corporal Jacobs held them up, so Brian could see they had been removed. Brian taxied to the run-up area to do his pre-takeoff engine checks.

Once airborne and configured to climb, Brian switched his radio to Sector Control, checked in for a training flight, and received an area and block of altitudes. He started through a familiar sequence of maneuvers to give him a feel for the aircraft's performance – turns, dives, climbs, standard aerobatic maneuvers and common combat maneuvers. He also did a full range of stalls and spins to make sure he felt the aircraft's signs and recovery procedures should he ever find himself departed from controlled flight. He also pushed the aircraft out to its maximum 'red line' airspeed and up to the service ceiling. Once he felt pretty good about the flight characteristics, he requested and obtained clearance out over the North Sea, found some flotsam on the water surface, and made numerous passes firing his guns at his 'target.' Lastly, he took advantage of some fair weather cumulus clouds to maneuver around just like he enjoyed doing so much with Malcolm Bainbridge when he was still learning to fly near Wichita, Kansas. When he was satisfied and with his fuel getting low, he headed back to Church Fenton. He obtained clearance for four touch-and-go landings before he took a full-stop landing and returned to the squadron parking area.

His flight debriefing was quick and painless. Baggy accepted his readiness.

Behind his closed office door, Squadron Leader Churchill said, "I've made arrangements with your old squadron for you to visit them tomorrow. Stack has agreed to have a couple of his Spitfires for you to play with up there. I want you to get a good feel for what you must do to make the Buffalo work against our best fighter."

"Good idea. Thank you, sir."

"I would also like you to keep this little exercise between you and me, for the time being."

"As you wish, sir."

Brian joined the other pilots. They talked about what pilot's always talk about – flying. Brian absorbed what the other pilots thought of the Buffalo as well as the Hurricane. The squadron remained at Available status for another couple of hours. Once they were released, they headed to the Mess to prepare for Brian's 'christening' into the squadron. Not bad for a first day.

———

Tuesday, 12.November.1940
Cabinet War Rooms
Whitehall, London, England
United Kingdom
16:00 hours

"Thank you for waiting, Prime Minister," said 'C,' as he entered Churchill's small private study and closed the door. "We just cleared an important message this afternoon," he continued and placed the Buff Box manacled to his left wrist on the desk. "I think you will understand why I asked you to wait before going into your scheduled War Cabinet meeting."

Churchill retrieved his key, opened the secure case, and found a single piece of paper in the 'Top of the Box' folder.

MOST SECRET - ULTRA

```
SECRET
DATE: 12 NOVEMBER 1940
TO: OKL
FROM: OKW
BEGIN
OPERATION MOONLIGHT SONATA BREAK OPERATION TO
CONCENTRATE ALL AVAILABLE FORCES ON DESIGNATED
TARGET BREAK ATTACK WAVE TIMING TO BE EXECUTED
PRECISELY FOR MAXIMUM DESTRUCTIVE EFFECT BREAK
AIR CREWS MUST BE FULLY TRAINED AND PREPARED TO
USE BROKEN LEG IF INCLEMENT WEATHER ENCOUNTERED
BREAK OUR LEADER WILL BE ASSESSING SUCCESS OF
THIS MISSION SPECIFICALLY BREAK AIRCRAFT AND
AIR CREWS MUST BE READY TO EXECUTE OPERATION
TWO NIGHTS EITHER SIDE OF FULL MOON AND EXECUTE
WITHIN SIX HOURS OF ORDER BREAK ALL AIR FLEETS
REPORT READINESS OF EVERY INVOLVED SQUADRON
AIRCRAFT AVAILABLE BOMB INVENTORY AND CREW
STATUS BREAK HAIL HITLER
END
SECRET
```

MOST SECRET - ULTRA

"This message is dated today," observed Churchill.

"This is a good day. We got lucky, to be candid. We broke the plug board and wheel settings shortly after midnight, about an hour after they went into effect."

"So, we shall have at least one bountiful day."

"Yes sir."

"When is the next full moon?"

"The 15th."

"This message corroborates information derived at Trent Park. Several of the senior captured pilots suggested a major air operation near the time of the full moon."

The Combined Services Detailed Interrogation Centre moved to the renowned country mansion at Trent Park and began operations on 12.December.1939. All captured *Luftwaffe* pilots were processed, interrogated, and then held there with a complex system of surreptitious listening devices to record, transcribe and analyze their conversations in a more casual setting.

"Do we know the target?"

"No. The analysts at Trent Park are convinced the air force officers they have do not know the specific target. Given the content of this decrypt, there will likely be at least one more message that will specify the target and *Knickebein* details. As noted in this message, they will get only six hours notice to execute their plan, which in turn means the best we can hope for is the same six hours, if we are lucky that day. If we are not so fortunate, we may not decipher the execution order until after the event. Analysts at Broadway House offer their best target estimate as central London, likely Whitehall or Westminster, Greater London, the Thames Valley, Kent or the Essex coast."

"We cannot hope to defend all of that with the assets we have."

"Quite so. Everyone at Station 'X,' Broadway House and Trent Park will remain ever so vigilant and will disseminate the relevant information as soon as it is available."

Prime Minister Churchill kept his head and eyes down on the sheet of paper in his hand, as if answers might burst forth from the spaces between the words at any moment. Colonel Menzies chose not to disturb the Prime Minister's contemplation. He eventually raised his head and responded. "This one is going to be a close run thing, I'm afraid. As we discussed last Friday at Ditchley, we are far too close to exposure for my liking. Do you have the complete access list?"

"Not complete, as yet. I expect the final names from Denniston tomorrow, as promised."

Churchill nodded his head, and then shook his head as if disagreeing with his own thoughts. "I am and will remain deeply concerned about any potential leak – even one seemingly minor transgression. A cipher clerk and analyst handling this material might have family, relations or friends in the target area, if we know the target in advance as we hope, and he might be tempted to warn his loved ones of the danger. As much as I understand the sentiment, we cannot tolerate and we must be absolutely ruthless in protecting this source."

"Yes sir."

"Anything else?"

"No sir, not yet."

"Very well, thank you for the information. No one else is to see this."

"As you wish, sir."

Colonel Menzies retrieved the message, returned it to the folder and box, locked the case and departed.

Churchill took a moment to gather his thoughts, left his office as well, and walked down the corridor to the main conference room. The combined War Cabinet and Defense Committee as well as their staff support filled the confined room to capacity, except for the prime minister's chair at the center head of the U-shaped conference table.

"My apologies, gentlemen. Late breaking news, I'm afraid." Churchill did not wait for Sir Edward to take control of the meeting. "Pray tell, A.V., do we have the results of Operation JUDGMENT?"

"Yes. Admiral Cunningham issued his preliminary report a few hours ago. Sir Andrew continues to gather post-operation intelligence and assessments, so revisions remain possible for the next few days. Sir Dudley, if you would be so kind to do the honors."

Vice Admiral Sir Andrew Browne 'ABC' Cunningham KCB, DSO with two bars, had been Commander-in-Chief, Mediterranean, in command of all naval forces in the region since the beginning of the present war. He gained considerable recognition and acclaim for the successful Mers-el-Kebir raid to neutralize the French Fleet the previous July.

The First Sea Lord Admiral of the Fleet Sir Alfred Dudley Pickman Rogers Pound, GCB, GCVO, GBE, began his report. "I believe Sir Andrew would agree in summary the raid on the Italian Fleet at Taranto was a resounding success. Our naval air forces under Sir Andrew's command have sunk one battleship, seriously damaged two additional battleships and two heavy cruisers. We recovered all our aircraft except for two. Two crew members were confirmed killed, and we suspect two other crew members may have been captured. We do not, as yet, have a casualty count for the enemy; however, it is certainly greater than our losses. Sir Andrew defied air attacks to be ready for engagement of any enemy warships that might attempt to sortie from the harbor. None have, as yet, made such an attempt. Also, Sir Andrew asked me to mention the exemplary planning carried out by Admiral Lyster, who was in command of the naval air forces aboard *Illustrious*. He ensured the involved air crews were trained meticulously for the mission. I do believe I can safely say, Admiral Lyster's operations plan was about as flawless as any combat plan can be and the air crews executed the plan exceptionally well."

Rear Admiral Arthur Lumley St. George Lyster, CVO, DSO, was commander of Mediterranean Aircraft Carrier Forces under Admiral

Cunningham. First Sea Lord Admiral Sir Dudley Pound had specifically tasked Lyster in 1935, with preparing a detailed attack plan for the Taranto anchorage.

"Well done to Admiral Cunningham, Admiral Lyster, the mission air crews, the fleet and the Admiralty," pronounced Prime Minister Churchill.

"Not bad for a bunch of old Swordfish, torpedo biplanes," Air Chief Marshal Sir Charles Portal.

"Indeed," responded A.V. Alexander.

"I assume General Wavell has been informed of these results," Churchill said.

"Yes. All defense ministries and commands."

"Thank you. Taranto should give that thug Mussolini something to think about." Churchill turned to the Cabinet Secretary. "Did the Home Office submit their report on the progress of the 'Double Cross' Committee?"

From the war's outset, the Security Service carried out aggressive counter-espionage operations under the central control of Department 20, also called XX or 'Double Cross' Committee. MI5 used the full breadth of assets to collect information from captured German spies, Nazi sympathizers, captured soldiers, airmen and sailors interrogated, watched and listened to at Trent Park and other sites as well as intelligence developed by MI6 – the Secret Intelligence Service. The secret Double Cross Committee had begun working double agents against the Germans. MI5 was under the ministerial supervision of Home Secretary Herbert Stanley Morrison, PC, and Member of Parliament for Hackney South.

"Yes," Sir Edward responded. "The full report is in your administrative box. Their efforts have begun to yield results. They picked up two more German agents last week. It appears their process of carefully feeding specific catalytic information back to the Germans via the double agents gave them sufficient information to make the arrests."

"While I am impressed with the successes of MI5 and their Double Cross Committee, I simply must urge caution, not to overreach. What they have accomplished has become a unique and vital asset, like others, and we cannot risk exposure or compromise. While I know the War Cabinet and Defense Committee are keenly aware of the sensitivity, I must advise the staff officers present strongly that all words and information discussed in this room is most sensitive and vital to our war effort, and thus must not be discussed with anyone outside this room. Is that clear?" He received a chorus of "yes sir." "I shall study Morrison's report. Until then, please pass our congratulations to Morrison and the Home Office."

"Yes sir."

"Now, Archie, pray tell us of the Air Ministry's preparations for whatever this impending enemy operation is going to be."

"Basic traffic analysis suggests the date is near," began Sir Archie Sinclair. Churchill chose not to mention the intelligence information he saw earlier. "We know their attack is near, probably around the full moon on the 15th, but we still do not know their target. The Air Ministry's Intelligence Branch has been feverishly searching message traffic and radio signals for the specific details we need. As of this afternoon, we do not have what we need. We have considered Operation COLD WATER, the concentrated bombing of likely launch aerodromes for their attack, but such operations would be costly and timing would be critical. The ASPIRIN countermeasures are ready, if we can just gather the details. They have perhaps a dozen source sites from Brittany to Norway, double that many frequencies, and they can aim those beams to intersect anywhere they wish. Until we find a more reliable, efficient and dependable means to collect the necessary details for ASPIRIN to work properly, we are relegated to sifting through the haystack straw by straw. Hopefully, we will find it in time."

"What about going after the source sites?" asked Attlee.

"We know generally where the sites are, but we have not found the means to locate the transmitters – photographic reconnaissance, electronic scanning, even tasking MI6 field agents. We have not been successful, as yet. They have camouflaged the transmitters well. They must expect us to be looking for them."

"Keep on it. We know something is coming. We do not know where, yet. We do know their time window of four to six days. Everyone is looking, listening and searching. Now, we must pray we get lucky."

The meeting concluded. The assembled ministers dispersed.

—

Wednesday, 13.November.1940
RAF Catterick
Catterick, North Yorkshire, England
United Kingdom
11:15 hours

Jonathan and several of the No.609 Squadron pilots watched the odd, stubby aircraft with 'XR-G' tail letters land and taxi to the operations building.

"What is that thing?" asked Victor Clegg.

"It's a Buffalo," answered 'B' Flight and Red Section Leader Flight Lieutenant Robert Gates 'Sparky' Morrow.

"It's got RAF markings."

"That's because it is an RAF fighter, you twit."

Jonathan watched the shutdown and pilot extract himself. As the pilot cleared the tail and removed his headgear, Jonathan recognized him. "That's Hunter." The two friends walked toward each other. "What the hell are you doing here?"

"I'm here on a mission."

"What is that thing?" Jonathan asked, gesturing with his head toward Brian's aircraft.

"That my dear fellow is a Brewster Buffalo Mark I."

"Can I take a look?"

"Certainly. We have time."

The two friends returned to Brian's aircraft. Several other pilots joined them. Brian provided a guided tour, not that he was an expert, but he had one more day and had at least flown the aircraft.

"Ugly soddin' machine," commented Clegg.

"Yeah, she's not particularly attractive, but she has half inch guns – more bite."

"Quite so," Jonathan said. "Surely you did not fly up here to show off your new aeroplane."

"Nice thought, but no. I'm not particularly proud of her, but I was sent by my new skipper to fly against your Spits to see how I can do against a superior aircraft."

"Stack hasn't said anything about it."

"Then, I guess we'd better go have a chat with Stack."

Squadron Leader Long-Roberts confirmed his conversation with Squadron Leader Churchill. After lunch, Jonathan and Victor would once again face off against Brian, but this time, Brian would be flying his Buffalo rather than a Spitfire.

The plan played out as expected. Brian worked much harder than he did last Friday. There was no doubt the Buffalo was no match for the Spitfire, and by inference the German fighters. Brian held his own against the superior aircraft, but he also lost a few of the engagements, or at least would have if bullets were flying. The pilots managed another sortie with different engagement setups. The results were essentially the same. Brian could not find any advantage. He could not out turn, out climb, out dive or out run the Spitfire, which in turn meant he would not have an advantage against the German Bf109 – not a comforting feeling.

Brian debriefed both flights with his former squadron mates. He did not want to wait too long. Sunset came much earlier these days, and he did not want to force himself into a night landing, if he could avoid it.

After refueling, Brian took off, kept his aircraft low as the landing gear retracted to gain speed as quickly as possible, and waited until he had to pull up. He rolled his aircraft twice, leveled off and headed south.

—

Wednesday, 13.November.1940
Cabinet Room
No.10 Downing Street
Whitehall, London, England
United Kingdom
22:15 hours

Despite the temporary repairs, scattered workman's tools and persistent dust, Prime Minister Churchill insisted upon using the historic rooms of No.10 for the conduct of business by His Majesty's Government. The temporary wallboards did not help the heating of the Cabinet Room, and Churchill seemed impervious to or simply ignored the chill in the air. This was one of the many little ways Churchill chose to shake his fist at the now nightly bombers of The Blitz. Plus, he was not particularly shy about expressing his paucity of fondness for the facilities of the underground bunker known as the Cabinet War Rooms.

The closed door meeting this evening was a special gathering called by Churchill with little notice to discuss the most current information regarding the looming major night raid by the German Air Force. Present for the meeting were the Chief of the Secret Intelligence Service 'C' Menzies, War Minister Anthony Eden, Air Minister Sir Archie Sinclair, Home Secretary Herbert Morrison, Chief of the Air Staff Air Chief Marshal Sir Charles Portal, Air Ministry intelligence specialist Doctor Reginald Victor 'R.V.' Jones, and science advisor to the Prime Minister Professor Frederick Alexander Lindemann, FRS, often simply referred to as 'The Prof.'

"So, pray tell me our status for the great raid looming over us this night," began Churchill.

"I believe those of us familiar with the intelligence to date," responded Menzies, "agree the Moonlight Sonata raid is not likely tonight, based on the traffic analysis we have, which does not reflect the associated preparations for a major raid . . . at least not beyond their nightly operations of late."

Traffic analysis involved monitoring the frequency and source locations of routine, un-coded, radio messages being monitored by the signals intelligence branch. Occasionally, the listeners picked up key words that gave them more information.

"We have not heard anything other than the usual pre-mission communications. The Moonlight Sonata raid is coming, of that we are fairly certain, probably around midnight or shortly after. They are changing their planned strike to avoid consistency."

"But, they are coming," growled Churchill.

"Yes sir. We have no information to suggest otherwise."

"Then, what of our preparations to counter the Hun's brutal rendition of Beethoven's magical orchestration?" A few soft chuckles could be heard.

"Doctor Jones, if you please," said Sir Archie.

"Yes, well," Jones began, "as of an hour ago, our night ground and air search for the beams have not yielded any results, which would tend to confirm 'C's assessment."

"Could it be that we have simply missed the beams?" asked Morrison.

"Possible," Jones responded, "but not likely. Our search equipment has improved significantly in the last fortnight or two. The evidence we have suggests they will not utilize the beams tonight."

"They have the moon for their illumination," Sir Charles offered in muffled comment.

"Yes, it is a clear night," continued Jones. "While we are expecting scattered clouds in the next few days, the cloud cover will not likely be sufficient for obscuration."

"Do we know the target, yet?" Churchill asked.

"No sir," answered Menzies. Churchill knew that meant Bletchley Park either had not decoded or did not have relevant information in their deciphered message traffic. "We continue to listen."

Churchill turned to Lindemann. "Do you agree with Doctor Jones, Prof?"

"Yes, I do. We visited the ground intercept stations last week, as well as the airborne search teams. Doctor Jones is spot on correct. I will go slightly farther, with the current state of their equipment and their search techniques, if the beams are switched on, they will find them."

"Any progress with your beam-bending hypothesis?" the Prime Minister asked Doctor Jones.

"We have tried to simulate the beams to test our process, but we are not confident we have a workable system. We need to time with the actual German beams. To the best of our knowledge and understanding, we believe our beam-bending technique will work, but I am afraid we will not know for certain until we are successful with the actual beams."

Churchill nodded his head in acknowledgment. "Any changes in our air defense preparations?" he asked.

Sir Archie looked to Sir Charles and nodded his head for the chief to answer.

"We took delivery of another half dozen of the new Beaufighters, yesterday."

"Hardly enough to stem the tide."

"No sir, but every little bit helps in this endeavor. We have been using our available aircraft to train crews in anticipation of these deliveries. The three available night fighter squadrons are currently deployed for London. We can reposition them, if or when we determine the target."

Prime Minister Churchill lowered his eyes and head, as he contemplated what should be done with their situation. The room remained still and quiet – not even a cough – as they left their leader to his thoughts. Several minutes passed with not even a twitch. "We must be very careful with our response. I hold out hope we may get lucky and learn the target before the attack . . . if or when the attack comes. I want to emphasize to all of us involved in this situation that our response to whatever we face must be within the range of our demonstrated capabilities . . . those we have been able to deploy so far."

"What are you saying here, Winston?" asked Morrison.

Churchill stared at the Home Secretary. Morrison was not read into ULTRA, and neither was Doctor Jones. Winston considered how he was going to answer the question. "We have a sacred responsibility to protect our citizens, to protect the realm. In wartime, that responsibility transcends the individual. Occasionally in this war, we will possess a surprisingly enhanced capability. We must make the hard choices for the greater good. It appears this event may come down to the wire. It is in this light, I shall say the decision to redeploy our assets for the Moonlight Sonata event will rest with me and me alone. There will be no debate or deviation, until the situation passes or changes; again, I will decide when that point has arrived. For now, the details of this situation and our discussions related to this matter shall remain most secret sensitive and restricted to this group and this group alone. Am I quite clear regarding this matter?"

Morrison opened his mouth, as if he wanted to press the Prime Minister. After a few moments, he wisely chose not to do so. "Yes," he responded simply.

Churchill looked to each man in the room and waited until he received a verbal or gestured affirmation of his guidance. "We have done as much as we can tonight. We shall reconvene in the morning to reassess our position and any new information we may have received. Please remain attentive and press on with all of our preparations."

"Yes sir," came a unison of responses.

"'C' . . . a word, if I may," Churchill said to his intelligence chief. Menzies waited until the cabinet room door closed and the two men were alone. "Denniston knows how close this will be?"

"Yes, he does, Winston. We discussed this several times in the last few days, the last time just after supper. He has moved as many people as he is able, to work on messages we suspect might be involved. They are working around the clock on this. I must say, for your information only, this intensity cannot be sustained for more than a few more days. We are consuming our capacity to decipher communications in other important areas."

"I understand that, Stewart. Yet, we know whatever the Huns are planning, it is likely bigger than anything we have seen so far. There is no telling what destruction they may wreak, if they focus their bombardment with those damnable beams."

"We understand the seriousness, Winston. We truly do."

"I know. I just worry. To be candid and rather blunt, I am more concerned about not exposing ULTRA than I am about what the damn bloody Germans are going to do to our precious citizens – sad but true."

"I do not envy the decisions you are about to make, Winston. We shall do our level best to give you the most accurate information we can as quickly as we can."

"I know you will. I do not need to keep you any longer tonight. Try to get some rest. I will see you in the morning. Good night, Stewart. Thank you for your extraordinary work. Let us hope, the Good-Man-Above brings us some luck our way soon."

"Thank you, sir. Good night."

—

Chapter 4

Let men decide firmly what not to do,
and they will be free to do vigorously
what they ought to do.

- Mencius

Thursday, 14.November.1940
Prime Minister's Office
No.10 Downing Street
Whitehall, London, England
United Kingdom
11:15 hours

"**A**ir Officer Commanding-in-Chief, Fighter Command, Air Chief Marshal Sir Hugh Dowding for your scheduled appointment, Prime Minister," announced his duty Private Secretary John Miller Martin.

Winston Churchill did not look forward to this discussion. He feigned attention on the papers before him to gird himself for what he knew had to be done. Archie Sinclair had consistently and persistently pressed his position that the venerable Air Officer Commanding-in-Chief Air Chief Marshal Sir Hugh Caswall Tremenheere Dowding, GCVO, KCB, CMG, no longer presented the energy and capacity to lead Fighter Command through the troubled times in which they were immersed and that lay ahead. Archie wanted this change. Yet, Winston felt enormous loyalty to Dowding and repeatedly credited him personally and singularly with defying the gale force, pre-war headwinds to prepare Fighter Command. He found the way to get the Chain Home radio direction finding system developed and deployed – a vital, if not singularly essential, element of the Air Defense System of Great Britain. He pushed the development and production of Hurricane and Spitfire fighter aircraft. Winston remembered that particular Cabinet Meeting last May, when Sir Hugh stood virtually alone before the War Cabinet to argue calmly, precisely and successfully against the sea of contrarian voices in the room that day, including his own rather strident insistence. That one confrontation required a leader who knew the situation, had command of the facts, and held the self-confidence in presenting his case. Winston took in a deep breath and looked up to Martin still in the doorway.

"Please show Sir Hugh in, if you will John." Churchill extended his hand to Sir Hugh before he was fully in the room. After their warm salutations, Winston motioned to the comfortable chairs. "I know you are a very busy man, Sir Hugh, so I shall not dawdle about or waste your time."

"I am at your service, Prime Minister."

Churchill nodded his acknowledgment. "To be direct, I have a new, very important mission for you."

"More important than Fighter Command and the air defense of the Home Islands?"

"Yes, more important than all that. I would like you to lead the British Air Mission to the United States."

"What is that exactly, if I may ask?"

"As you well know, we cannot produce aircraft fast enough for the current combat intensity, and we are not developing new models to conduct offensive operations on the Continent in the near future," Churchill explained. "We have turned to the Americans for that supply, among other acquisitions. They will soon become a vital resource for our war effort. Another keen interest I would ask you to closely monitor and influence as you are able is the airborne intercept RDF kit development now undertaken by the Americans within the joint team created by Sir Henry's technical exchange mission to the United States, last summer."

Sir Henry Thomas Tizard, KCB, FRS, had led several key Air Ministry committees on advanced aeronautics and air defense technologies before the war and was chosen to lead the Technical and Scientific Mission to the United States – the unilateral transfer of the country's most secret and vital military technologies.

Churchill continued, "We simply must improve our night fighter capability as quickly as possible. I will also say, Sir Hugh, you personally are highly regarded not just in this country, but in the United States as well, from President Roosevelt on down. I have asked Lord Lothian to set up a tentative meeting for you with the President as soon as we can get you across the pond. The embassy and consulates are primed and prepared to assist you on your mission. You will work closely with a variety of senior officials of His Majesty's Government and of course the United States, including the ambassador, Lord Beaverbrook and his Ministry of Aircraft Supply, and specifically Bill Stephenson. I think you have met Bill, have you not?"

"Yes sir. He escorted the American envoy Bill Donovan on his fact-finding tour last July."

"Precisely. I do not wish to and do not think it necessary to delve too deeply into Bill Stephenson's mission in the United States. Let it suffice to say, he is on assignment directly from me and the office I hold."

In June 1940, Churchill had asked his friend and former Canadian newspaper publisher William Samuel 'Bill' Stephenson, MC, DFC, to carry out a special and personal intelligence mission within the United States and to maintain direct contact with the various intelligence branches in the American military service departments and the Federal Bureau of Investigation (FBI). To carry out his mission, he established an office called British Security Coordination (BSC) under the cover of the British Passport Control Office, which he did, taking out a long-term lease of the 35th and 36th floors of the International Building, Rockefeller Center, in New York City. Stephenson's office operated outside but coordinated with the Secret Intelligence Service (SIS, or MI6) and the British military service intelligence branches.

At nearly the same time Stephenson took up his assignment, William Joseph 'Bill' Donovan had reluctantly taken an extended leave of absence from his successful and prestigious Wall Street law firm – Donovan, Leisure, Newton & Irvine, of which he was a founding partner. For the last dozen years, his law practice had taken him far and wide nationally and internationally, and enabled him to meet influential people on both sides of the present conflict. Donovan was a member of the Republican Party in good standing and leaned to the conservative end of the political spectrum. He saw the President's intelligence need and knew he could help fill the gaps. As Donovan's assignment expanded, the two Bills began a deep collaboration and developed an abiding friendship. Donovan was, on occasion, nicknamed 'Wild Bill' in reflection of his decisiveness to act, and between the two Bills, Donovan was often referred to as 'Big Bill' in contrast to his friend and colleague who was called 'Little Bill.'

"As I am sure you are aware, Prime Minister, I am well past retirement age." He was 58 years old at the time and eight years younger than the Prime Minister.

"But, you are still young, Sir Hugh."

"Do I have the option to consider your offer as well as the potential to enter the retired rolls?"

Churchill studied Dowding's calm, unemotional eyes. "I shall not beg, Sir Hugh, but yes, take a few days to reflect upon my offer."

"Thank you, sir. When is my removal from command to be effective?"

"Please do not think of this change in those terms, Sir Hugh. Your contributions to the defense of the realm are irreproachable. I know you have many more years of exemplary service ahead of you. We . . . I . . . need your skills, experience and stature for this mission." He paused to let that sink in for a moment. "Your reassignment is to be effective on the 24th of this month. I would like to announce your new assignment for His Majesty's Government at that time."

"Yes sir. You shall have my decision by the end of this week . . . before the beginning of next week. Who is to replace me, if I may ask?"

"Douglas . . . William Sholto."

Air Vice-Marshal William Sholto Douglas, CB, MC, DFC, had served as Deputy Chief of the Air Staff since April 1940.

"Good man – Bill. Sir Charles will work well with him." The two men sat in silence. Dowding stared out the newly replaced window overlooking the gnarled and pocked garden behind No.10, damaged by a near-miss German bomb. Churchill kept his eyes on Dowding. Sir Hugh looked back to Winston. "Again, if you will permit me to ask, what of Air Vice Marshal Park?"

Winston considered whether to answer Dowding's question directly. In these leadership changes within Fighter Command, Air Vice-Marshal Keith Park was to be replaced next month by his nemesis in the whole Big Wing debate, Air Vice-Marshal Trafford Leigh-Mallory, CB, DSO, and that would not go down well. Dowding probably viewed Mallory's conduct in that whole affair as disloyal – not an admirable attribute among warriors. Park was to be sent off to lead the air defense of Malta – the beleaguered bastion of British naval power in the central Mediterranean region. In the end, he decided to fib. "That is for Douglas and Portal to decide."

Dowding nodded his head, although this time his eyes conveyed his disappointment.

Churchill recognized and understood the brief expression for the one fighter group commander who stood in the breech during the worst of the German aerial assault during the past summer. The Prime Minister hoped at this juncture that his nephew would not be caught up in all these changes. Air Commodore John Spencer had been handpicked by Park to be his operations chief of No.11 Group at the peak of the German attacks, when invasion seemed to be looming over them by the day or hour.

"Thank you, Prime Minister. If you have nothing more for me, I should leave you to the weighty affairs of state. Lastly, thank you so very much for your recommendation to the King for my Knight Grand Cross. It is always appreciated to be recognized for one's service to the Crown."

"Well deserved, I must say. I cannot promise a peerage, Sir Hugh, but I can tell you what you have done for Fighter Command and especially the months of the battle." Churchill stood. Dowding followed. "I, for one, am most grateful for your steady hand through these troubled waters. I shall anxiously await your decision, Sir Hugh. Good day, and as we in the nautical services say, Godspeed and following winds."

Dowding nodded. They shook hands. "Thank you, sir. If it comes, I shall be grateful. However, I shall hold no expectations. Good day, sir." Dowding turned and was gone.

So, the nasty business was done. Winston had to replace many competent military leaders who were simply not the correct men for the task ahead, and he would undoubtedly replace many more in the months and years ahead, but this particular one bothered him the most of those that had gone before. Churchill was convinced this was the worst of backbiting among the flag officers, and a good man just lost the command he had built virtually from scratch over the last five years. The bitter after-taste would pass. There was a war to fight. Winston turned his thoughts to other challenges before him and the people.

John Martin appeared in the doorway.

"Please inform the Air Minister and Chief of the Air Staff their disgusting dirty work is done."

"Surely, you do not mean verbatim?" asked Martin.

Churchill connected to John's eyes, smiled, and answered, "I am tempted, but alas no. Proper decorum must be maintained in these sordid affairs. A simple, innocuous message should be sufficient. They were both waiting for this to be done, no need to explain or embellish."

Martin nodded his head and closed the door to allow the Prime Minister a few minutes of quiet time before the next scheduled meeting.

———

Thursday, 14.November.1940
Cabinet Room
No.10 Downing Street
Whitehall, London, England
United Kingdom
13:10 hours

The Defense Committee waited in the Cabinet Room for the Minister of Defense to arrive. They had been given information by the duty private secretary that the Prime Minister would be a few minutes late since he was tending to urgent business. The military ministers and service chiefs remained unusually silent as they waited. They were all still dressed in their ceremonial attire, having just returned from the funeral ceremony for the former Prime Minister Neville Chamberlain, who had passed five days earlier after what seemed like a short but swift battle with bowel cancer. The ceremony had been a proper but subdued affair due predominately to the wartime exigencies of damaged London.

Prime Minister Churchill entered the conference room still dressed in his formal attire as well. They all stood. Churchill motioned for them to be seated. "We do not have much time. However, we have important matters to discuss," he said before he was seated.

"First, if I may, Prime Minister," said the War Minister. He waited for Churchill's consenting nod. "Your eulogy for Prime Minister Chamberlain was exceptional, heartfelt and generous."

"Hear, hear," chimed in the others.

"Thank you. We lost a good man, and a blessed and proud servant of the Crown. While his policies may have been misguided in light of the facts in Germany, they were most certainly well intentioned. His magnanimous heart was taken advantage of and abused by an evil and duplicitous man. My words were the least I could do for a man of his stature. Again, thank you all for your sentiment." Churchill looked around the room. "I am afraid I must ask all but the ministers, chiefs and General Ismay to retire to the lobby for a few minutes." The few staff officers for each service chief left the conference room. The doors were closed. Churchill waited another minute. "We just received confirmation that the German Moonlight Sonata mission will happen tonight. The ULTRA message deciphered an hour ago, sets the commencement time at nineteen hundred hours tonight. Unfortunately, we still do not have the location, so there is little we can do with the information. Broadway House has passed the basic information as likely from unnamed, reliable sources to the three service ministry intelligence chiefs. Station X is still working feverishly to ascertain the target. They still believe the most likely target remains London. I suspect the Huns may try for Whitehall and Westminster . . . for a knockout blow, so I urge each of you to quietly and discretely as possible protect your people. You must couch your actions in some other form other than foreknowledge of an impending attack. Duty staffs must be maintained, unfortunately, to protect the source. They can react accordingly once the physical attack has begun. It is my intention to depart later this afternoon for Ditchley. I shall monitor tonight's action from there. So, with that piece of sensitive information out of the way, are there any questions?"

"What instructions would you care to pass to the ASPIRIN team?' Sir Charles asked, for the beam search units and the electronic counter-measures group.

Churchill held Portal's eyes as he considered his answer. "We do not know anything that can assist their efforts. Let them continue their processes. We must have faith in their skills. They might get lucky on their own. If we learn the target in time, we can provide refined search guidance without exposing our source. And, I cannot emphasize enough, anything we do henceforth tonight must offer not the slightest hint of foreknowledge."

"Very well."

"I will need to know precisely where each of you will be tonight," he said, "and, presumably not in the same location. Please notify John Martin directly with no other indications." They all nodded their heads in agreement. "Anything else?" Seeing or hearing no sign, Churchill continued, "General Dill, since you are closest to the door, would you be so kind to recall your staff so we can conclude this meeting and be on our way."

Chief of the Imperial General Staff General Sir John Greer Dill, KCB, CMG, DSO, left the room and returned, followed by a dozen or so staff officers and support personnel. It took several minutes for everyone to settle back in their chairs.

The Prime Minister's thoughts remained on the looming attack, now expected tonight, while the gathering discussed the military situation in North Africa, the naval situation in the Atlantic, and the nightly losses in the transformed air battle that was The Blitz. The anti-aircraft defensive measures seemed almost surreal in the context of tonight. The various staff officers conducted the briefings. The ministers and chiefs remained uncharacteristically quiet and pensive, as though their thoughts were on Moonlight Sonata as well. The Defense Committee meeting concluded on time despite the Prime Minister's late arrival. Churchill confirmed the committee's meeting time tomorrow, although none of them knew what tomorrow would hold.

—

Thursday, 14.November.1940
Prime Minister's Limousine
London, England
United Kingdom
15:20 hours

The polished, spotless, black, 1939 Rolls-Royce Phantom III limousine remained in front of No.10 with the engine running. Detective-Inspector Thompson stood beside the open door. The mostly cloudy sky darkened the street before dusk. Prime Minister Churchill sat patiently in the automobile lost in his thoughts. General Ismay sat beside the Prime Minister, motionless and wordless, so as not to bother Churchill's contemplation.

"This may be a long night, Pug," mumbled Winston.

"Yes sir," Ismay answered. "We are as ready as can be."

"Perhaps," Churchill whispered and lapsed back into his thoughts, once again.

They waited another five minutes. Assistant Private Secretary Jock Colville burst out of No.10 with the usual black dispatch box in hand. He had assumed the weekend duty a day early, so that John Martin could attend a family funeral.

"My most humble apologies, Prime Minister," Jock said as he took the jump seat in front of Churchill.

Winston held up his hand. He did not want any discussion, just yet. Thompson closed the door behind Colville, and then bounced around the car to take the passenger seat beside Sergeant Stanley 'Stan' Carrick, the Prime Minister's newly selected, handpicked driver from the Royal Army Service Corps. Carrick had driven race cars before the war and Inspector Thompson made certain he understood the necessary defensive driving skills from the Metropolitan Police, should they be needed. The car moved as soon as everyone was settled. Carrick drove expertly through the damaged streets of London.

They had passed Uxbridge and were into the country by the time Churchill broke out of his contemplative state. "Well done, Sergeant Carrick," Churchill pronounced. "We have not witnessed expert driving such as this in quite some time, if perhaps ever. Well done, indeed."

"Thank you, sir," Sergeant Carrick acknowledged.

"Right, then," the Prime Minister said, turning back to Colville, "what have you in our box?"

Jock Colville opened the dispatch box. "There is one message in the Top of the Box, sir." Colville handed the single piece of paper to the Prime Minister.

SECRET

```
ZZZZ/8471MMX5017/AM-PM-WC/JJRBZTOP/554/ZZZZ
DATE: 14.11.40 1445 HOURS
FROM: AIR MINISTRY
TO: PRIME MINISTER
SECRETARIAT
WAR CABINET
SUBJECT: ASPIRIN
BEGIN
BEAMS DETECTED. INTERSECTION INDICATES COVENTRY
IS THE TARGET. NO OTHER BEAMS DETECTED. NO
INDICATION TIME HAS CHANGED. ASPIRIN ACTIVATED.
INSUFFICIENT TIME TO REDEPLOY NIGHTFIGHTER
ASSETS PER PM ORDER. EVERY ATTEMPT TO BE MADE
FOR COUNTER MEASURES TO ALTER OBJECTIVE.
```

END

ZZZZ/8471MMX5017/AM-PM-WC/JJRBZTOP/554/ZZZZ

SECRET

"Turn around," Churchill commanded, as he handed the message to Ismay.
"Sir?"

"Turn around, now. Head back to Number Ten as swiftly as you are able."

Thompson turned to see the Prime Minister. Churchill nodded his head. Walter turned back forward to help Carrick find a turn around.

"Perhaps, we should press onto Ditchley, to ensure you are safe."

Churchill scowled at Ismay. "We have been through this before. I have no intention of keeping my person safe, while our people suffer."

"Yes sir. Then, perhaps, we should stop at Eleven Group to use their communications center," offered Ismay. The No.11 Group headquarters and operations center was not far off their return route.

"Good idea, Pug, but no. I appreciate your concerns for my safety. There is not much we can do at this late hour. Let us get back to Number Ten, where we have all the facilities of command."

"Yes sir."

"Would you care to go through the rest of the box?" asked Colville.

Churchill stared at Jock. "I doubt there are any messages in our box as vital as this one." Winston handed the paper back to Colville, who returned it to the folder and closed the box.

Sergeant Carrick performed his role exceptionally well. They arrived at No.10 in not quite half the time as the outbound portion of the journey. Churchill was grateful for Carrick's skills.

—

Beginning at 19:20 [Z] British Double Summer Time (BDST), on the evening of Thursday, 14.November.1940, the German pathfinder aircraft of the experimental / developmental squadron *Kampfgruppe 100* dropped incendiary bombs using the *Knickebein X-Gerat*, instrument, precision, bombing system to physically mark the target for the first and subsequent waves of *Luftflotte 3* medium bombers. The first wave dropped high explosive bombs on Coventry, and what was commonly and euphemistically called aerial mines, massive high explosive devices, to break up structures. Subsequent waves of bombers dropped a combination of high explosive and incendiary bombs, and even that latter group was mixed with phosphorous and petroleum devices. This night's attack lasted 13 hours, until nearly dawn the following day. The anti-aircraft guns fired thousands of rounds throughout the night, and night fighter aircraft made numerous attempts to intercept the waves of bombers during their approach and withdrawal. Not one German bomber would be shot down during the night's attack on Coventry. The fires in the city center could be seen for hundreds of miles around the city, assisted by the blackout and despite the cloud-shrouded full moon. The raid became the archetype for Allied bombing raids on Germany and Japan, and the symbol for revenge, more so than all the attacks on London.

—

Monday, 18.November.1940
Cabinet Room
No.10 Downing Street
Whitehall, London, England
United Kingdom
13:10 hours

"**W**ell, gentlemen," announced Prime Minister Churchill, "you have had four days to ascertain what happened." He chose not to be more definitive, as he considered the topic abundantly obvious for the Defense Committee. "Pray tell, let us have your reports."

Home Secretary Herbert Morrison cleared his throat to take the initiative. "The last of the fires were finally extinguished last night. Over five hundred citizens were killed during the raid. Nearly thirteen hundred were injured, some seriously, which may raise the death toll before this is all over. More than two thirds of the city has been destroyed beyond use. They intentionally broke up buildings and homes, and then set the rubble alight. The inferno created its own wind, updrafts that fueled and enhanced the fires. Many other buildings have been damaged – broken windows, burn damage, and such – but they are habitable and usable. All in all, this was the most focused and destructive raid we have experienced to date."

"Thank you, Herbert," Churchill said, and turned to and simply stared at the Air Minister.

"Yes, well, the destruction in Coventry is nothing short of tragic. In short, the Royal Air Force should have been able to do more. As we have discussed previously, the ASPIRIN counter-measures were activated that night. The search teams detected and localized the intersecting beams from source stations in Germany and Belgium. The relevant operational information – frequency, modulation and location – was passed to the ASPIRIN transmitters.

Unfortunately, during the initial pathfinder attack, they noticed no apparent effect of the beam-bending transmitters. As they hurriedly tried to figure what was happening, they discovered that a transcription error had been made – two digits had been transposed. The transmitters had the incorrect frequency. By the time they discovered the error and made the proper correction, the attack was well underway, and they no longer needed their *Knickebein* system to find their target."

"Well, that is not encouraging news, Archie."

"No, I'm afraid it is not. We have already taken steps to ensure the accuracy of information passed from the search teams to the counter-measures chaps."

"Rightly so."

"Yes. I might also add my personal opinion here. Perhaps we piqued their intensity too much. Everyone was keenly aware that something big was about to happen by virtue of our persistent inquiry, and they acted with unreasonable haste in their attempt to do their part to stop whatever it was that was about to happen."

"This is wartime, Archie. We have a dreadful and bloody long way to go before this thing is done. They had better get used to the intensity. It will not go away until the Huns have surrendered unconditionally." The Cabinet Room fell stone cold silent – not so much as a swallow could be heard. "Several thousand of our innocent citizens died or were injured four nights ago . . . due . . . due to a . . . a . . . a clerical error." Again, silence enveloped the room for what seemed like minutes. No one sought to speak, and Winston withdrew into his thoughts. "I want to ensure the individuals involved understand the consequences of what happened, but I do not want them abused for doing what they believed was their level best. I want them to be encouraged, on behalf of the Defense Committee and indeed the War Cabinet, to improve their processes, to strive to do better the next time, as most assuredly there will be many more next times before we savor the sweet embrace of victory in this war."

"Yes sir. Sir Charles and I will see to it personally. They are good men, who have been overworked and stretched thin. It is our task to improve their lot in this war."

"It is vitally important, Archie."

"Yes sir."

"We must institute the necessary changes to ensure this never happens again. We came very close to beating them last Thursday night, but we failed." Churchill turned to Morrison. "Herbert, pray notify my office as soon as the Emergency Services have secured the city. I must journey to Coventry as soon as physically possible. I must see the devastation for myself, before the cleanup is too far along. They are a strong people. They shall rebuild faster than we expect. They must see me with them in this."

"Yes sir. We anticipated as much. Word from Coventry indicates Wednesday or Thursday may be appropriate. I shall keep your office informed of their progress."

"Thank you, Herbert. We will plan for Wednesday." Churchill looked around the room. "Unless there is other urgent business, I think we have had enough punishment this afternoon. We shall reconvene tomorrow. Pray let us have a thorough status report from the Admiralty on the Battle of the Atlantic. I see the daily shipping numbers, but we need to know more about what the Navy is doing to thwart these damnable U-boats." The First Lord nodded his head, followed by the First Sea Lord. "Very well, gentlemen, we are adjourned."

——

Monday, 18.November.1940
Oval Office
The White House
Washington, District of Columbia
United States of America
11:00 hours

"Good morning, Mister President," Secretary of State Cordell Hull cheerily said upon entering the famous office alone. The door was closed behind him.

"Good morning to you, Cordell. So, you have news," Roosevelt answered and gestured toward the straight back wooden chair to the right of his desk.

"I just received word from the Foreign Minister via the Ambassador that the Germans have sealed off the so-called Jewish ghetto in Warsaw. According to the information we have been provided, MI6 has confirmed from multiple sources the German action of two days ago."

"What does that mean?"

"It means they have physically closed . . ."

"I know what sealed off means," the President interrupted, "but why did they do that? They have already been seriously restricted in their ability to travel anywhere."

"There was no further information from Lord Lothian. I can query Lord Halifax directly to see if they know anymore information regarding the purpose . . . or objective, or any other elements."

"Yes, please do. As I recall, the Germans began rounding up and transporting Poles of Jewish descent to enclaves in the major cities shortly after the Polish surrender."

"Your memory is precisely correct. Our ambassador confirmed that fact through the Polish government-in-exile in London a year ago. The Germans claimed it was a quarantine for unspecified health reasons. It seemed a bit odd, but there were many other higher priority issues occupying everyone in those days."

Roosevelt stared at Hull, as he considered his words, and did not speak. "This cannot bode well for the Jews."

"I suspect not. A health reason for such an action would affect everyone, not just the Jews."

Again, Roosevelt turned his wheelchair around, gazed out the window and lapsed into contemplation. Hull did not intrude. After several minutes, he turned back around. "That incident last year with the SS *St. Louis* and the Jewish refugees did not go down well, Cordell."

In June 1939, before the war in Europe ignited into full blaze, 936 Jewish refugees from Germany and other adjacent European countries sought asylum in the United States. Secretary Hull decided against issuing them tourist visas since they had no return address for the application—a technicality many criticized as heartless. The rejection sent the ship back to Germany and the consequence the refugees sought to avoid.

"Mister President, before you go too much farther with this, I am compelled to remind you that we cannot be the haven for all the abused peoples in this world."

Roosevelt started to respond and stopped, and looked directly into Hull's eyes. "What happened to 'Give me your tired, your poor, your huddled masses yearning to breathe free'?"

"Mister President, it is a noble concept and worthy inscription. However, we have practical limits. We cannot absorb all of 'the wretched refuse' of the world. We must draw the line somewhere."

Roosevelt considered Hull's words in the light of the most recent news. "Very well. Let's keep as close an eye on events in Poland as we can. I would like to know the answers, if any, we can get from the British."

"As you wish, Mister President."

"Anything else?"

"No sir."

"Thank you. Good day, Cordell," Roosevelt said dismissively. "Please ask Harry to join me at his earliest convenience."

Hull nodded his head and departed. Roosevelt returned to the papers on his desk.

—

Tuesday, 19.November.1940
RAF Church Fenton
Tadcaster, North Yorkshire, England
United Kingdom

"Gather around, gentlemen, and I use that term loosely," announced Squadron Leader Churchill. There was grumbling, but no specific or discernible words. Several pilots returned to the Dispersal Hut from the chill outside and closed the door behind them. "We have arrived at the point in our training program for a relevant experiment and exercise. 'Roley' has completed his transition familiarization, and we are now a full squadron, finally. This morning, we will launch the entire squadron. We will run a series of engagement scenarios with 'A' Flight versus 'B' Flight. Each flight has one Hurricane and one Buffalo section, so we will evaluate our ability to coordinate the fight with dissimilar aircraft. Then, this afternoon, we will repeat the engagement set-ups with the two Hurricane sections versus the two Buffalo sections to see if the dissimilar aircraft problems persist. In the afternoon exercise, Hunter will lead 'B' Flight, and Whitey, your Red Section will be with me."

Pilot Officer Michael 'Roley' Rigby from Detroit, Michigan, joined the squadron three days after Brian. Also, like Brian and others in the squadron, he learned to fly in the United States, trading aircraft and general maintenance work for flight instruction and flying time in a variety of biplane aircraft. He did not have as much time as some of the pilots, but he had more than most of their contemporaries. Roley arrived at the squadron directly from the advanced training unit with a good recommendation. He would fly right wing in Rusty Bateman's Yellow Section.

Baggy completed the briefing with their assigned training area and operating altitudes along with radio frequencies to be utilized. They would fly armed; just in case a rogue German aircraft found its way to the Midlands, but their armament systems would be switched off. 'B' Flight would be the 'bad guys' for the morning exercise, and the 'A' Flight would take that roll for the afternoon events.

The weather remained a near perfect fall day with scattered fair weather cumulus cloud below their operating altitudes. They flew six engagements during each sortie with a break for lunch in between the two sessions. They encountered no interference or distractions during either mission. They all worked hard, had some fun, and learned more than they imagined they would.

Baggy Churchill gathered them up at the end of their flying day to debrief the exercise. "Well done, lads. We had a good workout today. So, what did we learn from the day's events?"

"We learned Hunter is a slippery devil who cheats," pronounced Horse Harrow.

They all laughed. Those closest to Brian gave him a friendly punch in the shoulder.

"All's fair in love and war, they say."

"We also learned Hunter can make a piece of shit airplane smell like roses," said Salt Morton.

"So, your kinky self has smelled a few piles of shit, have you Salt?" Rusty Bateman jabbed.

Again, everyone laughed and this time punched Salt Morton in the shoulders. Morton did not respond.

"You seem to be the man of the hour, Hunter. Would you be so kind to give us your assessment of the day's exercise?" Baggy asked.

"I think we all can clearly see the Buffalos cannot keep up with the Hurricanes. The speed differential would be even worse if we had Spitfires. Once the engagements began, the distance between the sections opened up to such an extent that we could not support the Hurricane sections. If we get into a real, shooting fight with the Germans, we might get lucky to get one pass, if we find surprise or distract them for just enough time, and then we must run as fast as we can. Perhaps we can work on a coordinated engagement technique to use the Buffalos as bait."

"Oh great," commented Rusty Bateman. "We are given inferior aircraft, and now, our resident ace wants us to intentionally get shot at."

The comment struck Brian wrongly at precisely the worst moment. "Rusty, let me ask you, how many One Oh Nines have you faced?"

"None," he whispered.

"Right, so as I was attempting to answer the Skipper's query, we must find a way to negate our lack of performance. I cannot stand toe-to-toe with the One Oh Nine and an average pilot. Unfortunately, we must assume the pilot of every One Oh Nine we face has Werner Mölders or Adolf Galland at the controls."

"We can set up an experiment with one of the other refit squadrons," said Churchill. "What other options do you see? We are expected to receive the rest of our Hurricanes in the next two months. We may well be declared operational before we fully transition, thus we must find the means to do the best we can with the assets we have. In that light, let us hear from the rest of you." Baggy waited. "Now, now, gentlemen, don't everyone speak at once. No need to be shy. We are all family here."

"I'm with Hunter on this one," answered Whitey.

"How about we leave the Buffalos on the ground until the replacement Hurricanes arrive," Rusty added.

Everyone laughed, although a few nervous, uneasy giggles could be heard.

"Yes, well," Baggy interrupted, "a ship in harbor is safe, but will never accomplish its purpose. Leaving the Buffalos on the ground is not an option either." Churchill looked to each pilot. Most were too inexperienced to have developed a broader appreciation of tactics . . . in time, but not yet. They had gusto and panache. They had savior-faire and energy. They had audacity and confidence. What they did not have just yet was the experience of a hunter – the knowledge of understanding their prey. "Over the next few weeks, we will combine our training work with some experiments. We will evaluate Hunter's suggestion, and versions thereof. I challenge each of you to think about how to use our tools to accomplish our mission . . . and protect each other so that we survive this war. We were not promised an easy road. We shall ask for none. Now, Corporal Harris, if you would, please notify Sector and Group that Seventy-One – The Eagle Squadron – is complete for the day."

"Yes sir." He lifted the handset.

"Therefore, gentleman, we are done. Thank you for a good day. We took another step forward today."

"Sir, Sector and Group have been notified. We are released."

"Hang up your kit," said Baggy. "We shall reconvene in the Mess to celebrate a good day."

They laughed and joked. They felt good. Tonight would be a family affair. They would make the most of their night without combat, or even the sounds of bombs or distant cannons.

—

Wednesday, 20.November.1940
Cabinet Room
No.10 Downing Street
Whitehall, London, England
United Kingdom
17:30 hours

Only the War Cabinet and those members of the Defence Committee cleared for access to the ULTRA material were in the closed Cabinet Room. All such members were present.

"You called this special meeting, Archie," announced the Prime Minister. "You have the floor."

A broad smile blossomed on Sir Archibald's face. "We finally have some good and encouraging news." He paused. No one spoke and all eyes were on him. "As we discussed yesterday, ULTRA gave us the target for last night's enemy air raid . . . Birmingham. The ASPIRIN lads localized the beams and confirmed the German target. The necessary details were checked, rechecked, crosschecked and confirmed. The Chain Home tracking of the inbound first wave enabled us to precisely refine our countermeasures timing." He smiled more broadly. "I am so happy to report the system worked perfectly and as expected. The bombs from all three waves impacted in a rural area five miles from the city. The area had been evacuated without incident or disclosure. Not one single life was lost. There were some injuries, and the local fire brigade is dealing with the resultant fires in several spots of the affected area."

"Well done," Clement Attlee burst out exuberantly.

"Indeed," added the Prime Minister. "Our heartfelt congratulations must go to all members of the team without disclosing results, or means and methods."

"I think we can comply with that," Sir Archie responded.

"The Wizard War has finally saved incalculable lives. While the nation cannot know what they have done on their behalf, the people they saved will one-day cheer their accomplishment. Now, I am compelled to caution, we must engage the Press to avoid reference to the Germans missing their target and especially discourage any supposition as to why they missed. If we need to invoke the War Secrets Act, we must do so promptly and definitively. If the Germans gain even a hint that we have developed countermeasures to their Broken Leg bombing system, they will seek alternate means to perform their vile mission."

"I will inform and coordinate with Herbert," volunteered Lord President of the Council Sir John Anderson, GCB, GCSI, GCIE, PC, Member of Parliament for the Combined Scottish Universities, and Herbert Morrison's predecessor as Home Secretary. "My experience suggests we can properly engage the Press to protect our capabilities for the time being."

"Thank you, John. Do you have any other good news, Archie?"

"Yes, as a matter of fact I do. The nightfighters had perhaps the best night of hunting since the war began. They accounted for not quite a dozen enemy aircraft during ingress and egress."

"Excellent," proclaimed the Prime Minister. "Things appear to be coming together quite nicely. We must gird ourselves for future failures, but it is certainly sweet to savor a victory now and then."

Applause erupted spontaneously among the senior members of His Majesty's Government.

Churchill continued, "I shall seek an audience with The King to inform him of this victory in the long battle. Once again, I must remind everyone that we cannot divulge a word of what we know and how we know it. These means are far too important to our ultimate victory."

"Should we inform the Americans?" asked Sir Archibald.

Churchill thought for a moment. "If they ask and they are appropriately cleared for such information, we should answer their queries directly and truthfully. At this stage, I would not suggest volunteering this information. We are too early in this game, and we may experience failures in the future. The proper time will come. They are not threatened as we are."

"Understood," responded Sinclair.

"Hopefully," Churchill said, "this will be the first of many successes. Well done all the way around. One point of curiosity," he changed the subject and looked to the First Lord of the Admiralty, "I think we have the final destroyer transfer from the Americans coming up soon, do we not?"

"Yes," Alexander answered, "in just under a week's time . . . the last of the agreed to 50 destroyers. I must say, only a little more than half have actually made it to convoy service."

"But, every little bit helps," quipped Churchill.

"Quite so. We are most grateful. We are still working to get the remainder to proper operational status, and I must say, we could use another 50 or more."

"It was a stretch for the President to risk at 50. I would not encourage him taking additional risk at this stage. I can assure you, we will keep an eye out for an opportunity to acquire more."

"We can ask for no more," A.V. said.

"Is there any other urgent business we must tend to?" asked the Prime Minister. Several shook their heads in the negative. No one spoke up. "Hearing none, we shall adjourn."

The ministers and service chiefs departed, and the Prime Minister returned to his office down the hallway.

—

Chapter 5

Always, Sir, set a high value on spontaneous kindness.
He whose inclination prompts him
to cultivate your friendship of his own accord,
will love you more than one whom
you have been at pains to attach to you.

- Samuel Johnson (1781)

Tuesday, 3.December.1940
USS Tuscaloosa *(CA-37)*
Municipal Pier No.3
Miami, Florida
United States of America

The heavy cruiser tied up at dockside remained a most impressive warship that had not yet seen combat and was comparatively new, having been commissioned in 1934. Franklin Roosevelt held an affinity for these gray ships from his youth, long before he became Assistant Secretary of the Navy, and then President of the United States and Commander-in-Chief. He also appreciated the extra wide, covered gangway to enable his embarkation without the torture of walking with his braces locked.

The Boatswain's pipe whistled the unique notes followed by "United States arriving," over the 1 Main Circuit, ship-wide, broadcast system, commonly referred to as the 1MC, to inform the ship's company the Commander-in-Chief was coming aboard. The Officer of the Deck called the quarterdeck to attention.

Despite being carried aboard in his wheel chair, President Roosevelt saluted and said, "Permission to come aboard, sir."

The cruiser's captain, Captain Lee Payne Johnson, USN [USNA 1909], returned the President's salute and replied, "Permission granted. Welcome aboard *Tuscaloosa*, again, Mister President."

The four seamen lowered the President gently to the deck. "Thank you very much, Captain Johnson. It is once again an honor for me to be aboard your magnificent warship. Are all my people aboard?"

"According to the manifest provided by Mister Hopkins and the White House, yes sir. The personnel and footlockers have been accounted for, each and every one."

"I concur, sir," whispered Harry Hopkins from behind Roosevelt.

"Do you have all of the necessary permissions and information for the various ports of call on this journey?"

"Yes sir. We have made direct communications with the harbormasters for each port on your itinerary. The Royal Navy has been most helpful. Everything appears to be in order."

"Excellent, then shall we get underway?"

"We are ready and at your command, sir. I will say, if I may, we have a midday meal prepared for you in the Flag Mess, if you would care to eat while we set sail."

Roosevelt smiled broadly. "I just love that term. If it is not an imposition, I would like to observe our departure from Miami."

"No imposition at all." Payne looked and nodded to someone behind the President. "We shall inform your chief steward to keep things warm for you. Your best view will be on the Flag Bridge. As we make the channel, I shall join you on the Flag Bridge, if that is an acceptable arrangement, sir."

"That should do just fine. Thank you very much, Captain Johnson."

"My pleasure and honor, sir. Now, if you will excuse me, Mister President, we'll get our mooring lines singled up, while our escorts precede us out of the harbor. The Flag Bridge is set for you to listen to our commands, as we depart."

"Let us proceed."

Captain Johnson departed leaving a lieutenant to assist the President as might be required. The President, his carrier seamen and Hopkins followed the lieutenant to the Flag Bridge. By the time the President was situated, he could see two destroyers in trail slowly moving through the harbor channel toward the open sea. The various commands to the deck crew and linesmen could be easily heard over the bridge speaker. Two tugs pulled the heavy cruiser away from the dock and maneuvered the warship into the channel behind the destroyers. The lines to the tugs were cast off and they were underway. True to his word, Captain Johnson joined the President.

"The lead destroyer is the *Mayrant*, followed by the *Trippe*," announced Johnson.

"Those are different destroyers than were with us for the Panama Canal voyage last winter."

"Yes, they are. Good memory, sir."

As they approached the channel entry buoys, the two destroyers had spread out and presumably begun their work to ensure no bad guys were lurking outside the Port of Miami. In short order, they were clear of the channel, turned initially southeast and increased speed. The destroyers initially held station off the cruiser's port side until they were well beyond landfall, and then shifted their positions to several miles off the port and starboard bow of the cruiser.

"Would you care to join me for lunch, Captain?"

"I would be honored, Mister President."

—

Wednesday, 4.December.1940
Cabinet Room
No.10 Downing Street
Whitehall, London, England
United Kingdom
15:00 hours

The service ministers and military chiefs were all present at the appointed hour. In addition to the immediate Defense Committee, the Prime Minister had invited Professor Lindemann, his scientific advisor, and Sir John Andersen, who served as the supervisory minister for the British Technical and Scientific Mission to the United States of America led by Sir Henry Tizard. The Tizard Mission, as it had come to be known, had undertaken a comprehensive transfer of precious, highly secret, military technology to the United States three months ago. While the original intent of the mission had been the protection of those secrets given the seriousness of the invasion threat the British faced the previous summer, the joint British-American team had begun to yield results almost immediately. The combination of technologies showed great promise once the veil of secrecy had been removed for the joint team—one and one made five.

"Pray tell, let us have the report from America," began the Prime Minister with a hint of impatience. "Wait, before we begin, where is Sir Henry? I should think this is his child."

The Air Minister answered, "He is working with Doctor Watson-Watt and deeply into an improvement to the Chain Home system."

"He could not afford an hour of his time for this discussion?"

"He begs your forgiveness, but no . . . and I agreed with him."

"Very well," Churchill said and gestured for them to move on. "Proceed."

Sir Archibald Sinclair continued, "We received information from various sources late yesterday evening regarding the initial test results of the first production Mark Two Air-to-Surface Vessel or ASV RADAR unit that combines our cavity magnetron and the American duplex switch. A Navy PBY Catalina flying boat equipped with the Mark Two kit took off yesterday morning from Anacostia airfield near Washington, DC, climbed to 5,000 feet altitude over the Chesapeake Bay and began searching with the ASV RADAR. They detected, in short order, a capital ship 60 nautical miles into the Atlantic Ocean. Not only did they determine the location, but also precisely established the course and speed of the warship. The test conditions for both aircraft and target warship were varied numerous times throughout the duration of the two hour test. The results were validated multifold times."

"A double-edged sword for the Navy," interjected the First Sea Lord.

Churchill turned to Admiral Pound, "How so?"

"Yes, this kit will improve our search capability, but it will also increase the vulnerability of our ships should the technology fall into the enemy's hands."

"What is that old Admiralty saying about a ship in port?"

"A ship in harbor is safe, but that is not what ships are built for," Admiral Pound responded. "Quite so."

"We must protect this technology . . . all of our technology . . . as best we can, but that task must not cower us from putting this equipment to use as quickly and effectively as possible."

The First Lord A.V. Alexander chimed in. "We also understand the U.S. Navy immediately placed an order for 7,000 units with the Philco Corporation with an urgent priority demand."

"Presumably, some significant portion of that order is earmarked for our use," Churchill said.

"That has not been precisely determined or defined, as yet, however I intend to contact Secretary Knox immediately for that purpose."

"Excellent. Please do not let any grass grow under your feet. Also, I urge you, and pray give me confirmation as soon as possible, to contact Lord Lothian and Bill Stephenson in New York. Let us get them working on this matter as well."

"We will certainly do so," the First Lord responded.

"We will also direct Coastal Command," added the Air Minister, "to consider space, weight and power provision in their search aircraft . . . to be ready for immediate installation and use as soon as the Mark Two units become available."

"And," interjected the Chief of the Air Staff, "we are coordinating with the Americans to begin training our air crews ahead of time."

"Excellent. This must be our number one priority."

War Minister Anthony Eden said, "Everything cannot be number one priority, Winston."

Churchill waved his hand vigorously. "Yes, yes, Anthony, but you know what I mean. This is very important. We may not be able to find a surfaced submarine at 60 miles, but it will damn sure be at greater range than we currently achieve at present."

"Yes," said Admiral Pound, "I believe they have picked up a submarine in the range of 10 to 20 miles. If achieved operationally, such a capability may well shift the Battle of the Atlantic in our favor."

"Finally. We have suffered too long at the mercy of those gray wolves." Churchill looked to each of the attendees in the room. "Do we have any further business for the Defense Committee to discuss at this moment?" He looked again to each attendee. "Hearing none, we are adjourned, gentlemen. Have a good evening."

—

Thursday, 5.December.1940
RAF Manston
Ramsgate, Kent, England
United Kingdom
08:00 hours

Twelve 'PR' Spitfires of No.609 Squadron, Brian Drummond's original unit, landed safely at the battered but still operational aerodrome, taxied to their directed parking area and shutdown. During the worst days of the battle, in late August, Prime Minister Churchill visited the air base when the base commander decided to close the aerodrome after his ground crews could not repair the bomb damage as fast as the Germans were churning up the landing area with their bombs. RAF Manston had the unfortunate distinction of being the closest air base to France and Belgium, which made it a convenient target for the German bombers to drop their payloads, to claim they fulfilled their mission, and then run for home to avoid the British fighters. Churchill relieved the base commander that afternoon and charged the new commander with keeping the air base open and working.

The squadron had departed RAF Catterick early this morning well before dawn. They had seen the first sprays of dawn during their cruise flight at 12,000 feet on their way south. The River Thames had been unmistakable, and the shades of gray of blacked-out London had given them just enough detail to see the capitol city to the west of their track.

The pilots gathered in the nearby, makeshift, dispersal tent, while their fighters were refueled for their real mission. Half the pilots chose not to sit after the 85-minute flight down from RAF Catterick. They knew the next sortie was likely to be a long flight and some intensity likely. Their mission was to make a squadron fighter sweep into France.

"Listen up, gentlemen," Squadron Leader Long-Roberts said, and waited for quiet and their attention. "Today, our rest and refit period ends. As soon as our aeroplanes are ready, we head across the Channel. We are not the first squadron to take the fight to the enemy, but this will be our first opportunity. We will make the most of it. Before we do the mission briefing, if anyone has bodily functions to attend to, now is the time. Once we begin the mission briefing, we will be confined to this tent until we mount up." Stack looked and pointed to each of his pilots, and received a verbal or gestured negative response. "Very well, then. Let us begin. We will fly a joint mission with Six Four Squadron. You probably noticed their 'SH' Spitfires down the line. They will fly high cover for us. Their call sign is Freema, for those who don't already know it. Our mission is to attack two aerodromes in France . . . ." Spontaneous cheers broke out among the pilots. Stack raised his hand. He waited for quiet. "We will shoot up anything that moves or looks like it might move. These are both forward German fighter bases; one is Marck Aerodrome at Calais, and the other is Mardyck at Dunkirk." More cheers interrupted Stack. Again, he waited for quiet. "We will make the run across the Channel at low level, so we will have to watch our coolant temperatures. We will keep our speed down until we make landfall on the French coast, and then we will increase speed. You must ensure your coolant gates are wide open, or you will overheat for sure and could compromise the mission. Blue and Green Sections in echelon left. 'B' Flight will trail by no more than half a mile with Red and Yellow Sections in echelon right. Each section will spread their formation to give each pilot time to scan for enemy fighters and pick out their targets. Try to stay in your lane, so that we can hit as many targets as possible. We take one pass only at Marck, and then adjust our flight path direct for Mardyck. We will use the same attack formation for our pass at Mardyck. From there and depending upon Gerry's reaction, we will turn for Manston, stay low to minimize anti-aircraft fire, and once we are several miles into the Channel, we will climb and throttle back to cool the engines. Any questions, so far?"

"Yes Skipper," 'Sparky' spoke up. "So, this is why we were issued pistols for our kit."

"Yes, precisely. Other squadrons began conducting fighter sweeps last month. The German reaction has been quite mixed. The Air Ministry is still working on determination of their radio detection capabilities. Other squadrons have had the best results with these tactics. We are not likely to encounter large caliber anti-aircraft fire at these low altitudes, but we must expect small arms and machine gun fire. We will be over enemy territory. Losing an engine over there . . . well . . . a pistol won't help against a squad of infantry. If you go down, get away from the wreckage as fast as you can. Try to mask your tracks, as you are able. Hide and seek the assistance of the locals you can find."

Jonathan 'Harness' Kensington, Brian's best friend and former squadron mate, listened intently. This would be the first mission over enemy territory for most of the new squadron, and the first for him and the other veterans since the air operations over the Dunkirk beaches during the evacuation last June. He could feel the tension building in his gut. This was not going to be an easy mission, but there was also an undeniable good feeling, as well. They were taking the fight to the enemy, giving them a taste of the punishment they meted out last summer.

"Six Four Squadron will follow us at Angels Eight to attract the attention of the German radio detection operators and hopefully buy us some time. They will also handle the fighter reaction should we encounter any. So far, these fighter sweeps have produced a fighter counter-attack about half the time. You must continue to scan for fighters. We will all be on the same frequency, so any bogey call goes to everyone. Other than that, let us try to keep radio silence. Also, if your coolant temperature approaches the red line, you must keep your engine running. Call out your situation. Your section will cover you."

Squadron Leader Long-Roberts completed the briefing with radio frequencies, call signs for those facilities and units involved, the coordinates of their targets, and the enemy dispositions at their targets and in the area. Each of them marked their maps accordingly.

They did not have to wait long for the signal from the ground crew chief that their aircraft were fully fueled and checked.

"Very well, then, gentlemen. Let us mount up and have a successful mission. Keep your heads on the swivel. Do not succumb to target fixation. Good luck."

The pilots grabbed whatever kit they had removed. Most had only removed their leather helmets, goggles and oxygen mask, so they could hear the mission briefing.

Jonathan touched the grip of his pistol in its shoulder holster under his left arm. His 'PR-K' Spitfire Mark IA stood ready. They started their engines on Stack's signal. The ground was not particularly smooth as a consequence of all the bomb damage repairs, but it was good enough. They took off to the southeast. Stack kept the squadron low as they cleaned up their aircraft and throttled back for a comfortable, low altitude, cruise, power setting. As they crossed the cliff's edge, they followed him in a turn to the south and began a gradual descent to perhaps 50 feet above the wave tops. They passed along and parallel to the famous white cliffs of Dover. Jonathan positioned his Green Section off to the left and behind Blue Section. Ten minutes later, the French coastline came into view. He increased his throttle setting to maintain position, checked his coolant temperature and coolant gate switch full open, and then turned his head over both shoulders to make sure his wingmen were in position. Stack turned them almost due east, now, for their run in to the first target. Jonathan checked his guns were armed, his gunsight switched on bright, and this gun camera switch was in the armed position to be activated by the firing button. They spread out a little farther. Jonathan continued to scan the sky around them as he maintained his position and quickly checked his map to ensure he knew their location.

They adjusted their height above ground to skim across the treetops. It had to be an awesome sight on the ground – 12 sleek Spitfire fighters with their Merlin engines at full throat and high speed barely over a tree's height off the ground. Jonathan continued to scan the sky – still empty and crystal clear. They were minutes from their target. They should see the airfield any time . . . there it is. He checked his gunsight as a marker to pick out his target. Oh yes, he said to himself. He had a large building on the far side of the field and a Ju-52, three-engine transport plane with large, black crosses on the tail. Jonathan lined up the pipper of his gunsight short of the transport's left wing. He opened fire. The stream of bullets from his eight machine guns shook his aircraft and produced sparks across the entire wing that also burst into flames. Jonathan just missed the edge of the fireball and kept his firing button down, putting his stream of bullets into what he thought was a hangar. A bright flash illuminated his cockpit from behind. He did not dare look back. The concussion wave shook his aircraft, causing him to quickly adjust his controls to avoid hitting a church steeple near his left wing. He still had position on Blue Section. He quickly scanned. Both wingmen were still with him and in position. The sky remained clear.

Stack adjusted their flight path to the east-northeast. Jonathan manipulated his controls to maintain position and looked to make sure his wingmen had done the same. At their speed, they were only eight minutes from their next target. Still the sky was clear. There it is. Mardyck had bomb-damaged buildings all around the airfield, *probably from the fighting in June.* A Bf-109 with a black nose and propeller spinner was taxiing across the field. Tracers streaked across his nose and over him. Jonathan quickly adjusted his gunsight to slightly ahead of the German fighter and opened fire. His target's left main landing gear strut collapsed. The aircraft burst into flame and luckily the explosion came after Jonathan passed. Another fighter on the far end of the field had just started its engine. He never got to move as Jonathan dispatched him quickly.

Again, Jonathan scanned the sky. Then, he heard the first radio call. "Sorbo, this is Freema. Bogeys closing from the south. We'll take care of them. You should be clear for home. Nice shooting."

"Thanks, Freema."

They crossed the coastline. Stack kept the squadron low and their speed up, and then turned northwest. Jonathan checked his coolant temperature; he still had margin. Once they were well out into the Channel, Stack throttled back and began a gradual climb. Jonathan continued to scan the sky for enemy fighters and listened. There was nothing he could detect. *We did some damage and we got away free.* Fifteen minutes later, the white cliffs emerged from the haze and became easily discernible.

The entire squadron landed safely back at RAF Manston. The pilots were jubilant. Stack called Hornchurch Sector Control to give them a safe arrival and mission accomplished call.

"Gather up, gentlemen," Stack shouted from inside the tent. Half the pilots outside joined the others. "First, well done. We all made it back safely. We may have some shrapnel or small arms damage, but we had no losses. Sector has put us on Available in 30 Minutes status, so we can refuel and rearm. They are going to hold us here until early afternoon, to see if they will need our services anymore. We will have our intelligence chaps download our gun cameras for processing and brief when we get back to Catterick. We should get some lunch."

They deposited their flight kit on the row of hooks conveniently provided, adjusted their uniforms, and then walked the short distance to the makeshift officer's mess. The two flying sergeants had to split off and continue a little farther to the enlisted mess.

Through lunch and into their Available waiting period, they talked as pilots do after a mission. Jonathan learned from the other pilots who were flying behind him that the flash and explosion he noted had apparently been an ammunition storage facility of some kind. The explosion knocked several aircraft off their flight path and gun runs to avoid damage to their aircraft from flying debris. Collectively, they had apparently destroyed several dozen aircraft, mostly enemy fighters and the transport aircraft Jonathan hit. They would have to wait for the intelligence debriefing and the gun camera film assessment to know for sure.

—

Thursday, 5.December.1940
Over-Seas League
Park Place, St James's Street
Mayfair, London, England
United Kingdom
12:30 hours

None of the other No. 71 Squadron pilots, who had flown combat missions during the summer months of the Battle of Britain, had been ordered to the Over-Seas League. Only the four surviving American pilots were to attend a luncheon in honor of the American volunteer pilots of the Eagle Squadron. The polished brass plaque on the walled entryway to a small courtyard proved easy enough to find. Rusty Batemen was the most senior and oldest of the four, and assumed the leadership of the small group. Red Burns and Dusty Langford, along with the youngest among them—Brian—walked from the street entryway, through the asphalt courtyard, to the double doors that were obviously the entrance to the distinguished four-story building. The elegantly appointed lobby offered a pleasant, warm ambiance. They went directly to the receptionist's standing desk, behind which an elderly, well-dressed man stood.

"The four of us were ordered to appear here," Bateman said.

The receptionist looked at all four RAF officers in a critical, verging on unapproving, manner, and then said, "Your names, sir?"

"Bateman, Burns, Langford and Drummond."

The old man checked his list, apparently found their names when he nodded his head slightly, and said, "Yes, here we are. You are guests of Lady Astor for today's luncheon."

"If you say so," mumbled Bateman.

"My dear man, I presume from your accent you are Americans."

"Yes, we are . . . all four of us."

"Then, you may not know who Lady Astor is."

"Never heard of her. Sorry. We were just told to be at this address before one for some kind of ceremony."

The old man visibly seemed to chuckle, but no sound was heard. "Please allow me to inform you. Lady Astor is actually Viscountess Astor and is the first woman to sit in the House of Commons – a Member of Parliament and a rather important person, I should say."

Nancy Witcher Shaw née Langhorne of Danville, Virginia, married Waldorf Astor in 1906 – a second marriage for both of them. When her husband ascended to the peerage as 2nd Viscount Astor with the passing of his father in 1919, Waldorf relinquished his seat in Commons representing Plymouth, Sutton Division. Lady Astor stood for her husband's Commons seat. She was elected and became the first woman in history to take her seat in Commons as a Member of Parliament for Plymouth-Sutton, which she continued to hold.

"What do we call her?"

Again, the silent chuckle. "Lady Astor is her proper title in conversation. Now, if you will kindly follow my steward," he said, motioning with his open hand toward a young man in the same attire, who had silently appeared behind them, "he will show you to the banquet room, where you are expected. Good day, sir."

The four RAF pilots followed the young man up a flight of stairs to the first floor. The steward stopped on the far side of an open doorway, turned, and gestured into the room.

"Thank you," Brian whispered, as he passed the steward.

"You are most welcome, sir" he answered softly.

A long, comparatively narrow table that could easily seat 20 people dominated the fairly large, well-appointed, dining room. The room offered ample standing room, mostly on either end of the table. Several service personnel were making the final arrangements. A distinguished, middle-aged, silver-haired woman in a conservative dress accented with a double string of pearls and pearl earrings approached them.

The woman extended her right hand and said in a clear southern drawl, "Welcome. I am Nancy Astor, and my guess is you four young men are our Eagle pilots, our guests of honor."

Rusty took her hand. "Yes, Lady Astor. We are from Seventy-One Squadron. I am Flying Officer Bateman."

"Excellent."

"May I introduce my brethren? This is Pilot Officer Burns, Pilot Officer Langford, and the shy one behind them is Flying Officer Drummond."

Lady Astor shook each of their hands. She turned and gestured to a younger, but still middle-age man behind her, dressed in a dark, conservative suit and blue necktie. "I would like to introduce Under Secretary for Air Balfour of the Air Ministry. He is our speaker for today's luncheon celebration."

What celebration? Brian asked himself. *Celebration of what exactly? I wish someone had told us what this was all about before sending us all the way down here.*

Parliamentary Under Secretary of State for Air Harold Harington Balfour, MC with bar, Member of Parliament for the Isle of Thanet. Balfour was a decorated fighter ace from the Great War and reported directly to the Secretary of State for Air Sir Archibald Sinclair.

Balfour greeted each of the pilots and shook hands with them. When he reached Brian, he smiled broadly and said, "It is an honor to meet you finally." The confused expression on Brian's face was a little too obvious. "Forgive me; in my position, I have inside information, as the traders say." The other three pilots stared at Brian, at Balfour, and then back to Brian.

At that moment, Air Commodore John Spencer entered the room. He greeted Lady Astor and Balfour as if they were close and intimate friends. He was introduced to each of the pilots and shook their hands, but he embraced Brian. "Great to see you, again, Brian." Neither Balfour nor Astor seemed surprised. However, the three other pilots were now dumbstruck.

Balfour picked up on his statement. "John, I was about to tell young Brian, here, why I have been watching his service from afar and I am so pleased to finally meet him."

"Carry on, Minister."

"I served in Forty-Three Squadron during the Great War along with my savior," he said, motioning to John.

"You saved me more than a few times, Harold."

"So," interjected Brian, "you know Malcolm Bainbridge, then."

Balfour smiled broadly. "Yes, my dear fellow, the three of us served together in the skies above France and Belgium." His smiled disappeared in an instant. "My condolences to you, Brian, for the loss of your mentor and friend. John told me some time ago that Malcolm taught you to fly."

"Yes sir. Thank you, sir."

"You could not have had a better, more capable instructor, Brian. You are a most fortunate young man. John also told me that he and Malcolm were co-conspirators in getting you over here to join our little band of merry men a year ago June."

"Yes sir. Air Commodore Spencer has picked up the lance as my mentor."

"The honor is mine, Brian," John added. "You have vastly exceeded our already high expectations."

"Excuse us, Lady Astor and gentlemen," Balfour said, looking to each of them. "This is a reunion we do not often enjoy these days."

"Quite all right, Harold," Nancy responded. "These stories and your connections to each other are absolutely fascinating. We are blessed to share your reunion. I simply had no idea the links went so deep."

"Indeed they do," Balfour answered.

Lady Astor continued, "We are expecting two more for lunch . . . ah, yes, here they are."

Two men entered the room – one dressed in an expensive, blue suit with a white shirt and red silk necktie, and the other in the uniform of an RAF flight lieutenant.

Lady Astor made the introductions. "May I introduce Mister Charles Sweeny and Flight Lieutenant Peterson."

Charles Francis Sweeny was a wealthy and prominent ex-patriot American businessman living in London. He was the nephew of Colonel Charles Sweeny – a rather colorful character from the Great War and the Spanish Civil War, whose current prominence came from his open defiance of the U.S. Neutrality Act and from his acting as one of the principal recruiters of American pilots for the Royal Air Force. Colonel Sweeny was working closely with his nephew in London and others in North America, including the renowned Great War ace Royal Canadian Air Force Air Marshal William Avery 'Billy' Bishop, VC, CB, DSO & Bar, MC, DFC, with 72 confirmed aerial combat victories. Charles was also the older brother of Robert Charles Sweeny, Sr., and uncle to Robert Charles Sweeny, Jr., who served with Brian in No.71 Squadron.

Chesley Gordon 'Pete' Peterson had been trained by and flown with the United States Army Air Corps, left the Army, and was working at the Douglas Aircraft Company in Long Beach, California, when he was recruited by Colonel Sweeny to join the Royal Air Force. Peterson arrived in England, last August, completed his transition flight training at the end of November, and was expected to join No.71 squadron shortly.

Small world, Brian thought. *I wonder how he got to be a flight lieutenant? There must be much more to his story.*

"I do believe the lunch service is ready," Lady Astor announced and gestured toward the table. As they found their designated seat, Nancy added, "The club has done the best they can within the restrictions of war rationing. The meal may not be as stimulating as we might wish; however, I am certain it will be well prepared."

The four Eagle Squadron pilots were interspersed among the other guests. The meal was simple – roasted lamb chop, roasted potato slices and Brussels sprouts. Their table conversation remained on the light side and avoided the war.

When the dishes had been cleared, Lady Astor stood, gestured to the door and positioned herself at the head of the table. A half dozen journalists and several photographers were allowed into the room. She waited for everyone's attention. "Thank you all for attending our modest recognition ceremony. We are specifically to recognize the contributions of the American volunteer pilots, who took considerable risk just to join us. We have with us this afternoon, Mister Charles Sweeny, who with his uncle Colonel Charles Sweeny, has worked tirelessly with His Majesty's Government to create the first of what many of us believe will be many Eagle Squadrons in Fighter Command. We also have Flight Lieutenant Chesley Peterson, who is the senior American volunteer pilot and expected to join Seventy-One Squadron in the next week or two. The four other Fighter Command pilots with us this afternoon flew combat missions during the epic aerial battle last summer and survived. Four other American pilots did not survive the battle. May God rest their immortal souls. Lastly, we are honored to have as our guest speaker Parliamentary Under Secretary of

State for Air, the Gallant and Honorable Harold Balfour. Secretary Balfour, if you please."

Lady Astor took her seat and Balfour replaced her at the head of the table.

"Thank you so much, Lady Astor. On behalf of the Prime Minister and the Air Minister, I answered your invitation." He nodded his head to Lady Astor. "I will add one important bit of information to Lady Astor's offering. We have two-dozen American volunteer pilots with us in flight status today. Ten are members of Seventy-One Squadron – the Eagle Squadron – including these four gallant young men. The remainder are at various stages of their training and preparations to join operational squadrons. Further, with genuine and deep gratitude, we must first thank Mister Sweeny and his colleagues for the Eagle Squadron we celebrate this afternoon and the stream of additional pilots from the United States of America they are working tirelessly to acquire for us. With that stated, I offer a toast of gratitude to our precious American volunteer pilots." They all stood and raised a glass. "May God bless you and protect you through the ordeal ahead. Here is to our intrepid aviators. Our hearts and prayers are with you."

"Hear, hear," everyone said in unison as flash bulbs popped and glasses clinked.

"May we ask questions, sir?" one of the journalists asked.

"This is not a news conference," barked Balfour. "You have your photographs and you may quote what you have heard here this afternoon. Thank you for your reporting." Balfour's statement must have been some unspoken, implied dismissal. The reporters and photographers departed. Balfour waited for them to clear the doorway and disappear from view. He turned to their hostess. "Now, Lady Astor, if you will forgive me, I am afraid I must return to the Air Ministry and the business of this war."

"Yes, of course, Minister," responded Lady Astor.

"Gentlemen, I look forward to seeing each of you again soon and your doing of great things. Good day." Balfour left the room.

Lady Astor thanked each man and said good-bye. She saw Brian last. Astor spoke softly. "It was a genuine pleasure meeting you, Brian. I look forward to hearing more of your exploits in the not too distant future. Thank you for attending our little luncheon ceremony."

"Thank you, Lady Astor. It is always rewarding to have our efforts recognized."

Brian paid his respects to John Spencer and offered his best wishes to Mary and their yet to be born baby. The pilots reversed their route. They walked the short distance to Green Park Station. They would take either the

Victoria Line to Oxford Circus Station or the Jubilee Line to Bond Street Station, whichever arrived first, and then they would transfer to Central Line out to South Rulslip Station. From there, they would walk to the flight line at RAF Northolt. They would start up their three Buffalos and one Hurricane for the return flight to RAF Church Fenton. They were nearly to the Green Park Underground station when Rusty stopped and faced Brian.

"What the hell was that all about back there, Hunter?" Bateman asked, as if he had been duped.

"I think they just wanted to say thank you for what we do."

"No, not the luncheon, you idiot. How the hell do you know those people?"

"Well, John Spencer hel . . ."

"No! How old are you?"

"What does that matter?" Brian responded.

"Well?"

"I'm 19."

"Did you go to college?"

"No."

"Then, how the hell did you get to know an air commodore, a deputy air minister, and Red says you even know the bloody fucking prime minister?"

All three pilots stood and stared at Brian like he was some freak. "Why are you pissed off at me? I've done nothing wrong."

"Answer my damn question!"

"First, I have no obligation to answer your question. Second, we need to get back to Church Fenton before sunset. So, how about we get on the train and I'll answer your question."

Rusty hesitated. His mouth opened like he was going to reject the recommendation. He turned and stepped out smartly. Brian and the others followed. The Jubilee Line train was the first to arrive. The rail car they chose was a quarter full. They found four seats next to each other. Rusty looked at Hunter, raised his eyebrows and canted his head, as if he was saying . . . well?

"My first flying lesson happened when I was nine years old. I traded odd jobs and maintenance work for flight time. An old guy within easy bicycle distance of my home had a good size ranch and owned a half dozen airplanes. That old man was Malcolm Bainbridge, who as you heard was squadron mates with John Spencer and as I learned just this afternoon with Harold Balfour. They flew together with Four Three Squadron in the Royal Flying Corps during the Great War. Malcolm was credited with shooting down eight airplanes and two observation balloons. He was awarded the Distinguished Flying Cross.

Anyway, Malcolm not only taught me how to fly, eventually he taught me fighter combat tactics and thinking. He was a demanding teacher."

"I'll be damned," Langford said.

"Go on," added Bateman.

"I remember being out at Malcolm's place drinking lemonade after flying and Mrs. Bainbridge, his wife, telling us to listen to the radio. The CBS broadcast was talking about the Munich Accord in the fall of '38. Malcolm was convinced the agreement meant war for certain rather than peace as the radio folks were saying. Malcolm also told me about the new monoplane fighters that Great Britain developed and were now flying. So, I . . . ," Brian stopped as the train slowed for the Bond Street Station. "This is our transfer."

The four pilots disembarked and followed the signs to the Central Line. They reached the platform as the next train braked for its stop. They boarded and were again lucky enough to find four seats together.

"You left off at so I," Rusty said with discernible impatience.

"I told Malcolm I wanted to fly the Spitfire. Actually, I think I used the word 'have.' Malcolm resisted for months, and unknown to me, he had contacted his mate from the war days. He was a group captain when I first met him. Malcolm had me flying in air meets in the Midwest. I thought it was just for fun, but it wasn't really. He worked with Walter Beech . . ."

"Damn, man, where does this end?"

"I can stop here," Brian responded promptly.

"No, you twit, how many people do you know? That's a rhetorical question."

"A what?"

"Never mind, continue with your tale."

"We modified a Beech Mystery S monoplane to remove the wing stay wires, to clean up the fuselage and to up-engine the aircraft. I flew that aircraft at four or five air meets, the last one in St. Louis, in May of '39. I did not learn until it was all over that Group Captain Spencer had observed the whole meet. John . . . ,"

"John, is it now?" Bateman interjected. "You are getting rather familiar with a senior officer, don't ya think."

"He has been like a benevolent older brother to me. We flew a mock combat flight with Group Captain Spencer and a pilot by the name of Sales, Bobby Joe Sales, who owned a couple of surplus Grumman FF-1 aircraft. I guess he was satisfied with what I showed him. Group Captain Spencer made all the arrangements for me. All I had to do was get to Windsor, Ontario, Canada, which I did the following May. I made it through OTU and was ordered to a

Gladiator squadron. Again, Group Captain Spencer to the rescue. I joined Six Zero Nine Squadron in October of last year."

"Well, then, that explains how you got a commission with no college degree."

"Perhaps. I have no idea. It just was from my perspective."

Bateman looked at Burns, and then back to Brian. "Red here says you know Churchill."

"John Spencer is Churchill's nephew."

"Damn, so it's true?"

"Well, now, that may be a bit of a stretch. I've met him a few times."

"Damn, man! That's a few more times than all the rest of us combined. I doubt the Skipper has met the Prime Minister and his bloody family name is Churchill."

Dusty Langford decided to join the inquisition. "Is it true you have 19 kills?"

"So they say."

"And, you already have a DFC and a Military Cross." Brian glanced down at the ribbons below his wings and above the left breast pocket of his uniform tunic. "Oh yeah, sorry. Then, what is the other one?"

"A CBE."

"Which is?"

"Commander of the Most Excellent Order of the British Empire."

"And, he got it from the King himself," Frank Burns chimed in.

Brian nodded his head to acknowledge Reds statement.

"For a comparatively young guy, who never went to college, you have gotten around, haven't you?" Bateman added.

"I've been lucky is all."

They sat in silence for the last 20 minutes of their journey nearly to the end of the Central Line. From the Underground station, which was above ground out this far, they walked back to the flight line at RAF Northolt and their waiting aircraft. After checking their fuel level and donning their flight kit, they took off to the north and their return to RAF Church Fenton. They let Dusty Langford lead the flight of four. The flight was uneventful, and they landed just before sunset.

—

Thursday, 5.December.1940
RAF Manston
Ramsgate, Kent, England
United Kingdom
15:15 hours

No.609 Squadron had remained on the ground fully refueled and rearmed just in case the Germans tried a retaliatory attack. The ground crews had managed to make a few repairs to the damaged aircraft while they waited. Apparently, the Germans had decided not to play, or they had other more pressing tasks in front of them.

Sector Control had just released them for their return flight to RAF Catterick. Baggy briefed the squadron for the flight back north. In a rare instance these days, all 12 fighters took off together. Baggy wanted to do a squadron, high speed, low pass to thank the aerodrome personnel who had tended to them during their stay, but they needed the fuel reserve for the long flight north.

They landed by section just after sunset, during twilight, and parked their fighters in their area.

The squadron intelligence folks were waiting for them on their arrival. The debriefing took another couple of hours. None of the pilots were happy about the debriefing keeping them from their anticipated celebratory beers. Squadron Leader Long-Roberts insisted they get the chore done, so they could have a fresh start tomorrow. They expected to have a day on alert. They did not see many attacks this far north, but they did occur from time to time.

Several aircraft still had minor shrapnel damage that had not been fixed at Manston and would be repaired overnight. It had been a good day for No.609 Squadron. Tonight, they would celebrate in the traditional manner.

—

Chapter 6

America was named after a man
who discovered no part of the New World.
History is like that, very chancy.
- Samuel Eliot Morison

Friday, 6.December.1940
RAF Church Fenton
Tadcaster, North Yorkshire, England
United Kingdom
16:15 hours

Much to Brian's surprise, Charles Sweeny was standing outside the squadron dispersal hut. The well-dressed businessman stood out sharply with his dark gray suit in the forest of RAF blue uniforms and tan coveralls the ground crews used to protect their uniforms and offer some additional warmth during the winter months. He seemed to be pleased, having observed the squadron's return from another training mission. Baggy was the first to reach Sweeny as Brian was extricating himself from the Buffalo. The two men shook hands and were smiling.

We just saw him yesterday. What on earth is he doing up here the next day?

Brian was one of the last pilots to join the huddle around Sweeny. Several pilots appeared to already know him. Sweeny and Sweet embraced as family would.

"Listen up, lads," Baggy shouted. "For those of you who do not know him, this is Mister Charles Sweeny, Sweet's uncle and the man along with his father's brother, is singularly credited with the formation of this squadron." Several cheers or words of encouragement punctuated Churchill's statement. "Let's stow our flight kit and gather inside. Mister Sweeny would like to address the squadron."

"May I have a private word, first, Squadron Leader Churchill?" asked the elder Sweeny.

"Certainly." Sweeny followed Baggy into his office. The door closed behind them.

"We met your uncle yesterday in London," Dusty pronounced to Sweet.

"So I hear."

"We are just learning all kinds of things, aren't we," Rusty said with as much sarcasm as he could muster.

"About half of us have met your great uncle and were recruited by him back home," Rocket Downing added.

"Good man," said Roley Rigby.

"My great uncle is a bit of a rogue – the family black sheep. He flew in the Great War, bagged a few Germans, and got shot down several times. He also flew for Franco during the Spanish Civil War – a bit of a mercenary, I'm afraid. He knows a bunch of the Germans who flew for the Condor Legion – Mölders, Werner Mölders among them."

"Yeah, but he is still a good man," Horse Harrow interjected. "The colonel arranged for me to get some extra training with a combat pilot, which in turn helped me get into Fighter Command. He took care of everything. Good man," Horse repeated.

Baggy opened his office enough to stick his head out. "Whitey . . . a word, if you please."

Oh my, he's going to inform Whitey he will be transferred soon and replaced by 'Pete' Peterson. Shoot, I hardly got to know him.

They were not in there long. All three emerged.

"Let's gather up, gentlemen," commanded Baggy. When he had everyone's attention, he continued, "Mister Sweeny would like a few words with us, so please pay attention."

"Thank you, Squadron Leader Churchill. I saw a few of you yesterday, renewed our connection, and met Brian Drummond for the first time. Of course, my family would never forgive me if I did not keep an eye on my nephew."

"That's not an easy task," someone mumbled. Everyone laughed.

"Quite so. Anyway, now seemed like a good time to come check on my squadron. Once France fell and some of our pilots made their way here, I began working with the Air Ministry to form an American volunteer squadron, much like the squadrons created for the ex-patriot Polish and Czech pilots. For several months, the ministry did not believe we could attract enough pilots to form, set aside maintain, an all-American squadron. Thanks to you guys," he said, waving his arms as if to embrace the lot of them, "we proved them wrong. We have at least enough pilots at various stages of recruitment, transport and training to create one, maybe two, more squadrons, hopefully early next year. We will continue to recruit pilots until the U.S. enters the war, as most assuredly they will. It is only a matter of time. I have high expectations for you, gentlemen. God bless America, and God save the King."

They applauded. The telephone rang. There was immediate deathly silence.

Corporal Harris lifted the handset to his ear, listened for a few seconds, and simply said, "Yes sir." Harris nodded to Baggy.

"Does anyone have any questions for Mister Sweeny?" asked Churchill.

Langford raised his hand. Baggy nodded for him to proceed. "Are we going to get our back pay from our time with *le Armée de l'Air?*"

That sounded like pretty good French to me, not that I would know.

"We are working on that, Paul . . . for all of you who served in France. As you know, the French were supposed to pay us, and then in turn, we would pay you. To date, we have not received payment. We have made contact with the government in Vichy. The best I can say, we are in negotiations. I travel to Vichy next week . . . by a rather circuitous route, I'm afraid . . . for that very purpose. We are working as hard as we can to get all of you paid. You have every right and deserve to be paid for services rendered to the French government."

Dusty nodded his head and did not answer.

"Anyone else?" asked Sweeny. No one responded.

"Very well, then. We are released for the day. Mister Sweeny will join us at Mess and will knock back a few beers with us after dinner."

They shuffled out and walked toward the Officer's Mess. They nearly cleared the exterior corner of the Dispersal Hut when Brian heard from behind him. "Brian, may I have a word with you?"

Brian turned to see that Charles Sweeny had stopped just outside the door. Brian nodded his head and walked toward the elder Sweeny.

Corporal Harris closed and locked the door. "Good evening, gentlemen."

"Good evening to you, Corporal Harris," Brian responded. "See you in the morning."

"Yes sir."

"It was a pleasure meeting you yesterday, Brian. Lady Astor was so gracious to arrange that little luncheon, and I am grateful you could take time to join us. The press coverage for the squadron has been exceptional, and we all need to nurture that relationship."

"Thank you, sir."

"I had a nice chat with Air Commodore Spencer – interesting man, I must say."

"He has been extraordinarily generous with me."

"The two of you seem pretty close."

You have no idea how close. "Yes sir. I would say we are."

"Excellent. Would you mind if I call on you from time to time, if I need help with some bureaucratic roadblock?"

"I have no idea how I might be able to help you. You seem to me, far better connected than I am."

"You undersell yourself, Brian. You hold a unique place here. The King, personally, made you a Commander of the British Empire. That is one step short of knighthood . . . not that it is much use to us as Americans. Many more people, powerful people in this country and in the United States, know your name and some of your accomplishments. I am not asking you for anything, and I shall endeavor to avoid burdening you with my administrative stuff. I guess my point here is, I would like to build our friendship and trust in one another, and I will certainly promise you not to abuse our friendship."

"I have no objection

"Excellent, Brian. Thank you and thank you so very much for your efforts in the defense of freedom. We will rid this planet of Hitler's scourge. It is only a question of time."

"Yes sir."

"Then, let us be off. We do not want to be late for supper."

The two men walked to the Mess. They both avoided words of war and focused on the more personal aspects of sharing between friends. *He seems like a good guy, but I need to be careful.*

—

Friday, 6.December.1940
Marine Air Terminal
New York Municipal Airport
East Elmhurst, Queens, New York City, New York
United States of America
13:20 hours

Bill Donovan and his wife Ruth Rumsey Donovan had been married since 1914. They had endured long separations in their younger years and his Army service – the Mexican border incursion of 1916, and his deployment for combat in France during the Great War from 1917 to 1918. They sat quietly, both of them ruminating with the thoughts and images of the long journey ahead through war torn Europe. The last trip in July had been a couple of weeks. This one was planned for three months and would likely be extended, depending upon what Bill found. Ruth would remain in Manhattan, tending the luxurious town home.

Bill completed his check in and handed over his baggage 20 minutes earlier. It was a little less than an hour to boarding time when he spotted Mary and Bill Stephenson entering the reception hall, heading toward the check-in counter. The two Bill's made eye contact and nodded their recognition.

"Bill and Mary just arrived," Donovan said softly, leaning toward Ruth.

"I am only going to ask one last time, Bill, do you really think this is wise. London is being bombed every night."

"I would prefer not, my dear, but you know Franklin, he can be quite persistent and persuasive."

"Then he should go."

"Ruth, that is not fair. You know perfectly well he has far greater issues to deal with in these troubled times."

"Yes, well, perhaps so, but it is my husband who is being shipped off to war without a rifle."

What Bill Donovan could not tell his wife, or any other human being beyond Franklin Roosevelt and Frank Knox for that matter, was that his current mission had grown from the July visit to Great Britain under the aegis of Secretary of the Navy Frank Knox, and focused primarily upon the question of strategic intelligence for the President of the United States. The two service branches had very capable intelligence divisions, but they remained staunchly parochial and incapable of taking in the far broader perspective needed by the President. His cover for this journey was a tour of British military facilities. He would quietly connect with various intelligence operations at each location to gain a broader view of the war and more importantly develop a structure for filling in the intelligence gap the President clearly recognized.

The Stephensons completed their check-in and approached the Donovans. Bill stood and then Ruth. They greeted each other as old friends, which they were rapidly becoming. 'Little Bill' would accompany 'Big Bill,' or 'Wild Bill' as he was occasionally referenced, as far as London. Stephenson would remain with Donovan until after Christmas. From that point, Lieutenant Colonel Vivian Dykes from the War Cabinet Secretariat would replace Stephenson as Donovan's chaperon and vanguard on the remainder of his tour. Little Bill would return to the United States, while Big Bill would depart for Gibraltar – the first planned stop outside England.

A series of three tones signaled an impending message. "Pan American Airways is pleased to announce the boarding of the Yankee Clipper to Lisbon, Portugal, with scheduled stops in Bermuda, and Horta, Azores. All passengers please make your way to Gate Three at this time."

The Donovans and Stephensons stood. The men faced their partners. They embraced and shared their good-byes. Both men carried leather, hand cases. The two Bill's joined 25 other passengers on the overnight trans-Atlantic flight. Bill Donovan allowed Stephenson to precede him. As he approached the doorway, Bill looked back to see Ruth waving to him. He returned the wave and blew her a kiss before stepping through the doorway, another room with a pathway cordoned off by rope lines between stanchions, and then a covered dock.

The massive, Boeing Model 314 flying boat sat solidly moored to the boarding platform. With tickets checked against the manifest, a steward led the two Bill's through the aft boarding hatch, two passenger compartments, the galley and to the forward first class compartment. The steward gestured to the port side, forward-facing seat for Stephenson and the opposite rear-facing seat for Donovan.

The steward informed them, "You gentlemen will be our only first class passengers on this flight, so you are welcome to occupy any seat you wish. Would either of you gentlemen care for champagne and a bowl of warm, mixed nuts before we takeoff?"

"Yes, please," answered Donovan. Stephenson nodded his head.

Both men looked out the portal adjacent to their seat, as if they might see their wives waving to them. After the steward delivered a champagne flute and a small bowl of nuts, Stephenson said, "I received a message from Colonel Dykes this morning. He confirmed your itinerary. All arrangements have been completed. He has a letter of authority from the Prime Minister, so you should have no difficulty adjusting your schedule, as you deem appropriate, based on the circumstances you encounter or discover."

"Excellent."

"Winston asked that we join him and his family at Ditchley for the weekend prior to Christmas."

"Weekends with Winston are always entertaining and informative."

"Indeed. He has always been an intriguing character, from the very first day I met him prior to the Great War."

"I've not been to Ditchley Park."

"I have only been there once. It is a beautiful estate, owned by Nancy and Ronald Tree. 'Ron' is a Conservative MP and a friend of Winston's. Nancy is an American, by the way – a Virginian, as I recall. They offered the Prime Minister the use of Ditchley House and the large land holdings, when The Blitz began and worries mounted that Chequers, like Chartwell, was too easily discernible from the air. In essence, Ditchley is less of a target in the light of a full moon."

"Sounds quite reasonable and wise to me."

They both felt the flying boat move. They looked out the portal and they were drifting slowly away from the pier. The first Curtis-Wright R-2600 Cyclone 14 engine started and rumbled to a smooth fast idle. The remaining three engines started in succession. They taxied toward the northwest channel. The steward came to collect the glasses and bowls, and asked them to fasten their seat belts in preparation for takeoff. Several minutes later, the engines were advanced to full power and they surged forward. The aircraft passed Rikers Island on the starboard side. The ripples of the surface chop disappeared, and they were airborne and on the way.

"Another by the way, my friend, Nancy Tree's maternal aunt is none other than Lady Nancy Astor – the first female MP," said Stephenson. "You never know when such relationships might prove useful."

"Thank you for that little tidbit, Bill."

They banked left and headed south-southwest down the Hudson River. They watched the distinctive skyline of Manhattan pass quickly behind them. Soon, only the ocean could be seen, and they banked left, again, heading now southeast toward Bermuda, their first way station.

Both men opened their cases and began working through their paperwork. They would have nearly two days in transit by the current plan, and plenty of time to chat. Best to get the paperwork done first. For Bill Donovan, he had several State Department reports to read and absorb before they arrived in London.

—

Saturday, 7.December.1940
USS Tuscaloosa *(CA-37)*
At sea, Caribbean Sea

The knock at the door of the flag stateroom broke Roosevelt's concentration on the latest shipping report from the Navy Department. "Enter," the President responded robustly.

Captain Johnson with a single beige folder with a red striped border, stood in front of the desk, and handed the classified message folder to the President. "Sir, I thought I would deliver this message personally. The first message is short but an urgent communication." Roosevelt read the first sheet.

TOP SECRET - PRESIDENTIAL

```
WH
RAXHT MQP NR 1426
U 071905Z DEC 40
FM WHITE HOUSE
TO POTUS ABD TUSCALOOSA
SECNAV
SUBJ WILD BILL
BT
```

```
T O P      S E C R E T      P R E S I D E N T I A L
WILD BILL AND INTREPID AWAY ON SCHEDULE BREAK
POTENTIAL WEATHER IN EASTERN ATLANTIC MIGHT
AFFECT FLIGHT PLAN BREAK WILD BILL WILL
SEND SAFE ARRIVAL CALL BREAK ALL PLANNED
ARRANGEMENTS CONFIRMED
BT
NNNN
```

TOP SECRET - PRESIDENTIAL

"The second is much longer. This is without a doubt the largest, longest message any of us, including me, have ever handled. This message saturated our encryption equipment for more than an hour. I must ask whether you might anticipate any further messages of this magnitude? If so, we need to make arrangements for additional equipment and operators be delivered to us promptly."

President Roosevelt quickly leafed through the 20-page message and saw who the message was from – Prime Minister Winston Churchill – another personal message and indeed a big one. "First, to answer your question, I need some time to read and study this message. I suspect I know the content; however, I am not aware of any expectation of a message such as this. I just don't know. Second, if you would be so kind, please find Harry Hopkins and ask him to see me as soon as he is able. Third, I offer my apologies to your communications room personnel, and to you and your crew. I know my presence aboard your warship is a burden. I can only say we shall do our best to minimize that burden. If additional cipher gear eases that burden, we shall do our best to get you that equipment as soon as possible. I shall also talk to our communications officer to see what we can do to lessen our burden on your ship. Lastly, what is our next port call?"

"Port Castries, St. Lucia, tomorrow morning, sir."

"Very well, Captain. Thank you for expressing your concern. I do appreciate your candor. Now, if you will, get me Harry Hopkins and we will get you an answer and perhaps some help as soon as possible."

"Yes sir . . . right away," Captain Johnson replied and departed.

Roosevelt turned his attention to the big message.

TOP SECRET - PRESIDENTIAL

NO3A

AA RAA NR 507

P 080152Z DEC 40

FM WHITE HOUSE

TO POTUS ABD TUSCALOOSA

SUBJ RETRANSMISSION OF TELEGRAM FROM PM UK

BT

T O P   S E C R E T   P R E S I D E N T I A L

BEGIN

MOST SECRET AND PRIVATE

LONDON

DECEMBER 8TH 1940

MY DEAR MR PRESIDENT

BEGIN BODY

AS WE REACH THE END OF THIS YEAR I FEEL THAT YOU
WILL EXPECT ME TO LAY BEFORE YOU THE PROSPECTS
FOR 1941 BREAK I DO SO STRONGLY AND CONFIDENTLY
BECAUSE IT SEEMS TO ME THAT THE VAST MAJORITY OF
AMERICAN CITIZENS HAVE RECORDED THEIR CONVICTION
THAT THE SAFETY OF THE UNITED STATES AS WELL AS
THE FUTURE OF OUR TWO DEMOCRACIES AND THE KIND
OF CIVILISATION FOR WHICH THEY STAND ARE BOUND
UP WITH THE SURVIVAL AND INDEPENDENCE OF THE
BRITISH COMMONWEALTH OF NATIONS BREAK ONLY THUS
CAN THOSE BASTIONS OF SEA-POWER UPON WHICH THE
CONTROL OF THE ATLANTIC AND THE INDIAN OCEANS
DEPENDS BE PRESERVED IN FAITHFUL AND FRIENDLY
HANDS BREAK THE CONTROL OF THE PACIFIC BY THE
UNITED STATES NAVY AND OF THE ATLANTIC BY THE
BRITISH NAVY IS INDISPENSABLE TO THE SECURITY OF
THE TRADE ROUTES OF BOTH OUR COUNTRIES AND THE
SUREST MEANS TO PREVENTING THE WAR FROM REACHING
THE SHORES OF THE UNITED STATES END
BEGIN PARA 2 THERE IS ANOTHER ASPECT BREAK IT
TAKES BETWEEN THREE AND FOUR YEARS TO CONVERT
THE INDUSTRIES OF A MODERN STATE TO WAR PURPOSES
BREAK SATURATION POINT IS REACHED WHEN THE
MAXIMUM INDUSTRIAL EFFORT THAT CAN BE SPARED

FROM CIVILIAN NEEDS HAS BEEN APPLIED TO WAR
PRODUCTION BREAK GERMANY CERTAINLY REACHED THIS
POINT BY THE END OF 1939 BREAK WE IN THE BRITISH
EMPIRE ARE NOW ONLY ABOUT HALF-WAY THROUGH THE
SECOND YEAR BREAK THE UNITED STATES I SHOULD
SUPPOSE WAS BY NO MEANS SO FAR ADVANCED AS
WE BREAK MOREOVER I UNDERSTAND THAT IMMENSE
PROGRAMMES OF NAVAL MILITARY AND AIR DEFENCE ARE
NOW ON FOOT IN THE UNITED STATES TO COMPLETE
WHICH CERTAINLY TWO YEARS ARE NEEDED BREAK IT
IS OUR BRITISH DUTY IN THE COMMON INTEREST AS
ALSO FOR OUR OWN SURVIVAL TO HOLD THE FRONT AND
GRAPPLE WITH NAZI POWER UNTIL THE PREPARATIONS
OF THE UNITED STATES ARE COMPLETE END
BEGIN PARA 3 THE FORM WHICH THIS WAR HAS TAKEN
AND SEEMS LIKELY TO HOLD DOES NOT ENABLE US
TO MATCH THE IMMENSE ARMIES OF GERMANY IN ANY
THEATRE WHERE THEIR MAIN POWER CAN BE BROUGHT
TO BEAR BREAK WE CAN HOWEVER BY THE USE OF SEA
POWER AND AIR POWER MEET THE GERMAN ARMIES IN
THE REGIONS WHERE ONLY COMPARATIVELY SMALL
FORCES CAN BE BROUGHT INTO ACTION BREAK WE MUST
DO OUR BEST TO PREVENT GERMAN DOMINATION OF
EUROPE SPREADING INTO AFRICA AND INTO SOUTHERN
ASIA END
BEGIN PARA 4 THE FIRST HALF OF 1940 WAS A PERIOD
OF DISASTER FOR THE ALLIES AND FOR THE EMPIRE
BREAK THE LAST FIVE MONTHS HAVE WITNESSED A
STRONG AND PERHAPS UNEXPECTED RECOVERY BY GREAT
BRITAIN FIGHTING ALONE BUT WITH INVALUABLE AID
IN MUNITIONS AND IN DESTROYERS PLACED AT OUR
DISPOSAL BY THE GREAT REPUBLIC END
BEGIN PARA 5 THE DANGER OF GREAT BRITAIN BEING
DESTROYED BY A SWIFT OVERWHELMING BLOW HAS FOR
THE TIME BEING VERY GREATLY RECEDED BREAK IN ITS
PLACE THERE IS A LONG GRADUALLY MATURING DANGER
LESS SUDDEN AND LESS SPECTACULAR BUT EQUALLY
DEADLY BREAK THIS MORTAL DANGER IS THE STEADY
AND INCREASING DIMINUTION OF SEA TONNAGE BREAK

WE CAN ENDURE THE SHATTERING OF OUR DWELLINGS
AND THE SLAUGHTER OF OUR CIVILIAN POPULATION
BY INDISCRIMINATE AIR ATTACKS AND WE HOPE TO
PARRY THESE INCREASINGLY AS OUR SCIENCE DEVELOPS
AND TO REPAY THEM UPON MILITARY OBJECTIVES IN
GERMANY AS OUR AIR FORCE MORE NEARLY APPROACHES
THE STRENGTH OF THE ENEMY BREAK IT IS THEREFORE
IN SHIPPING AND IN THE POWER TO TRANSPORT ACROSS
THE OCEANS PARTICULARLY THE ATLANTIC OCEAN THAT
IN 1941 THE CRUNCH OF THE WHOLE WAR WILL BE
FOUND BREAK IF ON THE OTHER HAND WE ARE ABLE TO
MOVE THE NECESSARY TONNAGE TO AND FRO ACROSS THE
SALT WATER INDEFINITELY IT MAY WELL BE THAT THE
APPLICATION OF SUPERIOR AIR POWER TO THE GERMAN
HOMELAND AND THE RISING ANGER OF THE GERMAN AND
OTHER NAZI GRIPPED POPULATIONS WILL BRING THE
AGONY OF CIVILIZATION TO A MERCIFUL AND GLORIOUS
CONCLUSION END
BEGIN PARA 6 OUR SHIPPING LOSSES HAVE BEEN
ON A SCALE ALMOST COMPARABLE TO THAT OF THE
WORST YEARS OF THE LAST WAR BREAK IN THE 5
WEEKS ENDING NOVEMBER 3RD THE LOSSES REACHED A
TOTAL OF 420300 TONS BREAK OUR ESTIMATION OF
THE ANNUAL TONNAGE WHICH OUGHT TO BE IMPORTED
IN ORDER TO MAINTAIN OUR WAR EFFORT AT FULL
STRENGTH IS 43000000 TONS BREAK THE TONNAGE
ENTERING IN SEPTEMBER WAS ONLY AT THE RATE
OF 37000000 TONS AND IN OCTOBER AT 38000000
TONS BREAK WERE THE DIMINUTION TO CONTINUE
AT THIS RATE IT WOULD BE FATAL UNLESS INDEED
IMMENSELY GREATER REPLENISHMENT THAN ANYTHING
AT PRESENT IN SIGHT COULD BE ACHIEVED IN TIME
BREAK ALTHOUGH WE ARE DOING ALL WE CAN TO MEET
THIS SITUATION BY NEW METHODS THE DIFFICULTY OF
LIMITING THE LOSSES IS OBVIOUSLY MUCH GREATER
THAN IN THE LAST WAR END
BEGIN PARA 7 THE NEXT SIX OR SEVEN MONTHS BRING
THE RELATIVE BATTLESHIP STRENGTH IN HOME WATERS
TO A SMALLER MARGIN THAN IS SATISFACTORY BREAK

```
THE BISMARCK AND THE TIRPITZ WILL CERTAINLY BE
IN SERVICE IN JANUARY BREAK WE HAVE ALREADY THE
KING GEORGE V AND HOPE TO HAVE THE PRINCE OF
WALES AT THE SAME TIME BREAK THESE MODERN SHIPS
ARE OF COURSE FAR BETTER ARMOURED ESPECIALLY
AGAINST AIR ATTACK THAN VESSELS LIKE THE RODNEY
AND NELSON DESIGNED TWENTY YEARS AGO END
BEGIN PARA 8 WE HOPE THAT THE TWO ITALIAN
LITTORIOS WILL BE OUT OF ACTION FOR A WHILE AND
ANYWAY THEY ARE NOT SO DANGEROUS AS IF THEY
WERE MANNED BY THE GERMANS BREAK PERHAPS THEY
MIGHT BE BREAK WE ARE INDEBTED TO YOU FOR YOUR
HELP ABOUT THE RICHELIEU AND THE JEAN BART AND
I DARESAY THAT WILL BE ALL RIGHT BREAK BUT MR
PRESIDENT AS NO ONE WILL SEE MORE CLEARLY THAN
YOU WE HAVE DURING THESE MONTHS TO CONSIDER FOR
THE FIRST TIME IN THIS WAR A FLEET ACTION IN
WHICH THE ENEMY WILL HAVE TWO SHIPS AT LEAST AS
GOOD AS OUR TWO BEST AND ONLY TWO MODERN ONES
BREAK THUS EVEN IN THE BATTLESHIP CLASS WE ARE
AT FULL EXTENSION END
BEGIN PARA 9 THERE IS A SECOND FIELD OF DANGER
THE VICHY GOVERNMENT MAY EITHER BY JOINING
HITLERS NEW ORDER IN EUROPE OR THROUGH SOME
MANOEUVRE SUCH AS FORCING US TO ATTACK AN
EXPEDITION DESPATCHED BY SEA AGAINST FREE FRENCH
COLONIES FIND AN EXCUSE FOR RANGING WITH THE
AXIS POWERS THE VERY CONSIDERABLE UNDAMAGED
NAVAL FORCES STILL UNDER ITS CONTROL BREAK
IF THE FRENCH NAVY WERE TO JOIN THE AXIS THE
CONTROL OF WEST AFRICA WOULD PASS IMMEDIATELY
INTO THEIR HANDS WITH THE GRAVEST CONSEQUENCES
TO OUR COMMUNICATIONS BETWEEN THE NORTHERN AND
SOUTHERN ATLANTIC AND ALSO AFFECT DAKAR AND OF
COURSE THEREAFTER SOUTH AMERICA END
```

Harry Hopkins had entered the flag stateroom, but Roosevelt read through to the end of the paragraph before he looked up to acknowledge his closest advisor.

Roosevelt held up the lengthy message. "This is from Churchill . . . very long . . . and I haven't finished my first read through as yet. This is a very important statement by Winston. I might even say it is extraordinary. I want your opinion before I read it a few more times. So, if you wouldn't mind, grab a cup of coffee. It's fresh and very good. There are a few sandwiches," he said, pointing to a sideboard-serving table, "over there. I would like your first blush impression. Also, so I do not forget this and please do not let me forget, Captain Johnson voiced serious concern about the burden of this message on the ship's communications center. He asked if we expected to send or receive any messages of this length while we are aboard. I suspect not, but please check with our specialist to see if there is anything we can do to assist the ship's capability."

"I can do that now, Franklin, while you finish your reading."

"No, please stay. I would like to get through this first reading for both of us as soon as possible. I told Captain Johnson we would have an answer within an hour or so."

"No problem."

"Also, please send an acknowledgment to the White House Communications Center and to Winston that we have received his message and we are considering our response. Also, let us not, I say not, chastise anyone for forwarding Winston's lengthy message. They made the correct decision to send it to me by the most expeditious means. This is a very important message, perhaps a critical or pivotal message for our relationship with the British and for the war raging around us."

"As you wish."

"From what I've read so far, I suspect we will not respond until we return to Washington."

"I'll take care of those items as soon as we are done here." Hopkins turned to the sideboard and the coffee urn.

"Would you mind freshening my coffee as well?"

Roosevelt nodded his head and returned to his reading. Hopkins took the President's mug, refilled it, and returned the mug to his desk.

```
BEGIN PARA 10 A THIRD SPHERE OF DANGER IS IN
THE FAR EAST BREAK HERE IT SEEMS CLEAR THAT
THE JAPANESE ARE THRUSTING SOUTHWARD THROUGH
INDO CHINA TO SAIGON AND OTHER NAVAL AND AIR
BASES THUS BRINGING THEM WITHIN A COMPARATIVELY
SHORT DISTANCE OF SINGAPORE AND THE DUTCH EAST
```

INDIES BREAK IT IS REPORTED THAT THE JAPANESE
ARE PREPARING FIVE GOOD DIVISIONS FOR POSSIBLE
USE AS AN OVERSEAS EXPEDITIONARY FORCE BREAK WE
HAVE TODAY NO FORCES IN THE FAR EAST CAPABLE OF
DEALING WITH THIS SITUATION SHOULD IT DEVELOP
END

BEGIN PARA 11 IN THE FACE OF THESE DANGERS
WE MUST TRY TO USE THE YEAR 1941 TO BUILD UP
SUCH A SUPPLY OF WEAPONS PARTICULARLY AIRCRAFT
BOTH BY INCREASED OUTPUT AT HOME IN SPITE OF
BOMBARDMENT AND THROUGH OCEANBORNE SUPPLIES AS
WILL LAY THE FOUNDATION OF VICTORY BREAK IN
VIEW OF THE DIFFICULTY AND MAGNITUDE OF THIS
TASK AS OUTLINED BY ALL THE FACTS I HAVE SET
FORTH TO WHICH MANY OTHERS COULD BE ADDED I
FEEL ENTITLED NAY BOUND TO LAY BEFORE YOU THE
VARIOUS WAYS IN WHICH THE UNITED STATES COULD
GIVE SUPREME AND DECISIVE HELP TO WHAT IS IN
CERTAIN ASPECTS THE COMMON CAUSE END

BEGIN PARA 12 THE PRIME NEED IS TO CHECK OR
LIMIT THE LOSS OF TONNAGE ON THE ATLANTIC
APPROACHES TO OUR ISLANDS BREAK THIS MAY BE
ACHIEVED BOTH BY INCREASING THE NAVAL FORCES
WHICH COPE WITH ATTACKS AND BY ADDING TO THE
NUMBER OF MERCHANT SHIPS ON WHICH WE DEPEND
BREAK FOR THE FIRST PURPOSE THERE WOULD SEEM TO
BE THE FOLLOWING ALTERNATIVES END

BEGIN SUBPARA A THE REASSERTION BY THE UNITED
STATES OF THE DOCTRINE OF THE FREEDOM OF THE
SEAS FROM ILLEGAL AND BARBAROUS WARFARE IN
ACCORDANCE WITH THE DECISIONS REACHED AFTER
THE LATE GREAT WAR AND AS FREELY ACCEPTED AND
DEFINED BY GERMANY IN 1935 BREAK FROM THIS THE
UNITED STATES SHIPS SHOULD BE FREE TO TRADE
WITH COUNTRIES AGAINST WHICH THERE IS NOT AN
EFFECTIVE LEGAL BLOCKADE END

BEGIN SUBPARA B IT WOULD I SUGGEST FOLLOW THAT
PROTECTION SHOULD BE GIVEN TO THIS LAWFUL
TRADING BY UNITED STATES FORCES I E ESCORTING

BATTLESHIPS CRUISERS DESTROYERS AND AIR
FLOTILLAS BREAK PROTECTION WOULD BE IMMEDIATELY
MORE EFFECTIVE IF YOU WERE ABLE TO OBTAIN BASES
IN EIRE FOR THE DURATION OF THE WAR BREAK I
THINK IT IS IMPROBABLE THAT SUCH PROTECTION
WOULD PROVOKE A DECLARATION OF WAR BY GERMANY
UPON THE UNITED STATES THOUGH PROBABLY SEA
INCIDENTS OF A DANGEROUS CHARACTER WOULD FROM
TIME TO TIME OCCUR BREAK HITLER HAS SHOWN
HIMSELF INCLINED TO AVOID THE KAISERS MISTAKE
END
BEGIN SUBPARA C FAILING THE ABOVE THE GIFT LOAN
OR SUPPLY OF A LARGE NUMBER OF AMERICAN VESSELS
OF WAR ABOVE ALL DESTROYERS ALREADY IN THE
ATLANTIC IS INDISPENSABLE TO THE MAINTENANCE
OF THE ATLANTIC ROUTE BREAK FURTHER COULD NOT
UNITED STATES NAVAL FORCES EXTEND THEIR SEA
CONTROL OVER THE AMERICAN SIDE OF THE ATLANTIC
SO AS TO PREVENT MOLESTATION BY ENEMY VESSELS
OF THE APPROACHES TO THE NEW LINE OF NAVAL
AND AIR BASES WHICH THE UNITED STATES IS
ESTABLISHING IN BRITISH ISLANDS IN THE WESTERN
HEMISPHERE BREAK THE STRENGTH OF THE UNITED
STATES NAVAL FORCES IS SUCH THAT THE ASSISTANCE
IN THE ATLANTIC THAT THEY COULD AFFORD US AS
DESCRIBED ABOVE WOULD NOT JEOPARDISE CONTROL
OVER THE PACIFIC END
BEGIN SUBPARA D WE SHOULD ALSO THEN NEED THE
GOOD OFFICES OF THE UNITED STATES CONTINUALLY
EXERTED TO PROCURE FOR GREAT BRITAIN THE
NECESSARY FACILITIES UPON THE SOUTHERN AND
WESTERN SHORES OF EIRE FOR OUR FLOTILLAS AND
STILL MORE IMPORTANT FOR OUR AIRCRAFT WORKING
WESTWARD INTO THE ATLANTIC BREAK IF IT WERE
PROCLAIMED AN AMERICAN INTEREST THAT THE
ATLANTIC ROUTE KEPT OPEN FOR THE IMPORTANT
ARMAMENTS NOW BEING PREPARED FOR GREAT BRITAIN
IN NORTH AMERICA THE IRISH IN THE UNITED STATES
MIGHT BE WILLING TO POINT OUT TO THE GOVERNMENT

OF EIRE THE DANGERS WHICH ITS PRESENT POLICY IS
CREATING FOR THE UNITED STATES ITSELF END
BEGIN CONT PARA 12 HIS MAJESTY'S GOVERNMENT
WOULD OF COURSE TAKE THE MOST EFFECTIVE STEPS
BEFOREHAND TO PROTECT IRELAND IF IRISH ACTION
EXPOSED IT TO A GERMAN ATTACK BREAK BUT I DO
NOT DOUBT THAT IF THE GOVERNMENT OF EIRE WOULD
SHOW ITS SOLIDARITY WITH THE DEMOCRACIES OF THE
ENGLISH SPEAKING WORLD AT THIS CRISIS A COUNCIL
OF DEFENCE OF ALL IRELAND COULD BE SET UP OUT
OF WHICH THE UNITY OF THE ISLAND WOULD PROBABLY
IN SOME FORM OR OTHER EMERGE AFTER THE WAR END
BEGIN PARA 13 THE OBJECT OF THE FOREGOING
MEASURES IS TO REDUCE TO MANAGEABLE PROPORTIONS
THE PRESENT DESTRUCTIVE LOSSES AT SEA BREAK
TO ENSURE FINAL VICTORY NOT LESS THAN
THREE MILLION TONS OF ADDITIONAL MERCHANT
SHIPBUILDING CAPACITY WILL BE REQUIRED BREAK
ONLY THE UNITED STATES CAN SUPPLY THIS NEED
BREAK LOOKING TO THE FUTURE IT WOULD SEEM THAT
PRODUCTION ON A SCALE COMPARABLE WITH THAT OF
THE HOG ISLAND SCHEME OF THE LAST WAR OUGHT TO
BE FACED FOR 1942 END
BEGIN PARA 14 MOREOVER WE LOOK TO THE
INDUSTRIAL ENERGY OF THE REPUBLIC FOR A
REINFORCEMENT OF OUR DOMESTIC CAPACITY TO
MANUFACTURE COMBAT AIRCRAFT BREAK WITHOUT THAT
REINFORCEMENT REACHING US IN A SUBSTANTIAL
MEASURE WE SHALL NOT ACHIEVE THE MASSIVE
PREPONDERANCE IN THE AIR ON WHICH WE MUST RELY
TO LOOSEN AND DISINTEGRATE THE GERMAN GRIP ON
EUROPE BREAK THE DEVELOPMENT OF THE AIR FORCES
OF THE EMPIRE PROVIDES FOR A TOTAL OF NEARLY
7000 COMBAT AIRCRAFT IN THE FIGHTING SQUADRONS
BY THE SPRING OF 1942 BACKED BY ABOUT AN EQUAL
NUMBER IN THE TRAINING UNITS BREAK BUT IT IS
ABUNDANTLY CLEAR THAT THIS PROGRAMME WILL NOT
SUFFICE TO GIVE US THE WEIGHTY SUPERIORITY
WHICH WILL FORCE OPEN THE DOORS OF VICTORY

BREAK IN ORDER TO ACHIEVE SUCH SUPERIORITY
IT IS PLAIN THAT WE SHALL NEED THE GREATEST
PRODUCTION OF AIRCRAFT WHICH UNITED STATES OF
AMERICA ARE CAPABLE OF SENDING US BREAK MAY I
INVITE YOU THEN MR PRESIDENT TO GIVE EARNEST
CONSIDERATION TO AN IMMEDIATE ORDER ON JOINT
ACCOUNT FOR A FURTHER 2000 COMBAT AIRCRAFT A
MONTH BREAK OF THESE AIRCRAFT I WOULD SUBMIT
THAT THE HIGHEST POSSIBLE PROPORTION SHOULD BE
HEAVY BOMBERS THE WEAPON ON WHICH ABOVE ALL
OTHERS WE DEPEND TO SHATTER THE FOUNDATIONS OF
GERMAN MILITARY POWER END
BEGIN PARA 15 YOU HAVE ALSO RECEIVED
INFORMATION ABOUT THE NEEDS OF OUR ARMIES BREAK
IN THE MUNITIONS SPHERE IN SPITE OF ENEMY
BOMBING WE ARE MAKING STEADY PROGRESS BREAK
WITHOUT YOUR CONTINUED ASSISTANCE IN THE SUPPLY
OF MACHINE TOOLS AND IN THE FURTHER RELEASE
FROM STOCK OF CERTAIN ARTICLES WE COULD NOT
HOPE TO EQUIP AS MANY AS 50 DIVISIONS IN 1941
BREAK BUT WHEN THE TIDE OF DICTATORSHIP BEGINS
TO RECEDE MANY COUNTRIES TRYING TO REGAIN THEIR
FREEDOM MAY BE ASKING FOR ARMS AND THERE IS NO
SOURCE TO WHICH THEY CAN LOOK EXCEPT TO THE
FACTORIES OF THE UNITED STATES BREAK I MUST
THEREFORE ALSO URGE THE IMPORTANCE OF EXPANDING
TO THE UTMOST AMERICAN PRODUCTIVE CAPACITY FOR
SMALL ARMS ARTILLERY AND TANKS END
BEGIN PARA 16 I AM ARRANGING TO PRESENT YOU
WITH A COMPLETE PROGRAMME OF MUNITIONS OF ALL
KINDS WHICH WE SEEK TO OBTAIN FROM YOU THE
GREATER PART OF WHICH IS OF COURSE ALREADY
AGREED BREAK AN IMPORTANT ECONOMY OF TIME
AND EFFORT WILL BE PRODUCED IF THE TYPES
SELECTED FOR THE UNITED STATES SERVICES SHOULD
WHENEVER POSSIBLE CONFORM TO THOSE WHICH HAVE
PROVED THEIR MERIT UNDER ACTUAL CONDITIONS OF
WAR BREAK IN THIS WAY RESERVES OF GUNS AND
AMMUNITION AND OF AEROPLANES BECOME INTER

CHANGEABLE AND ARE BY THAT VERY FACT AUGMENTED
BREAK THIS IS HOWEVER A SPHERE SO HIGHLY
TECHNICAL THAT I DO NOT ENLARGE UPON IT END
BEGIN PARA 17 LAST OF ALL I COME TO THE
QUESTION OF FINANCE BREAK THE MORE RAPID AND
ABUNDANT THE FLOW OF MUNITIONS AND SHIPS WHICH
YOU ARE ABLE TO SEND US THE SOONER WILL OUR
DOLLAR CREDITS BE EXHAUSTED BREAK THEY ARE
ALREADY AS YOU KNOW VERY HEAVILY DRAWN UPON
BY PAYMENTS WE HAVE MADE TO DATE BREAK INDEED
AS YOU KNOW ORDERS ALREADY PLACED OR UNDER
NEGOTIATION INCLUDING EXPENDITURE SETTLED OR
PENDING FOR CREATING MUNITIONS FACTORIES IN
THE UNITED STATES MANY TIMES EXCEED THE TOTAL
EXCHANGE RESOURCES REMAINING AT THE DISPOSAL
OF GREAT BRITAIN BREAK THE MOMENT APPROACHES
WHEN WE SHALL NO LONGER BE ABLE TO PAY CASH
FOR SHIPPING AND OTHER SUPPLIES BREAK WHILE
WE WILL DO OUR UTMOST AND SHRINK FROM NO
PROPER SACRIFICE TO MAKE PAYMENTS ACROSS THE
EXCHANGE I BELIEVE THAT YOU WILL AGREE THAT
IT WOULD BE WRONG IN PRINCIPLE AND MUTUALLY
DISADVANTAGEOUS IN EFFECT IF AT THE HEIGHT
OF THIS STRUGGLE GREAT BRITAIN WERE TO BE
DIVESTED OF ALL SALEABLE ASSETS SO THAT AFTER
VICTORY WAS WON WITH OUR BLOOD CIVILISATION
SAVED AND TIME GAINED FOR THE UNITED STATES TO
BE FULLY ARMED AGAINST ALL EVENTUALITIES WE
SHOULD STAND STRIPPED TO THE BONE BREAK SUCH A
COURSE WOULD NOT BE IN THE MORAL OR ECONOMIC
INTERESTS OF EITHER OF OUR COUNTRIES BREAK WE
HERE WOULD BE UNABLE AFTER THE WAR TO PURCHASE
THE LARGE BALANCE OF IMPORTS FROM THE UNITED
STATES OVER AND ABOVE THE VOLUME OF OUR EXPORTS
WHICH IS AGREEABLE TO YOUR TARIFFS AND DOMESTIC
ECONOMY BREAK NOT ONLY SHOULD WE IN GREAT
BRITAIN SUFFER CRUEL PRIVATIONS BUT WIDESPREAD
UNEMPLOYMENT IN THE UNITED STATES WOULD FOLLOW
THE CURTAILMENT OF AMERICAN EXPORTING POWER END

```
BEGIN PARA 18 MOREOVER I DO NOT BELIEVE THE
GOVERNMENT AND PEOPLE OF THE UNITED STATES
WOULD FIND IT IN ACCORDANCE WITH THE PRINCIPLES
WHICH GUIDE THEM TO CONFINE THE HELP WHICH
THEY HAVE SO GENEROUSLY PROMISED ONLY TO SUCH
MUNITIONS OF WAR AND COMMODITIES AS COULD BE
IMMEDIATELY PAID FOR BREAK YOU MAY BE ASSURED
THAT WE SHALL PROVE OURSELVES READY TO SUFFER
AND SACRIFICE TO THE UTMOST FOR THE CAUSE AND
THAT WE GLORY IN BEING ITS CHAMPION BREAK THE
REST WE LEAVE WITH CONFIDENCE TO YOU AND TO
YOUR PEOPLE BEING SURE THAT WAYS AND MEANS WILL
BE FOUND WHICH FUTURE GENERATIONS ON BOTH SIDES
OF THE ATLANTIC WILL APPROVE AND ADMIRE END
BEGIN PARA 19 IF AS I BELIEVE YOU ARE CONVINCED
MR PRESIDENT THAT THE DEFEAT OF THE NAZI AND
FASCIST TYRANNY IS A MATTER OF HIGH CONSEQUENCE
TO THE PEOPLE OF THE UNITED STATES AND TO THE
WESTERN HEMISPHERE YOU WILL REGARD THIS LETTER
NOT AS AN APPEAL FOR AID BUT AS A STATEMENT OF
THE MINIMUM ACTION NECESSARY TO THE ACHIEVEMENT
OF OUR COMMON PURPOSE END
BEGIN I REMAIN YOURS VERY SINCERELY WINSTON S
CHURCHILL END
BT
NNNN
```

TOP SECRET - PRESIDENTIAL

"Your turn, Harry." Roosevelt handed the classified message folder to Hopkins. He sipped his tepid coffee and took another bite from his half eaten sandwich. "Read it through. Do not react until you are done. I want your first blush impression to the whole message."

"Certainly, Franklin." Hopkins returned to his chair and began reading.

President Roosevelt watched Hopkins' expression for several minutes, saw nothing, and picked up the next document in his 'to-do' stack. The two men read for several minutes, until Hopkins looked up and stared out the portal. He could only see cloudless blue sky, but he was not staring to see. Franklin waited for his friend and advisor to be ready.

"Good to know Donovan and Stephenson are on their way. I sure hope Bill is successful learning what he needs to answer the root question."

"That is my hope. Now, what are your thoughts of Churchill's message?"

"First off, the date is wrong. It is dated the eighth, but today is the seventh," Hopkins stated. "Is this a draft or advance copy, or just an error?"

"I don't think so. They must have sent the original after midnight London time. The British are on Double Summer Time for the war years, which means they are six hours ahead of Washington. My guess is our folks noticed as soon as they started deciphering the message that it was an important communication and began preparing to resend it to us as quickly as possible. Nonetheless, unless we are told otherwise, we will use the date of this message for our reference."

Hopkins nodded his head. "I know Churchill and the British are understandably focused on the Germans, but it is reassuring to see his analysis of the situation in the Pacific and Far East with Japanese aggression." Roosevelt nodded his head. "Also, I understand the British predisposition with Ireland."

"Historic."

"Yes. There is no debate with his logic. Operating bases on the western coast of Ireland would dramatically improve their coverage of the sea-lanes. Given the persistent tension between the British and the Irish, I cannot imagine getting into the middle of that quarrel."

"I cannot imagine the difficulty in finding enough citizens of Irish heritage to stand behind strong-arming Ireland into helping the British. I suspect our efforts will more likely be exerted to keep Ireland from joining Germany. We are going to leave that one in the box."

"Clearly, Winston is quite concerned with the whole Battle of the Atlantic."

"We are all concerned."

"Yes, Franklin. As I'm sure you will recall, I did not believe you would succeed with the surplus destroyer deal last summer, and in fact, I thought it might well derail your re-election campaign at the worst possible time. I was wrong on both counts."

"That is quite all right, Harry. To be candid, I was not convinced we could do it either, but we did."

"But, these requirements," Hopkins said, holding up the message, "are way beyond the destroyer deal. Those were surplus, Great War and arguably obsolete destroyers. He is essentially asking for general mobilization, or at least industrial mobilization. I cannot imagine how we are going to get that past Congress and withstand the Press and public pressure against such an action." Roosevelt nodded his head as he considered Harry's words. "Do you really think we can swim up such a swift stream?"

"I don't know. You are quite correct, the gale force headwinds and mountainous seas are daunting to say the least. I will reserve my opinion until after you complete your assessment."

"U-boats ravaging convoys are bad enough, but battleships. My God, Franklin."

Roosevelt stared intently at Hopkins, and then he said softly, "Naval Intelligence has confirmed his assessment."

"Any destroyers we can provide are no match for a battleship and her escorts." Franklin nodded his head. "I am struck by his knowledge of our munitions production – all forms. How on earth can he know that much detail?"

"One word . . . Intrepid."

"Stephenson, really?"

"J. Edgar has kept a closer eye on 'Little Bill' than I have been comfortable with."

"So, you are OK with the British spying on us?"

Franklin shook his head in disagreement as he considered his words. "I do not want any of this discussed beyond you and me. Understood?" Hopkins nodded. "What other observations do you have?"

"I'm not sure what his reference to the Hog Island Scheme is suggesting? I'm not familiar with it."

"When I was assistant secretary of the Navy, we developed, negotiated and implemented a massive shipbuilding program to support the U.S. war effort. That effort was centered at Hog Island, near Philadelphia, Pennsylvania. The facility became the world's largest shipyard with 50 slipways, 28 outfitting berths, and 80 miles of rail track to support production, and employed modern shipbuilding techniques that enabled the yard to lay a new keel every five days. The shipyard delivered its first ship in early August 1918, and reached its peak in 1919. Hog Island built 122 ships before being abandoned, dismantled and sold off, as a consequence of the post-war drawdown and the Washington Naval Arms Treaty. Winston wants us to flip the switch and pick up where we left off."

"Can we do that?"

"No. It took us nearly two years to get things running and that was with a supportive Congress and population. We will need several Hog Islands before this war is done, but that path forward is not yet clear to me. We received some very advantageous bases in exchange for those surplus destroyers. I don't know how we will swing this deal."

"Do you want to?"

"Again, I'll reserve my opinion for the moment. What else do you have?"

Hopkins thought for a moment. "I guess that is it for my first reading. Now, if I may ask, what is your opinion?"

"You did not comment on the financial paragraph. While you hit the major points fairly well, the root problem is money. Until now, they have been on a cash-and-carry basis. Churchill has been extraordinarily candid with us. Bankrupting Great Britain will not win the war. We need the British to remain viable and solvent. We will ultimately need England as a training and launch site for any invasion of the European continent. We need the British more than they need us."

"What do you want to do?"

Roosevelt looked at Hopkins as he thought. Neither man moved. "Think," Franklin simply said.

"Then, I should leave you to it. You do your best thinking without interference from anyone, including me. It is getting late and past my bedtime. Is there anything I can get for you before I leave you, Franklin?"

"Please see to the receipt acknowledgment messages before you retire. Also, would you ask the duty steward to make me up a fresh sandwich and perhaps some orange juice, if they have it."

"Certainly. Good night, Franklin."

"Good night, Harry, and thank you for your observations."

Harry Hopkins nodded his head and departed. President Franklin Roosevelt would spend more time, into the early morning hours, deep in his thoughts, except for the brief interlude when the duty steward delivered his requested sandwich and orange juice. They had to find a path and the means to assist the British. They would have to carry the heavy burden until the United States could be prepared for the inevitable war that had already swallowed up most of the world.

—

Chapter 7

What shall become of us without any barbarians?
Those people were a kind of solution.

- Constantine Cavafy

Thursday, 12.December.1940
USS Tuscaloosa *(CA-37)*
Mayaguana Island, British West Indies
10:35 hours

Harry Hopkins entered the flag stateroom after a single quick knock and without waiting for a response. "We just received this message," he said and handed the single piece of paper to President Roosevelt.

CONFIDENTIAL

```
WH
RAXHT MQP NR 1457
P 121310Z DEC 40
FM WHITE HOUSE
TO POTUS ABD TUSCALOOSA
SUBJ LORD LOTHIAN
BT
C O N F I D E N T I A L
BRITISH AMBASSADOR TO THE U S THE 11TH MARQUESS
OF LOTHIAN PASSED AWAY SUDDENLY EARLY THIS
MORNING BREAK HE WAS PRONOUNCED DEAD AT 0200
EST AT THE BRITISH EMBASSY IN WASH DC BREAK
CONDOLENCES SENT TO HRH KING GEORGE VI AND HMG
LONDON BREAK CHARGE TO ASSUME RESPONSIBILITIES
UNTIL REPLACEMENT ARRIVES BREAK REPLACEMENT
UNKNOWN AT PRESENT
BT
NNNN
```

CONFIDENTIAL

"Oh dear," responded Roosevelt. "This is a terrible loss. He was a very good man, a tireless servant of his country, and a true friend of the United States. Didn't he convert to Christian Science?"

"Yes . . . several years ago. As I understand his conversion, Nancy Langhorne of Virginia, Lady Astor, Viscountess Astor, was instrumental in his conversion."

"I hope that was not a contributor to his passing."

"Me either."

"Would you be so kind to prepare a personal message from me to the King? If memory serves, he never married and his parents are deceased."

"Yes sir. I checked our file. You are correct. I will contact State to see if there are any close family members for your condolences."

"Thank you, Harry. What is the next stop on our sunshine adventure?"

"We are in the process of departing Mayaguana Island. We stop at Long Island," he smiled, "the one in the Bahamas Archipelago, this afternoon. We are scheduled to arrive at Eleuthera Island, tomorrow morning, where you will host a luncheon aboard ship for the Governor General of the Bahamas, His Royal Highness, the Duke of Windsor."

"That should be interesting."

"Yes, it should."

"Winston is barely tolerant of his pro-Nazi and anti-Semitic politics. They won't allow him to return to England, at least until the war is over. The King is very insistent as well. So, here he sits, in the sunshine and solitude, with his divorcee, commoner mistress and now wife."

"Isn't that rather thick, Franklin? He's the King's older brother."

"Perhaps, but I think you will find the facts are correct. Winston has been very candid with me, and his views. For your ears only, Harry, MI5 is in constant contact with the FBI. Edward has been and will remain under constant surveillance at Winston's request. Winston is quite concerned about Edward's potential to contact or assist the Germans in some manner, which would be intolerable and probably result in his mysterious death."

"Really? That is very cloak and dagger, don't you think?"

"And serious, Harry."

"Then, why are we meeting him?"

"We have been traipsing through his domain. It is the courteous and proper thing to do. Plus, I want to develop my own assessment of the man. Winston might appreciate my perspective."

"The luncheon and meeting are scheduled and confirmed. We anchor at Eleuthera Island tomorrow morning. The Duke is due to arrive with his aide at 11:00 tomorrow morning. We expect him to be with us until midafternoon. We will depart later in the afternoon and dock in Charleston the next morning. An express train will be waiting to whisk us back to Washington, as you requested."

"Excellent. Now, in the interest of a timely response, please go draft that message to King George. When you return, I want to talk to you about Winston's message and my revelation last night."

"Oh my, I can't wait. I'll be back shortly."

The drafting took an unusually short time. Harry returned with another single sheet of paper.

"See if this satisfies your intention," Harry said, as he handed the paper to the president.

```
FOR TRANSMISSION TO HIS MAJESTY, THE KING OF
ENGLAND:
USS TUSCALOOSA - AT SEA -
I AM SHOCKED BEYOND MEASURE TO HEAR OF THE
SUDDEN PASSING OF MY OLD FRIEND AND YOUR
AMBASSADOR, THE MARQUESS OF LOTHIAN.  THROUGH
NEARLY A QUARTER OF A CENTURY, WE HAVE COME
TO UNDERSTAND AND TRUST EACH OTHER.  I AM
VERY CERTAIN THAT IF HE HAD BEEN ALLOWED BY
PROVIDENCE TO LEAVE US A LAST MESSAGE HE WOULD
HAVE TOLD US THAT THE GREATEST OF ALL EFFORTS
TO RETAIN DEMOCRACY IN THE WORLD MUST AND WILL
SUCCEED.
(SIGNED) FRANKLIN D. ROOSEVELT.
```

"Perfect, Harry. Send it via State and Foreign Office."

"Yes sir. Let me get this on the wire, and I'll be right back to hear about your revelation."

"You do know we do not have wire out here, don't you?"

"Yes sir. Figure of speech."

Roosevelt waved his hand, palm down, like he was shooing a fly or gesturing for Hopkins to skedaddle. Again, Harry returned in short order.

"Your condolence message will be sent in the next 15 minutes. The Comm Center estimates it should be delivered this afternoon. So, now, I am ready to listen."

"Thank you for tending to that so promptly, Harry. Now, to Churchill's message, in all those words, three words struck me last night on reading the whole message for the umpteenth time – loan or lease. My revelation, Harry, is that those words may well be the key to the whole problem, theirs and ours.

We have already begun issuing contracts under the Rearmament Act and the Defense Appropriations Act. We have begun our industrial expansion. British orders of the magnitude in Winston's message will give an even greater customer base for the expansion, well beyond the Hog Island Scheme in the last war. We will need legislation, let's call it the Lend-Lease Act. We will issue contracts under the authority of the legislation and will lend the equipment to the British, to be returned to the rightful owner when the need has passed. Everybody wins! Industry makes money. They expand rapidly. The British do not have to further deplete their reserves and assets. And, we keep the British in the fight until we engage."

Harry Hopkins smiled more broadly than Franklin could ever remember seeing him smile. "Brilliant! Absolutely brilliant!"

"As I said . . . a revelation. The hard part will be crafting the language to give us maximum flexibility to adapt to the changing needs of the war. We are going to press Henry Morgenthau, Frank Knox and Henry Stimson to get as many Republicans as possible. We don't even have a draft bill, yet, and we need to get this passed in a month or two."

Secretary of the Treasury Henry Morgenthau, Jr., of New York, had been in his position since 1934. He was a Democrat, and a vociferous and vehement anti-Nazi, who had already proven himself instrumental in the material support of Great Britain.

"That is a very tall order, Franklin."

"Yes, I know . . . I know quite well how hard this will be, but we simply must get it done. The British need all the equipment in that message yesterday. We need them to have everything they need to defend themselves and take the fight to the Germans. That said, I want to send you to London right after the New Year, to personally and privately inform him what we are doing. We are going to need a ramrod, a trail boss to drive this herd to market. Let's start with Senate Majority Leader Alben Barkley of Kentucky to sponsor the bill. We will need the votes of all the Democrats and as many Republicans as Frank and Henry can muster up for us. We need to get back to Washington as soon as possible, no time to waste."

"Yes sir. We might be able to get an aircraft to fly you back. That would be quicker."

"No need. Remember, I want to make a quick stop at Warm Springs, and the train ride will be more inspirational. Now, I need to find the words necessary to sell this thing to an isolationist Congress."

"My only point was, we have the means to return you to Washington quickly, if you wish."

"Yes, yes, I understand that. The current itinerary will be sufficient. I assume all arrangements for the Duke's visit are settled. By the way, I must say, we will discuss neither Winston's message nor our proposed response with the Duke, or anyone else for that matter, until we have discussed this with Congress, or at least the leadership. We cannot tolerate any surprises. And, there is no need to muddy the water, if Edward is talking to the Germans."

"Yes sir. My lips are sealed."

—

Thursday, 12.December.1940
Cabinet War Rooms
New Public Offices
Whitehall, London, England
United Kingdom
17:45 hours

The War Cabinet meeting had been extended this day a little longer than usual in dealing with a wide variety of issues, not least of which was the passing of Lord Lothian. The financial situation for Great Britain had dominated the day's discussions in terms of time, having reached a dire level. They had yet to receive a response from President Roosevelt, but they all knew that Churchill's message of the 8th could not have been easy to absorb and deal with given the isolationist political mood, so prevalent in the United States at present. The King's Treasury had just tallied up the War Cabinet's shopping list reflected in the message of the 8th as well as contractual orders recently placed in the United States. The debt to date totaled US$ 9 billion – a valuation that exceeded the liquid assets of His Majesty's Government.

"Might I have a word, privately?" Churchill asked, looking directly to the eyes of Foreign Minister Lord Halifax.

"Certainly, Winston."

The two men waited for the conference room to clear and Sir Edward Bridges to close the door behind him. Churchill motioned for Wood to take a chair, as did Winston, turning his chair to face Lord Halifax.

"Let us discuss replacements for Philip."

"As you wish."

"Who do you have in mind?"

"The popular choice at the moment is the Duke of Windsor."

"Seriously?"

"Many in the Foreign Office favor him and he is practically in America already. He seems to get on well with the Americans, and his wife, the Duchess, is a native-born American after all."

"The Duke has a meeting with President Roosevelt tomorrow in the Bahamas, as the president is nearing the end of his Caribbean cruise. I encouraged Franklin to take the meeting to get a measure of the man himself. I have not shared with him this potential. Who else?"

"Any one of my three senior diplomats – Vansittart, Cadogan and Sargent – would make an excellent choice as well. There are undoubtedly others, if I am given time to think things through and vet some candidates."

"As you well know, time is not on our side at the moment. We need a very capable man, respected on both sides of the Atlantic, and comfortable with the rough and tumble manner of the Americans, and we need him there today. We have too many critical matters in play with the Americans, not least of which are the acquisition programs and the technical exchange program initiated by Sir Henry."

"It sounds like you already have a candidate in mind."

Churchill smiled broadly, perhaps too much like the Cheshire Cat. "Yes, I do, in fact. You."

Halifax seemed a bit stunned by Winston's statement. "You can't be serious."

"Oh, but I am . . . quite serious."

"I am flattered by your confidence in me, Winston, but I would prefer to stay at the Foreign Office and continue my work in the House of Lords."

"I am certain you would. I would as well given your position and stature. However, the exigencies of war time dictate a different course."

"Winston, again, thank you, but I would prefer to stay in London. If you must move me from the Foreign Office, I would understand and accept it . . . abundantly. I truly enjoy my work as Leader of Lords, and I am quite reticent to relinquish my position in the House of Lords, as I would have to do on such an assignment."

"I will not make a contest of this, Edward; however, I must say I am prepared to go to the King, if need be."

"You are serious."

"Stone cold."

Lord Halifax stared at Churchill for several seconds. "No need to bother the King with my trivial preferences. I would be honored to assume that important post. Who do you favor to replace me at the Foreign Office?"

"Anthony Eden."

Halifax considered Churchill's choice. "Anthony is certainly familiar with the office. I know I have been a thorn in your backside, Winston, but I must ask, aren't any of my senior diplomats worthy?"

"Quite the contrary, Edward. They are all highly qualified. The problem for me is, I desperately need the best man we have in Washington, DC, to nurture our relationship with the Americans and coax them on the way to becoming full partners in this affair. In the vacuum of your departure, I need fresh blood. If you think it would be helpful, I will talk to each of the three to sooth any hurt they may feel."

"Thank you for that, Winston. I do not think that will be necessary. I am probably best positioned to ease this transition. How soon do you wish to make this effective?"

"Today, if I could. I have not talked to Anthony, as yet, so that is a priority. You have considerable arrangements to make for the transport of you and Dorothy. All your children are grown, but I do not know if you would take any of your children with you. It is your choice entirely. To ensure your safe arrival, I propose we transport you, your family and your household goods aboard one of our fast battleships. My private secretary will see to the coordination with Admiralty. To answer your question, I would propose we make the transfer of the foreign secretary effective Sunday the 22nd, and your transport to your new assignment in January, once all arrangements have been completed."

"As you wish. I stand ready to collaborate with Anthony as soon as you give me the signal, so that he is ready before the 22nd."

"Thank you, Edward. You are a genuine gentleman."

"I have one piece of news I chose not to bring before the War Cabinet with the rather full agenda this evening. 'C' received word from 'Intrepid' that they have been stranded in Bermuda for nearly a week now due to severe weather in the Azores – their next scheduled stop."

"When do they expect to take to the air on their journey?"

"According to the message, in the next day or two. They had to wait for the storm to clear not only the Azores but also their route of flight."

"Well, that throws off the time table somewhat. I had planned to entertain Donovan and Stephenson at Ditchley on their arrival. We will have to amend that to the following weekend, prior to Christmas, if they are able to complete their journey by then. Bill Donovan and Colonel Dykes are scheduled to depart on their extended tour on Boxing Day. It is wartime after all, so we will adapt. I would prefer they are safe rather than prompt."

"That is the plan. The Foreign Office has informed all sites and all ambassadors involved. Colonel Dykes has been fully engaged and has received detailed briefings from each of the relevant desk chiefs. We are fully prepared to support Donovan's tour. The only dicey portion of their itinerary, other than the threat of enemy action, of course, is Donovan's insistence on two days in Vichy. The new American ambassador to Vichy, France, Admiral Leahy, is expected to present his credentials in early January. There are a thousand ways that portion of the journey could go off the rails."

Admiral William Daniel 'Bill' Leahy, USN [USNA 1897] had been the prior Chief of Naval Operations (CNO) – Admiral Stark's predecessor. After serving a full career in the Navy, he had taken on the assignment as Territorial Governor of Puerto Rico, before being asked by the President to become the U.S. ambassador to Vichy, France.

"There are always risks. We must do everything possible to support and ensure the success of Donovan's mission. Franklin and I have not discussed Donovan's future since his visit last July, but I strongly suspect Franklin favors Donovan as his chief of intelligence. This tour is quite likely a preparatory process."

"That is 'C's read of it as well. Menzies likes the man . . . thinks he can get on well with Donovan should the American become his counterpart."

"That is my understanding as well. We shall do our part."

A few moments silence punctuated their conversation. "Is there anything else you wish to discuss with me, Winston?"

"That should do it, I do believe. Thank you for your cooperation in all this, Edward. You are a cherished colleague."

"Thank you, Prime Minister. The honor to serve is mine."

Lord Halifax stood, nodded his head and departed, closing the door behind him and leaving Churchill alone with his thoughts. *That went better than I expected; now, onto Anthony and the next phase.* Churchill stood and headed back to his office. There were several things he must attend to before supper with Clementine in the Annex dining room.

—

Sunday, 15.December.1940
RAF Church Fenton
Tadcaster, North Yorkshire, England
United Kingdom

No.71 Squadron had no flights and no other training scheduled on the daily calendar. There was only one item represented – the visit of newly promoted, Air Officer Commanding-in-Chief, Fighter Command, Air Marshal Douglas. According to Squadron Leader Churchill, Douglas wanted to gain a measure of each member of the squadron and intended to meet with each pilot personally and privately.

Brian acknowledged that such visits were necessary, as the Eagle Squadron had become somewhat of a novelty in Fighter Command, in the Royal Air Force, and indeed the whole of Great Britain – young, brash Americans. He preferred to be flying. They were supposed to be training and preparing for combat, but they seemed to have more of these no-fly days than he ever remembered in No.609 Squadron. They did have another, at least more acceptable, excuse for not flying – they were in their final transition from the Buffalos to the Hurricane. Brian was the last pilot scheduled to make the transition later in the coming week.

"Attention!" barked Baggy Churchill, as Air Marshal Douglas entered the Dispersal Hut.

"As you were gentlemen," responded Douglas. Several pilots sat. Brian remained standing at the far wall.

"Welcome to Seventy-One Squadron, sir," Baggy said.

"Thank you, Squadron Leader Churchill." He gestured for everyone to be seated. Brian found an open chair, again at the back of the room. "I know you would rather be flying, as would I." Several grumbled, muted and unrecognizable remarks from the pilots punctuated his statement. "Yes, quite so. I appreciate your tolerance. As the only squadron in Fighter Command, or the Royal Air Force, for that matter, with American volunteer pilots, you hold a rather unique position. I am sure you are thankful to be nearly complete in your transition to the Hurri. It is a damn sight better aeroplane than the Brewster Buffalo."

"Got that right," grumbled Roley Rigby, which produced a sharp, un-approving glare from Baggy.

Air Marshal Douglas smiled and glanced at Squadron Leader Churchill.

"I decided to come here myself for several reasons. First and foremost, to assure you that as soon as you are declared operationally ready, you will be moved south and join your sister squadrons. We have begun flying fighter sweeps into France and Belgium. We are taking the fight to the Germans. We intend to harry them and avenge the destruction they have wrought on this country."

"When?" asked Salt Morton.

Air Marshal Douglas smiled, again, but it was not a smile of humor or happiness. Brian saw his expression as one of irritation and annoyance. He was apparently not accustomed to being interrupted by young pilots.

"When you are ready, you will have your chance."

Salt decided to press his point. "Half our pilots have combat experience; some in last summer's epic air battle. Hell, sir, we have the third highest scoring ace in all of Fighter Command in our squadron."

"That's enough," barked Squadron Leader Churchill. "This is not a debate. The Air Marshall was gracious enough to visit us up here. We will treat him with the respect he deserves."

"Thank you, Baggy. This is a rowdy bunch isn't it?"

"My apologies, sir."

"No need," Douglas said to Churchill, and then turned back to the pilots. "Thank you for the reminder, young man. I can assure you, I am well aware of the accomplishments of some of your brethren. There are other factors involved in all decisions, gentlemen. Rest assured, you will be brought to Category 'A' status as soon as conditions are met. His Majesty's Government remains most grateful for your voluntary service. Now, I would like to move onto the next segment of my purpose here today. I intend to meet each of you privately, to get to know you a little better than just your record. I will start with Squadron Leader Churchill, Flight Lieutenant Whittington, and then Flying Officer Drummond. Then, Baggy, if you will, you can determine the order from there."

"As you wish, sir," Baggy responded.

Air Marshal Douglas stood, followed immediately by Baggy, Whitey and Hunter. The others were very slow to rise and a few did not stand at all. The modest disrespect bothered Brian, but he said nothing. Baggy followed the AOC into his office and closed the door.

"Gentlemen," said Whitey, "in the Royal Air Force, you stand when a senior officer stands. Are we clear?"

A couple of muffled yes sir replies came, but most just nodded their heads.

Brian walked outside into the chilly, winter air. There was no snow on the ground, yet, but Brian could feel that it was close. Snow on the ground would curtail their operations even more than these incessant visits and show events. Red Burns joined him.

"Damn cold," Red observed.

"The fresh air feels good."

"For a while, I suppose. I'm sure it gets this cold in Kansas, as it does in Ohio."

"Much colder than this, and add in a brisk north wind, the cold cuts through you like a knife."

"What did you think?" Red asked, changing the subject.

"About?"

"Air Marshal Douglas?"

"He seems reasonable. I'm just not too keen on 'Stuffy' Dowding getting cashiered for Douglas."

"What do you think he meant by 'other factors'?"

"I have no idea, but if I was to guess, I would say discipline."

"What do you mean?"

"Just what we demonstrated this morning with those outbursts. I cannot believe Fighter Command will accept a bunch of unruly, disrespectful pilots, no matter how good they think they may be, into combat operations where split second, life or death, decisions and reactions are critical for the whole operation."

"Do you think it was really that bad?"

"It was not good. I am just like everyone else. I came here eager to fly and with no military experience. I had the advantage of being here for nearly a year before the serious shooting started. I suppose the senior officers who make such decisions are waiting to not only see how we fly, but also how we work with others and how we act as members of the Royal Air Force."

Burns thought about Brian's words. Hunter started to walk down the flight line, more just to move in the cold air than for any other purpose. Red walked with him. They reached the end of their flight line, and then turned to walk back.

As they approached the Dispersal Hut, the door opened and Baggy's head poked out. "Hunter, you're up."

"Here we go," Brian muttered and picked up his pace, leaving Red Burns behind.

Whitey was already out. Brian went directly to the commanding officer's door and knocked twice. He waited for a muffled, 'Enter.'"

Brian opened the door, entered, shut the door firmly, took two paces forward, stomped his right foot, coming to attention, and saluted crisply and smartly. "Flying Officer Drummond, sir."

"At ease, Brian. Take a seat." Brian did as he was instructed. "I understand you know Air Commodore Spencer fairly well."

"Yes sir. I suppose as well as a junior officer can know a senior officer."

"I suspect you are understating your relationship, but that is neither here nor there. I also understand your mentor has introduced you to the Prime Minister."

Where is this going? Why is he asking me about John Spencer? Is there something incorrect about being friends with a senior officer? I'm not feeling real good about this so far.

"Pardon me, Brian. I sense you may be raising some caution. This is not an inquisition. I know what your record says," Douglas remarked, as he leafed through pages in an open folder in front of him. "I am just trying to fill in some blanks, to know you better."

"Yes sir. I have met the Prime Minister several times since I joined the Royal Air Force. I met him the first time before he returned to the government."

"Again, understated. Let it suffice to say, you have made quite an impression on Mister Churchill, and here I mean the Prime Minister, although the same is true for your commanding officer."

"Thank you, sir."

"I also understand none other than Malcolm Bainbridge taught you to fly."

"Yes sir, he did."

"I wish you could have seen Malcolm and John work together in the air during the Great War. It was artistry of the highest order. I was so very sorry to hear of his passing, and if there is any consolation in death, he was doing what he loved best. My belated condolences to you, Brian, for your loss."

"Thank you, sir."

"And, apparently, you have made a most favorable impression on the King, as well. It is rather unusual and rare for a young officer, and even more so a young, American, volunteer pilot, to receive a CBE at the insistence of the King. Please tell me a little about your relationship with Mrs. Charlotte Palmer."

Brian stared at Air Marshal Douglas, who intently stared back. "That is personal, sir."

"Quite so, Brian. Again, I have no hidden purpose. I am simply curious. She is a holder of the George Cross for risking her own life to save a pilot from certain death; the widow of Royal Navy Lieutenant Ian Palmer; a substantial land owner and daughter of a Great War hero; all this contributes to who you are."

"She will be my wife . . . when the war is over, sir."

Douglas chuckled modestly. "That could be a long wait, my boy. Why wait, if I may ask?"

"Not my choice, sir. I wanted to marry her several months ago." Douglas shrugged his shoulders, canted his head and raised his eyebrows, as if to say, OK, why not. "She has suffered terrible loss in her life, and she has a pretty good idea how risky is the work I do."

"Not unlike many women, I'm afraid. Well, I wish you the best of luck and my genuine prayer that we shall make quick work of this affair, so that you can marry her. Now, one last personal question, and then I have a few things I would like to share with you." Brian nodded his head. "What do you see yourself doing when the war is over . . . besides marrying Charlotte Tamerlin?"

Oh wow, he used her family name. He has done his homework. Brian smiled. "I have not thought that far ahead to be truthful, sir. But, I suppose, I would like to stay here and help Charlotte on the farm, while we raise our children. There is not much for me back in Wichita, other than my parents."

Douglas smiled, nodded his head, and jotted down a few notes in the folder. "Quite so. Thank you for sharing that Brian." He closed the folder, which probably signified the get-acquainted segment was over. "What I am about to say, I must ask you to treat as confidential . . . between us. Well . . . I have shared my thoughts with Baggy, so other than that connection, these are private thoughts I trust you with here. Is that understood?"

"Yes sir."

"I chose not to engage Sam Morton on his challenge for good reason. I want you to know why? Whether you like it or not, you are the *de facto* leader of this squadron.   Churchill and Whittington have the rank and position, but they are British, and they know it by themselves and from me. These are not a gaggle of individual pilots. This is a squadron, or supposed to be. They must act like a squadron, before we can possibly risk placing them on the line. I must ask you to help them become a squadron, to work together and with other squadrons. You are an American volunteer fighter pilot, the very first in this war, as Malcolm was in the last war. I know you are capable. You are the third highest scoring ace in all of Fighter Command, in the whole Royal Air Force. You know what it means to fight in the air." Brian nodded his head in recognition, more so than acceptance. "Further, and this is crucial, the relationship of His Majesty's Government with the United States is essential to victory for a host of reasons I will not enumerate here. Let it suffice to say, we, and by the plural pronoun I mean the British people, cannot risk failure. The potential for damage to public relations with an isolationist minded American populace is simply too great at this moment in our combined history. Seventy-One Squadron is and will be held to a higher standard simply because of that risk. What do you think of what I have told you?"

"To be frank, sir, it is disappointing. The guys are feeling we are simply for show, like we are some dog and pony show in the circus. We came here to fly, to fight for freedom. Americans have died here. Each one of those guys out there," Brian said, motioning with his right thumb over his right shoulder, "thinks the same way. We all risked being banished by our government, having our countrymen turn their backs on us, just so we could fly in these fights and do our part to beat the Germans. The Brits fight because they have to fight. It is their homeland that is threatened. The Poles, Czechs, French, they all fight because they have nowhere else to go and their countries have been overrun by the Germans. We Americans are here in defiance of our government and our people because we believe that much in freedom. If we do not defend England, we will be fighting the Germans in Kansas."

"Well now, even I am impressed. You are both well informed and quite articulate, Brian. Thank you for your candor and sharing your perspective. I cannot and will not quibble with your assessment. In fact, I would say you are spot on. We, or at least most of us, recognize the sacrifice you and your brethren have made to join us. We shall do our best to stand with you in the brotherhood, and to do right by you. That said, are you up to the challenge of helping your American brothers to become the best squadron in the Royal Air Force."

"I am not as old as these guys . . ."

"You are the youngest in this squadron, Brian," Douglas interjected. "But, that does not diminish your experience in aerial combat. There are very few, and none in this squadron, who have the practical combat experience that you possess. That counts far more than age, which is just a number."

"Yes sir. Thank you, sir. All I can say is, I will do my best to fulfill your expectations."

"I can ask nothing more. Now, I would love to continue our chat. You are a delightful human being. However, I have already taken too much time, and by doing so, I will have drawn unwanted attention to you. So, let me close by saying, do your best.. I have faith in you."

"Thank you, sir." Brian stood and saluted. Air Marshal Douglas returned the salute, stood and extended his right hand to Brian. They shook hands and Brian departed.

Rusty Bateman was standing just outside. "It's about time, Hunter."

"Your turn," Brian answered and did not wait for a follow-up statement. He walked directly outside and down the flight line, again. He did not want to talk at the moment. He had much to think about, to consider from the most recent conversation concluded. Surprisingly, the other pilots must have understood and let him walk alone with his thoughts.

—

Tuesday, 17.December.1940
Oval Office
The White House
Washington, District of Columbia
United States of America

"Thank you for joining me, gentlemen," began President Roosevelt, as White House Press Secretary Stephen Tyree 'Steve' Early, himself a former journalist, shepherded nearly two-dozen journalists and a handful of photographers into the famous office. They deployed in a broad semi-circle around the President's desk. The President had decided that he must prepare the American people for what would become his program proposal to expand American assistance to the United Kingdom. Early took up his position beside Harry Hopkins and the main entry door, opposite from the President, so they could pick up any signals from the Commander-in-Chief. President Roosevelt waited for the room to quiet, and then continued, "I would like to offer a short statement. I will be happy to take your questions after I've had my say." Not a sound was heard other than the click of camera shutters and pop of flash bulbs.

"Since my return from the tour of our new bases in the Caribbean region, I have been trying to catch up on quite a number of other things. I don't think there is any particular news, except possibly one thing that is worth and explanation from me. In the present world situation, of course, there is absolutely no doubt in the mind of a very overwhelming number of Americans that the best immediate defense of the United States is the success of Great Britain in defending itself; and that, therefore, quite aside from our historic and current interest in the survival of democracy, in the world as a whole, it is equally important from the selfish point of view of American defense, that we should do everything to help the British Empire to defend itself against external aggression.

"I have read a great deal of nonsense in the last few days by people who can only think in what we may call traditional terms about finances. In my memory and in all history, no major war has ever been won or lost through lack of money.

"I go back to the idea that the one thing necessary for American national defense is additional production facilities; and the more we increase those facilities—factories, shipbuilding ways, munition plants, et cetera, and so on—the stronger American national defense is.

"Orders from Great Britain are therefore a tremendous asset to American national defense; because they automatically create additional facilities. I am talking selfishly, from the American point of view—nothing else. We must encourage expanded production.

"All I can do is to speak in very general terms, because we are in the middle of it. I have been at it now three or four weeks, exploring other methods of continuing the building up of our production facilities and continuing automatically the flow of munitions to Great Britain. I will just put it this way, not as an exclusive alternative method, but as one of several other possible methods that might be devised toward that end.

"It is possible—I will put it that way—for the United States to take over British orders, and, because they are essentially the same kind of munitions that we use ourselves, turn them into American orders. We have enough money to do it. And thereupon, as to such portion of them as the military events of the future determine to be right and proper for us to allow to go to the other side, either lease or sell the materials, subject to mortgage, to the people on the other side. That would be on the general theory that it may still prove true that the best defense of Great Britain is the best defense of the United States, and therefore that these materials would be more useful to the defense of the United States if they were used in Great Britain, than if they were kept in storage here.

"Now, what I am trying to do is to eliminate the dollar sign. That is something brand new in the thoughts of practically everybody in this room, I think—get rid of the silly, foolish old dollar sign.

"Well, let me give you an illustration: Suppose my neighbor's home catches fire, and I have a length of garden hose four or five hundred feet away. If he can take my garden hose and connect it up with his hydrant, I may help him to put out his fire. Now, what do I do? I don't say to him before that operation, 'Neighbor, my garden hose cost me $15; you have to pay me $15 for it.' What is the transaction that goes on? I don't want $15—I want my garden hose back after the fire is over. All right. If it goes through the fire all right, intact, without any damage to it, he gives it back to me and thanks me very much for the use of it. But suppose it gets smashed up—holes in it—during the fire; we don't have to have too much formality about it, but I say to him, 'I was glad to lend you that hose; I see I can't use it any more, it's all smashed up.' He says, 'How many feet of it were there?' I tell him, 'There were 150 feet of it." He says, 'All right, I will replace it.' Now, if I get a nice garden hose back, I am in pretty good shape.

"In other words, if you lend certain munitions and get the munitions back at the end of the war, if they are intact, haven't been hurt—you are all right; if they have been damaged or have deteriorated or have been lost completely, it seems to me you come out pretty well if you have them replaced by the fellow to whom you have lent them.

"I can't go into details; and there is no use asking legal questions about how you would do it, because that is the thing that is now under study; but the thought is that we would take over not all, but a very large number of future British orders; and when they came off the line, whether they were planes or guns or something else, we would enter into some kind of arrangement for their use by the British on the ground that it was the best thing for American defense, with the understanding that when the show was over, we would get repaid sometime in kind, thereby leaving out the dollar mark in the form of a dollar debt and substituting for it a gentleman's obligation to repay in kind. I think you all get it."

A journalist in the center of the scrum asked, "Mr. President, that suggests a question, all right; Would the title still be in our name?"

The President smiled. "You have gone and asked a question I have told you not to ask, because it would take lawyers much better than you or I to answer it. Where the legal title is would depend largely on what the lawyers say. Now, for example, if you get mixed up in the legal end of this, you get in all kinds of tangles. Let me ask you this simple question: You own, let us say, a house, a piece of property, a farm, and it is not encumbered in any way—there is no mortgage on it, but you have had some troubles, and you want to borrow four or five thousand dollars on it. You go to the bank and you say, 'I want to borrow four or five thousand dollars on my house or my farm.' They say, 'Sure; give me a mortgage.'

"You give them a mortgage, if you think you will be able to pay it off in three or four years. In your mind, you still think you own your own house; you still think it is your house or your farm; but from the strictly legalistic point of view, the bank is the owner. You deed your house over to the bank; you pledge it, like going to the pawnbroker. Let's take the other side of it: The title to your gold watch is vested in the pawnbroker. You can redeem it; you can pay off your mortgage and get title to your house.

"On this particular thing—let's say it's a ship—I haven't the faintest idea at this moment in whom the legal title of that particular ship would be. I don't think that makes any difference in the transaction; the point of the transaction is that if that ship were returned to us in first-class condition, after payment of what might be called a reasonable amount for the ship during that time—the other people might have had a legal title or the title might have remained in us; I don't know, and I don't care.

Another journalist asked, "Let us leave out the legal phase of it entirely; the question I have is whether you think this takes us any more into the war than we are?"

"No, not a bit."

"Even though goods that we own are being used?"

"I don't think . . . ," the President paused to consider his words, "you go into a war for legalistic reasons; in other words, we are doing all we can at the present time."

"Mr. President, did you mean naval craft?"

"No, no! I am talking about merchant ships."

Another journalist to the left of the President interjected, "Is this a safe conclusion on what you have said, that what the British are interested in is to have us lend them the supplies?"

The President turned his head to look at his inquisitor. "That's the point. I am trying to eliminate the dollar signs."

The journalist followed up immediately. "Does this require Congressional approval?"

"Oh, yes, this would require various types of legislation, in addition to appropriations."

"Mr. President, before you loan your hose to your neighbor you have to have the hose. I was wondering, have you any plans to build up supplies? There has been a good deal of discussion about lack of authority to tell a manufacturer he should run two or three shifts a day. There is no one now who has that authority.

"Isn't there?"

"I don't believe so," the man responded rather sharply.

"I think so, yes," Roosevelt said sternly. "After all, you have to follow certain laws of the land." He continued, "The number of perfectly crazy assertions that have been made in the last couple of weeks by some people, who didn't grow up until after the World War is perfectly extraordinary. They have assigned all kinds of authorities and powers to people in the World War that never existed, except in the figment of their imagination. I went through it; I happen to know."

Another man asked, "Mr. President, do you expect to place this general idea before this session of Congress?"

"Either that or something similar."

"Within a few days?"

"No, probably not until the 3rd, because the thing has not only to be worked out here, but in London, too."

"Mr. President, is there any plan under consideration for building up our Defense Program because of this?"

Roosevelt smiled with a slightly irritated twist. "Perhaps you have forgotten about the two, large, defense rearmament bills I signed into law a few month ago. As the world crisis worsened earlier this year, we recommended and the Congress saw fit to improve our defense preparedness multifold. That process will continue unabated until the situation is well-in-hand or the crisis has been resolved."

"Mr. President, various sources indicate the whole Defense Program is lagging pretty severely; do you see anything in this picture that would require you to extend the present limited emergency?"

"No."

Early picked up the President particular gesture—a glance to him and a raised left eyebrow. "One more question, gentlemen," 'Steve' Early announced. "The President has a very busy schedule today, and we are falling behind."

"Mr. President, on this defense setup, do we understand you to mean that you are not interested in appointing a chairman of the national defense?"

"I would not draw any inferences on that sort of detail. Thank you very much for your time, gentlemen. Have a good day."

Roosevelt turned his attention to the papers on his desk, ignored a couple of attempts at additional questions, and pretended not to hear. Early completed the removal and closed the door behind him.

Hopkins approached the President's desk. "I think that went better than expected."

"How so?"

"There were no questions about being drawn into the war. I would say that is a major step forward with the Press and most likely with the American people."

Steve Early returned. "Well done, Mr. President."

"Thank you, Steve. I must ask you to follow-up on every question and please monitor closely the yield in the Press as a consequence of this session. We will need to take aggressive action at the first hint of any deviation from the program."

"Understood, Mr. President. I shall see to it."

Both aides departed leaving Roosevelt to his work and his thoughts.

—

Wednesday, 18.December.1940
RAF Church Fenton
Tadcaster, North Yorkshire, England
United Kingdom

After lunch, the pilots remained inside the Dispersal Hut. The coal-burning space heater did reasonably well at keeping the interior comfortable. Brian looked out one of the few available windows and the only window overlooking the flight line and alighting area as the British called it. The last two, primary, Hawker Hurricane fighters were due to land at any time, now. Rusty Bateman and he were the last two pilots to transition. Brian was more than ready to get a more capable aircraft than the Brewster Buffalo.

"Guess you're as ready for the Hurricane as I am," said Rusty, who came up to stand beside Brian, gazing out the window.

"You got that right. There was just no way we would stand much of a chance in a Buffalo against a One Oh Nine. We might have done OK against a One Ten, but we would not have been able to catch them."

"You got that right. I flew a brand new Dewoitine D.520 in France before the collapse – a very capable machine – and flew Hurris with One Five One Squadron in The Battle, not quite the Five Twenty, but still a helluva lot better than a Buffalo."

"I've not flown that one, either, yet." Brian noticed two specks on the distant horizon. "I think those may be ours," he said, nodding his head out the window.

"Yeah."

Both pilots watched intently as the two specks became recognizable. They were Hurricanes, and as they made their approach for landing, they appeared to be brand-new Hurricane fighters with no tail designator markings.

Most of the squadron had beat-up, hand-me-down aircraft that were still serviceable, but had clearly seen a better day. These two would be the first and only brand-new, out of the factory aircraft. The two fighters landed together and smoothly. When they turned toward the Seventy-One flight line, Brian grabbed his heavy, fleece, flight jacket and headed outside. Bateman followed.

Brian looked for Corporal Jacobs and spotted him at the open spot where Brian's Buffalo had been parked after the morning training sortie.

"This one's ours," announced Jacobs. "She looks brand spanking new, Mister Drummond."

"Yes, she does."

They watched as the pilot expertly parked the Hurricane, shut down the engine, pulled the canopy back, and got out of the aircraft. The ferry pilot was a woman – a rather attractive woman at that. "This one must be yours," she said. "She's an excellent machine – a new Mark Two."

"I do believe so," Brian answered.

"Good hunting. She's armed . . . just needs petrol," she added, and then turned to Jacobs. "You have two Buffalos for us."

"Yes ma'am. Both are at the end of the flight line," Jacobs responded, pointing to the right. She only nodded her head in acknowledgment.

The other ferry pilot, also an attractive female, walked past them and was joined by her colleague.

Brian and Henry watched the two ferry pilots walk away from them.

Jacobs turned back to Brian. "I removed the tail designator from your aircraft after you returned from this morning's flight, sir. We are going to tow the aircraft into the hangar, warm it up a bit while we give her a good inspection, and we will paint on the tail designator. I believe you will retain the 'XR-G' marking."

"Fine."

"She should be back out here in an hour, two at the most, for you to take her up, if you wish."

"I think that is the plan."

"Brilliant. Then, we'll step out smartly," Jacobs answered, and then turned to begin his work.

Brian watched the crew work for a minute, and then returned to the warmth of the Dispersal Hut. Bateman was already inside.

"Skipper wants to speak with you, Mister Drummond," announced Corporal Harris, as Brian closed the door behind him.

Hunter went to the commander's office. The door was open. Brian knocked on the door jam. Churchill looked up. "So, you got a new machine," he said.

"You are welcome to it, Skipper. You are the commanding officer, after all."

"Yes, I am, but no. She is yours. When will Jacobs have her ready for you?"

"In an hour or two, he said."

"Plenty of time to take her up for a run out."

"Yes sir. If you don't mind, I'll take the opportunity to run up to Catterick."

"Kensington?"

"Yes sir, if that's all right with you."

"Quite well with me. Are you ready?" Brian knew that meant had he studied the Pilot's Notes on the Hurricane. Brian nodded his head. "Enjoy."

Bateman's new 'XR-D' aircraft was the first out. "See you later," he announced, as he grabbed his flight kit and headed off for his flight.

Brian watched Rusty take off and head west. It took another 20 minutes before Brian's new 'XR-G' aircraft was towed to the flight line. "Mark me out," Brian said to Harris.

"Do you need us to go with you, Hunter?" asked Bulldog Tolly.

"No, not this time . . . just a familiarization flight," Brian responded, as he headed out.

The Hawker Hurricane Mark II had the up-rated, 1,480 horsepower, Merlin XX engine. The main difference between the Hurricane and Spitfire, other than appearance, was the wood and fabric empennage with metal skinned wings. The cockpit instrumentation was essentially the same as the Spitfire, and the operational procedures were the same. Take off was quick and easy, the same as the Spitfire.

Brian took his new aircraft up to 20,000 feet, stepped through a quick series of aerobatic maneuvers, and a few hard turns to get the feel for the aircraft.

He liked what he felt. Catterick was only 40 miles north of Church Fenton, so this familiarization exercise took longer than the transit. Brian took his descent to and landed at RAF Catterick. He taxied to the No.609 Squadron flight line, found an open parking spot and shutdown his engine.

Jonathan Kensington was waiting for him at the left, aft, wing root as Brian extricated himself from the cockpit. "So, you have a new machine," said Harness.

"Yep, first flight for me, so I asked the Skipper if I could come see my buddy."

"Well, congratulations, Brian. I'm sure she's a damn sight better than the Buffalo you had."

"To say the least. This is a Mark Two. She has a four-inch nose extension and a new Merlin Twenty engine – nearly 1,500 horsepower. She feels good. This is my first flight, so I've not had her in a fight, yet."

"Well, we'll get you topped off with petrol. You still have your gun port tapes, so no ammunition needed."

"Thanks, mate."

"You want to go inside?"

"I don't have much time, Jonathan. I just wanted to come up and say hi. We don't get to see each other so much these days. I heard that the squadron carried out your first fighter sweep into France."

"Yes, we did . . . nearly a fortnight ago. Very successful mission, I must say. It is so sweet to finally get to shoot up the Germans for all the punishment they meted out to us last summer."

The ground crew had the fuel bowser at the nose and began refueling his aircraft. They also checked all the fluid levels. The crew chief gave Brian a thumbs-up signal that everything was OK.

"We received a newsletter that your squadron got a visit from the chief the other day."

"Yes, we did . . . a rather strange visit. He talked to each of the pilots. He knew an awful lot about my history. It seems like we are spending more time in show and tell than we do flying, like we are a show squadron of Americans rather than a combat squadron."

"Did you say that to Air Marshal Douglas?"

"Yes, I did."

"Damn, boy . . . rather ballsy of you, don't you think? What did he say?"

"He listened . . . not much else," Brian answered, avoiding any violation of his commitment to Air Marshal Douglas. "How is your sister?" he asked, changing the subject.

Jonathan laughed hard. "You are practically married, you rogue . . . unless you already got married in secret, without including your best friend."

"Not married."

"My sister is just fine. In fact, she is at home for Christmas break from university. I would offer to make a run up to Carlingon Castle, so you can reunite with her, but I will not contribute to your delinquency."

Brian smiled. "Thank you for your concern, my friend. Please say hello for me."

"Will do. How is Charlotte?"

"Doing well. I talked to her a week ago. We were informed that the squadron will be taken off line for the Christmas and New Year's holiday."

"Lucky you. We might get a day or two. I'll go home whenever I get a break. I hope to bring Linda up and introduce her to my parents."

"Sounds serious, Jonathan."

"We have discussed marriage."

"You will probably do it before Charlotte and me."

"She is sticking to her end of the war *dictum*."

"Yes, so far."

"Then, yes, we probably will be well after you."

The leading aircraftman crew chief walked up to Brian. "You are refueled and ready to go, sir."

"Thank you." Brian turned back to Jonathan. "You'd better make sure I get an invitation whenever you decide to make her an honest woman."

"You know you will."

"Thanks mate. I'd better get back."

"Great to see you, Brian. Be safe."

"No fun in that. See you next time, Jonathan. You can stop in at Church Fenton anytime you get a chance."

The two men embraced and said good-bye. Brian mounted up. He taxied out but chose to wait for a section of Spitfires to take off on a mission. As had become his practice, Brian obtained permission from the control tower to make a low-pass on the field, which he did, although this time he was much closer to the No.609 Squadron flight line, so his former squadron mates got the full effect of a high speed pass. He rolled once left and once right, and then continued his climb away. Brian yanked the aircraft around a few more times before landing at RAF Church Fenton.

—

Friday, 20.December.1940
Ditchley Park
Enstone, Oxfordshire, England
United Kingdom

"Welcome to Ditchley House," said Prime Minister Churchill. "I suspect this is the first visit for both of you."

"It is for me," responded Bill Stephenson.

"And, for me as well," Bill Donovan added.

"Ronald and Nancy Tree, whom you will meet later this weekend, were gracious and generous enough to offer us the use of their country manor house when The Blitz began and my protectors became overly concerned with the vulnerability of Chequers to aerial attack, especially in the light of a full moon."

"Surely, the Germans could bomb this place as well," interjected Donovan.

"Quite so. However, the Air Ministry felt the associated landmarks were less recognizable on a moonlit night and thus somewhat more difficult to hit. I was not convinced, but I agreed to placate the worriers around me late last summer. I've come to have great affection for this place. Very peaceful, I must say."

"So far, so good, from the appearance of the magnificent surrounding park," Stephenson said.

"Yes . . . so . . . we have a few hours before dinner. Let's retire to the study for a whiskey before supper. I am simply itching to hear of your adventure in getting across the Atlantic. It has to be one of the longest journeys across the Atlantic since the days of sail, I do believe." Winston laughed. The two Bills joined in.

Stephenson and Donovan followed Churchill down the long hallway and into the elegant study/library. A servant poured them each a drink, as they wanted it. They sank into plush, leather chairs arranged in a semi-circle centered on the modest but warming fire in the large stone fireplace.

"Now that I think of it that way, Winston, I do believe you may well be correct," Little Bill responded. "It took us 12 days in total, for what should have been a one or two day affair."

"It was a rather tortuous adventure," added Big Bill Donovan.

"Pan American World Airways . . . the pilot, told us about a rather rare, cyclonic storm moving off of Africa they were watching. He also said, they were going to try to beat the storm to the Azores. By the time we arrived at Bermuda and refueled, the leading edge of the storm was already beginning to affect conditions at Horta. They ferried us into Hamilton and put us up in a nice hotel for what we hoped was an overnight stay."

"Didn't turn out that way," interjected Donovan.

"Indeed! Day after day, they kept telling us the same thing – any day now. First, the storm hit the Azores, and then they believed it was tracking along our route of flight. Second, the storm was too big to go around. And third, we were carrying nearly full passengers and extra cargo. As the days wore on, they apparently considered off loading the cargo, and eventually even off-loading some passengers to take on extra petrol to make Lisbon directly. By that time, the storm was approaching Bermuda. The pilot told us they might have to fly back to New York to avoid weathering the storm while moored off Darrell's Island, their big seaplane base. Fortunately, for all of us and our mission, the storm turned north before reaching Bermuda. We only felt the outer edges of it. On the eighth day, we finally took off for Horta. It was a little bumpy on landing at Horta, but we made it safely. The next morning, we took off for Lisbon and arrived there in fine fashion. I must say, Winston, travelling first class on the Yankee Clipper is quite the experience – very gentlemanly. Unfortunately, we were so far off schedule by the time we reached Lisbon, our RAF transport had returned to England."

"We tried to convince, and then buy flight time to have the flying boat take us on to Southampton or Bristol," said Bill Donovan. "But, we were not successful."

"The embassy was most helpful in communicating with the Air Ministry. We spent two more days in Lisbon, before they managed to get us an Armstrong Whitley medium bomber out of Bomber Command. They configured two hammock chairs in the bloody bomb bay. Our baggage and we were suspended from the bomb racks. It was not a comforting feeling."

"And, it was neither pressurized nor heated."

"They gave us extra blankets, but they were not sufficient to keep us warm. It was very cold. I do not know what altitude we flew at, but it was quite cold."

"And loud."

Stephenson laughed. "Yes, and that, too. We were next to each other, and we had no hope of sharing a word, and it was black with barely any light. Despite the rigors of our transit, we finally landed in England at St. Eval, the Fighter Command and now Coastal Command aerodrome in Cornwall. The aircraft and crew were taken care of, but they struggled trying to figure out how to extricate us from the bomb bay. They eventually found a bomb loader trolley they hoisted up, and then lowered us one at a time to the ground. It took another day to make our way to the rail station in Bristol and into London. At the end of the day, we are here now."

"That is the most incredible story, Bill. I am so glad you are at least here safely."

"Things happen," Donovan said.

"It would have been faster by ship," commented Churchill.

"We didn't think it would turn out as long as it did. When we were into our fourth or fifth day, we did consider switching to a ship, but Bermuda is not on the shipping lanes, and a ship was not readily available. On the positive side of our . . . our . . . ordeal, we enjoyed plenty of time to discuss my mission."

"I eagerly await what you are able to share with me, with us," Winston said.

"Secretary Knox, and I think it is safe to say President Roosevelt, has charged me with expanding my assessment from my July visit. The *prima facie* question is the viability and sustainability of Great Britain in the war with Germany, as well as my prognosis if Japan should attack British territory in Asia. As I have shared with Bill, I think underlying the principal question is the development of a strategic intelligence capability, or perhaps agency, to fill in the gaps left by the segmented intelligence generated by the military branches."

"A noble purpose, I must say. While I would be less than forthright if I claimed no apprehension regarding your *prima facie* mission, as you say, but more so your implied mission. I think we have proven and demonstrated our resolve to stay in this fight and to be victorious in the end. It is your implied mission that portends far greater impact on not only the war's impact, but far more importantly on the war's duration. To be frank and rather blunt, Bill, the sooner the United States realizes her destiny, the sooner this dreadful affair will be over for all of us."

"That is way beyond my pay grade, Prime Minister."

"You are an intelligent man. I prefer Winston between us. Please do not sell yourself short in the name of humility. What Franklin is missing, and he knows it, is precisely what you may well be chartered to provide the president – strategic intelligence – the larger, broader view. It will be through the information you and your future agency will provide that President Roosevelt will be able to find that successful path. Our task in this is to assist you in your mission, and through you to help the President and your country. Also, I think Little Bill has informed you, we have assigned Lieutenant Colonel Dykes of the War Cabinet Secretariat to be your escort and problem solver for your tour."

"Yes, he has," Donovan answered.

"I briefed Big Bill with respect to all the information your office provided," Stephenson contributed.

"Including my granted, unlimited authority."

"Yes. We also met with Colonel Dykes for most of the day yesterday while you were busy with your visit to Harrow School. If I may speak for the absent Colonel Dykes, I believe all of us are in agreement that the arrangements are set."

Winston looked to Donovan. Before the American could answer, the butler announced that dinner was ready. This night, only the three of them would dine. Clementine was expected tomorrow afternoon, along with the Trees. Winston stood, followed by the two Bill's. Winston turned to face Donovan. "You were going to say?"

"'Bill' is spot on, as you say. This is a necessary and hopefully rewarding, if not bountiful, tour of your territory, facilities and other stops. I shall also acknowledge everyone's concern about my side visit to Vichy. The concern is understood and appreciated, but my orders are quite clear."

"Then, so be it. Now, let us go enjoy some of Mrs. Landemare's exquisite culinary artistry," he said and turned to walk. Winston continued his words on their way to the dining room. "Wartime rationing and shortages have made her efforts to feed us properly a great deal more difficult. She is a veritable magician. She never ceases to amaze me. "

This evening's fare included a delightful oyster stew, or perhaps it should be called a thin soup, along with muttonchops with a nice gravy, roasted new potatoes, and mushy peas with an extra tang. She prepared her famous bread pudding with fresh homemade vanilla ice cream for dessert.

Into their meal, Churchill picked up the conversation. "With the tortures of your journey, I'm not sure if you heard of Lord Lothian's passing."

"Yes," answered Stephenson. "We were informed by the embassy staff in Hamilton, Bermuda, before we finally departed. Have you decided upon his replacement?"

"Yes, as a matter of fact, I have. Lord Halifax will replace Lord Lothian. Anthony Eden will move from War to the Foreign Office, and David Margesson will take over as Minister of War."

Henry David Reginald Margesson, MC, PC, Member of Parliament for Rugby, had served as a captain in 11th Hussars in France during the Great War and held the position of Parliamentary Secretary to the Treasury and Government Chief Whip since 1931. He was an accomplished parliamentarian.

Both Stephenson and Donovan must have shown puzzlement in their facial expressions. "I know, Lord Halifax may seem like an odd choice, given Edward's alignment with Neville during the appeasement years."

"I don't think I would have been so generous with the description," Stephenson said.

"Edward is a good man. He knows the government and he knows diplomacy. I have faith that he will perform admirably. He may not exhibit the . . . what shall I say . . . enthusiasm as Philip did, but he shall account well of himself and the vital relationship between our two countries."

"Does the President know?"

"He was informed two days ago. I might add, for your edification alone and in confidence, there was a substantial faction on both sides of the Atlantic who lobbied for me to appoint the Duke of Windsor as His Majesty's Ambassador to the United States. At my behest, President Roosevelt met the Duke during an anchorage stop on his cruise of our Caribbean bases earlier this month. Let it suffice to say, despite all the efforts to help the Duke, President Roosevelt detected Edward's unmistakable pro-fascist leanings. He simply cannot rid himself of his admiration of Herr Hitler. Needless to say, the Duke's, and his wife's for that matter, barely hidden German bias disqualifies him from such a vital position. To be frank, and perhaps risk being overly candid, the King has made it abundantly clear his older brother is no longer welcome while the Kingdom is at war with Germany."

"So, that is why you shipped him off to the backwaters of the Bahamas," observed Stephenson.

Winston smiled. "Precisely, I'm afraid. We are keeping a close eye on him to make sure the Duke does not complicate our war efforts . . . which I must say have improved in the last few days."

"How so, if I may ask?' Big Bill said.

"I surmise you are not aware of the recent communications between Franklin and me, since both of you had begun your odyssey." Donovan shook his head in the negative. "Earlier this month, I sent a rather long telegram treatise to the President regarding out situation and war needs. He has crafted a rather ingenious program, from my perspective, to supply us those materiel needs until the United States can prepare for war."

"Did he actually state that last element?" asked Donovan.

"Prepare for war?"

"Yes."

"No. He did not precisely say that. It was my supposition . . . or perhaps even just wishful thinking." Donovan nodded his acknowledgment. "I recognize the very fine line he is walking. However, three days ago, the President held a press conference. He used a masterful analogy—lending a garden hose to a neighbor to fight a fire—that perfectly describes the program developing for the lending of war materials to sustain us in the fight against Germany and Italy. He has begun preparing Congress and the American people for a substantial increase in the country's industrial war effort. So, let me ask you, do you not see the entry of the United States in the fight against

Nawzee Germany?"

"Respectfully, Prime Minister, it does not matter what I think. My task is to collect facts. It is the President's place to decide what to do with those facts."

"You sell yourself short, Bill. Whether you recognize or acknowledge your developing roll as the President's chief intelligence advisor."

"I am just a concerned citizen, who was asked to make some observations by a mutual friend."

"Humility is an admirable human trait, Bill. I shall not debate your future roll. That is the President's decision entirely."

Donovan studied Churchill's face and eyes. "First, to be direct and perhaps rather blunt, I have no defined assignment in the current administration or any other. Second, I am extraordinarily grateful for your support and tolerance of my intrusion into the affairs of His Majesty's Government on behalf of the Secretary of the Navy. Lastly, I have a successful and lucrative law practice that I had to step away from to perform this task as requested. I thought I could help with the immediate problem, but I have no interest in government service."

Churchill smiled. "I laud your candor. So much of what is going to happen in this sordid affair will depend upon personal relationships—an efficiency of communications, if you will. You may well not be privy to communications Franklin and I have shared for several years. He has shared with me his concerns about strategic intelligence. I do not presume to know what the future holds . . . well, other than our ultimate victory in the present endeavor. Perhaps, I see the vision of your future better than you."

This time, it was Bill Donovan who smiled. "I am not bosom buddies with President Roosevelt. We are from opposite political parties, although I will concede to running in similar circles."

Churchill chuckled. "Similar circles, indeed."

Donovan changed the subject. "That was a delightful meal, Winston. My compliments to Mrs. Landemare. I must say, you seriously understated the exceptionalness of her bread pudding."

Winston again smiled broadly. "I am so glad you enjoyed it. She does an exemplary job, doesn't she? Now, if you have had your fill, shall we retire to the study for a brandy and cigar? I believe we have a new release, American movie for tonight's entertainment, but for the life of me, I cannot recall the title. Nonetheless, I am certain it should be most enjoyable."

The three men managed to laugh and joke about various aspects of the last several weeks. Winston chose to keep their first night together on the lighter side. There would be plenty of time to discuss the more serious elements of the war before Donovan departed on Boxing Day.

—

Chapter 8

So we grew together,
like a double cherry, seeming parted,
but yet a union in partition;
two lovely berries moulded on one stem;
so, with two seeming bodies, but one heart.

- William Shakespeare

Monday, 23.December.1940
Headquarters, Secret Intelligence Service
54 Broadway
Westminster, London, England
United Kingdom

Commander Alastair Denniston, Royal Navy, walked confidently, with purpose but not urgency, up Broadway from St. James's Park Underground Station. The rail journey from Bletchley on the London Midland Railway Line to Euston Station had been quite routine and rather pleasant on this second day of winter. The unscarred countryside soon gave way to the bomb damage of the capitol city. There was no direct Underground line between Euston Railway Station and St. James's Park Underground Station, and several transfer routes were available. Denniston had taken them all at one time or another. On this particular late morning, his timing was perfect. He took the Northern Line to Embankment Station, and then the Circle Line to St. James's Park.

He was just another uniformed man moving to and fro through London. Some of the officers and enlisted men carried similar leather cases. His was the only case manacled to his left wrist and contained an unseen, hardened, interior case with an elaborate lock for a key he was forbidden to carry on his person. Denniston was not aware of any particular threat to his case or to him, but he remained attentive to everyone moving on either side of the street and in either direction. The pistol under his uniform jacket was uncomfortable physically, but reassuring to his churning mind.

As he approached the modest, well-kept, 10-story office building that was his destination, he quickly touched the simple brass plaque near the entryway door--Minimax Fire Extinguisher Company. Denniston smiled, as he always did. He loved the façade moniker for the far more serious organization that occupied the building above the ground floor.

Denniston moved smoothly through the various checkpoints and security screening procedures throughout the building, rigorously enforced for all, even the Director, Government Code and Cypher School.

"'C' is ready for you, Commander Denniston," announced the private secretary and gatekeeper to the office of the Director-General, His Majesty's Secret Intelligence Service, otherwise known as MI6.

Denniston knocked once and did not wait for permission. He opened the door and closed it behind him.

"So, you have something of interest, do you now, Alastair," said Menzies. As Director-General SIS, he continued the usage of code letter 'C' for his position. The practice has been a *de facto* implementation by the original director-general and founder of MI6.

"I do believe this qualifies," Denniston responded, as he placed his case on 'C's desk, to be unlocked by the director. "It took us five days and nights, and no small portion of good fortune, to break this one. The traffic analysis desk suspected this one was important, and once again, I do believe they were correct." Menzies extracted several pages from Denniston's case. "This is a notification summary. The formal order to the various commands is apparently being sent by letter and courier."

Menzies nodded his head in acknowledgment and began reading.

MOST SECRET - ULTRA

```
SECRET
DATE: 18 DECEMBER 1940
TO: OKH OKM OKL
FROM: OKW
BREAK
DIRECTIVE NUMBER 21 OPERATION BARBAROSSA
BEGIN
THE ARMED FORCES MUST BE PREPARED TO CRUSH
SOVIET RUSSIA IN A QUICK CAMPAIGN EVEN BEFORE
THE CONCLUSION OF THE WAR AGAINST ENGLAND BREAK
BREAK
FOR THIS PURPOSE THE ARMY WILL HAVE TO EMPLOY
ALL AVAILABLE UNITS WITH THE RESERVATION THAT
THE OCCUPIED TERRITORIES MUST BE SECURED
AGAINST SURPRISES BREAK BREAK
FOR THE AIR FORCE IT WILL BE A MATTER OF
RELEASING SUCH STRONG FORCES FOR THE EASTERN
CAMPAIGN IN SUPPORT OF THE ARMY THAT A QUICK
COMPLETION OF THE GROUND OPERATIONS CAN BE
```

ACHIEVED BREAK THE MAIN EFFORT IN THE EAST IS
LIMITED BY THE REQUIREMENT TO PROTECT COMBAT
AND ARMAMENT AREAS BREAK FURTHER OFFENSIVE
OPERATIONS AGAINST ENGLAND PARTICULARLY AGAINST
HER SUPPLY LINES MUST NOT BE PERMITTED TO BREAK
DOWN BREAK BREAK
THE MAIN EFFORT OF THE NAVY WILL REMAIN
UNEQUIVOCALLY DIRECTED AGAINST ENGLAND EVEN
DURING THE EASTERN CAMPAIGN BREAK BREAK
THE LEADER SHALL ORDER THE CONCENTRATION
AGAINST SOVIET RUSSIA POSSIBLY 8 WEEKS BEFORE
THE INTENDED BEGINNING OF OPERATIONS BREAK
BREAK
PREPARATIONS REQUIRING MORE TIME TO GET UNDER
WAY ARE TO BE STARTED IMMEDIATELY AND ARE TO BE
COMPLETED BY 15 MAY 1941 BREAK BREAK
IT IS OF DECISIVE IMPORTANCE HOWEVER THAT THE
INTENTION TO ATTACK DOES NOT BECOME DISCERNIBLE
BREAK BREAK
THE MASS OF THE RUSSIAN ARMY IN WESTERN RUSSIA
IS TO BE DESTROYED IN DARING OPERATIONS BY
DRIVING FORWARD DEEP ARMORED WEDGES AND THE
RETREAT OF UNITS CAPABLE OF COMBAT INTO
THE VASTNESS OF RUSSIAN TERRITORY IS TO BE
PREVENTED BREAK BREAK
THE ARMED FORCES SHOULD PLAN FOR ACTIVE
PARTICIPATION OF ROMANIA AND FINLAND IN THE
WAR AGAINST SOVIET RUSSIA BREAK USE OF SWEDISH
RAILROADS AND HIGHWAYS FOR NORTHERN OPERATION
SHOULD BE EXPECTED BREAK BREAK
THE OBJECTIVES FOR OPERATION BARBAROSSA ARE
AS FOLLOWS BREAK FOR ARMY GROUP NORTH SECURE
LENINGRAD MURMANSK AND ARCHANGEL BREAK FOR
ARMY GROUP CENTER SECURE MOSCOW AND EAST TO
URAL MOUNTAINS BREAK ADVANCE INTO THE URALS
AND BEYOND IS NOT AUTHORISED BREAK ASIATIC
RUSSIA FROM URALS TO PACIFIC REMAINS THE
DOMAIN OF IMPERIAL JAPAN BREAK FOR ARMY GROUP
SOUTH SECURE DONETZ BASIN AND BAKU OIL FIELDS

```
BREAK OPERATIONS BEYOND URALS AND CAUCASUS ARE
RESERVED TO THE LEADER ALONE BREAK BREAK
ALL OPERATIONAL ORDERS TO BE ISSUED BY THE
COMMANDERS IN CHIEF ON THE BASIS OF DIRECTIVE
21 MUST CLEARLY INDICATE THAT THEY ARE
PRECAUTIONARY MEASURES FOR THE POSSIBILITY
THAT RUSSIA SHOULD CHANGE HER PRESENT ATTITUDE
TOWARD US BREAK THE NUMBER OF OFFICERS TO BE
ASSIGNED TO THE PREPARATORY WORK IS TO BE KEPT
AS SMALL AS POSSIBLE BREAK ADDITIONAL PERSONNEL
SHOULD BE BRIEFED AS LATE AS POSSIBLE AND
ONLY TO THE EXTENT REQUIRED FOR THE ACTIVITY
OF EACH INDIVIDUAL BREAK OTHERWISE THERE IS
DANGER THAT MOST SERIOUS POLITICAL AND MILITARY
DISADVANTAGES MAY ARISE BREAK BREAK
THE LEADER ANTICIPATES FURTHER CONFERENCES
WITH THE COMMANDERS IN CHIEF CONCERNING THEIR
INTENTIONS AS BASED ON THIS DIRECTIVE BREAK
REPORTS ON THE PROGRESS MADE IN THE PROPOSED
PREPARATIONS BY ALL SERVICES OF THE ARMED
FORCES WILL BE FORWARDED TO THE LEADER THROUGH
THE ARMED FORCES HIGH COMMAND BREAK BREAK
BY ORDER OF THE LEADER HAIL HITLER
END
SECRET
```

MOST SECRET - ULTRA

"Bloody hell!" exclaimed 'C.'

"My reaction precisely."

Menzies stared at Denniston for several minutes as his mind ground through the ramifications of this extraordinary message. Several times he looked down to the message and back to Denniston's eyes. "The PM will need to see this as soon as we can get it to him."

"Where is he?"

"We will confirm with Number Ten, however, I believe he is at Ditchley for the holidays."

"Not exactly on my way back to Bletchley; yet, I shall go there directly. What about the Foreign Minister?"

"That is Anthony Eden, now, in case you did not know. The change was effective yesterday. I shall find him and inform him verbally myself. We shall leave it to the PM to decide upon dissemination. Until then, no copies, no disclosure." Menzies lapsed into thought, again. "We are not likely to find a paper copy of the full directive, but we can at least make sure our field agents are attentive. I shall task the German Desk to alert all of our field operatives, indirectly, as we can make no reference to our knowledge of Directive Two One. Who knows what might turn up?"

"Seems prudent to me," added Denniston.

"This means the likelihood of a cross-Channel invasion attempt in the spring has nearly vanished. Clearly, they intend to press their bombing campaign on us as long as possible. Diminishment or curtailment of their air operations against us should give us confirmation that their push to the east is imminent."

"You don't think they will try to do both?"

"Given that man's delusions of grandeur, anything is possible." Menzies smiled. "This," he said holding up the ULTRA message, "may well be the bite he chokes on."

"We can only hope."

"No, we can do more. When you see the PM, please inform him the Secret Service has begun preparing a plan to exploit what we now know."

"Is there a possibility this is a disinformation initiative to coax us into looking in a different direction?"

Menzies considered the words of his chief codebreaker. "We can never discount such action entirely, Alastair. However, as you know, we have seen signs since late October that the Germans were withdrawing or diverting their assembled invasion forces. We did not know why, exactly. Directive Two One would explain their redeployments."

"As you say, then."

"Also, the PM may ask our opinion on what we may pass to the Russians. If so, please let him know, our recommendation for that element will be part of our proposal to him and the War Cabinet. It may take us several days to a week to put everything together. Also, if you would be so kind, suggest to the PM, there may be opportunities for SOE to work their mischief in Western Europe as the Germans collect their resources for BARBAROSSA."

"Yes sir."

"Well done, Alastair. Please convey my heartfelt appreciation to your cipher team. Exceptional work, I must say. This would not have been easy."

"No, it was not. Our luck turned when a simple, lower priority, administrative message from the same day gave us the box setup. We still do not have a reliable means of determining the daily settings."

"Every operational unit of our armed forces have standing instructions to capture the box and the code book, and more importantly, to protect such capture, when it occurs, with the utmost secrecy."

"We can use all the help we can get."

"It will happen. I have faith."

"Very well, then. We shall persevere until that day arrives."

Denniston returned the message to his case.

"Wait," said Menzies. "You will need to transfer that message to the Buff Box for the PM."

"Oh yes, good catch, 'C'."

"Also, call me on the secure line after your visit with the PM."

"Yes sir."

With Menzies assistance, Denniston's original case was released from his left wrist, the message transferred to the PM's Buff Box, and the hardened steel cuff attached to his left wrist. The Buff Box was a little less ordinary in appearance, but this was not the first time Denniston had used the box to carry sensitive messages to Prime Minister Churchill. Once secure, Denniston departed for his journey north. 'C' jumped into the delicate process of aligning the intelligence agency he was responsible for in this war. The situation of the United Kingdom had just taken a dramatic and positive turn thanks in full measure to the megalomania of the German chancellor.

—

Tuesday, 24.December.1940
Standing Oak Farm
Winchester, Hampshire, England
United Kingdom

"Stop here, please," Brian said.

The taxi driver did as he was requested, just past the crest of the last ridgeline. "Is there a problem, sir?"

Brian shook his head, and then responded, "No, not at all." Brian smiled. "Isn't that just the most glorious scene?"

"Yes sir. Mrs. Palmer has always kept her family's farm in fine form."

"Quite so. Now, I do believe the lady of the manor is waiting on my arrival. Let us proceed on down."

The vehicle moved down the road. Brian saw no one moving around the house or the barn. He was a little surprised Charlotte was not outside, waiting to greet his return. Even Horace and Lionel were nowhere to be seen, but it was after morning milking, so they could be anywhere on the farm, or on some errand in town. The driver stopped near the front door – still no Charlotte. Brian paid the fare plus a handsome gratuity. He looked around the visible portion of the property, as he watched the taxi drive up the hill and disappear over the ridgeline.

Brian looked around Charlotte's farm, again. He saw no one. Brian knocked on the door. No answer. He opened the door and walked in.

"Welcome home, Brian." He heard Charlotte's voice.

Brian turned the corner from the entryway. There before him stood Charlotte Palmer in all her glory, not even a pair of socks to warm her feet from the chill of the stone floor. Her abdomen had become round and protruded. Her breasts were larger, and her nipples and areolas were darker. His smile must have displayed his excitement.

"I thought you would appreciate this," she said, moving her hands up and down both sides of her body.

"An understatement of the century, my darling."

Charlotte extended her arms toward him. Brian dropped his satchel, sprang to her, and wrapped his arms around her, feeling her softness and swollen belly.

"My God, woman. You are amazing . . . and you feel so good."

"I should hope so. Now, pick me up. My feet are cold. Take me to bed. We have business to tend to first."

"As you command, my darling," he answered and scooped her up. He smelled the delightful scent of her hair. She kissed him passionately.

Brian laid her gently on the bed and undressed quickly. His excitement and eager anticipation was readily discernible.

"I see you have missed me," she giggled.

Brian looked down, and then back to her eyes with a smile. "Again . . . an understatement." He lay next to her, embraced and kissed her, and rolled away slightly to rub her moderately distended abdomen. "Are you sure this is OK?"

Charlotte grasped him gently and stroked him a few times. "Yes, Brian. We might not be able to enjoy some forms of our past pleasures, temporarily, but I know you will not hurt the baby or me."

Brian needed no further encouragement. They jumped into their reunion and carnal pleasures. By the time they reached a point of mutually sated exhaustion, they were fitted together like two puzzle pieces. Brian wrapped his arms around her with one hand on her distended belly and the other cupping her right breast, with their legs intertwined like ornamental vines. Brian simply loved the feel, smell and taste of her. She shivered. Brian pulled the top sheet, blanket and comforter over them before they retreated into slumber.

Brian had no idea how long they had been asleep.

"Mrs. Palmer."

Brian heard the muffled call. "Charlotte," he whispered at her ear and nudged her.

"What?" Then, she heard the call herself. "Mister Morgan," she said loudly, "go ahead without me, if you please."

"Are you well, ma'am?"

"Yes, yes, quite well," she shouted. "Please go ahead without me this afternoon."

"As you wish, ma'am."

Charlotte giggled. "I can only imagine what he must be thinking."

"He shall know soon enough when we appear together later."

She giggled, again. "That may not be until after Boxing Day. I've given them both the two days off to spend with their families." She turned slightly to kiss Brian. "Merry Christmas, Brian."

"Merry Christmas to you, my dear."

"Oh my, we must have fallen asleep."

"A measure of our love, I do believe."

"You are so sweet. Lionel and Horace must have returned for the afternoon milking. I should really go help them."

"We!"

Charlotte smiled and kissed him. "Yes, we should go help them. But, this feels so good and right, to be snuggled up with you finally back home."

"Whatever your wish, my darling."

Charlotte thought for a moment. Brian felt her warm feet against his legs. They lay together peacefully and quietly, drifting off again in their contentment. It was completely dark inside and outside when they next stirred to consciousness. Brian's stomach growled loudly. They both laughed.

"We need to feed you . . . us," said Charlotte. "I need to draw the blackout curtains before we switch on any lights. We never know if some German bomber is out there looking for a wayward light in the darkness." She wrapped herself in her robe, donned her warm slippers, and closed the bedroom curtains first. She proceeded to the other windows, expertly navigating furniture and other obstacles in the dark.

Brian had to grope around the bedroom in the dark to find the robe Charlotte had laid out for him. By the time he found it, she had switched on a small lamp in the kitchen. He joined her.

"I need to go check the barn to make sure everything is done."

"You will need something on your feet, darling," she said and laughed.

Brian returned to the bedroom, found the slippers he had used before, and rejoined her near the entryway blackout curtains. They stepped through. Brian made sure the curtain returned to its proper overlapped position.

"Let's give our eyes a moment to adjust," she said in the dark.

They groped at each other and giggled in their play. Charlotte opened the door. The light of a quarter moon and half a sky of stars offered quite a bit more light. The walk to the barn was easy and without incident. They went to the small side door.

As Charlotte opened the door, she said, "Grab the torch, if you will."

Charlotte had already transferred from her slippers to her muck boots by the time Brian switched on the flashlight with the lens covered, except for a small slit, like blackout lights on automobiles. It gave off enough light to see objects a short distance ahead. Brian changed to his muck boots. The boots used by Horace and Lionel stood empty. They had completed their work and departed. Brian held the flashlight for Charlotte as she checked the log for the afternoon's yield and supply consumption. Satisfied, she quickly checked the storage vat and milk cans. Three were missing, which meant Horace or Lionel took the evening yield into town for sale. Charlotte nodded her head that all was in order.

They reversed the process as they returned to the house. Once inside and everything in place, Charlotte switched on a few other lights.

"I will work on something to eat, if you would stoke the fire," she said.

Brian added some kindling and a couple of split logs to the fireplace. He used the adjacent bellows, as he had done many times before, to flare the embers and light the kindling. He had a modest fire going in short order. Charlotte had partially sliced a loaf of bread, baked earlier in the day, some sliced cheese made on the farm and sliced chicken, pickles and homemade mustard on that table. She also had a pot of fresh brewed tea and a bottle of wine, a bit of a rarity for wartime England.

"How is your flying going?" she asked, as they sat down at the kitchen table. *Wow! What has changed? She never asks me about flying or the war.* "I finally got to transition to a brand new Hurricane Mark II from the Buffalo – a real dog of an airplane, the Buffalo. Neither airplane is as good as the Spitfire, but the Hurricane is much closer. So, I would say things are looking up. Fighter Command still has not declared us operational, so we continue to train and fly pretend missions. We have been doing far too much of what the lads call dog-and-pony shows – like circus animals – every visiting dignitary or journalist wants to talk to us or get their picture taken with us. It seems like we are just a showcase squadron, rather than a working squadron."

"I'm fine with that," she said and smiled. "Do you think it will change?"

"We are not much help with this damn night bombing the Germans have been up to since September, and there is no sign of them letting up on that. I talked to Jonathan the other day. They have made several squadron sweeps into France to shoot up the Germans. I suspect they gave us a week off for the holidays because they will declare us operational next month."

"You know how I feel."

"Yes, I do."

"I am so happy to have you home. I do not care about tomorrow. I am certain you will let me know when your status changes or you move closer to the fighting. Until then, I shall enjoy every moment we have together."

"Likewise."

They finished eating, cleared and washed the dishes, and refilled their wine glasses.

"Let's sit by the fire," Charlotte suggested.

Brian poked the fire and put another split log in the fireplace. Rather than take separate chairs, Charlotte chose to sit across Brian's lap.

"I've done quite a bit of thinking, since you were here last." She chuckled. "I know that can be dangerous." They both laughed, but Brian knew she had serious words to say and wondered what she was about to say. She took his hand and placed it on her belly. "I am four months along with our first child. I have decided that I must put my fear aside. I want to get married before you have to return to duty."

Brian grinned broadly. "Really?"

"Yes, really, you twit."

"Then, let's do it tonight."

Charlotte laughed heartily. "This is Christmas Eve, silly. The earliest would be next week, or at least after Boxing Day."

"That's Friday."

"There are arrangements that must be made. I am told by the minister at our church in Winchester that you must inform or apply at the American Embassy in London, so that our marriage is legal and proper for you."

"I will call on Friday, to see what must be done."

"Are you sure, Brian?"

He pinched her, which caused her to yelp. "I was serious last September, when I first asked you."

"Do you recall me telling you last month that I wanted to introduce you to Ian's parents in Devon?"

"Yes."

"Well, that is one other requirement I would like to fulfill before we marry. I know all of this would have been easier if a year of mourning had passed and I was not visibly pregnant with our child; however, I do not want them to find out or be informed after the fact."

"I understand. That should be no problem."

"Excellent. Then, if you will take care of your embassy requirement on Friday, I will make arrangements for us to visit the Palmer's this coming weekend. Horace and Lionel can tend the farm, as they did this afternoon. It is a bit of a journey, given the wartime constraints, so we should plan to spend the weekend with them."

"Are you sure it will be OK?"

"Yes. They are good people. I suppose the essential question is, will you be comfortable? After all, they are strangers to you."

"If you are comfortable, I will be comfortable."

Charlotte pulled him tightly to her and kissed him passionately. "I think they will take an instant liking to you, as I have. I love you, Brian, very much."

"I love you, Charlotte." Brian held her eyes. "How about we pick up where we left off this afternoon."

"Oh you naughty boy." She reached into his robe to offer her response with a gentle caress.

Charlotte rose, followed by Brian. He placed the spark screen over the face of the fireplace. They switched off the lights and walked hand-in-hand to the bedroom, where they would spend the next few hours in carnal bliss before sleep claimed them.

—

Saturday, 28.December.1940
Palmerton Close
Yelverton, Devon, England
United Kingdom

The journey from Winchester by railway had taken the better part of a day. Fortunately, an air force station, RAF Harrowbeer, was located on the southwestern outskirts of the village, and Brian had worn his uniform. There was no taxi service in this part of the country. Thanks to a courteous airman from the station, an RAF supply truck took them to the Palmer farm a little more than a mile to the east of the village. The property sat on the periphery of the Royal Dartmoor Forest—a forest largely in name only as most of the trees had been removed to build ships back in the days of sail. The trees on the Palmer's property had been maintained over the centuries of private ownerhip.

The Palmer manor house was modest, well kept, and situated in a picturesque setting among the trees and in what had to be a colourful garden during the spring and summer.

Edith and Derek Palmer owned several acres of the remaining private forest along the River Meavy, with a dozen acres of adjacent farmland they utilized for their supply and sale of the excess. Mister Palmer was a successful shipping merchant, who operated his small cargo fleet out of Plymouth. Palmer's ships were now operating in service to His Majesty's Government, as Derek's father had done during the Great War 20 years earlier.

The Palmers greeted Charlotte warmly and with unusual affection, and welcomed Brian with respect for his uniform and service to the Crown. By Charlotte's arrangements and coordination, she and Brian would spend the rest of the day visiting with the Palmers and stay the night, since they would be unable to return to Standing Oak Farm until tomorrow.

The senior Mrs. Palmer was the first to broach the observation of Charlotte's baby bump after their comparatively sumptuous evening meal. Charlotte spent the remainder of the evening explaining her situation and decision. She conveyed enormous respect for Ian and her abiding love for them, as she told the story of her unexpected love for Brian. The revelations cast a demonstrable chill on the conservation, yet the Palmers respected Charlotte's initiative and courage for being forthright with them. Neither of the Palmers raised the specter of her shortened mourning period or her intervening pregnancy. Charlotte offered to inform Ian's siblings; however, Derek insisted they would handle that task.

The assessment of the weekend's visit and disclosure would occupy the entire journey back to Charlotte's farm the following day. She had held no illusion the Palmers would be pleased with the news, but felt it had gone better than expected and she felt relieved to have that burden removed from her consciousness. Charlotte concluded that she had fulfilled her perceived obligation and was ready for their planned event on Monday.

—

Sunday, 29.December.1940
Headquarters, No.11 Group
Uxbridge, Middlesex, England
United Kingdom
21:25 hours

The tracking board in the well of the Group Operations Room began to present red 'H' blocks over Northern France and Belgium. This was going to be yet another long night. The primary question, as always, was what was the target for this night's raid in the continuing Blitz?

Air Commodore John Spencer liked being closer to the pointy end of the sword than the oppression of the incessant paperwork of Fighter Command Headquarters, but even the job of Chief Operations Officer and Chief Controller was a long way from the cockpit of a fighter airplane. John checked the status board for each squadron in the Group on the wall opposite his balcony desk. The day squadrons were Not Available and would be of no use this night at any rate. The night squadrons stood at Available status.

Spencer glanced at the array of colored telephones on his desk, and then looked to his assistant controllers, who were all looking at him. "Bring up Six Oh Four and Nine Six squadrons to Standby," John said softly but firmly. The associated controllers called their sector controllers to alert the designated squadrons. He raised the red handset that was a direct line to the Air Officer Commanding-in-Chief, No. 11 Group, Air Vice-Marshal Trafford Leigh-Mallory, who had assumed command of the Group on the 18th of the month. From John Spencer's perspective, Leigh-Mallory was a decent enough fellow, yet he truly resented what the man had done during the summer and fall of the great aerial battle. His obstinate, persistent and under-the-table undermining of Sir Hugh Dowding and his immediate previous boss, Keith Park, had resulted in Dowding being relieved and shipped off to America in November, and Park relieved just 11 days ago and reportedly on his way to Malta, of all places. Leigh-Mallory did not deserve command of the premier fighter group in the Royal Air Force for that simple reason – disloyalty and deceit; yet, he was here and in command. John could not afford any conflict or confrontation with the man, regardless of what he thought. He would not resort to the same tactics to get ahead – simple as that.

"Sir, we have a major raid heading into the Channel. The initial vectors suggest London, tonight. I've brought two of the night fighter squadrons up to Standby. Yes sir."

Ten minutes later, as the first wave of German bombers approached the southeast coast, Leigh-Mallory joined John at the senior controller's station.

"So, it's London tonight," said Leigh-Mallory.

"Yes sir. I've brought two more squadrons to Standby. We launched Six Oh Four and Nine Six Squadrons five minutes ago. The London gun batteries are at the ready."

"I assume we have made all the appropriate notifications," meaning the government, emergency services, medical facilities, and transportation services.

"Yes sir . . . as soon as the target became clear."

John concentrated on the movement of the red and blue blocks on the tracking board. By the time the night fighter squadrons began to engage the

German bombers, the first signs of a second wave forming began to appear over Northeast France and Belgium. *This is going to be a very long night.*

—

Monday, 30.December.1940
Ditchley Park
Enstone, Oxfordshire, England
United Kingdom
02:45 hours

Winston sat in the large, overstuffed, leather chair focused on the flames in the fireplace as he waited for Roosevelt's scheduled radio broadcast. Pug Ismay and Jock Colville sat behind him by the radio, listening to CBS Radio with the volume so low that they could barely hear the programming and would not disturb their prime minister. *They are good and loyal troopers, each in his part.* He expected this to be the boldest statement, yet, by the United States in the present war. Winston did not expect a declaration of war or a partner in the war, finally. However, his message of a week ago was very encouraging. And now, his most trusted confidante, Mister Harry Hopkins – Mister Root of the Matter – was now scheduled to visit London next month. Winston held his partially burnt but now extinguished cigar with his lips as he gently swirled his third dose of cognac in his snifter. The fragmentary news from across the pond had been cryptically encouraging. *I wonder what the President will say publicly, for everyone to hear, including us . . . and the Germans, Italians, and Japanese. He has to be concerned about what Congress will do with his proposal. I suppose we shall know soon enough. We need their participation, whether the American people recognize the need or not.*

"Sir," said Jock. Winston looked over his shoulder to Colville. "The President is about to speak."

"Yes, yes," Winston said, as he rose to join Pug and Jock around the radio, taking a straight back chair undoubtedly saved just for him. "Turn up the volume. Let's hear what the President has to say, tonight."

Colville did as he was requested. The volume was certainly loud enough now to be heard outside the study.

Churchill stared at the radio console before them and tolerated the occasionally scratchy audio of the short wave transmission from across the Atlantic Ocean. He listened intently for all 37 minutes of the broadcast. All three of them did. Winston did not move and made no attempt to wipe away the tears of relief, of pride, of gratitude, descending down his cheeks and dripping onto his light blue, siren suit – his preferred, quick-don, overalls named for their use when the air raid sirens wailed and he needed to dress quickly. Churchill had become so accustomed to the simplicity and comfort of his siren suits they had become his preferred choice of casual wear.

When the announcer concluded the broadcast, Churchill lowered his head in thought, if not prayer. Jock first turned down the radio, and then switched it off. Neither Ismay nor Colville stirred beyond that, giving the Prime Minister time to absorb the President's words of encouragement.

Several minutes passed. Winston raised his head, wiped the remnants of his tears away, and looked into the eyes of both his companions. "I think those are the most moving words I have ever heard," Winston pronounced.

Both Ismay and Colville nodded their heads in agreement, not wanting to contradict their prime minister or break the euphoria of the moment.

"It was an impressive and encouraging speech," added Ismay.

"An understatement of the first order, I must say Pug. We could not have asked for more. After his press conference of a fortnight ago and with those words, he has committed American industry to our cause. We finally have an ally in this fight. They may not be contributing soldiers and sailors, just yet, but they are no less committed."

"He clearly wants to keep us in the fight."

"Precisely. I am good with that. With American materiel support, we shall choke the bloody Nawzees and that foul, odiferous leader of theirs until they are devoid of life. Did you hear those magnificent words . . . great arsenal of democracy . . . indeed!"

"Yes sir."

"And, the very altars of modern dictatorship . . . he has acknowledged the Nawzees use of concentration camps to suppress dissent and any semblance of opposition. He knows!"

"So it would seem."

A knock at the door broke the mood of the moment, as if reality had disturbed the exquisiteness of the idyllic upland meadow. Colville rose to attend the disturbance. Churchill, followed by Ismay, rose and returned to the fire.

"General, if you will," Colville spoke with uncharacteristic firmness.

Ismay turned toward the door. Both men stepped out and closed the door behind them, leaving the Prime Minister alone with his thoughts.

As the minutes passed, Churchill began to wonder what had become so urgent in the middle of the night. Just when he was about to go see what the problem was, General Ismay and Jock Colville returned with grim expressions. *This cannot be good. What must now spoil my joy with the President's speech?*

The two men sat. Colville now held papers in his left hand.

"Sir," began Ismay, "we apparently have a dreadful situation unfolding in

London." Churchill waited for his military aide to continue. "The German bombers hit London hard . . . two waves already, and apparently a third wave on its way to strike before dawn. We have been informed they got lucky tonight. They destroyed a water pumping station and managed to cut several main water lines. The fire brigade has no water pressure. The Germans firebombed the city with incendiaries and high explosives. Emergency Services are gathering as much hose as they can find and pumpers from around the city to draw water from the Thames. Several of the fires have become uncontrolled and joined. All available night fighter squadrons in Ten, Eleven, and Twelve Groups are now on their third sortie of the night."

"Have they asked anything from us?"

"No sir. The message received by the communications section simply wanted to inform you."

"Then, there is not much we can do to assist their heroic efforts tonight."

"We are also informed that the Home Secretary and the Air Minister will journey to Ditchley tomorrow to personally brief you on the status of this night's bombing raid. They will bring the latest information from the morning's assessment. They expect to arrive in early afternoon, after lunch time."

"Anything more?"

"I'm afraid not, sir. That is the extent of what we know so far."

"Then, we should try to get some sleep. It is going to be a long day tomorrow." Churchill stood. He poked at the glowing coals in the fireplace to ensure they were safe for the night. Winston led his companions out of the study. None of them would enjoy a restful night's sleep, but they had to try.

—

Monday, 30.December.1940
Winchester Register Office
Castle Hill, High Street
Winchester, Hampshire, England
United Kingdom
11:00 hours

Charlotte and Brian arrived at the appointed time, by arrangements agreed to the previous Friday. Brian was dressed in his RAF uniform with medals rather than ribbons. Charlotte wore a modest and well tailored, light blue, woolen suit that was slight too tight across her abdomen.

The duty magistrate was present and prepared to perform the simple, civil marriage with Lionel, Horace and Jacob as witnesses to the ceremony. Brian presented his military identification papers as well as the notice of acknowledgment he had obtained from the U.S. Embassy. The process took all of ten minutes to complete. They signed the marriage registry book beside their names and they were done. Charlotte was now Mrs. Brian Drummond.

They paid their small fee, and then the five of them rode in Charlotte's delivery truck with Brian driving, Charlotte beside him and the three men riding on the back bed between the stake railings. They celebrated the wedding with several bottles of chilled champagne that Charlotte had saved up from before the war and their signature farm cheese. Laughter and joyous words punctuated the happy occasion. Brian and Charlotte were finally husband and wife.

—

Monday, 30.December.1940
Ditchley Park
Enstone, Oxfordshire, England
United Kingdom
14:45 hours

Lunch had been unusually quiet, sparsely attended and simple in cuisine, by standards common for Winston Churchill, especially on weekends away from Whitehall at Ditchley House and Chequers Court. The Prime Minister had decided to extend his stay at Ditchley, having been advised that their various routes into Whitehall were blocked with emergency services personnel who continued their struggle to gain control of the fires, clear streets and achieve some level of normalcy for the city.

The Prime Minister paced in his study, uncharacteristically fidgety and anxious with the news headed his way. The staff made several telephone calls into London only to be informed by the operators that various lines had been cut or were inoperable, and when they did get through, the fragments of information ominous rather than helpful. Jock Colville and the set of duty stenographers feverishly stepped through the mid-day correspondence as they waited. Jock was nearly complete with the contents of the morning dispatch box when the knock at the door broke the process.

"Excuse me, sir."

"Yes, yes, see who it is."

The task did not take long. "Sir, Secretary of State for Air Sir Archibald Sinclair and Home Secretary Herbert Morrison to see you."

Churchill waved impatiently. Colville opened the door for the two ministers. The two stenographers instinctively knew it was time for them to leave. "Jock, I think we may need you. Please stay. No, first, please find General Ismay. He needs to hear this as well."

"Yes sir." Colville closed the door behind him, as he departed to retrieve General Ismay.

The Prime Minister and two cabinet ministers sat at a small conference table near the entry door. "Let's have it. I've been as anxious as a caged lion all morning. We have not heard much since last night's message from the Home Office. We were informed this morning that we could not return to Whitehall as most of the roads were damaged or blocked. How did you get out of the City?"

Pug Ismay and Jock Colville returned, positioned and sat in two straight back chairs behind the Prime Minister.

"It has been a very bad night," began Morrison, "and, I'm afraid we have not yet seen the worst of it. To answer your query, Winston, we had to commandeer a launch from the Admiralty and make our way up the Thames to Richmond before we could transfer to a Royal Air Force staff vehicle from Uxbridge, Archie was kind enough to arrange for our transport here. Not to be melodramatic, the fires were burning to the river's edge on both banks."

"Dear God above. Our beloved city."

"Unfortunately, Prime Minister, it is my duty to inform you that the fires are still growing by the minute. What the Germans started last night may well exceed the Great Fire of 1666."

"That is dreadful. Why in bloody hell was last night so bad?"

"They managed to score direct hits on two of the principal pumping stations supplying water pressure to the city. Further, for the stations that did survive, numerous bomb craters severed main supply lines. The fire brigades had no water pressure and no water beyond what little they carried in their lorries. They were relegated to rigging up supply lines from the Thames, and even then it took precious hours to gather the necessary hoses. On top of that several of the river lines sucked up mud. Low tide occurred early this morning, complicating the river supply operation. The engineers had to quickly devise a means to keep the suction ports off the river bottom as well as clean out the already clogged hoses. We did not make headway against the fires until nearly dawn. The fire brigades and other emergency services personnel braved the continuing bombardment all through the night to help as many people as possible. The subsequent bombardment and fires trapped some units. Rescue operations were still underway when we departed. Many of the fires have now joined, and the heat is creating its own wind, fanning the fires ever more."

"What happened to our air defense?" Winston barked at the Air Minister.

"We did better last night than any previous night."

"It certainly does not sound that way, Archie."

"Gerry got extraordinarily lucky, last night."

"Lucky, indeed!"

Archie chose to continue. "All of the night fighter aeroplanes in the three southern groups flew at least three long, productive sorties last night, with few flying four and a couple flying five sorties into the twilight hours this morning. They achieved their highest number of night victories last night, since we introduced night fighters last summer. Even the gun batteries managed to knock down more bombers last night. The fires illuminated the subsequent waves better than the searchlights could."

"There are blessings in tragedy."

"Yes sir."

"What is our casualty count?"

Morrison responded, "Our sole focus has been gaining control of the fires. We know there are dead and injured. Regrettably, we cannot reach most of them, which likely means the death toll will be higher than usual for The Blitz. We are working to evacuate those people who may have sheltered at Underground stations in the areas of the largest fires. The process continues as we speak."

"Is there anything we can do?"

"Pray," answered Morrison.

"I have done that and I shall do more."

"We shall inform you once the fires are under control and waning."

Churchill turned to Sinclair. "What are you doing to prepare for tonight's raid, as the Hun will surely return in an effort to compound the destruction?"

"We considered moving the northern and Irish squadrons, but that will take more than a day to complete and would leave them devoid of night defense fighter coverage in those areas. We have temporarily halted day fighter operations and ordered those ground crews to service the night fighter aircraft, to give the flight and ground crews the maximum rest we can. Fighter Command's controllers are prepared for tonight, should they return to London. This effort will make us perilously thin over the Midlands and North Country."

"It is a risk we must take."

"Yes sir. I must add a footnote, Winston; your nephew performed his role perfectly last night. He had worked all day on cross-Channel offensive operations, and then orchestrated a masterful defense all through the long night. He literally collapsed from exhaustion once the enemy retreated at dawn and the last of the squadrons landed safely. They covered him up with a blanket on the floor, to let him sleep."

"Thank you for your kind words, Archie. John is a good man with a bright future."

"Indeed."

"Do you have any questions, Pug?"

"No sir."

Churchill looked back to the two ministers. "You are welcome to hole up with us out here in the country, gentlemen."

"Thank you, sir," answered Morrison. "We must return." Sinclair nodded his head in agreement.

"I am sorely tempted to go with you."

"Please do not," interjected Herbert. "To be blunt, Winston, your presence would be a distraction at this critical stage. We shall do our best to keep you informed."

"Then, we need to set up a radio network, as the telephone lines have apparently been seriously damaged as well."

"I will see to it," Archie Sinclair answered.

"Excellent. Then, as we say in the nautical services, Godspeed and following winds."

"Thank you, sir," the two ministers answered in unison.

All four men departed, once again, leaving Winston Churchill alone with his thoughts. *We shall learn from this. We will improve our defenses. And, I vow to return this wonton destruction of a great city in full measure when the time comes. This insult shall not go unanswered. Their day of reckoning is coming.*

Monday, 30.December.1940
Springwood Estate
4097 Albany Post Road
Hyde Park, Dutchess County, New York
United States of America
11:10 hours

The manor house that served as Franklin Roosevelt's sanctuary presented a unique combination of Dutch colonial architecture tweaked with New York country practicality. He truly smiled every time he saw the house as they drove up the driveway. He had another few days left on the scheduled holiday break from the demands of Washington and the rigors of the approaching war.

Senior Military Aide to the President Major General Edwin Martin 'Pa' Watson, USA [USMA 1908] had been in his position since Franklin had become President in 1933, and since he had been a colonel. He had picked up his nickname from his classmates at West Point, having been in and out of the Military Academy several times before he managed to graduate. He was also the holder of the Silver Star for valor in combat during the Great War. Roosevelt had become comfortable with Watson and relied on his experience and judgment . . . and if truth be told, he liked Watson's backchannel connections into the Army and the War Department. Watson had the holiday duty, largely to give Harry Hopkins a long holiday break before departing on his mission to London. Watson joined the President in his study.

"Sir, we have information from the London Embassy."

"Do tell, 'Pa.'"

"The Germans carried out a multi-wave, incendiary attack last night until dawn. Major fires are still burning. The Embassy sustained some blast damage from bomb impacts nearby, but not significant or serious damage to our buildings, and all personnel are safe . . . no injuries. They did note they have no water service and suspect the Germans managed to damage the water supply system, which may be contributing to the spread of the fires. They have been unable to make their usual contacts in the government to obtain a more accurate picture. The telephone system has apparently been seriously damaged as well."

"Where is Churchill?"

"We did ask about the Prime Minister. The latest information available to the embassy staff indicated he was safe in the country at Ditchley House."

"Good. I cannot imagine how events might turn at this precarious moment if something happened to him in all this."

"Yes sir."

"What is the prognosis?"

"The embassy has none from the government. They have such limited information so far. The extent of their available sources appears to be limited to personal observations from the rooftop of the embassy building. They even tried to send a runner – a messenger – to the Home Office, but he was turned back by emergency services personnel, who stated that all streets were blocked."

"That is dreadful . . . absolutely tragic . . . such a great and magnificent city."

"Yes sir. We told them we needed information as soon as they could acquire it. It is late afternoon in London. They can see fires all around them . . . the smoke is very thick. Based on what little we know, it may be several days, if not longer, for the fire services to gain control of the fires. Then, they will have to deal with the dead and injured they cannot yet reach, and certainly unexploded ordnance to be made safe. Frankly, given what we are hearing so far, recovery from last night's raid may take weeks."

"And, I doubt the Germans will let up on what the Press is calling The Blitz."

"If I was them, I would not let up a minute. They appear to have had a significant success last night. The principles of warfare dictate the exploitation of successes."

"Then, I suppose the best we can hope for is the Germans may not recognize their success for several days and turn their attention elsewhere."

"I suppose there is always hope, Mister President. However, hope is not a bank-able commodity in warfare."

"Is there any we can do to help them?"

"Short of attacking Germany to divert attention and resources . . . no. We can certainly ask the Chief of Staff to see if the Army has any ideas."

Franklin Roosevelt held Watson's eyes while he considered the options. "No, no need to bother them during the holiday break. We all have families, even you, 'Pa.'"

"It is my honor to serve, Mister President. Harry leaves in a few days and he needs the rest."

"Yes, but we should have had Frances come up here with you. Eleanor would have appreciated the feminine company."

"Thank you, sir. She is spending the holidays with her family. She knows quite well that you keep me pretty busy," he said and chuckled slightly to accentuate his words.

"Yes, well, I am most grateful for your service, 'Ed' . . . and I am appreciative of your wife's sacrifice to allow your service."

"Thank you, again, Mister President. If there is nothing else, I will go check to see if communications has received any further information. I'll also poke the duty staff at the War Department to see what they may know."

"Thank you, 'Ed.'"

Watson departed and closed the door behind him. Franklin could not and did not want to even imagine what Londoners were going through, and the whole of the British people for that matter. *Hopefully, Harry will be able to convey our commitment to Winston and the British. We simply must get this lend-lease legislation passed as quickly as humanly possible. I do not want to find out the answer to the question of how long they can hold out against this atrocious and damnable Blitz, as they call it?*

—

Chapter 9

Vision is the art of seeing things invisible.

- Jonathan Swift

Wednesday, 1.January.1941
Ditchley Park
Enstone, Oxfordshire, England
United Kingdom
10:35 hours

"Jock," Churchill called from his bed.

His duty assistant private secretary opened the bedroom door within seconds. "Yes sir?"

"I think I have recovered from last night's celebration of the New Year after a comfortable sleep. I'll take my breakfast now, and please fetch one of the ladies."

"Yes sir. Right away."

By ladies, Jock Colville knew the Prime Minister meant one of the ladies from the duty stenographer pool that constantly attended to his transcription needs virtually 24 hours per day, every day. Colville immediately called the kitchen. They would stop their preparations for lunch and immediately prepare Churchill's usual breakfast—two eggs, sunnyside up, fried diced potatoes and wheat toast with marmalade. He also knew Churchill's valet, Frank Sawyers, would be waiting in the kitchen to deliver the bed breakfast tray to his employer. Next, Colville called the staff office and asked for a stenographer.

Miss Jennifer Scores, one of Churchill's longer serving stenographers, arrived at the Prime Minister's bedroom door within minutes and before his breakfast tray. "Anything special?" she immediately asked Jock sitting outside at a small desk.

"No, not that I'm aware of. It should be fairly simple, since he did not ask for more than one."

Scores asked, "May I go in?"

"Yes please. His breakfast is due up shortly."

Scores took a deep breath, knocked twice on the door and entered. "Good morning, Prime Minister, how may I be of service?"

"Good morning to you, Miss Scores." He gestured impatiently to the duty, straight back, wooden chair next to his bed. Jennifer took up her station, flipped open her steno-book and held the first of her half dozen, sharpened, graphite pencils in the ready position.

"Before we begin, I simply must tell you I heard the most extraordinary radio broadcast, early New Year's Eve morning. President Roosevelt gave one of his exceptional fireside chats to the American people, and we were listening attentively. Did you happen to hear it?"

With an expressionless face, she looked at Churchill and answered, "I believe I was asleep."

"Yes, yes, it was quite early in the morning at our time. Jock and Pug stayed up with me to hear it. A most impressive speech I must say. Anyway, enough frivolity, I need to send a personal note to President Roosevelt. Please date it today—New Year's Day.

"My dear Franklin," he began. Scores focused on her notepad. "First and foremost comma Clementine and I genuinely wish you and Eleanor a happy and delightful New Year period new paragraph I listened with rapt fascination to your latest fireside chat to the American people period I was truly and unabashedly brought to tears dash the great arsenal of democracy comma indeed exclamation point I can think of no better term for your place on the world stage period I have been so moved by your personal response to my impassioned plea of eight December period Your creation of this lend dash lease program is genius dash pure genius period new paragraph Thank you for so very much for the courtesy of keeping me informed of your legislative plan and progress for passage period Lord Lothian . . ." The knock at the door interrupted his dictation. "Yes, yes," he shouted. "Let's have it." Colville opened the door for Sawyers to enter, carrying the breakfast tray. "Where was I?" he asked Scores, as Sawyers placed the tray over the covers across Churchill's lap."

"You began a new sentence with 'Lord Lothian,'" responded Scores.

Sawyers uncovered the dish. Churchill did not touch his breakfast. Sawyers departed the room and closed the door.

"Yes. Lord Lothian's unfortunate passing does complicate this situation period The chargé in Washington shall remain ready to assist in any manner you may decide period Indeed comma all of His Majesty's Government is prepared to render support as you may wish period new paragraph Again comma we wish you and your family a productive comma prosperous and safe New Year period Yours truly in friendship." Churchill waited a few moments for her to finish her unique scribbles. "Please read it back for me."

Scores did as she was requested without the punctuation notations in flawless fashion.

"Excellent. Pray let me have that in short order."

"You shall have the transcription within the hour, Prime Minister."

"Very well. Excellent. Now, hop to it Miss Scores."

The stenographer rose and departed. Churchill stared at the door for several moments, and then turned to his breakfast before him.

—

Saturday, 4.January.1941
RAF Church Fenton
Tadcaster, North Yorkshire, England
United Kingdom
09:00 hours

"**W**elcome back, gentlemen," said Squadron Leader Churchill. "We are back to being a whole squadron, once again. I trust everyone enjoyed a nice protracted holiday break."

"You bet, Skipper. Best piece of ass I've ever had," offered Roley Rigby.

The Dispersal Hut erupted in laughter.

Baggy held up his hand. "No need for vulgarity, Roley. I think it safe to say you are a randy bunch."

"Got that right Skipper," Salt Morton added.

"Enough," shouted Baggy. "We are not here for your carnal pleasures. You are bloody fighter pilots. You have only one purpose . . . fly the aeroplanes His Majesty's Government provides you to kill Germans. The Air Ministry was gracious enough to give you extra time to rest. Whether you used that time for rest is not my affair. It is now time to get back to work." Churchill waited to see if any of his rowdy pilots wanted to spout off. "Fine. Now, pay attention. I trust each of you followed orders to pack your personal effects and place them on the lorry outside the Mess. We will depart shortly to our new base at RAF Kirton-in-Lindsey. We will remain in One Two Group and at least a little closer to the action."

"About damn time," Rocket Downing interjected.

"Be careful what you wish for. Most of you have been fortunate. As the veterans of The Battle will attest, only a few months ago, we were begging for relief, for sleep, for some rest from the relentless attacks. So, count your blessings. You are not in London." Again, he waited. "I am informed that we should expect to be declared operational upon arrival at Kirton and after we complete an area orientation training flight."

"Does that mean we're going to get into this fight?" Horse Harrow asked.

"Some of us have been in this fight," mumbled Rusty Bateman.

Churchill nodded his head. "Yes . . . certainly closer. I have not been informed of any specific plans, but once we are declared operational, we are fully available for combat operations. The night fighters are very busy each night. For the day fighters, we can expect to eventually participate in cross-

Channel raid operations. Until then, we will fly patrols and cover missions for those squadrons venturing into France and Belgium. I don't have any further information, yet. So, first things first."

Squadron Leader Churchill briefed the transit mission. The distance to travel was short – just 50 miles. The flight to RAF Kirton-in-Lindsey would take all of 15 minutes. They would take off as a squadron and land as a squadron. He covered the necessary radio frequencies and call signs. He expected to land at Kirton, occupy their new Dispersal Hut, and then fly their required orientation flight.

"Any questions?" Baggy looked to each pilot and receive a negative reply gesture. "Very well, then, grab your kit and let's mount up. Corporal Harris, if you would be so kind, please notify Group we are in transit."

"Yes sir."

"We will see you this afternoon at Kirton-in-Lindsey."

"Yes sir."

All of the pilots rose, to collect their flight equipment. Brian as well as most of the pilots already had their Sidcot suits on over their uniforms, while the remainder donned their Sidcot suits before leaving the Dispersal Hut. The insulated, overall, flight suit was first developed by and named for Wing Commander Frederick Sidney Cotton, OBE, during his service in the Great War, to lessen the effects of cold at altitude in the open cockpit airplanes of the day. The suits dampened the winter cold on the ground, much better than any overcoat. They all liked the new version of the Sidcot suit with its fur-lined collar. They had received the new flight suits just last month.

"Any special instructions, Boss?" asked Dusty Langford with Bulldog Tolly listening as they walked.

"Nope," answered Brian. "We'll fly our usual 'Vic' off the right wing of Blue Section." They both nodded their heads.

Baggy set a slow pace for their start, first flight of the day checks and take off. The transit flight south was indeed brief. They landed without incident. A 'follow me' vehicle led them to their assigned parking area. Several other Spitfire and Hurricane squadrons were located at the base – two Spit squadrons and No.71 made the third Hurri squadron. Brian recognized the 'QJ' designator of No.616 Squadron Spitfires and the 'SW' designator for No.253 Squadron Hurricanes, but did not see the designators for the other assigned squadrons. They shutdown and secured their aircraft. A skeleton segment of their ground crews chocked their wheels. A sign on the door of the small, nearby, green, clapboard hut marked their new Dispersal Hut.

Welcome
No. 71
Squadron

Someone had gone to the effort of lighting their coal-fired heater, giving the interior pleasant warmth to take a bite out of the winter chill.

A base sergeant gave the pilots a quick briefing on procedures and a short tour of the necessary facilities, the most important being the Officer's Mess and Bar. If they had not been told where they were, this could have been at any one of a dozen similar fighter bases in England. They all had similar construction, organization and feel to them. So, this would be home . . . until they were moved, again.

—

Saturday, 4.January.1941
RAF Kirton-in-Lindsey
Kirton-in-Lindsey, Lincolnshire, England
United Kingdom
10:30 hours

Squadron Leader Churchill clapped his hands sharply for attention. It took a few minutes for the pilots to settle down. "I know this is a bit rushed, but the weather guessers are suggesting we might have a spate of freezing rain this afternoon. So, I want to get the required area orientation flight completed and back here before lunch ends at the Mess."

Baggy moved to the wall-mounted map. He pointed to the key checkpoints they would pass. The emphasis clearly fell upon the coastal landmarks of the sector they would be expected to support. Brian remembered the shipping patrols during the missions of last July. Yet, flying was flying; Brian enjoyed it all.

"Let's get this done," Baggy concluded.

The clouds were darkening to the west as the pilots stepped out of their new Dispersal Hut. The pilots strapped into their machines, started their engines, completed their checks and taxied for takeoff. Once all the fighters were in the air, cleaned up and in position, Baggy turned the squadron to the west. The weather looked worse in the air. Fortunately, it was still beyond their intended route of flight. They passed south of Sheffield, skirted in eastern edge of Manchester, and the northern edge of Leeds and York. Baggy climbed the squadron to 15,000 feet altitude, as high as they could reasonably go and remain under the high overcast clouds. He turned them more northerly to pick up the eastern coastline at the Middleborough Inlet, and then turned southeast several miles off the coast. Baggy also spread the squadron formation, so each pilot could see the geographical landmarks of their expected area of operations.

When they passed Flamborough Head, Brian remembered his high school history lesson and the famous naval battle fought down there 161 years earlier. *How history turns. Two sail frigates fought a desperate battle down there. With his USS* Bon Homme Richard *devastated and when the demand for his surrender came, Captain John Paul Jones famously and defiantly shouted, "I have not yet begun to fight!" By the tenacity of Jones and his crew, it was the captain of HMS* Serapis *that eventually surrendered. We were mortal enemies in that earlier battle, and now, here I am flying a Hurricane fighter in defense of Great Britain. I wonder if anyone else feels the irony and remembers the history made off Flamborough Head?*

They continued on south past the Humber Estuary, Hull and The Wash. Baggy initiated a wide, descending turn to seaward, off the coast from Norwich. He leveled them off at 500 feet, as they tracked back north along the coastline to give each pilot a low angle view of the landmarks. Baggy throttled back to avoid overheating the engines and save fuel. Once they reached Middlesbrough Inlet, again, they turned south, heading direct to Kirton-in-Lindsey.

The overcast had come down substantially during their flight. Rain spatters began to appear on Brian's windscreen. Brian checked both wings to see if he was picking up ice. So far, so good. He checked both wingmen and received a thumbs-up as the visibility began to decrease and the rain picked up. Baggy increased their speed. As they passed York, they popped out of the rain band. A few minutes later, they spotted their new home base.

Baggy set them up for a squadron landing that was accomplished in fine fashion. Brian kept his canopy closed to minimize the chill in the unheated cockpit. The first drops of rain appeared on the canopy as the engine and propeller stopped, and Brian completed the shutdown of his aircraft. He unstrapped from the seat and his parachute before he slid the canopy back. Brian jumped out and immediately closed the canopy to protect the interior from the approaching rain.

"No squawks," Brian shouted to his crew chief, Corporal Henry Jacobs.

"Very well, sir. We'll have to wait for the rain to stop before filling her with petrol."

Brian jumped down off the left wing. "That should work. I think we are done for the day." He jogged toward the Dispersal Hut.

"Very well, sir," Jacobs shouted to the retreating form of Flying Officer Drummond.

Once all the pilots were inside, Corporal Harris informed them. "Skipper is on the tellie to Group. Please remain here."

"It's lunchtime, James," protested Horse Harrow.

"I understand that, Mister Harrow. I am simply informing you of Squadron Leader Churchill's order."

Several intermingled, inaudible grumbles punctuated the exchange. They waited not so patiently. When Baggy finally appeared from his office, the pilots quieted.

"Well, gentlemen, after our tortuous months of training, Fighter Command has seen fit to declare our humble squadron operational."

The pilots cheered and offered shouts of bravado to each other. Brian did not participate. He knew quite well what the announcement meant, and he still held doubts about the cohesion of this squadron. They still seemed to be individuals, pretending to be a fighter squadron.

Churchill held up his right hand for calm. "Group has released us for the afternoon. We have a patrol mission in the morning. Let us get over to the Mess for lunch before the steward's stop serving. We have the afternoon to celebrate this milestone. We are back at it tomorrow morning. I implore you . . . don't do anything stupid."

They secured for the day. Unfortunately, the rain had become steady. At least it was not freezing, yet. Corporal Harris called Transport for a covered lorry. They waited five minutes and quickly loaded on the truck. Corporal Harris closed the door behind him and was the last man on the truck. The debate as to whether to brave the rain for the journey to their favorite public house up the B1398 roadway to the edge of the village would come after lunch. They all wanted to eat.

—

Sunday, 5. January. 1941
RAF Kirton-in-Lindsey
Kirton-in-Lindsey, Lincolnshire, England
United Kingdom

Fortunately, the weather system from yesterday passed through quickly without the freezing rain the meteorologists had forecast, leaving them with a clear, crisp day. They launched on their first operational mission as No.71 Squadron – a convoy escort patrol. They picked up Convoy SNOW just south of The Wash – 15 merchant ships out of London with two destroyers as their naval escort. The squadron took their station in a long racetrack pattern, displaced to seaward, so they could keep an eye on their charges, scan the North Sea for the slightest sign of a U-boat lurking about, and the sky for some stray airborne attacker that might have slipped through the Chain Home radar network. These patrols were always rather mundane, but they carried their own tension as well, largely for what might happen, what they did not see.

"Eagle Leader, this is Boxer calling."

"Go ahead, Boxer. This is Eagle Leader."

"We have a possible bogey southeast of your position, 25 miles, angels two two."

"Roger, Boxer. Break. Eagle Yellow Leader, this is Eagle Leader, dispatch to intercept the bogey."

"Roger, Eagle Leader."

Brian glanced over his left shoulder, past Bulldog Tolly's 'XR-J' Hurricane, just in time to see Rusty's 'XR-D' Hurricane roll right more sharply than usual and Roley Rigby's 'XR-L' Hurricane barely initiated his roll. Roley bunted, pushing the stick forward hard, causing his engine to sputter from fuel starvation. Rusty's fighter just missed Roley's machine. Then, Brian was shocked to see Roley arrest his bunt, to re-fire his engine, and roll right in an apparent attempt to regain his position off Rusty's right wing . . . his attention probably on his section leader. Sweet Sweeny had also rolled, unfortunately with his attention on Bateman as well. They most likely never saw the other, when Sweet's left wing struck Roley's canopy. Both aircraft, now damaged, shuddered, shook and twisted, nearly hitting each other again.

"Impact," Brian broadcast. "Eagle Leader, Eagle Green, Roley and Sweet have collided. I'm breaking off. Eagle Green rolling left, Two, Three, spread right echelon, keep your eyes out."

"I've got it," radioed Rusty.

"Your section, Rusty. We'll cover you."

Brian kept his section in an over-watch position. Roley's Hurricane had entered a slow spin. Sweet's Hurricane was still gyrating. He was struggling with control.

Brian broadcast, "Rusty, stay with Sweet. See if you can get him back to base. I'll see if we can help Roley." Brian checked on his wingmen, rolled and moved toward Roley's spinning Hurricane. Brian could hear Rusty talking to Sweet, but his attention and focus were now on Roley. He closed and slowed his fighter to match Roley. "Eagle Green Two and Three, stand off and orbit clear."

"Roger, Green Leader," Dusty radioed.

Brian noticed them executing his command. He maneuvered his aircraft closer. "Roley, anti-spin controls. You need to stop your spin." Brian checked their altitude. They were passing 8,000 feet. "Roley do something, do anything. You've got to get out of the spin." Brian tried to see Roley's condition. He slowed even closer to the aircraft's stall speed, risking his own loss of control. He caught a glimpse in Roley's cockpit. His head was bloodied and displaced at an odd, unnatural angle by the centrifugal force of the spin. "Eagle Leader,

Eagle Green, call sea rescue. Roley is unconscious."

"Will do. Break. Boxer, this is Eagle Leader. We have an injured pilot. We need Sea Rescue to Eagle Green Leader's position."

"Roger, Eagle Leader. This is Boxer. Eagle Green Leader, hit your Pipsqueak."

Brian switched hands on his control stick, quickly glanced down to his transponder panel, found the squawk switch, and pushed it ON. "Mark, mark."

"Eagle Green Leader, we have you. Sea Rescue is enroute to your position."

"Roley, if you hear me, bale out. You need to get out."

Brian saw Roley several more times. There was no change. They were now passing 3,000 feet. Brian knew this was not going to end well. "Eagle Green Two and Three, maintain angels five."

"Eagle Green Two, roger."

Brian stayed with Roley all the way to the end. There continued to be no change until Roley's damaged Hurricane impacted the North Sea. Brian increased his speed for a safer margin, maintained 500 feet altitude, and set up a circular orbit around the foam of Roley's impact spot. Brian noticed a high-speed boat heading straight toward his position . . . probably out of Grimsby at the mouth of the Humber Estuary. He watched as the rescue boat slowed and stopped at Roley's impact site. They clearly searched the surface. After several minutes and the bubbles had disappeared, the rescue boat crew signaled no signs of a survivor. Brian maintained his orbit for another ten minutes, watching the rescue boat. The boat captain signaled the end of their search. Brian throttled up, leveled his wings, and as his speed increased, he rolled and dove for the water. He adjusted his heading to make a high-speed pass, just off the water surface and ahead of the rescue boat, now headed back to the station. As he passed the boat, he saw the crew wave to him. He pulled up, rocked his wings, and then initiated a climbing, right turn.

"Eagle Green Two and Three, join up as I pass your altitude."

"Eagle Green Two, roger."

"Eagle Leader, this is Eagle Green, no joy on Roley. We will rejoin you shortly."

"Negative, Eagle Green. Return to base."

"Eagle Leader, this is Eagle Green. Wilco." Brian checked to see both wingmen in position. "Boxer, Eagle Green Leader, we are RTB."

"Eagle Green Leader, this is Boxer. Roger. Your vector is good."

Thirty minutes later, Brian called Kirton Tower for landing. Green Section landed, taxied, parked and shutdown. Brian noticed Rusty Bateman's 'XR-D' Hurricane parked in its usual position.

"No squawks, Henry," he said.

"Very well, sir. We will fill her up. If I may ask, sir, what happened up there?"

"We lost Pilot Officer Rigby this afternoon."

"Combat?"

"No . . . a mid-air collision."

"Oh dear."

"Yes, a real tragedy. Skipper is still out with Red Section."

"We'll watch for them, sir. I'm sure the intelligence folks will need to talk to you."

"An understatement, I do believe."

"We'll make things right, sir."

"Thanks, Henry."

Brian walked toward the Dispersal Hut. He really did not want to see Batemen, but the meeting was unavoidable. Langford and Tolly joined him.

"What do we do, now, Boss?" asked Tolly.

"Well, Bulldog, we just put one foot in front of the other and keep doing that until we reach the Hut, and then we step inside."

"So funny, Hunter. You know damn well what I mean."

"Yeah, I know what you mean. I don't know. This has never happened to me. We'll just have to see how this plays out."

They did not speak. They entered the Hut. Bateman was in the corner with his head in his hands. Langford turned toward Bateman. Brian stopped him, shook his head, and turned to Corporal Harris. "Report Green Section Available, once the crews show us refueled."

"Very well, sir."

Brian hung up his flight equipment. He walked back to the door, looked at Corporal Harris, and nodded for their operations clerk to join him outside. James closed the door to the Hut behind, as he stepped outside with Brian. Hunter walked to the end of the building, and then turned to face Corporal Harris. "Where is Pilot Officer Sweeney?"

"He is at the Dispensary for treatment, sir."

"Treatment . . . for what?"

"His right main undercarriage collapsed during landing. I was told he received several cuts and perhaps a broken arm. They are tending to him now."

"Where is his aircraft?"

"The crash crew got the aircraft up on its undercarriage and towed it to Hangar Number Two."

"What is going on with Flying Officer Bateman?"

"The intelligence chief told me they are waiting for Squadron Leader Churchill's return. He has been in the corner since he arrived. What happened up there, if I may ask, sir?"

"Mid-air collision. Pilot Officer Rigby did not make it."

"I am so sorry, Mister Drummond. No wonder Mister Bateman is so withdrawn."

"Yes . . . well . . . it was his mistake, I do believe." *Damn, I should not have said that. What was Rusty thinking . . . rolling in like that?*

"Oh my."

Six Hurricane fighters approached and landed together – the remainder of the squadron. Brian watched the process. Their gunport tapes were still intact. *Whew! Thank goodness . . . no combat.* He looked to Corporal Harris, "You'd better get inside to your station. I suspect the Skipper will not be in a good mood."

"Yes sir. Thank you, sir."

Harris did as he was instructed. Brian remained outside, although the chill was beginning to bite.

Churchill jumped out of his aircraft before the propeller stopped and did not acknowledge his crew chief. He strode purposefully and with anger to his gate. As he neared Dispersal, he looked and gestured to Brian. "Mister Drummond, in my office, if you please." He did not wait for an answer.

Why the hell is he mad at me? I'm not the one who killed one of our pilots.

Brian knocked and entered the squadron leader's office. Churchill gestured for him to close the door. He did not motion for Brian to sit, so he came to attention.

"Of all the pilots, I least expected you to break discipline. This has been a rowdy and unruly bunch from the outset. You have more flight experience and as much combat experience as I do. You hold a DFC, Military Cross and a bloody CBE for your combat contributions, for God's sake. You know better than to break formation like that. We had a mission, which we managed to complete without you and your section, I might add. I am disappointed, Brian. I am depending on you to help these lads be better, not offer them a bad example."

"I am sorry, sir."

"Bugger all, you bloody well should be. I do not want you to make a mistake like that, again. Am I clear?"

"Yes sir."

"Now, I said what I had to say. Beyond your initial mistake, I want to thank you for sticking with Roley. I did not see what happened, but the outcome speaks for itself. What the bloody hell happened?"

"When you ordered Yellow Section to intercept the bogey, I think Rusty was a little too eager. He rolled into Roley faster than expected. Roley bunted to avoid the collision, coughed his engine, and then pulled up to restart and return to his position. Sweet rolled to keep up with Rusty and probably never saw Roley trying to recover. Sweet's right wing struck Roley at the canopy. Based on what I saw, as best I could, while Roley's machine was in a spin, I think the impact broke his neck. There was blood everywhere. I focused on trying to help Roley, which proved worthless. I understand from Corporal Harris that Rusty and Sweet made it back home, but Sweet's right main undercarriage collapsed during landing. Sweet is apparently being treated at the Dispensary. Rusty is stuck in a corner."

"Thank you for your report. I was going to send you up with Rusty, but based on your report, you will need to debrief with the intel guys. I believe you may be the only witness. I'm going to send Whitey out with Rusty in an attempt to not lose another pilot in this tragedy."

"Yes sir. Again, sir, I offer my apology for breaking formation without your direction."

"I appreciate your concern for Roley. I trust you will learn from your mistake."

"Yes sir. Certainly, sir."

"Now, an administrative note, while I have you. Flight Lieutenant Chesley Peterson, a countryman of yours and the highest ranking American in the RAF, is supposed to join us tomorrow."

"I met him last month in London."

Churchill nodded his acknowledgment. "He was supposed to relieve and replace Whitey. Now, I'm going to convince Fighter Command to leave Whitey for the time being. I'll make Peterson Yellow Section leader, and Bateman, if he holds up, will take Roley's position."

"He won't like that, sir."

"Yes, well, he should consider himself fortunate, if he retains his wings."

"Yes sir."

"You are a good man, Brian, and a gifted pilot. You will have your own squadron in due course. We all make mistakes, but it is what we do with those mistakes that really matters."

"Yes sir . . . lesson learned."

"I should hope so. Now, get out of here. Send Whitey in, and get your debriefing completed."

"Yes sir." Brian left and did as he was ordered. This had been a crazy day already, and it was not over, yet. Another pilot lost, and this war was a long way from being over.

—

Monday, 6.January.1941
House of Representatives
Capitol Building
Washington, District of Columbia
United States of America

President Roosevelt entered the House Chamber through the side door to the right of the Speaker's dais. The Members of Congress and the spectators stood as they recognized the President. He ambled into the Chamber with the assistance of General Watson. The process of negotiating the few steps to the Clerk's lectern – the mid-level tier of the Speaker's dais – was not easy for the disabled president. The House remained quiet and patient. When the President was ready at the lectern, he glanced over his left shoulder and nodded to Speaker of the House Samuel Taliaferro 'Sam' Rayburn. President of the Senate Vice President 'Cactus Jack' Garner stood to the Speaker's right – his last State of the Union event. After a contentious last few years, Garner had been replaced on the Democratic Party ticket by Henry Wallace, and 'Cactus Jack' would leave office in a few weeks as Roosevelt began his unprecedented third consecutive term as president on the 20th of January.

The Speaker raised his right hand and waited for quiet. He banged his gavel two times. "Members of Congress, I have the high privilege and distinct honor of presenting to you the President of the United States."

The audience applauded. The shuffling of several hundred people taking their seats replaced the clapping of hands.

The President waited for quiet in the House Chamber. "Mister President, Mister Speaker, Members of the Seventy-seventh Congress, I address you at a moment unprecedented in the history of the Union. I use the word 'unprecedented,' because at no previous time has American security been as seriously threatened from without as it is today.

"Since the permanent formation of our Government under the Constitution, in 1789, most of the periods of crisis in our history have related to our domestic affairs. Fortunately, only one of these – the four-year War Between the States – ever threatened our national unity. Today, thank God, one hundred and thirty million Americans, in forty-eight States, have forgotten points of the compass in our national unity.

"We need not overemphasize imperfections in the Peace of Versailles. We need not harp on failure of the democracies to deal with problems of world reconstruction. We should remember that the Peace of 1919 was far less unjust than the kind of 'pacification' which began even before Munich, and which is being carried on under the new order of tyranny that seeks to spread over every continent today. The American people have unalterably set their faces against that tyranny.

"Every realist knows that the democratic way of life is at this moment being directly assailed in every part of the world – assailed either by arms, or by secret spreading of poisonous propaganda by those who seek to destroy unity and promote discord in nations that are still at peace.

"During sixteen long months, this assault has blotted out the whole pattern of democratic life in an appalling number of independent nations, great and small. The assailants are still on the march, threatening other nations, great and small.

"Therefore, as your President, performing my constitutional duty to 'give to the Congress information of the state of the Union,' I find it, unhappily, necessary to report that the future and the safety of our country and of our democracy are overwhelmingly involved in events far beyond our borders.

"Armed defense of democratic existence is now being gallantly waged in four continents. If that defense fails, all the population and all the resources of Europe, Asia, Africa and Australasia will be dominated by the conquerors. Let us remember that the total of those populations and their resources in those four continents greatly exceeds the sum total of the population and the resources of the whole of the Western Hemisphere – many times over.

"I have recently pointed out how quickly the tempo of modern warfare could bring into our very midst the physical attack, which we must eventually expect, if the dictator nations win this war.

"That is why the future of all the American Republics is today in serious danger.

"That is why this Annual Message to the Congress is unique in our history.

"Our national policy is this:

"First, by an impressive expression of the public will and without regard to partisanship, we are committed to all-inclusive national defense.

"Second, we are committed to full support of all those resolute peoples, everywhere, who are resisting aggression and are thereby keeping war away from our Hemisphere.

"Third, we are committed to the proposition that principles of morality and considerations for our own security will never permit us to acquiesce in a peace dictated by aggressors and sponsored by appeasers. We know that enduring peace cannot be bought at the cost of other people's freedom.

"Therefore, the immediate need is a swift and driving increase in our armament production.

"Leaders of industry and labor have responded to our summons. Goals of speed have been set. Actual experience is improving and speeding up our methods of production with every passing day. And today's best is not good enough for tomorrow.

Once more, applause caused the President to pause, but he did not move, other than the turn the page on his script.

"I ask this Congress for authority and for funds sufficient to manufacture additional munitions and war supplies of many kinds, to be turned over to those nations which are now in actual war with aggressor nations.

"Our most useful and immediate role is to act as an arsenal for them as well as for ourselves. They do not need manpower, but they do need billions of dollars' worth of the weapons of defense.

"Let us also say to the democracies: 'We Americans are vitally concerned in your defense of freedom. We are putting forth our energies, our resources and our organizing powers to give you the strength to regain and maintain a free world. We shall send you, in ever-increasing numbers, ships, planes, tanks, and guns. This is our purpose and our pledge.'

"In fulfillment of this purpose, we will not be intimidated by the threats of dictators that they will regard as a breach of international law, or as an act of war our aid to the democracies, which dare to resist their aggression. Such aid is not an act of war, even if a dictator should unilaterally proclaim it so to be."

General applause punctuated the President's speech, again.

"When the dictators, if the dictators, are ready to make war upon us, they will not wait for an act of war on our part. They did not wait for Norway, or Belgium, or the Netherlands to commit an act of war."

Applause filled the House Chamber.

"I have called for personal sacrifice. I am assured of the willingness of almost all Americans to respond to that call.

"A part of the sacrifice means the payment of more money in taxes. In my Budget Message, I shall recommend that a greater portion of this great defense program be paid for from taxation than we are paying today. No person should try, or be allowed, to get rich out of this program; and the principle of tax payments in accordance with ability to pay should be constantly before our eyes to guide our legislation.

"In the future days, which we seek to make secure, we look forward to a world founded upon four essential human freedoms.

"The first is freedom of speech and expression.

"The second is freedom of every person to worship God in his own way.

"The third is freedom from want – which means economic understandings which will secure to every nation a healthy peacetime life for its inhabitants.

"The fourth is freedom from fear – which means a world-wide reduction of armaments to such a point and in such a thorough fashion that no nation will be in a position to commit an act of physical aggression against any neighbor."

Respectful applause came from the audience.

President Roosevelt continued, "That is no vision of a distant millennium. It is a definite basis for a kind of world attainable in our own time and generation. That kind of world is the very antithesis of the so-called new order of tyranny, which the dictators seek to create with the crash of a bomb.

"To that new order, we oppose the greater conception – the moral order. A good society is able to face schemes of world domination and foreign revolutions alike without fear.

"Since the beginning of our American history, we have been engaged in change – in a perpetual peaceful revolution – a revolution, which goes on steadily, quietly, adjusting itself to changing conditions – without the concentration camp or the quick-lime in the ditch. The world order, which we seek, is the cooperation of free countries, working together in a friendly, civilized society.

"This nation has placed its destiny in the hands, and heads, and hearts of its millions of free men and women; and its faith in freedom under the guidance of God. Freedom means the supremacy of human rights everywhere. Our support goes to those who struggle to gain those rights or keep them. Our strength is our unity of purpose. To that high concept, there can be no end save victory."

The entire chamber – both houses and both parties – stood and applauded the President's speech. Roosevelt nodded his head in appreciation and waved his hand several times. He awkwardly turned, took a difficult step toward the upper tier of the Speaker's dais, and then shook the proffered hands of Speaker Rayburn and Vice President Garner. President Roosevelt signaled to General Watson to come help him. 'Pa' Watson moved swiftly and deftly to the President's side. Roosevelt waved a few more times, took Watson's arm, and together, they made their way out of the House Chamber.

Tuesday, 7. January. 1941
Off Folkestone
Folkestone, Kent, England
United Kingdom

The entire squadron launched at mid-morning and had taken up their long, racetrack, holding pattern just off the southeast coast. 'Pete' Peterson had indeed joined the squadron yesterday, as the Skipper had indicated, and he was currently flying as Yellow Section leader with Rusty Bateman relegated to 'Pete's right wing position. 'Pete' had successfully flown his orientation flight with the commanding officer. Rusty seemed to take the change in stride and risen from the hole of depression he had dug for himself.

They were flying as the covering force for his old squadron that was flying another cross-Channel fighter sweep of German airfields in Northern France. They waddled along at maximum endurance thrust and airspeed. These missions were not much more exciting than protection of shipping missions, but they had more potential these days. Brian had heard the stories directly from Jonathan and Jeremy Morrison, who had led his squadron on the most successful fighter sweep to date, destroying seven bombers, two fighters on the ground and another one in the air, as well as shooting up hangars, maintenance vehicles and most spectacularly an ammunition bunker that nearly swallowed up one of his pilots.

"Eagle, Lumba calling."

"Lumba, Eagle, go ahead."

"Primary extended. No opposition noted. You will be extended for cover. Don Two alerted, prepared for your bingo and quick turn."

"Roger, Lumba."

Baggy did not need to explain the instructions. They would continue their holding orbit waiting on No.609 Squadron to return. *They must be having a good hunt to extend their mission into their aerial combat fuel reserve. I can't wait to hear Jonathan's stories.* Brian kept his sight scan on the southern approaches looking for their sister squadron and object of this mission. RAF Hawkinge was now their designate divert base for refueling, since they had nearly reached the bingo fuel level – the remaining fuel to return to their base. So, they droned on as they waited.

The winter weather was clear with only a few middle altitude clouds off to the east. During one turn back to the east, Brian looked off to the west, down the coast. He could see Brighton. *Amazing what these coastal villages have seen. These waters were crowded with ships, boats, and almost anything that would float back last May and June. That was quite some weekend.* Brian had met Rosemary Kensington, Jonathan's sister, at the beachside resort town. *Now, that had been some weekend. Whoa, I need to get back to Charlotte. Get your mind back on your work, you idiot.*

It took a few more turns before someone broadcast, "Tally ho!" Brian quickly scanned to the south. Sure enough, 12 Spitfires in perfect formation tracking north, several thousand feet below them. Brian searched the sky behind the returning squadron – above and below. He could not see any pursuers. That had to be a good mission.

Baggy held their orbit as the No.609 Squadron Spitfires passed ahead of and below them. "Lumba, this is Eagle Leader calling."

"Eagle Leader, this is Lumba. Go ahead."

"Lumba, Eagle, primary back feet dry. No pursuit."

"Roger, Eagle Leader. You are released to bingo Don Two."

"Roger Lumba."

Baggy did not alter this throttle setting and simply began a gradual descent. He showed no sign of urgency, which meant he would take them into RAF Hawkinge for fuel and probably a bite of lunch before heading back north to RAF Kirton-in-Lindsey. *Another uneventful, boring mission.* Yet, Brian knew instinctively that unexciting missions would eventually give way to more serious, action-packed sorties; perhaps, not as exciting as last summer, but certainly equally as serious. *We did what we were directed to do, and we did it well, by the numbers.*

—

Thursday, 9.January.1941
Cabinet War Rooms
New Public Offices
Whitehall, London, England
United Kingdom

"Excuse me, Prime Minister, Mister Hopkins has arrived," announced Assistant Private Secretary John Martin, who had the duty, tending to the Prime Minister's affairs.

"Please show him in, John."

Churchill waited in his private study underground for Martin to retrieve their distinguished guest. Winston waited patiently, feigned attention to the accumulated paperwork. The knock on the door marked the moment. The door opened just enough for Martin to appear.

"Sir, Mister Harry Hopkins."

Churchill nodded his head and moved around his desk to greet his guest. Winston knew precisely how important this rather frail, mousy looking man was to President Roosevelt, and thus to him and the British people. Winston extended his right hand, "I am honored to finally meet you, Mister Hopkins. May I call you Harry?"

Martin closed the door, leaving the two men alone for private discussions.

"By all means, Prime Minister."

"Please, please, Harry, I prefer Winston among friends."

"As you wish, sir."

Winston motioned for Hopkins to take a chair at the small conference table.

"Welcome to our underground world of perpetual light, without wind or sunlight. I must apologize for our humble accommodations, Harry. These are the times in which we live."

"What the Germans are doing to this beautiful and historic city is criminal and horrific," Hopkins stated.

"Yes, indeed, and yet we endure, as we have for four months of this damnable, nightly Blitz. Unfortunately, my dear Harry," Winston said and glanced at his desk clock, "in another hour, it shall be sunset, and the Huns will not be far behind. You are safe with us, as you will experience what Londoners have lived through every night."

"We heard about the Second Great Fire. The President received daily, almost hourly, reports on what happened that night."

"In some respects, the fires they started that night, not quite a fortnight ago, were worse than the Great Fire of 1666. Those fires consumed more of the city, but we had far fewer casualties than the Great Fire. It took the Fire Brigade nearly a week to extinguish the fires, all while the Huns tried to add to the destruction. The damage to our water system has still not recovered in some areas."

"Terrible . . . just tragic."

"As ugly as it is now, they shall reap the whirlwind soon enough . . . with your help."

Hopkins smiled. "Well, Winston, that is the primary reason the President asked me to make the journey on his behalf to personally convey his message. I am to inform you the so-called Lend-Lease bill is to be introduced in Congress tomorrow. This is the legislation that grew from your December message to the President and your subsequent communications. We can make no promises regarding whether or when the legislation will be passed, but we have done the groundwork with congressional leaders in both political parties to move this bill as quickly as possible. I must also say our efforts still have substantial opposition, not least of which are Charles Lindbergh and Joe Kennedy."

"Ah, my good friend . . . the former ambassador.

"One and the same."

"The gift that keeps on giving."

"Indeed. Yet, we believe the America Firsters do not have the influence or sway they did six months ago . . . before you beat back the German invasion. Sympathy is growing steadily as 'Ed' Murrow has described The Blitz to the American people."

Edward R. 'Ed' Murrow, born Egbert Roscoe Murrow, had joined CBS Radio in 1935, and had been assigned to cover European events for CBS Radio in 1937. As the Battle of Britain raged during the summer of 1940, Murrow began a near daily evening broadcast in August 1940, called *London After Dark*, as part of a joint venture between CBS Radio and BBC Radio that brought home the realities of modern warfare to listeners around the world and especially in the still isolationist bent United States.

"It was a close run thing, it should be said. I'm certain you and the President recognize we were extraordinarily vulnerable last summer. The bulk of our ground combat capacity was snatched from the jaws of humiliating defeat, and they came off those beaches in France and Belgium with none of their heavy armaments – artillery, armor, stockpiles of ammunition and fuel. We need those precious supplies from American arsenals and industry."

"The President has taken enormous political risk to provide the supplies you need. I was with the President when your words stimulated his epiphany. The one, single word in your long message that was 'loan.' We appreciate your candor regarding your financial situation, and frankly that was the issue that caused the President the most pause. That one word got us over the hump."

"We are extraordinarily grateful for the President's vision and commitment."

"The President is committed to doing his utmost to assist, but I must confess on a personal level that I worry he may be getting too far ahead of the American people. Fortunately, he was re-elected last November, and he begins his third term later this month, so he has more maneuvering room. I just urge you to be sensitive to the President's political position."

"I can assure you, Harry, I am quite sensitive to the President's position, and I have no intention of compromising the President's position."

Hopkins nodded his acknowledgment. "President Roosevelt approved the military staff exchange and coordination effort to begin later this month. He also asked me to inform you that Admiral Bill Leahy presented his ambassadorial credentials to Marshal Pétain, yesterday. The expectation is our ambassador to Vichy France will give us both an intelligence window into the Third Reich."

Churchill smiled. "Thank you for the staff exchange. Our new ambassador, Lord Halifax, will depart early next week. I would like you to make the journey with us to send off Lord Halifax. The assigned military staff officers for the exchange conference will travel with Lord Halifax aboard the battleship HMS *King George the Fifth*. Regarding your diplomatic overture to Vichy, I would encourage you to not hold much hope of that potential being realized. Our experience with the Vichy French has not been . . . shall we say . . . friendly, which precipitated our naval action at Oran and Mers-el-Kebir."

"Understood, but at least we can try."

"It is my understanding from Colonel Donovan's itinerary that he intends to meet with Ambassador Leahy later this month. He has completed his first external visit to Gibraltar Station."

Hopkins lapsed into contemplation. Winston felt the need to change the subject.

"I understand from Franklin's last communication that you will be with us for a fortnight."

"Yes sir."

"Where are you staying?"

"Claridge's in Mayfair."

"Excellent hotel. You should be quite comfortable. I trust your itinerary reflects joining me at Ditchley House this weekend."

"If that is acceptable, Winston."

"Acceptable," laughed Churchill, "I would like to insist, my dear friend. We have so much to discuss and for your task to collect all the information you seek to fulfill your mission for Franklin."

"I am at your service and convenience, Winston."

"Excellent, then I would like you to ride with me. We will leave here tomorrow afternoon by limousine. Once we are out of the city, the drive is less torturous and depressing, and usually takes two to three hours."

"I look forward to the journey and being your guest at Ditchley. It will be a new experience for me. I have not seen Ditchley Park, yet."

"Beautiful country, quite safe. The manor house and grounds were purchased by your countryman and now conservative member Ronald Tree."

The knock at the door interrupted them. John Martin poked his head through the cracked open door. "The War Cabinet has gathered, sir." Winston nodded his head to Martin and turned back to Hopkins.

"Ronald Tree . . . from the Marshall Field family," said Harry.

"Yes, precisely. Now, I have a War Cabinet meeting pending, and I would like you to attend as a distinguished observer."

"I would be honored, Winston. Thank you."

Churchill stood, followed by Hopkins. "With your permission, Harry, I would like to inform the War Cabinet of your news regarding the war material legislation."

"By all means."

"Excellent. Thank you for that. Now, let's attend to business."

Churchill and Hopkins left the Prime Minister's room, and walked back toward the entrance to the underground bunker and the Cabinet Conference Room. Harry Hopkins' official visit to England had begun.

—

Chapter 10

Don't quote Latin;
say what you have to say,
and then sit down.

- Duke of Wellington

Saturday, 11.January.1941
Standing Oak Farm
Winchester, Hampshire, England
United Kingdom

Charlotte walked from the barn to the front door of the main house as Brian's taxi approached. *Well, shucks, looks like I don't get the same welcome as last month.* She was dressed in her heavy winter work coat, overalls and muck boots. Brian paid the driver and thanked him for his service. The crunch of gravel faded as the taxi departed. They embraced and kissed.

"Welcome home, Brian."

"Thanks," he answered. "I was lucky to get a three-day pass. Is everything OK?"

"It's nearly lunch time," she said and turned toward the front door. "Are you hungry?"

Brian stopped.

Charlotte did not hear his footsteps with hers. She stopped and turned to him. "What's wrong?"

Brian stepped toward her, grasped both shoulders, looked into her gorgeous eyes, smiled and said, "There is nothing wrong with me. More importantly, what is eating at you?"

Charlotte tried to ignore his question and stare him down. Her strength broke. "I'm so sorry, Brian," she gurgled and began to cry. "What have we done? What have I done?"

"What do you mean? What happened? What did we do?"

Charlotte embraced him, and then stepped back. "I need to get out of these muck boots. Go inside. Make yourself comfortable. I baked some biscuits this morning. The plate is on the kitchen table. I'll come back and make us a pot of tea. Then, we can talk." She did not wait for an answer and turned to walk back to the barn.

Brian stepped to follow her. She must have heard his steps. Without looking at him, she raised her left hand and said, "No. Go inside. I'm just going to change shoes. I'll be there forthwith."

Brian stopped, watched her continue to the barn, and then did as she requested. He went inside. The sweet aroma of fresh bread and cookies greeted him, and oddly reminded him of home. His mother's cooking always made him feel good. Charlotte was an exceptional cook, managing delicious meals with scarce ingredients. Brian took off and hung up his overcoat and uniform tunic. He left his brimmed cap on the wall peg. *What the hell could possibly be eating at her? Whatever it is, it cannot be good.* Brian sat at the kitchen table and munched on one of Charlotte's delicious cookies. They did not have much sugar with rationing, so she used a honey glaze with all of the ingredients coming from her farm.

Brian heard the front door open. He stood. As soon as she entered, Charlotte waved at him to sit, which he did. She quickly brewed a large pot of tea and wrapped it in a cozy to keep it hot. *Oh, oh, this is going to be a long talk.*

Charlotte poured a cup of tea for each of them, and then sat across the table. She stared at Brian, expressionless, for several minutes. Brian gestured, as if to say, OK, what's the problem? Charlotte took a sip of tea, placed her cup down, and then lowered her gaze to the cup, as if divine guidance might emanate from the inanimate object and its dark liquid contents.

Charlotte looked again to Brian's eyes and said, "First, I want to say and you must know that I love you." Brian nodded his head in acknowledgment. "I thought our visit to the Palmer's last month went as well as could be expected. I could tell Mister Palmer was not enamored with our news, but I really thought he would warm quickly. Apparently, I was wrong." She paused. Brian did not respond and tried hard to keep his eyes and face expressionless, to let her finish whatever it was she needed to say. "He drove over here from Devon, took a day off from his business, to visit me and say what he needed to say. It was not good." Again, she paused, apparently waiting for Brian to say something, but he did not even twitch. "Mister Palmer felt compelled to tell me that he did not approve of me marrying you. He praised your service to the kingdom, but virtually condemned you as a 'Yankee mercenary,' in his words, fighting for blood money."

"I guess he does not know we are already married . . . and, probably doesn't know you are pregnant with our first child."

"I could not tell him. I was heartbroken. I respected him as a wise and generous man from the moment I met him years ago, but this . . . what he said . . ."

"I am sorry you had to endure that alone, Charlotte. I wish I had been here to set him right. In fact, now that I think of it, I should drive out to Bickleigh and talk to him directly. That was a very unfair thing for him to say to you."

"No, Brian, please do not do that. I am a grown woman, making a free choice. I wanted their approval, but I do not need their approval."

"Especially since we're already married and pregnant." They both laughed. Brian was the first to return to seriousness. "What exactly were his objections, if I may ask . . . besides being an ugly American mercenary . . . and cavorting with his adopted daughter, presumably?"

"Well, he thinks that you are too young, too tall and not of this land. He thinks you will use me for what you want and throw me away when you are done."

"Well, other than that Mrs. Lincoln, how did you like the play?"

"What?"

"Sorry, dark country humor from the colonies."

"Brian, please do not do that. You are a good man. He does not know you. I am fairly certain he does not know what you have done for this country, and he did not ask me how I felt about you. He just knows what he sees. To him, it was all about the appearance of things."

"OK, then, what do you want to do?"

Charlotte did not answer straight away, apparently to give herself time to think. "I guess there is nothing we can do, or perhaps should do, other than give him time . . . for us to prove him wrong."

This time Brian hesitated to think. *I'd still like to give that old bastard what for. He was wrong to do that to her. He is probably steeped in Victorian morality properness and can't see past his nose. She's right.* "That seems like the best approach, since you won't let me confront him about his unfairness and lack of vision."

Charlotte nodded her head in response. "But . . ."

"Oh, damn, there is a 'but.'" They both laughed.

"But, his visit and his words did make me think hard this past week. I am eight years older than you. I will be an old woman when you are still a young man."

"Rubbish! No more of that nonsense!"

"It is a fact, Brian. You are so young. How could you possibly know what you want? You have been with other women. There are many more women out there who would love to have a poke at you. We shouldn't be bringing an innocent child into this mess we are in. My mother never had a chance to teach me about pregnancy," she said rubbing her belly, "and what is happening to my body is driving me crazy."

"Looks pretty damn good to me," Brian responded and winked at her.

"You naughty boy, you just want to have a go."

"Yes, I do, and I'm not ashamed to admit it. Pregnancy has made you even more beautiful."

"You're just saying that to make me feel good."

"I sure as hell am not!" he protested. "It's true. Let's get naked and I'll show you."

"You are indeed a naughty boy. You'll get your bonking in due course, but I have more to say, and then we have the afternoon milking to do. I expect Horace and Lionel back anytime now from this morning's delivery. I do not want them finding us in bed in the afternoon, again." They both chuckled at the remembrance of his last visit. "We are going to have this child, but we must take precautions, Brian. I do not want the added burden of raising children alone. I want more than one child . . . just not more during this damnable war."

"As you wish, my darling. Wait . . . you said precautions. What do you mean by precautions?"

"In time, we will need to discuss those precautions, but for now, I am already pregnant and cannot get pregnant, again, for the time being. We shall enjoy our playtime, while I remain safe. I just wanted you to know how I feel."

"Duly noted."

"I want to make more children with you, Brian, when we both can enjoy them."

"I understand and agree. And, for the record, I may be younger than you, but there is no doubt in my mind . . . I know what I want. I would be lying to you if I tried to deny my attraction to the other women in my young life, even Mary Spencer."

"You are incorrigible, Brian Drummond."

"I'm not sure I know what that means, but I can guess. I just know how I feel when I see you, when I feel you, when I think about you."

"That is a lovely thought, Brian. Thank you."

The knock at the door interrupted their conversation. Horace Morgan opened the door, stepped inside and closed the door behind him.

"Mrs. . . . . oh Mister Drummond, great to see you, again. They gave you time off from the war, so soon after the holidays."

"Yes, Horace, nice to see you, again, as well. I try to take full advantage of any break I am offered. I love the mistress of the farm too much to stay away."

"Very well, sir. Mrs. Palmer, or is it Drummond now?"

"Which ever you prefer, Horace."

"Yes ma'am, we delivered the milk shipment. The dairy said they would deposit your compensation in the bank this afternoon. Mister Bridges went to the barn to prepare for the afternoon milking."

"Very good, Horace. We shall join you in a few minutes."

"My apologies for interrupting, ma'am. Just wanted you to know we had returned and everything was as it should be."

"Excellent. Thank you."

Morgan lowered his head and bowed, and then departed.

Brian waited for the front door to close. "Where were we?"

"We have more time to talk before you have to go back. Right now, we need to get you out of that nice uniform and into some proper work clothes. You will not escape the afternoon chores, this time."

"No escape desired . . . I love pulling on those tits."

Charlotte laughed hard. "You do indeed, my dear man, and I am grateful you do enjoy it so much."

The remainder of the afternoon, most of which was well after evening twilight during the winter months, stepped along routinely. None of the vestiges of war penetrated the idyllic farm nestled in the gentle hills of Hampshire. Brian truly appreciated the peace he felt with Charlotte and at Standing Oak Farm.

—

Tuesday, 14.January.1941
Prime Minister's Rail car
West Coast Main Line
Just past Stoke-on-Trent, Staffordshire, England
United Kingdom

Prime Minister Churchill moved through his special rail car to the secure, protected compartment. An army sergeant with the Buff Box manacled to his left wrist stood in the corridor in front of an armed guard, cradling a Thompson and both men had holstered pistols on their right hips. The sergeant crisply saluted Winston as he approached. Churchill returned the salute. They had made a special stop at Stoke to allow the courier to board the train. Churchill took the unusual step to accompany Lord Halifax to Glasgow and Gourock for his send-off aboard the battleship HMS *King George V* and his new post as His Majesty's ambassador to the United States. The journey gave the Prime Minister some quiet time to discuss relations with the United States. Circumstances enabled a perhaps unique opportunity to extend the special relationship, with President Roosevelt's personal representative Harry Hopkins joining the discussions with Lord Halifax. The discussions had gone exceptionally well, so far. It seemed to him that Harry and Edward were developing a warm rapport, and what he thought would be a fine working relationship. Yet, more immediate matters presented.

"What have you, sergeant?"

"Sir, 'C' insisted the message here," he said, patting the Buff Box, "be delivered to you as soon as possible."

"Very well. I'm sure you are not eager to join us on our journey. Let's get this done, so we can get you off this train, and back to your duty station and home."

"I am at your service, Prime Minister," the courier responded.

They stepped into the compartment. The sergeant closed the door.

"Please latch the door, and then turn about, if you would, sergeant." The courier did as he was commanded.

Churchill retrieved his special key from around his neck and straightened his shirt. "Very well, sergeant. Let's have your dispatch box." The courier placed the Buff Box on the small, wall desk. The Prime Minister used his key, unlocked the box, looked through the various folders, and found only one message in the Most Urgent folder.

MOST SECRET - ULTRA

```
SECRET
DATE: 12 JANUARY 1941
TO: OB WEST OKH
FROM: OKW
WITHDRAWAL OF AIR FORCE UNITS
BEGIN
BY THE LEADERS ORDER THIS DAY OKL WITHDRAWING
MAXIMUM NUMBER OF FIGHTER AND BOMBER UNITS
BREAK ARMY HIGH COMMAND WEST SHALL RETAIN
MINIMUM FIGHTER UNITS FOR AIR DEFENSE
AND SUFFICIENT BOMBER FORCES TO MAINTAIN
BOMBARDMENT OF GB PER PLAN 109 BREAK REMAINDER
AND RESERVE UNITS TO BE DETACHED WITHIN THE
MONTH AND RETURNED TO GERMANY FOR REST AND
REFIT BREAK EFFECTIVE DATE FIVE DAYS AFTER
MESSAGE DATE
END
SECRET
```

MOST SECRET - ULTRA

Churchill lifted the handset of the intercom telephone. "Jock, I need Lord Halifax straight away . . . and you and a stenographer. Thank you." He placed the handset back in its cradle. "Sergeant, I must ask you to step outside and remain away from the door. Please standby, as I may need you to carry reply instructions."

"Yes sir."

The courier latched the cover, grasped the box, unlatched the door and did as he was instructed.

Winston stared at the Enigma decrypt. *This may be the moment.*

The knock at the door interrupted his thought. Lord Halifax entered the compartment. "You wished to see me, Prime Minister."

Churchill handed the paper to Halifax. The former foreign minister and future ambassador to the United States looked up. "Well, now!"

"Quite so. We must not attach too much significance to a singular piece of intelligence; however, this date may very well be a pivotal turning point in the war."

"What do you think it means . . . in the broader sense?"

Churchill stared into the eyes of Lord Halifax. "By itself, not particularly significant. Yet, when combined with the intercept of last month, referencing Directive number 21, I would say this means the foul Nawzee leader has turned his attention eastward. We are not out of The Blitz, just yet, but they clearly are turning their focus from us . . . at least for the time being."

"What do you want me to tell the President or the Americans?"

"Nothing for the moment, but I need you to be aware of what is happening. We shall share this with our cousins, but not just yet. The spring will likely be confirmation, but to me, it appears the odoriferous bastard is going to take on his ultimate living space and ideological nemesis – the Soviet Union."

"That would relieve the pressure on us."

"Quite so. We shall know soon enough. Yet, my . . . our . . . most immediate concern is not the diminishing threat of invasion . . . rather, it is war materiel supply from the United States. We are not likely to gain American partnership any time soon, but we must have their industrial capacity. As Harry has told us, Congress has begun their deliberations on what Harry has referred to as their lend-lease bill. That must be your primary focus. Bill Stevenson can and should be a big help to you, but you are our principal agent in Washington. We need to do whatever we can do to get this bill passed and get the supply line flowing . . . more than it is at present."

"Yes sir. Should we warn the Soviets?"

Churchill considered Edward's question. "Do you believe we have confirmation that foul bastard is intent upon invading Russia?"

"No, I do not believe so, but the signs continue to mount and suggest that is his intention."

"I would agree in the main, but we must be on firm ground to make such a gesture. After all, at present, Stalin is aligned by treaty more closely with Hitler than with us. I suspect he really has his eyes on Baku to supplement his oil supply from the Romanian oil fields. He needs oil."

"Quite so."

"I need to get the courier off this train. You are welcome to stay." Halifax nodded his head. Winston went to the compartment door. Jock Colville and a female stenographer, whose name he could not remember, stood outside the compartment. He motioned with his head for them to enter. He closed and latched the door behind them. Winston extended his right hand toward Edward for the message, which Halifax delivered. Churchill looked down at the message, as his thoughts considered exactly what he wanted to do. *No, there is nothing to be done, and we cannot do anything directly with this information.* He sat at the table, took a fountain pen from the desk holder, and wrote – ensure War Cabinet only sees this message, WSC.

"I've changed my mind. Please ask the courier sergeant to step inside. No further action."

Colville stepped out and motioned for the courier. The stenographer departed without a word or expression. As the sergeant returned to the compartment, Churchill retrieved the key from his trouser pocket, opened the case, took one last look at the message and his handwritten response, and deposited the message back in the Urgent folder. "Return this to 'C' directly," commanded the Prime Minister.

"Yes sir."

"Jock, please see to it that the sergeant can disembark at the next appropriate stop, so that he can board a return train to London without delay."

"Yes sir."

Churchill gestured for everyone to shoo. "Lord Halifax, a moment please." They waited until everyone departed and the compartment door closed. "That was important information for us to know, but there is nothing we can do with it. I want to shout at the top of my voice, from the highest mountain top, WE WON!" He paused. No one spoke. Lord Halifax did not respond. "But, I cannot do what my urges suggest." Edward shook his head in agreement. "We shall not mention this with Harry, so let us both engage him on any other topic."

"I agree, Winston. In time, they must have access to ULTRA. Until then, we must remain steadfastly protective of our special source."

"Excellent. Now, let us return to our guest in the salon. We need him to feel a part of your mission, your journey, and your commitment. We need the Americans in this war, but we must be mindful to not push too hard. You will be at the front line in this effort, which is precisely why we must have our very best man out there. I trust Dorothy is not too angry with me."

"She is certainly not. She sees this assignment as a respite from this dreadful war . . . the bombings, the rationing, the displacement of our children, all of it. I am one who will miss my position in Lords . . . and in His Majesty's Government."

"You will be in perhaps the most vital position in the government."

"I appreciate you saying that, Winston, but there is no need for you to sugar coat things with me. I know we have not agreed on much for the last few years."

"Ed, please do not sell yourself short. I have considerable respect for you as a man, as a diplomat, and as my trusted representative in Washington, full stop. You must believe. I am entrusting you with this critical and essential mission."

"I understand, Winston. The best I can say, I shall do my best."

Churchill looked deeply into Edward Wood's eyes. "I know you will. Now, let's get back to our guest. We do not want him to feel neglected. We shall be in Gourock soon enough, and you shall board that magnificent warship for your journey."

Halifax nodded his head in agreement.

Winston led them forward to the main lounge compartment. They had several more hours before they were due to arrive at Gourock Station. *I want to be back in London before bedtime, but we need to send off Edward properly. I need to make nice with Dorothy – Lady Halifax – before we arrive. This mission is too bloody important.*

———

Wednesday, 22.January.1941
RAF Kirton-in-Lindsey
Kirton-in-Lindsey, Lincolnshire, England
United Kingdom

"What the hell is going on?" asked Salt Morton, as they waited. Corporal Harris knew nothing more than the rest of the pilots did . . . or, at least that he would confess to before the squadron pilots.

"We've done more visits, more interviews, more show events, than we've done flying," added Rocket Downing.

"You got that right," said Bulldog Tolly. "So, what do you think is going on, Hunter?"

"How am I supposed to know?"

"You've been in this business longer than any of the rest of us."

"But, I don't know any more about what is going on than any of the rest of us."

An RAF officer in a squadron leader's uniform with only pilot's wings above his left breast pocket on this tunic walked into the squadron Dispersal. He was a smallish, rather mousy looking man. "May I have your attention please," he said and waited for quiet. "My name is Taylor, Bill Taylor. You are probably asking yourselves, why is this bloke here? Well, I must inform you that Squadron Leader Churchill has been diagnosed with a very serious sinus infection. The flight surgeon has grounded him, and he has been placed on extended medical leave to recuperate. I have been assigned by the Air Ministry as your new commanding officer." Stunned silence greeted Taylor's words. "I am informed that his sick leave is listed as indefinite. I was told to assume my assignment is permanent. In essence, Squadron Leader Churchill is not expected to return to this squadron and will likely be reassigned once he has recovered."

"Excuse me, sir, are you taking questions here?" asked Salt Morton. Taylor nodded his head in the affirmative. "You have an American accent . . . not really a question . . . but kinda."

"I shall take it as a question. I am an ex-patriot American, as each of you are. My career, if that is what we call it, has been a sort of potpourri of military service. Short version: I transferred from the Royal Navy to the Royal Air Force last October, and here I am."

The story of William Erwin Gibson 'Bill' Taylor encompassed a broader spectrum than he disclosed to the squadron. He obtained his U.S. naval aviator wings in 1927, served in U.S. Naval Reserve, transferred to the Marine Corps Reserve, where he served until congressionally mandated budget cuts ended his service in 1933. After a stint in commercial aviation and the war in Europe flashing to full flame, Taylor joined the Royal Navy Fleet Air Arm, where he served until he was transferred to the Royal Air Force.

"What does all this mean to us?" Bulldog asked.

Taylor smiled, not a humorous smile but rather a really irritated smile. "Well, since you asked, we shall remain in operational status. We are going to be unofficially placed back in training status."

"Oh, great. We have only been operational for a couple of weeks, flown a couple of lame convoy missions, gotten one guy killed, and now, they push us back to training status."

"It's not quite like . . ."

"And," Bulldog continued after interrupting Taylor, "all we have done is train and be the one-trick pony in this circus.

"Pilot Officer Tolly, you are out of line," commanded Taylor.

Tolly shook his head in disbelief, but he did not respond. He just lowered his head and stared at his shoes.

Salt Morton picked up the lance. "Bulldog's right, Skipper. We have been a fighter squadron for almost four months. We were just declared operational a couple of weeks ago, and we do more VIP visits, press interviews, photographic sessions, and whatever other public relations the powers that be can think of, to roll us out . . . like we are for show rather than for combat."

Squadron Leader Taylor grinned, nodded his head, paced back and forth several times, before he turned back to face his pilots. "I am going to say this only once, so I suggest each of you pay attention." Bill looked to each set of eyes on him. "This is not some flying club, here for your pleasure. We are a military unit, part of a much larger military organization. We do what the leaders of this team need us to do." He paused, again, to look at each pilot. "If you cannot enthusiastically obey the orders we are given, I'm sure the Air Ministry will gladly transfer you to Coastal Command, or one of the support groups, so you fly a bus, or a truck hauling cargo for those of us who fly fighters." Once more, he paused to scan the pilots for any dissent. Brian quickly looked at the other pilots. No one moved. "Fine, then I will assume your silence indicates that each of you understands and accepts what I have said." He heard no dissent. "Now, I will speak plainly and frankly, as it appears that is the only way you appreciate circumstances. Fighter Command was not impressed with our last mission performance."

"Our?" someone grumbled.

"Yes, our! This is my squadron now and I am responsible for our performance. The combination of the dreadfully simple mistake as well as losing our commander, Fighter Command wants to see how you perform under my leadership." Taylor looked over his left shoulder. "Corporal Harris, report the squadron in training status."

"Yes sir."

As the squadron operations clerk performed his assigned duty, Bill Taylor turned back to the pilots. "The weather forecasters are predicting snow and ice tomorrow and Friday. We will fly two sorties today. First, this morning, we will launch as a squadron. We will fly a number of maneuvers as a unit and several tactical formation shifts. Then, in the afternoon, we will fly mock engagements between 'A' Flight and 'B' Flight. Any questions?" There were none. "Fine, then grab your kit and let's get this done before the weather gets here."

They all donned their Sidcot suits, as it was a rather cold, frosty day outside. About half the pilots, including Brian, put their leather flying helmets on with the oxygen masks attached to the left side only and their goggles on their forehead to keep their ears warm against the cold.

Brian did not like being pushed back to training status, but he understood why Fighter Command lost confidence in the squadron. His brethren and countrymen were a spirited bunch, but they still struggled with conformity. They had to learn to function as a team rather than a gaggle of individual pilots, who might be far more easily picked off by competent German fighter pilots. The midair collision that claimed 'Roley' Rigby's life still haunted him, more so than his last crash that nearly claimed his life. It was such a simple mistake. Rusty Bateman was not the first and certainly would not be the last to allow his eagerness to interfere with good judgment and procedure. Brian had discussed the accident numerous times with Dusty and Bulldog. He believed his Green Section had learned from Rusty's mistake. Now, they would bite the bullet, and go prove themselves, again.

As they walked to their aircraft, a wingman on each side of Brian, Bulldog Tolly asked, "Do you think the Skipper really meant what he said?"

"Yes, in a heartbeat," answered Brian calmly and softly.

"He would send us to fly transports?"

"Or, worse, a desk or deport us back home."

"Damn," interjected Dusty Langford.

Brian stopped and looked to both men. "He is spot on correct. This is not some flying club. We do what we are told to do. Now, we need to mount up and fly these machines the best we can and do what we are asked to do and get through this training phase, again. Understood?"

Both men nodded their heads in agreement. Brian watched both his wingmen settle into their cockpits, and then he tended to his. He strapped in quickly to his parachute and seat, turned on his oxygen diluter, and snapped his oxygen mask in place, so that he could close the canopy and at least eliminate the cold breeze adding to his chill. All three of them were ready to taxi their fighters for takeoff when Bill gave the signal. They would be in the air soon enough.

—

Friday, 24. January. 1941
United States Naval Academy
Annapolis, Maryland
United States of America

The distinctive profile of the battleship HMS *King George V* lay at anchor broadside across the mouth of Annapolis harbor, having arrived just after dawn, with two of her escort destroyers anchored beyond her. President Roosevelt remained inside his black, 1939, Lincoln K-Series limousine with its powerful V-12 engine and retractable roof, they popularly called the car the Sunshine Special. On this cold winter day, the top remained in place and the motor continued to idle for interior warmth alone. *I'm so glad those 14-inch main battery guns are stowed fore and aft. I cannot imagine what damage a full broadside from that warship would do.* The President thought nothing of his unprecedented presence at the arrival of a foreign ambassador. Despite Secretary Hull's advice and counsel to not attend, Franklin was determined to demonstrate the special relationship he had with the British prime minister, and between their two countries.

General Watson approached the car. Franklin rolled down the window. "Sir, the launch has cast off. The lieutenant stated their transit will take 15 minutes."

"Fine, Pa. Then, let's get me out of here. I want to be standing for the ambassador's arrival."

"Yes, certainly, Mister President." Watson knew exactly what needed to be done. He shielded the disabled president during his transition.

Roosevelt swung his withered legs out of the car, locked his leg braces and stood awkwardly. Grasping Watson's right arm firmly at the elbow, Roosevelt ambled toward the dockside where the admiral's barge from the battleship would moor and allow its distinguished passengers to disembark. The cold, winter morning did not make the laborious process any easier, but Roosevelt persevered, arriving at his intended spot as the launch slowed for its approach. The Royal Navy lieutenant and two able seamen crisply saluted the President. Roosevelt returned their salute. No words were exchanged. President Roosevelt watched the rather elegant launch expertly come about, placing the bow just off the dock, starboard side to, as the seaman at the bow cast a mooring line to his compatriot on the dock. The stern swung gracefully to the dock and the stern line cast across to the dock. In short order, the launch was securely moored. The two-dockside seamen along with two American seamen moved a small gangway to the launch.

A rather stern-looking, middle-aged woman, dressed conservatively in a dark blue, long, dress-suit was first up the gangway, followed and assisted by a tall, balding man, who Roosevelt recognized. The woman had to be Lady Dorothy Evelyn Augusta Wood née Onslow, Countess of Halifax, and wife of Lord Halifax. He readily recognized Lord Halifax, the former British foreign minister and now the King's ambassador to the United States. Dorothy smiled, and her generous smile warmed her appearance. Once firmly on the dock, she stepped aside to allow her husband to lead them to the President.

"Welcome to the United States, again, Mister Ambassador," Roosevelt boomed with vigor and confidence, and extended his right hand to Lord Halifax.

"You are most gracious and generous with your precious time, Mister President." Halifax shook hands with Roosevelt and Watson. "I am honored to introduce my wife, Dorothy. My dear, this is President Franklin Roosevelt and his Aide-de-Camp Major General Edwin Watson."

"Lady Halifax, a pleasure to finally meet you."

"The pleasure is mine, Mister President," Dorothy responded, shaking the President's proffered hand, and then turned to shake hands with General Watson. "A pleasure to meet you, General Watson."

"Nice to meet you, Lady Halifax."

Franklin turned to Halifax. "May I suggest we retire to the Sunshine Special, where it is warm and more comfortable. This cold is not kind to the steel that trusses my legs."

"By all means, Mister President."

Despite the President's handicap, Roosevelt insisted Lady Halifax enter the limousine first. She knew without asking where she should sit and took the aft-facing seat on the far side of the automobile. General Watson assisted the President in returning to his seat. Lord Halifax walked around the rear of the car and took the seat next to the President. General Watson was the last to enter, taking the seat next to Lady Halifax. As soon as everyone was seated, the President nodded his head and they were off for the drive back to Washington.

"I knew the *King George the Fifth* could not make it up the Potomac, so I thought we could put the final leg of your journey to productive use."

"Excellent idea, Mister President. Again, Dorothy and I are most honored for your courtesy and generosity."

"Nonsense, the honor is mine. You have large, deep shoes to fill from Philip's untimely and tragic passing." Lord Halifax nodded his head in acknowledgment, deferring to the President's thought. "I have every confidence in Winston's choice for his replacement, Ed . . . excuse me, I presume you will permit me the informality of your given name."

"By all means, Mister President. I am flattered."

"Then, I must insist, please call me Franklin, or even Frank, just not hey you." Everyone laughed. "Then, Ed it is. Our first order of business at the moment is the pending legislation in Congress. I imagine Winston has shared with you what we are doing."

"Yes, he has."

"With this lend-lease bill, the door will be open. We are late to the pitch, as you would say, but we expect our industry to mobilize quickly to fulfill your war needs. I signed three major, defense mobilization laws last year."

"Better late than never, as they say."

Roosevelt had essentially ignored the scenery of the magnificent stone buildings of the Naval Academy and the rather quaint architecture of Maryland's state capitol, but he did notice Dorothy's captivation with the new scenery and even Ed's occasional distraction, as this was a new location environment for them. It had to be an even more dramatic contrast for them, placed against the wartime damage to London and other British cities damaged by the Germans. They would soon be on the Route 50 heading west-southwest back into Washington, and the scenery would turn to defoliated, hibernated, deciduous trees and stands of conifers offering the only green in the winter landscape of Maryland.

"What is the prognosis for passage?" asked Halifax.

"I am reticent to ever predict what might happen in Congress. Our version of Parliament tends to be far less orderly and predictable, I'm afraid. Yet, if our friends in Congress are correct, we have a good shot at passage. My principal concern is time – how long it will take us to gain passage. Winston was very direct, clear and precise in this depiction of the situation. What struck me most in his December message was the economic and financial state. As I have tried to assure the Prime Minister, as I am certain you are aware, the United States must do everything in our power to support and sustain Great Britain."

"If I may be so bold, Mister President . . ."

"Franklin, please."

"My apologies. If I may be so bold, Franklin, what is the likelihood of the United States joining this war?"

"Well, now, I can answer as a knowledgeable and concerned American citizen, or as the President of these United States, or I can answer for the United States of America. In my answer, I must be equally precise as Winston has been. That said, in my mind, we are already in this war. We joined in a form when we sent that first arms shipment last July, and especially when we transferred 50 surplus destroyers to the Royal Navy. I know the level of our involvement was not the context surrounding your question. My personal opinion is not particularly relevant here. Again, I know you are aware of, and I believe you will become far more attuned to, the isolationist sentiment so prevalent in this country. I cannot ignore the mood of the people I represent."

"I fully understand, Franklin, and I can likewise assure you His Majesty's Government, who I now represent, are quite sympathetic to your . . . shall I say . . . situation. Yet, I must also say, you are without a doubt the most informed citizen in this country, thus your opinion certainly does matter."

Roosevelt smiled a friendly but wary grin. "Ah, yes, a diplomat's finely crafted words." Franklin did not look directly at either Edward or Dorothy, but he recognized that both sets of eyes were intently on him. Pa Watson tried to look distantly uninterested, or perhaps detached or uninvolved. Franklin glanced at Dorothy, who averted her eyes, and then directly to his left and engaged Edward's eyes. His smile had disappeared. "Please allow me to be equally diplomatic. I do not believe the Germans will allow us to remain a distant materiel supplier of Great Britain. The Japanese show no signs whatsoever of restraining their conduct in Asia and the Western Pacific. I have signed into law several actions in addition to the defense mobilization bills I mentioned earlier, including several counter espionage and subversion laws and our selective service law, to draft military age men. Congress passed those laws – all of them – before I approved them. I will also say that Congress is farther along the road of recognition and acknowledgment, but I must have time to bring the American people to the same awareness. I am not confident Hitler or Tojo will allow me the necessary time. Regardless of what they do, we cannot allow Britain to falter, stumble or fall – financially or militarily. It truly broke my heart to witness the fall of France so swiftly, and there was little we could do to assist at the time. This country is already different from where we were a year ago, and we will continue our preparations for what I believe is the inevitable."

"You have been most generous, Franklin. Thank you for your candor, and more importantly, for your tolerance."

"Again, nonsense. We are friends and now compatriots in a common struggle against a common foe. We must be candid, forthright, honest and thorough with each other, if we are to be successful in this endeavor. My only concern in choosing my words carefully is the risk of misleading you and your government into thinking I can do more than I am able. While I was elected handily last November, it serves no one to be too far ahead of the people. My obligation, my duty, is to help them understand and support what we must do. If there is one element I can and must impress upon you and Winston, it would be that simple but solemn task before me."

"We respect that reality, Franklin. I can assure you, His Majesty's Government will do its utmost to assist you in any manner you deem appropriate."

"Thank you, Ed. I also understand you have senior military officers with you."

"Yes, indeed. Our joint coordination staff will be disembarking later this afternoon to begin our agreed to military staff conversations. Our officers are: Rear Admirals Bellairs and Danckwerts, and Captain Clarke for the Royal Navy; Major General Morris for the Army; and Air Vice Marshal Slessor for the Royal Air Force. They are fully prepared to open the operational and planning dialogue with your staff officers to ensure the utmost coordination between our two military staffs. The Prime Minister asked me to convey his wishes that we establish a combined planning staff at your earliest convenience, to fulfill our mutual objectives."

"Excellent. They will be meeting early next week with our delegation comprised of: Major General Embick for our Army, and Rear Admiral Ghormley for our Navy. We have no separate air force, but General Embick will ensure a representative for our Army Air Corps will attend to coordinate for our aviation component. I must say I agree with Winston regarding the joint planning staff, but once again, the timing is not right. I am all in favor of and have agreed to this so-called staff conversations conference, but we shall have to be cautious regarding expansion of our combined military efforts for now . . . for the reasons I mentioned earlier. I trust you understand."

"Absolutely, Franklin. I think the Prime Minister's message was simply to convey our readiness for such joint planning work, when you are able to carry out those endeavors."

Roosevelt nodded his head in recognition and reached the end of his agenda. He looked to Lady Halifax. "My apologies, Dorothy, but business tends to get in the way of social graces these days."

"Quite understandable, Mister President, and I am accustomed to those priorities with Edward's work."

"Thank you for your tolerance. On behalf of the First Lady, we welcome you to this country. I hope and trust your stay with us will be comfortable and rewarding."

"I am certain it will, Mister President, and thank you for allowing me to listen into your conversation with Edward." Roosevelt nodded his head.

The remainder of the drive into Washington stayed at the superficial, social level of conversation. The transfer of Dorothy and Edward to the United

States was not their first visit for either of them. As soon as they settled into the ambassador's residence at their embassy and Edward presented his credentials, President Roosevelt invited them to a private dinner at the White House with he and Eleanor. They both commented numerous times about the contrast between wartime London and Washington. They all hoped it would remain that way, but none of them were willing to predict that it would. The realities of war tamped down such hopes.

—

Monday, 27.January.1941
No.10 Annexe
New Public Offices
Whitehall, London, England
United Kingdom

"**W**elcome to London," the Prime Minister greeted his luncheon guest at the first-floor lobby of the New Public Offices building and extended his right hand.

Wendell Lewis Willkie, the Republican presidential candidate in the last election three months previous, walked smartly to his host and grasped the proffered hand. The two men shook hands vigorously. "It is an honor to finally meet you, Mister Prime Minister."

"Winston, please."

"Very well, then, Wendell is my preferred given name."

"You are a brave man to have ventured out from the safety of the promised land to our now blemished capital city."

"Nonsense. I am but a humble servant performing his duty."

Churchill gestured toward the barely masked, reinforced walls of the Annexe that had become the Prime Minister's residence after the bomb damage to No.10 Downing Street. The Prime Minister led his guest to the modest dining room and gestured to his seat. The lunch service began as the two men continued their discussions.

"Thank you for taking the time to meet with me, Winston. President Roosevelt asked me to carry a personal note from him to you." Wilkie reached inside his jacket and extracted a small single piece of notepaper. He handed it to Churchill.

The Prime Minister unfolded and read the note.

The White House

Washington, DC

January 20, 1941

My dear Winston,

    I think this verse applies to your people as it does to us:

```
          Sail on, O Ship of State!
          Sail on, O Union, strong and great!
          Humanity with all its fears,
          With all the hopes of future years
          Is hanging breathless on thy fate.
```

*These are the first lines of Longfellow's poem <u>The Building of</u>
<u>the Ship</u>, written on November 18, 1849. 'The Ship' served as
an emblem for 'The Union,' which, at the time, was threatened
with secession by the South and the looming dark clouds of the
Civil War.*

    *I have asked Wendell to carry this note as his bona
fide and to represent me during his visit. While he initially
represented well his party's isolationist leanings, Wendell has
come around to the exigencies of the times in which we are
immersed. I believe he will become an essential spokesman
and advocate for the Lend-Lease Program we both are
seeking. Please extend to him your open arms. It is vital to our
purposes.*

    *I trust this note finds you in good health and wonderful
spirit.*

Your friend and

fellow traveller,

Franklin D. Roosevelt

Tears unabashedly streamed down Winston's face. He made no attempt
hide them or wipe them away.

"Have you read this note?" Churchill asked with considerable emotion
in his voice.

"No," Wilkie answered. "It was personal from Franklin to you . . . not
my place."

Churchill handed the note to Wilkie. His American guest read the note,
smiled and nodded his head, clearly impressed by the sentiment conveyed.
Wilkie placed the note on the table between them. Churchill gestured for
them to eat while their meal was hot. "I shall write Franklin today and thank

him . . . very typical of his generosity. I think I will also have this note framed and hung in my study . . . very symbolic and poignant." Wilkie nodded his head in agreement. "There," he said placing his hand on the note, "with the pleasantries aside, let me assure you that you shall have my authority to see anything and everything you wish during your visit. It is vital to both countries that you gain the knowledge you seek."

"Thank you, Winston."

"If I may, Wendell, what changed your mind regarding materiel support for our lone stand against that demon in Germany? As I recall, you were a staunch advocate for your country remaining behind your Atlantic moat just a few months ago during the election campaign."

"Fair question. I think my personal opinion mirrors the view of the American people. If I had to boil down my answer to two words, those words would be The Blitz. The reporting of 'Ed' Murrow and other journalists from here, the photographs bearing witness to this atrocity, and frankly your words that I dare say will become immortal have swayed public opinion and directly my opinion." Churchill ignored his meal to listen intently to his guest's response. "Franklin and I have had several private discussions. I now share his view as well as his proposed effort to provide the support you need. I represented a political party that maintained its position of opposition to foreign entanglements. The bitter pain and sacrifice of the last war remains quite vivid in the minds and consciousness of the American people."

"We had no choice," interjected Churchill with solemnity.

"Yes, quite so, but we have a choice. The war has not come to our shores. It is not personal for my countrymen."

"With respect, Wendell, the war came to your shores years ago." An expression of confusion bloomed on Wilkie's face. "Your government has been and continues to deal with active espionage activities in your country carried out by the Nawzee vermin. German submarines are sinking your ships. There should be little doubt that Hitler has ambitions beyond Europe. You may not be next, but your country is in their sights."

"You may well be correct, however, the United States is not prepared for war."

"Yes, yes," Winston said with some impatience. "My country was not prepared for war either, 17 months ago. Again, we had no choice. The President and Congress have begun the process of preparation with the rearmament and draft service acts of last year. With your help, we will stand the line and buy you precious time to further your preparations."

"Thank you. I am here, representing the President, to do my part. As I said, I am convinced the President is correct. I intend to help him convince Congress to quickly pass the Lend-Lease bill, which I am fairly sure you know has been introduced in Congress two weeks ago and is working its way through committee review."

"Yes, I am aware."

Neither one of them finished their meal. Churchill gestured to the steward for the service to be cleared.

"Would you care for a brandy?" asked Churchill.

"No, no thank you . . . a bit early for me."

"Very well. If you have no objection, I shall imbibe a wee dram of the golden elixir."

"Be my guest," responded Wilkie.

Churchill gestured toward the liquor cabinet. The chief steward knew precisely the meaning of the Prime Minister's signal. A small snifter was produced with two fingers of clear, amber-colored liquid. Churchill took a sip with discernible pleasure. "If I am properly informed, you will be with us for a fortnight."

"Yes, you are well informed. Franklin did forewarn me that I might be recalled early if the congressional committees begin taking testimony. He has asked me to add my voice on behalf of the government and for passage of the bill. I agreed to do so."

Churchill took another sip of his brandy as he considered his word choice. "Franklin has set a new high bar for political engagement in asking his opponent in the last election and the standard bearer for the opposition political party to represent him and even more so to testify before your colleagues on his behalf."

Wilkie smiled broadly. "I do believe that honor goes to you, Winston. After all, you have the leaders of your opposition parties in your government and sitting on the leadership War Cabinet, to boot, as well as your principle antagonist within your own party sitting on that very same War Cabinet."

This time, Churchill smiled. "Perhaps, but I was obligated to The King to form a wartime coalition government. Franklin has no such obligation."

"Yes . . . well . . . Franklin is a very persuasive man."

"That he is, Wendell. That he is."

"Thank you for lunch and the chat, Winston. I'm afraid it's time for me to be on my way. I have an action-packed schedule and I appear to be falling behind."

Churchill stood, followed by Wilkie. The two men shook hands. "I wish you good hunting. If you should encounter any obstacles, please call me immediately. I want you to be free to go, see, hear, ask and feel whatever you wish to do . . . to fulfill your mission for the President."

"Thank you, Winston. I appreciate your generosity and I shall ensure the President knows that as well."

The two men walked to the main entrance lobby and shook hands, again. Wilkie turned and departed the building. Churchill could see the black, U.S. Embassy Cadillac waiting for him at the curbside in front of the building. Winston smiled and nodded his head to no one in particular, as he turned and headed toward the stairway leading to the government's underground bunker and his sequestered office to prepare for his pending War Cabinet meeting.

———

Wednesday, 29.January.1941
Office of the Secretary of War
Munitions Building
Constitution Avenue & 20th Street
Washington, District of Columbia
United States of America
16:50 hours

Secretary of the Navy Frank Knox entered Henry Stimson's office after being announced. "Henry, I wanted to chat a bit before the others arrive," Knox said and sat on the couch facing Stimson's desk and across an elegant, inlaid, coffee table.

Stimson rose from his desk. "Good afternoon to you, Frank." Stimson said, as he repositioned to the matching leather couch facing Knox.

"I don't know about good. It's freezing out there and the sidewalks are still icy. I considered using the car, but that seemed a bit ridiculous for a two block distance."

"You appear no worse for the wear. What can I do for you?"

"This joint planning conference with the British may have taken on an even more important role than we considered."

"How so?"

"I happened to be in the Oval Office this afternoon to brief Franklin on our progress with the naval rearmament program we began last year. This whole Lend-Lease Program he has created has added considerable complexity to our planning. As you know, they introduced the bill in Congress nearly three weeks ago."

"Yes, yes," Stimson injected somewhat impatiently.

"He met . . ."

"He?"

"Franklin met Halifax in Annapolis as Halifax arrived aboard *King George the Fifth*, along with the British military officers for this joint staff conversations conference. If I read Franklin's words correctly, he may well direct the entire output of the rearmament program to be delivered to the Royal Navy."

"It's not just ships, Frank. The same is true for airplanes, howitzers and even rifles, for God's sake."

"So, what do we do with this conference?"

"First, let's hear what our representatives say about the first day's meeting. Then, I think . . ." A knock on the door interrupted Frank's statement. Both men looked to the door. Stimson's military aide appeared in the partially open door.

"Excuse me, sir. The Chief of Staff, Chief of Naval Operations, and other officers you requested are present and ready for your scheduled meeting."

"Give me another minute," Knox said softly to Stimson.

"Ask the generals to wait another minute or so," Stimson said. The colonel nodded his head and closed the door.

"As I was going to say," Knox continued, "I think we need to issue precise instructions to our representatives for these joint conversations."

"More precise than we already have?"

"My concern here, Henry, is the British may press for deeper involvement of our forces, especially in the Atlantic, which in turn will likely amplify pressure to deploy new destroyers in the protection of shipping role."

"What do you suggest?"

"We need our guys to avoid any semblance of commitment to expanding the role until the President has issued the appropriate guidance and funding."

"OK. I'll need some time to consider those instructions. The British will be here for two months by the current plan, so we have time . . . a little time to contemplate the proper words. I do agree. It would be quite easy to escalate things through these staff discussions. Now, we have generals waiting and we are already past our start time."

Knox nodded his head. Stimson went to his desk and simply pushed one of an array of buttons.

The door opened. General Marshall led the group of four flag officers into Stimson's office. Knox and Stimson greeted each general as they entered and gathered around the ten-place oak conference table. Chief of Staff General Marshall and Chief of Naval Operations Admiral Stark led their respective services. Major General Stanley Dunbar 'Stan' Embick, USA [USMA 1899] represented Stimson, Marshall and the War Department. Rear Admiral Robert Lee 'Bob' Ghormley, USN [USNA 1906] represented Knox, Stark and the

Navy Department. The service secretaries and chiefs had handpicked both Embrick and Ghormley; each of them had served previously as directors of their service's War Plans divisions. Ghormley had just temporarily returned from his assignment as Special Naval Observer in the United Kingdom for this conference.

Once they were all seated, Stimson nodded his head to Embrick to begin.

"The opening session was fairly routine," Embrick began. "After introductions, we jumped into sketching out the general purpose of the staff conversations, as they call it."

"Allow me to inject, General," said Knox. "Why is the conference referred to as staff conversations?"

Embrick answered, "Actually, Mister Secretary, Admiral Bellairs informed us that the title was suggested by Prime Minister Churchill in deference to our current political position of neutrality. He felt it was a less integrated, more informal term of reference."

Rear Admiral Roger Mowbray Bellairs, RN, CB, CMG, had been recalled to active duty from the retired list to lead the British mission, largely because of his war plans experience and the confidence the First Sea Lord held in him.

"Well . . . stated that way . . . my hat's off to the Prime Minister. Sorry for the interruption. Please continue."

"Yes sir. We are here to keep you informed regarding the content and progress of these staff conversations. Please ask your questions as they arise. We agreed to three general purposes. First, we will discuss in strategic terms the means of defeating Germany . . ."

"And Italy," interjected Knox.

". . . and liberating occupied lands," Embrick continued. "Yes, and Italy, although it is quite clear from the British contributions that Germany is their primary focus, and they are apparently convinced Italy cannot stand without Germany." Knox nodded his head in acknowledgment. "Second, we will discuss in broad terms how we might coordinate our forces, while respecting our neutrality, to achieve the primary objective. Third, military cooperation will be addressed along with the means to ensure our military operations at least do not interfere and preferably are coordinated to the common objective." Embrick looked to Stimson, apparently signally that was the extent of his remarks on this particular afternoon."

Stimson picked up the queue. "That sounds like a reasonable start. I know Bellairs from previous collaboration during the Great War. Tell us a little about the other British members."

"While Bellairs is chartered by their government to lead this mission, my counterpart is Major General Edwin Morris, formerly of the general staff studies group. He is between division command assignments and was diverted to this mission. They also have Air Vice Marshal 'Jack' Slessor of the Royal Air Force, who is slated to become Air Officer Commanding-in-Chief, Number Five Bomber Group. He was Director of Plans prior to this mission. By the way, after consultation with General Arnold, Colonel 'Joe' McNarney, Chief of the Air Component Branch of the War Plans Division has been tasked with representing the Air Corps and will serve as 'Jack' Slessor's counterpart for aviation matters." Embrick looked to Ghormley.

Admiral Ghormley picked up the description. "As General Embrick noted, Admiral Bellairs is serving as the chief of mission for these conversations. My counterpart is Rear Admiral Victor Danckwerts, who served as Director of Plans for the Admiralty and is currently awaiting command assignment. During my time in London and the UK, I met with Danckwerts numerous times . . . good man . . . with a solid understanding of contemporary naval operations and planning. I have also asked Admiral Turner, and Captains Kirk and Ramsey to join us for these discussions, as their line duties permit."

Rear Admiral Richmond Kelly 'Kelly' Turner, USN [USNA 1908] had just recently been promoted and taken up his current position as Director, War Plans Division for the Navy. Captain Alan Goodrich Kirk, USN [USNA 1909] had served as naval attaché in London since the war began in Europe, just this month been routinely relieved and was slated to take up his new position as director of Naval Intelligence (N-2) when the staff conversations conference concludes. Captain DeWitt Clinton 'Clint' Ramsey, USN [USNA 1912] currently served as chief of plans within the Bureau of Aeronautics.

"I also should add," Ghormley continued, "we have included Lieutenant Colonel Omar Pfeiffer to represent any expeditionary or amphibious planning that might arise from these staff conversations, and Captain Ramsey will address all naval aviation matters."

"Very well," Stimson said. "A good start, it seems to me. Frank, do you have any questions or anything you would like to say?"

Knox stared at Stimson as he considered his words. "No questions from me. These conversations are just beginning." Knox scanned the group. "Secretary Stimson and I may provide further guidance. Until that time, please proceed under the current instructions. Until these conversations take more defined positions, I will simply urge each member to be careful and conscious of our national neutrality. The President wants to do as much as we can to support the British defense . . . but, I just urge caution."

"I will join Secretary Knox's comments. General Marshall, Admiral Stark, do you have any questions?"

"No sir," the two senior officers said in unison.

"Thank you very much for keeping us informed of these discussions. Good luck and good evening." The military officers stood and departed Stimson's office. Knox remained seated. Stimson did the same with his colleague. They waited until the door closed. "You have more you wish to discuss, Frank?"

"From our preface talk, I think we started well. How about I give you a day or so to consider my earlier words and your position. I'll schedule a follow-up meeting for Friday afternoon, if that is acceptable."

"Fine by me, Frank. We need to get your concerns reconciled quickly. We cannot leave the team with any uncertainty. We both know how important Franklin sees this coordination with the British."

"Quite so." Knox stood and extended his right hand to Stimson, who stood and shook hands. "Thank you for hearing me out. Have a good evening, Henry."

"You as well, Frank."

Knox departed.

—

Chapter 11

Show me a hero
and I will write you a tragedy.
- F. Scott Fitzgerald

Saturday, 1.February.1941
Oval Office
The White House
Washington, District of Columbia
United States of America
10:45 hours

Harry Hopkins waited for the President to be wheeled to his desk by one of his duty Secret Service agents.

"So, this is it?" asked Roosevelt.

"Yes, Franklin, this is the off-the-books meeting we discussed last week and you requested be set up for today. Before Chennault arrives, I wanted a few minutes to cover the order, but first, I was informed by Frank Knox earlier this morning that General Order 143 has been issued and made effective today. The U.S. Fleet is abolished and replaced by the separate commands of the Atlantic, Pacific and Asiatic Fleets. Admiral Ernest King has been assigned as Commander-in-Chief Atlantic Fleet, headquartered at Norfolk. Admiral Husband Kimmel has been assigned as Commander-in-Chief Pacific Fleet at Pearl Harbor. And, Admiral Thomas Hart retains his command of the Asiatic Fleet in the Philippines."

"Very well. What of Admiral Richardson?" asked Roosevelt of the vocal, resistant predecessor of Admiral Kimmel.

"Richardson has been relieved of command and transferred to the Office of the Secretary of the Navy, where he is expected to retire from service once he has completed his assignment on the General Board."

"Very well." Roosevelt extended his right hand. "Let's see the order."

Hopkins handed the President a single sheet of paper.

```
                    MILITARY ORDER
      By virtue of the authority vested in
   me, as President of the United States and as
   Commander-in-Chief of the Army and Navy of the
   United States, it is ordered as follows:
```

1. The 1st American Volunteer Group (AVG) is hereby established.

2. The AVG shall report to and be under the operational control of the Central American Manufacturing Company (CAMCo) to further the purpose and overall objective of supporting the Chinese government in their struggle to defend their country against the aggression of Imperial Japan.

3. The director of CAMCo is authorized draw from current production orders 100 new Curtiss P-40 Warhawk pursuit planes and arrange for transport of those aircraft to place(s) deemed appropriate to the purpose stated in paragraph 2. Further, the director shall arrange for proper logistics support of these aircraft.

4. By this order, the director is authorized to seek qualified, rated pilots and ground crews from active duty military squadrons and units to operate the aircraft allocated in paragraph 3. To aid this selection process, the following guidelines are specified:

    a. Any individual who volunteers under this order shall retain their rank and time in service with their respective service.

    b. Each individual shall be compensated at their current rate and shall have such compensation adjusted in accordance with congressionally approved pay tables.

    c. When an individual's service is concluded, the individual shall have the right to return to his respective military service.

    d. No individual who volunteers under this order shall be penalized in any manner whatsoever.

```
       e.  This  order  shall  serve  as  the  contract
with  each  individual  who  volunteers  for  AVG
service.
       5.  All  military  commanders  who  may  be
called  upon  in  the  execution  of  this  order  are
directed  to  render  such  assistance  as  may  be
requested  by  the  director  of  CAMCo.
       6.  Claire  Lee  Chennault  is  hereby
appointed  as  Director  of  the  Central  American
Manufacturing  Company  with  the  equivalent  rank
of  colonel.
       7.  This  order  shall  remain  in  effect  and
valid  until  rescinded  or  superceded  by  this
office.
                    FRANKLIN  D.  ROOSEVELT
                      Commander-in-Chief
THE  WHITE  HOUSE,
February  1,  1941
```

"I believe this is what we agreed to with the service secretaries and Chennault," Roosevelt said.

"That is my understanding."

"Has Chennault seen the final order?" asked the President, holding up the order.

"Not in the present form. He has seen and agreed to the essential elements."

"OK. Then, we must give him time to review and consent to the order."

"Certainly."

"Very well. Check on Chennault. Let's get this done. This whole affair is farther outside the boundaries, but it simply must be done to keep the Japanese from overrunning all of China."

"Yes sir. I'll go check on his location."

Hopkins left the executive office for the outer office, reception area. He was gone for a couple of minutes. Upon return, Hopkins announced, "Mister Chennault has arrived Mister President."

"Please show him in Harry and join us." Roosevelt wheeled his chair to his usual position between the long couches.

Chennault entered the Oval Office and said, "Good morning, Mister President."

Roosevelt extended his right hand to Chennault and replied, "Good morning." The two men shook hands. Roosevelt gestured for Chennault to sit. Hopkins moved a straight back wooden chair to a position behind and to the left of the President, and sat. "Thank you for meeting with me. I expect this shall be our last meeting before we return you to China. Again, I must thank you for your steadfast support of the Chinese government. You have done extraordinary work."

"Thank you, sir."

"As we discussed a few months ago, I will authorize you to draw on production deliveries of pursuit airplanes and seek volunteer pilots to fly and ground crews to maintain those airplanes. General Arnold is fully informed on this program and will deal with any local commander who may present a problem to your recruitment efforts. Also, as we discussed, I shall sign the order that will serve as your authority. If you run into any obstacles you cannot resolve, please contact Harry Hopkins immediately. Lastly, this administration is extending military support to the Chinese through you in a climate of diminishing isolationism, but isolationism nonetheless. I must impress upon you the need for utmost secrecy and avoidance of public exposure. Do you understand and accept all of this?"

"Yes sir, Mister President."

President Roosevelt reached behind him with his left hand extended to Hopkins. Harry placed the military order in the President's hand. Roosevelt in turn handed the paper to Chennault. "This is the order I will sign. Please review it now to ensure it states the guidelines and authority you need to perform your mission."

Chennault took the paper and read the order several times. "Yes sir, I believe it does. I am satisfied."

"Very well. I will sign the order and get you on your way."

"One question, if I may, Mister President, before you sign the order." Roosevelt nodded his head in consent. "Does this authorize me to draw on the American volunteer pilots in the Royal Air Force?"

"Why do you ask . . . beyond the obvious?"

"They are the most experienced, combat fighter pilots we have . . . real combat. They have some very accomplished fighter pilots that would be perfect for this mission."

Roosevelt contemplated the question and his response, having not considered that option. "I'm afraid I shall have to insist that you avoid such contact or recruitment of those already in Great Britain and the Royal Air Force. While the strength of Fighter Command is improving and is substantially better than their situation last September, they are not out of the woods, yet. Further, recruitment of existing service pilots will have to suffice for one primary reason—we can control reaction via General Arnold."

"Very well . . . hands off the RAF. May I contact Colonel Sweeney or the other volunteer recruitment agents before pilots arrive in the UK?"

"Again, I must respond in the negative. They are predominately recruiting from the civilian pilot population. By confining your recruitment efforts to active, rated pilots, you have an exclusive pool. The RAF needs all the pilots it can get, and they are training those pilots who volunteer. We cannot interfere with that process. You should not have the same problem, since the pilots you are drawing from are already trained and experienced."

"Very well, sir. So be it."

"Do you have any other questions?"

"No sir."

Roosevelt nodded his head to Hopkins, who knew precisely the meaning of the President's gesture. Hopkins retrieved the order from Chennault, and then pushed the President's wheelchair back to his desk. With his fountain pen, President Roosevelt signed the order. Hopkins blotted the wet ink, and then placed the signed order in a folder.

Hopkins handed the folder to Chennault. "Here is the original signed order that you should retain and safeguard, since there will only be this one original copy. There are also 25 copies of the order for your use."

Chennault stood, came to attention facing the President and saluted the Commander-in-Chief.

Roosevelt said, "As we say in the nautical services, Godspeed and following winds."

"Thank you, Mister President. Good day." Roosevelt nodded his head, and then Chennault departed the Oval Office to continue his mission.

———

Wednesday, 5.February.1941
RAF Kirton-in-Lindsey
Kirton-in-Lindsey, Lincolnshire, England
United Kingdom

"**Y**our attention, gentlemen . . . and I use that term loosely," announced Squadron Leader Taylor, just outside his office. He waited for quiet, which took longer than it should have. "After your protestations of last week and your diligent performance during out latest training period, the Air Ministry this morning once again declared this squadron operational." Applause and cheers punctuated his announcement. Bill held up his right hand and quiet returned. "I am informed by Group that we can expect to launch on a convoy over-watch mission."

"Oh, great," Salt Morton said.

"Do you wish to request a transfer, Mister Morton, since you are apparently dissatisfied with the mission assignments we are given?" Salt did not respond. "Mister Morton, I asked you a proper question?"

"No sir, I do not wish to request a transfer."

"Fine. In the future," Taylor said, waving his hand across the room, "unless you have a relevant or contributory query, or you have something constructive to add to any discussion, I strongly suggest you keep your silly, juvenile comments to yourself. Am I clear?"

"Yes sir," came the unanimous response.

"As I was trying to say, before I was so rudely interrupted, we are going to fly a protection of shipping patrol as a squadron. We have spent several days practicing our formation changes and tactics. We all know we are ready. I urge everyone to keep a calm head, even if we get into a tangle with the Germans. Let's show headquarters and the Air Ministry we know what we are doing and we are ready for combat operations."

Squadron Leader Taylor provided their assigned operating radio frequencies and call signs, as well as the available intelligence on the convoy for which they would be providing fighter cover. Twelve ships departed the Thames estuary yesterday and were designated Convoy COTTON. Another eight ships from the Humber estuary joined them earlier this morning. No enemy activity had been directed at the convoy. A single destroyer provided surface escort. The squadron would relieve another unspecified squadron and fly conventional, maximum endurance, racetrack orbits behind and to seaward of the convoy, at an altitude of 12,000 feet.

"Are there any questions?" asked Bill. Hearing none, he concluded, "We will wait for our launch command. That is all." He took one last look at each of the pilots, and then turned smartly to return to his office.

Brian turned and leaned toward Dusty and Bulldog. "We're going to fly this mission perfectly, aren't we, lads?"

"You bet." "Yes sir." They answered together.

"We must do our part to get past this training and show phase. I am tired of doing interviews and photographs. I think we all came here to fly and to contribute to beating the Germans. But, our performance as a fighter squadron has been doubtful to Fighter Command and the Air Ministry. Our first objective is to gain sufficient confidence of our leaders that we can become a front line fighter squadron, rather than a second tier squadron stuck with convoy escort missions, and VIP and press events. We will not be taken seriously until we act and perform seriously."

Dusty looked askance at Hunter. "Are you serious?"

"And, what would lead you to think otherwise?"

"You're a bloody, fucking ace. What could be more serious than that?"

"I am only one pilot, one member of a team of pilots. It does not matter how good any one of us is. The only thing that matters is how we operate as a squadron. The controllers, the other squadrons, must have confidence in all of us as a unit. So, yes, I am very serious."

The telephone rang and everyone stopped their conversations. Corporal Harris listened, and then placed the handset back in its cradle. "Squadron to Standby."

Bill Taylor appeared from his office. "There you have it, fellas. It is time to go to work. Let's do this right."

All the pilots donned their Sidcot flying suits and inflatable flotation vests. They retrieved the remainder of their flying equipment. As was his practice in wintertime, Brian also fitted his leather helmet and earphones, with his goggles on his forehead and oxygen mask attached to the left side of his helmet. Each pilot walked to his respective aircraft.

Brian's ground crew – Jacobs, Hawking and Easton – stood at attention by the left horizontal stabilizer. They saluted. Brian returned their salute.

"Why the formality, Henry?"

"We are back out of training status, again. We want to send you lot of fly-boys off on your first operational mission in proper order."

Brian laughed. The men joined him in laughter. "Very well, then. Let's get this show on the road."

All of the pilots were soon strapped into their aircraft. They waited for Bill's start signal. As the minutes passed, Brian allowed his attention to drift off to the right, to the distant tree line. The trees appeared to be a similar conifer variety as Charlotte had on her farm. *I miss you woman. It has been too long since I've seen you, and I've no idea when I will see you again.*

"Mister Drummond," Corporal Jacobs shouted, bringing him back to the cockpit. "Start."

Brian nodded his head. Several other propellers were already turning. Brian stepped through the remainder of his start actions. He had his Hurricane fighter ready to go in short order and before Bill signaled for the squadron to taxi.

The mission went exactly as briefed. They flew very boring, elongated patterns along the 21-ship wakes that marked the passage of Convoy COTTON northbound through the North Sea. While the simple mission encountered no air, surface or subsurface threats, they had flown a flawless sortie. The long two-and-a-half-hour mission ended back where they began – no harm, no foul. They landed, taxied back to their squadron area, and shutdown their Merlin engines – their gun port tapes still in place and their fuel tanks nearly empty.

The debriefing process was short, direct and painless. There was not much to report. They had done their job as everyone expected. *Maybe we have finally turned the corner. Now, we just need to convince Fighter Command.*

"Now that your duties are complete," announced Corporal Harris, "we have mail." The operations clerk called out the names of nearly every pilot, except for Horse Harrow. Brian was the next to last. The envelope had an embossed return address of some law office in Wichita in the upper left corner, opposite the four postage stamps, and his address was typed. He stared at the envelope. *I wonder what the hell this could be . . . another attempt at my deportation? Do I really want to open this?* After several minutes, his curiosity overcame his resistance. He carefully opened the envelope, pulled out the single, folded sheet of paper, unfolded it and read.

The law offices of
Bender, Braddock and Sloan
Wichita, Kansas

January 9, 1941

Mr. Brian Arthur Drummond
No.71 Squadron
Fighter Command, Royal Air Force
Air Ministry, London, England

Dear Mr. Drummond:

It is with profound regret and deepest heartfelt condolences that is my duty to inform you of the passing of both your parents – Susan and George Drummond. A tragic automobile accident in the early morning hours of New Year's Day claimed their lives. As of this writing, the police have not completed their investigation; however, it appears they were returning home from a New Year's Eve celebration. As you were not available and I held a limited power of attorney from your parents, I decided to inter them in Maple Grove Cemetery.

I also offer my most humble apologies for the means of and delay in this notification. It took nearly a week to find what we believe is your current postal address in your parents papers.

Beyond notification as the next of kin, and as your parents' designated executor, I must also inform you that you are the sole surviving beneficiary designated in your parents' last wills and testaments. As such, we need your presence or instructions to close your parents' estate, after their debts and obligations have been concluded. You may not be aware, but they amassed a substantial estate that will significantly exceed the closing of their debts and obligations.

I understand and acknowledge your present employment in the defense of freedom. I have no idea what latitude you have to return to Wichita, to fulfill your obligations, yet, my counsel and first choice recommendation is for you to gain an extended leave of absence from your present duties to allow us to complete execution of your parents' wills. If you are unable to attend, we can engage a local attorney for you and work through a rather laborious set of legal communications to ensure your parents' wishes and yours are thoroughly represented in the final documents filed with the probate court.

Please inform us as soon as possible what your intentions are with respect to your parents' estate. We will work to whatever you are able to do in this matter.

Again, I offer my deepest condolences for your loss. I shall do my best to assist you in this tragic time. Please be safe.

```
With great respect,
your humble servant,
```

Jonas T. Braddock
```
                    Partner
```

Brian was in shock. He could not believe what he read. The words just did not make sense.

"Are you OK?" asked Dusty Langford. Brian did not respond. Dusty touched Brian's left shoulder and repeated softly, "Are you OK?" Brian turned his head toward Dusty, but did not – could not – see him. "You're white as a ghost. Bad news?" The letter slipped from Brian's hand. Langford took the liberty of retrieving the letter and read it. "Dear God above," Paul gasped.

"What's wrong?" asked Red Burns.

Langford did not respond. He simple put a hand under Brian's left arm and applied pressure to coax him to stand. Brian wobbled slightly. Langford escorted Brian to the Skipper's office. He did not knock or even request entry. He sat Brian in one of the chairs before Taylor's desk, and then handed Brian's letter to Squadron Leader Taylor.

Bill waved his hand to shoo away Langford and motioned for him to close the door. Taylor came around the desk, sat next to Brian and placed a hand on Brian's right shoulder. "I am so sorry, Brian. I'm going to take you off flight status for the rest of the day. I'll talk to you later to see what you want to do. I want you to go back to the Mess. Take some time to think. You might want to call Charlotte and talk to her, as well."

Brian nodded his head, stood, and walked out of Taylor's office and through the main room of their Dispersal building. He was still in a daze. No one said anything to him. Langford clearly had informed the other pilots. No one knew what to say in such a drastic situation. Brian walked instinctively toward the Officer's Mess, oblivious to the cold, winter air. His mind could not latch onto any particular thought. Everything was a haze.

—

Friday, 7.February.1941
Aérodrome d'Abbeville-Drucat
Abbeville, Picardy
Occupied France
14:10 hours

No.609 Squadron had begun the shooting portion of their RHUBARB fighter sweep as they flew at wave top height into the Somme estuary toward their primary target. The intelligence blokes told them, they might find a few remaining transport barges left stranded in the tidal flats at the mouth of the River Somme from last summer's invasion preparations. Indeed, there had been two barges lined up perfectly for Yellow Section. Jonathan Kensington had no idea whether they had taken the shots to chew up those stranded river barges. He had been focused on his flying task at this extraordinary low altitude above the water or the land. They encountered some tracers passing behind them from German anti-aircraft gunners, who had not been able to compensate for their speed and low altitude, and they would be firing at their comrades on the other side of the estuary.

They crossed over the marshes and into the farm fields and adjusted their direction slightly, heading to their target – the Abbeville airfield – the base of four German fighter squadrons. It seemed like their propeller tips were cutting the grass and clipping the tops of each tree line. Jonathan glanced at his coolant temperature gauge. He still had margin, but the temperature was rising, even with the cold air.

"There we go," Harness said aloud into his oxygen mask and to himself. The distinctive, nearly orthogonal, concrete runways jumped into view. "We got 'em," he said again to himself. His Green Section was assigned the south barracks area, fuel storage tanks, and the parking area for one or two of the enemy squadrons. As they cleared the last tree line on the north boundary of the airfield, half the Bf109 fighters were already moving. Two of them were airborne, cleaning up their configuration for combat. More importantly, half had not yet moved. Jonathan opened fire. All eight, wing, machine guns erupted with streams of bullets. He saw the tracers from his wingmen as well. Bullet impacts began just short of the closest parked fighter. His wingmen were in better position for the parked aircraft. Jonathan quickly adjusted his gunsight pipper slightly ahead of the nearest aircraft attempting to take off on the grass across one of the runways. The flashes on the wing, fuselage, engine and cockpit marked square hits before the aircraft exploded and spread burning remnants across the field and crossing runway. Jonathan noticed other explosions to his right, but did not look. His wingmen were finding success as well. He did not have much time to pick one more aircraft well into his takeoff roll. He achieved a few hits, but did not stop the fighter. Jonathan had very little time to jink to the right slightly to pick up their primary target, the barracks, a hangar, and three fuel storage tanks. His wingman had already fired on the barracks buildings. Bits and pieces were flying. Several small explosions and fire erupted. Jonathan could see men running from the barracks. He fired on them, undoubtedly hitting some, but he immediate shifted his focus on the fuel tanks. Harness opened fire early, kept his pipper on those tanks, and used his rudder to spread his bullet streams across all three large tanks. The other two Green Section Spitfires hit the tanks as well. All three tanks exploded into large fireballs. Jonathan banked hard left, and then hard right as he passed the fireball and returned to treetop height. He glanced to the right and saw two Spitfires going strong. *We did it.* They turned to the left, per their mission briefing, to their escape point south of Boulogne-sur-Mer.

Once they were clear of the airfield and on their egress leg, Jonathan picked up his altitude slightly, so he could scan the sky around. Some of the German fighters got airborne, and they would be looking for blood. There would probably be other fighter squadrons from other airfields scrambled to intercept them, especially since they had clearly been successful at Abbeville airfield.

—

Friday, 7.February.1941
Rue du Bois Bullon
Drucat, Picardy
Occupied France
14:22 hours

Trevor Andersen, known to British intelligence and the SOE as Agent 'Diamond,' rode in the large, single axle, horse-drawn cart with his long-time friend and colleague Jacques Merton, formerly a major in French Army intelligence and now a member of the fledgling resistance. They were working an intelligence task collecting German dispositions in the vicinity of Abbeville. They were dressed as farmhands – unshaven with dirty faces, hands and clothes. Their story was they were returning from a delivery of silo-ed wheat to Abbeville from the farm they worked on east of Drucat, and they used the aliases of François Deschamps and Yves Moulin, respectively.

They both heard the machine gun fire in the distance and the explosion followed by the red fireball amid the thick black smoke. Neither one of them spoke, but they both looked toward the large petroleum fire. Both of them and their horse were startled as 12 Spitfires roared just over their heads, their engines at deep-throated high power. They felt the wind of their passing and felt what seemed like the heat from their powerful engines. They watched as the aircraft continued a left turn, almost dragging their left wing tips in the furrowed field.

Trevor noticed movement in the sky above and to the south of the retreating British fighters. The shapes were clear – German Bf109 fighters. The enemy aircraft were diving toward the Spitfires. The Spitfires leveled their wings headed north-northwest and either did not see their German pursuers, or they were depending on their speed to outrun the Germans. In less than a minute, the British fighters disappeared behind a far tree line, but they could still hear the engines fading into the distance. It took several more minutes to calm their horse.

Trevor whispered to Jacques in French, "I guess our information was put to good use."

"Quite so. It is reassuring to know they are listening to us."

"We need to be alert and cautious. The Germans will not be happy, and they will be looking for anyone to blame and punish."

"Then, we must look very innocent and ordinary."

Jacques flicked the reins, and they began to move again.

Trevor looked back to the descending German fighters. Suddenly, the distinctive shapes of a dozen Spitfires arrived from the north, causing the diving Germans to pull up. The fight ensued at comparatively low altitude. They could hear a lot of distant machine gun fire.

"We need to get through Drucat, to the farm, and off the roads," Trevor said in French. "We need to hurry, but not look like we are hurrying. We don't need to give the Germans a reason to see us or stop us."

"Easy, my friend. Relax."

Drucat was not a big village. They made it through the town and into the countryside on the east side. They had a better view of the aerial fight above and ahead of them. By this time, they could see several smoke trails. Someone had been hit. Then, almost as quickly as the fight had formed, the Spitfires broke off toward the north. The Germans gave chase, but they pulled up and turned back. Within another minute, the sky was clear, and the sounds of the country returned – birds chirping, an occasional frog croaking, and a distant cow mooing or a horse baying.

They pulled off the roadway and onto the worn path in the grass leading to the farm that had become their base of operations in the area. The farm belonged to Madame Marie du Clerc – an elderly, widowed woman, who needed two strong men to help her run the farm. She also happened to sympathize with and support the resistance as best she could.

They unharnessed the horse, brushed him down, and returned him to his stall in the barn.

"We might have visitors," Jacques said, as he was looking out of the barn.

Trevor joined him at the partially open doorway. They both stood back, remaining in the shadows of the darkened interior, so that no one outside could see them.

A German Army Volkswagen *Kübelwagen* Light Multirole Armored Car, often referred to as a "Tub" car, sat crosswise at the farm entrance. The large, black *Wehrmacht* cross was clearly visible on the side of the ash gray vehicle. They were probably scanning the farm and discussing whether they should search the buildings and interrogate the inhabitants. After several minutes of contemplation and no detectable movement, they drove off. For all they knew, the farm was abandoned, and thus would be a waste of their time.

"Good," Trevor commented. "Gerry is probably going to be stirred up for several days." He checked his uniquely French, 'worker' watch. "Our next contact window opens at 15:10 this afternoon."

"We have not found the headquarters, yet."

"No, we haven't. We will have to report negative, but I also want to report the attack on the airfield. We were far too close, and they should have warned us."

"Perhaps, the mission was approved since our last contact."

"Perhaps. However, they must know we could have easily been caught up in that attack."

"As you wish . . ."

"Do you think I am wrong?"

"Trevor, I have known you for many years. I know some of what you have accomplished, but I recognize I have no way to know everything you have done. I trust your judgment, but this is war. Things happen in war. We have enough other high priority tasks ahead of us than complaining about being surprised. I am impressed they moved so quickly on the information we provided just a few days ago."

They heard movement outside. They both move swiftly and silently to observation points. Jacques stood back and looked to Trevor. "It is Marie returning," he said. They relaxed.

The barn door opened wider and Madame du Clerc walked her horse into the barn. She was a petite woman in her late 50's with gray highlights in her short, light brown hair. This day, she wore riding trousers, heavy boots and a heavy riding coat. Large fur earmuffs covered her ears, which she pulled off when she saw the two men. "You are back from your delivery," she stated in her native French, delightfully spoken.

"Yes, everything went perfectly," said Jacques.

"And, we almost got caught up in the attack on the aerodrome."

"That was rather spectacular, wasn't it?"

"Except, we were a little too close when it happened," Jacques said and nodded to Trevor in acknowledgment of his colleague's concern.

"Did you make any more contacts?" asked Trevor, seeking to change the subject.

"Yes, as a matter of fact, I have . . . several more in the neighboring villages."

"You do trust them . . . yes?"

Marie smiled. "Who can you ever trust these days? But, yes, I believe we can. I know them all. They are patriots, who want to see the *Boche* run out of our country."

"Do you feel comfortable running and expanding your local network?" asked Trevor.

"Yes, I would say so."

"Then, perhaps, we should tell London. If SOE agrees, we can send Jacques back to Paris, and I can head south for extraction."

"That is your choice," she responded.

"We haven't found the command center, yet," added Jacques.

"No, we haven't, but we can leave that task, as well as the others, to Marie and her new network."

"Again, as you wish, my friend."

"Excellent. Thank you. Then, if we are agreed, let us all three go for our communications window."

"I am ready," announced Marie.

Trevor looked to Jacques, who nodded his head in agreement. "Very well. I will make the first contact, so they recognize me, and I can call for my extraction instructions. Then, Jacques can send his concurrence, and you will send the remainder of our report. We will acknowledge the aerodrome attack and confirm your new resistance network, and lastly no success on objective two, as yet."

"I can do that."

"We have confidence in you, Marie."

"Yes, we do," added Jacques.

Marie smiled broadly. "Excellent. I'll go make some lunch. It will take us an hour to reach our next transmission site." The Germans had demonstrated early on in the war their keen ability for direction finding and triangulation. SOE used a sophisticated transmitter location-shifting technique developed by MI6 after the tragic Venlo Incident in 1939, and the capture of agents Stevens and Payne-Best.

"That will work. We'll take care of your horse, if you are going to make lunch. We will join you shortly."

Marie nodded her head and left. Jacques collected a bucket of oats for both horses, while Trevor unsaddled Marie's horse, brushed him down, and returned him to the adjacent stall. They completed their barn chores and took the rear doorway to join Marie in the main house.

—

Saturday, 8.February.1941
Standing Oak Farm
Winchester, Hampshire, England
United Kingdom
15:15 hours

Brian barely stepped out of the taxi when Charlotte leapt into his arms.

Charlotte whispered in his ear, "I am so very sorry for your loss, my darling."

"Thank you. I am still adjusting to the new reality."

"I know how you feel."

They remained locked in their embrace until the taxi disappeared over the entry ridge line. They released one arm to walk into the house.

"Thank you for calling me the night you received the news. How long will you be with me?"

Brian dropped his satchel. They walked to the living room with a modest fire in the fireplace and sat. "Everything happened so fast. I did not have an opportunity to call you with the rest of the news. We have two tickets on a Pan American flying boat tomorrow morning, leaving from Bournemouth."

"Brian!" Charlotte said in shock. She did not know what else to say.

I have been given four to six weeks to return to Wichita and settle my parents' affairs. We have talked about visiting my childhood home. While our original purpose has passed, I would still like you to see where I grew up. You have never been to the United States, and I would like you to see some of my country. Plus, you have dealt with this estate business with your parents' passing. I think you could be of great help to me."

"Brian, I am speechless. How did you possibly arrange all this? How will we get from wherever this flying boat lands to Kansas? How will we get back? Brian, I had no idea. There is so much to consider. I don't even know if my passport is current or valid. How can I leave the farm for that long?"

"Well, let me see if I can work through your concerns. I do not want to be presumptuous, but I thought Lionel and Horace could handle the farm while we were away."

"They can for a few days, but we are talking about a month, maybe more. They are both old men, Brian. I'm not so sure that is fair to them."

"Can we talk to them, Charlotte? Maybe they will feel differently."

"Yes, of course. It never hurts to ask."

"Anyway, I showed my letter to Squadron Leader Taylor . . ."

"He is your new commanding officer?"

"Yes, Squadron Leader Churchill was placed on some kind of extended medical leave. They decided to give me some time off. It was Air Commodore Spencer, John Spencer, who found the connection to this flying boat, leaving tomorrow. He says the trans-Atlantic crossing takes hours instead of days. They even made sure my passport was still valid after I received the President's pardon, and that you were recognized as my wife. I was told we can get you an emergency passport, if we need it. The flying boat takes off from Bournemouth tomorrow before noon and lands in New York the following day, instead of the seven to ten days by ship. Then, an Army Air Corps C-39 transport aircraft will take us from New York to Wichita. I've been very impressed with all the arrangements just for me, for us."

"What can I say?"

"Yes is all you need to say."

Charlotte giggled in a nervous way. "I so want to be with you, to see where you grew up, but truth be told, I am five months pregnant with our first child, my first pregnancy. I will be at six months upon our return. I feel the risk is too great, Brian. As much as I hate to say this, I am afraid you shall have to do this alone."

Brian stared at Charlotte. *This can't be happening. I was so sure she would jump at the chance. We may never get an opportunity like this again.* "Can we discuss this, to find a way to change your mind?"

"We can discuss it all you wish, but facts are facts," she said, as he patted her distended belly with both hands. "I would never forgive myself, if anything happened to our baby. I have never flown in an aeroplane before. I have no idea what effect that might have on me or the baby."

"I'm sure you are not the first pregnant woman to fly."

"Are you?"

Brian's thoughts raced through possible answers. *Well, no, I'm not.* "I can ask. I'm sure someone must know. Mary is pregnant. Maybe John and Mary have flown, and they could tell us if there are any risks, or perhaps they know more about such things."

"I know you want this to happen. I want this to happen. But, I must think of the baby. And, I do need to tend to the farm."

"Perhaps, I should not go either, then."

Charlotte looked off to some distant, unseen place, and returned to Brian. "That is your choice to make, my darling. You have lost both your parents. There are affairs that demand your presence. So many people have gone out of their way to see that you have the opportunity to take care of those affairs properly."

"I cannot argue with you."

"Good. Then, it is settled. I will drive you to Bournemouth. With the checkpoints, it will take a couple of hours to drive what should only take an hour."

"No need. Save your fuel. I have two tickets on the morning train from Winchester to Bournemouth."

"Then, I will go with you, to send you off properly. I would like to see this contraption you call a flying boat."

"OK. The train is scheduled to depart Winchester at 08:05, and arrive at Bournemouth 50 minutes later, which should be plenty of time to make the 10:30 boarding time for the flight."

"Agreed. Now, it is milking time, so change your clothes. You can join us in the barn."

They both rose. Brian went to the bedroom. Charlotte went to the barn. They would have a normal afternoon and evening. She was good about that, and Brian respected her more for that attribute. The cows would not wait for the foibles of their human caretakers.

—

Saturday, 8.February.1941
Chequers Court
Ellesborough, Buckinghamshire, England
United Kingdom
21:35 hours

Prime Minister Winston Churchill uncharacteristically sat alone in his study within the classic 16th Century, Gothic Tudor mansion at the foot of the Chiltern Hills. The manor house and surrounding 1,500 acres of land had been the prime minister's country retreat since the estate was deeded to the nation in 1917. The elegant mansion offered far more space with which to entertain guests as well as magnificent and immaculately kept grounds for a casual walkabout and quiet contemplation. There was peace at this place, even in wartime and with the threat of impending invasion. Evening meals, regardless of where he was located, were usually social or working events, especially at his weekend retreats to the prime minister's country estate or his wartime, de facto alternate at Ditchley Park. Dinner had been quiet – just Clemmie and him. After supper, she retired to her bedroom to read. He had completed his entire dispatch box of incessant paperwork before dinner. This evening, Churchill decided to re-read Harriet Beecher Stowe's seminal 1852 novel, "*Uncle Tom's*

Cabin – or, Life Among the Lowly." The embers of his half-smoked cigar had gone out, and his second snifter of brandy was nearly dry. He was a little over halfway through his reading, when a knock at the door interrupted his silent pleasure. He did not answer and waited for the door to open.

His duty private secretary John Martin poked in his head. "We have an urgent telephonic message from the Foreign Office, Prime Minister." Churchill stared at Martin, waiting for him to continue. "Ambassador Lord Halifax notified the Secretary a short time ago, the U.S. House of Representatives passed the lend-lease bill by a vote of 260-165."

"Well, I will be damned. We are one step closer. You said this information came from the ambassador, not Harry Hopkins?"

"Yes sir . . . the ambassador. Mister Hopkins is in Bournemouth with Mister Bracken. They left London earlier this afternoon, and Mister Hopkins is scheduled to depart by flying boat aeroplane tomorrow around mid-day, I do believe."

"Does Harry know about the House vote?"

"I do not know, sir. Would you like me to have the Foreign Office pass the information to Mister Bracken and Mister Hopkins?"

"No, John, I would like you to make the call directly to Harry Hopkins on my behalf."

"Yes sir. I will tend to it immediately, sir."

"Excellent. Before you leave, would you be so kind to reload my snifter? I have reason to celebrate."

"Of course, sir."

Martin brought the cognac level up to the desired quarter mark. He placed it beside the Prime Minister and ignited a lighter for Churchill's cigar.

Winston nodded his head, took several puffs to relight his cigar, and then raised his snifter. "We have cause to rejoice, John."

"Yes sir. Is there anything else, sir?"

"I need an audience."

"Would you like me to see what I can muster up for you?"

Winston laughed. "No, I shall hold my words for now."

"Very well, sir. If you will excuse me, I will call Mister Hopkins directly."

"By all means, John. Thank you."

When the door closed, Churchill stood with his brandy in his right hand and his wafting cigar in his left hand, and did a little jig. *One-step closer, indeed. Congratulations, Franklin . . . for all of us. The timing is perfect, could not be better. I am scheduled to give a broadcast war update tomorrow night, the first public broadcast in five months. The words feel good. Give us the tools, and we will finish the job. I am eager to deliver this particular speech.*

Winston paced the room, scanned the books on the shelves, puffed on his cigar and sipped his brandy. *Yes, this feels right, quite right . . . very right. I pray for your success, Franklin.*

Martin returned. Churchill shrugged his shoulders, as if to say, well? "I was able to reach Mister Hopkins. I informed him on your behalf of the House vote."

"What did he say? Well, come on, man, what did he say?" Churchill asked with clear impatience.

"He was grateful for the information and for your consideration. He informed me that he has made arrangements with the pilot captain of the aeroplane to receive your speech tomorrow night. They expect to be on approach to or at Lisbon by broadcast time."

"Excellent. I think he will appreciate the words. Fortuitously, the words are appropriately suited to this moment in history. There is no more business tonight, John. Go to bed. I am going to return to tonight's book – an old novel, but reflective of history, and then head to bed myself. Business is done for this night."

"Very well, sir. I am but a call away, should you need me. I will see you in the morning."

"Good night, John."

"Good night, sir."

John Martin left the Prime Minister, who stared at the door for several seconds, and then returned to his large, well-cushioned chair and this evening's book. Tomorrow was another day and would be a good day.

—

Chapter 12

> I always love to begin a journey on Sundays,
> because I shall have the prayers of the church
> to preserve all that travel by land, or by water.
>
> - Jonathan Swift

Sunday, 9.February.1941
Bournemouth, Dorset, England
United Kingdom
10:25 hours

Charlotte and Brian decided to walk the half-mile distance from Bournemouth Station to the Pier. Bomb damage had been cleared but not repaired. Well, some of the damage had been repaired, but most had not. The air was brisk and felt good . . . at least it was dry. People acknowledged his uniform without knowing who he was. Charlotte beamed with pride. They walked purposefully down Holdenhurt Road, and then Bath Road. As they cleared the last buildings onto Bath Road, opening up the scene to the coastline, they both noted the large airplane floating at a mooring several hundred yards off the shore.

"Oh my, that is big," noted Charlotte.

"Yes, much bigger than anything I have flown," Brian added. "That's it."

They stood admiring the gray aircraft with Pan American Airways System displayed in bold letters below the massive wing and Yankee Clipper painted on the nose.

Brian looked around to find a small, wooden building with a professionally painted sign beside the door that read 'PanAm Office.' He led them inside.

A middle-aged man in some kind of flight uniform smiled from behind a small desk. "You must be Flying Officer Drummond." Brian nodded. "We have been expecting you. Please allow me to offer my sincerest condolences for your loss. We are honored to be of service in your return home."

"Thank you." Brian presented both tickets.

"I am Chief Steward Haggler, John Haggler, for your flight." He looked to Charlotte. "And, you must be Mrs. Drummond."

"Yes."

"Welcome. I know you will enjoy your flight."

"Oh, I am not going. I just wanted to send off my husband properly."

"Oh dear, apparently, we misunderstood. We were instructed to reserve two seats for both of you."

"Yes," interjected Brian, "that was the plan, but we have decided that it is best if she does not travel, since she is with child."

"I see. Well, congratulations to both of you. Very well, then, we shall scratch Mrs. Drummond from the manifest, and we shan't be needing this one" Haggler said, handing Charlotte's ticket back to Brian.

"Thank you," answered Brian.

"You are officially checked in, Mister Drummond. We will handle your bag," Haggler said, as another steward took Brian's bag, tagged it, and placed it on a cart outside a side door. "We will be boarding the aircraft in half an hour. It is warmer in here, although there is not a great deal of space. Please remain close by for our boarding announcement."

Brian nodded his acknowledgment and turned to Charlotte. "Do you want to wait in here where it is warm?"

"Actually, no," she answered. "'Let's walk a little."

"Close by," Haggler reminded them.

"Yes, of course," Charlotte chuckled. "We shall not stray far."

This time Charlotte led them into the rising sun, which had begun to provide some warmth against the winter chill. Two good size launches were shuttling baggage and people back and forth between the pier and the aircraft. After walking in silence for 25 yards or so, Charlotte stopped and turned to face Brian. "I want to be going with you, Brian. I hope you know that."

"Yes, I do, and I also understand why you are not going."

"I love you, and I will miss you terribly." She wrapped her arms around his torso, pressed her body against his, and kissed him passionately. "Come home safely to me as soon as you can."

"I will. I'll get this done quickly."

"You take whatever time is necessary, so that you are comfortable with the arrangements. After all, you will be over here for however long this war lasts."

"True. Will you be OK going back to the farm by yourself."

Charlotte giggled. "Yes, my darling. I have made this journey more than a few times. I've spent practically my entire life in Hampshire and Dorset. I shall be just fine, I can assure you."

Brian laughed. "Yes, now, there is that."

Charlotte glanced around them. Brian instinctively looked around as well, expecting to see someone approaching them. He then felt her hand gently squeeze his groin. It startled him, and his body reacted instantly.

She giggled mischievously. "Remember what I do with that thing."

Trying not to react any more than he already had, Brian exclaimed, "Charlotte, damn!"

She grinned broadly at him, but did not let go. "Don't forget."

"Damn, woman. I don't worry about that. I could never forget you and what you do."

"That's my boy." She kissed him, again, and then let him go. "I will manage things until you return. Please cable me, if you need me or would like my advice."

"I can always do that. Thanks, Charlotte."

"Now, I got what I wanted, let's go back to the warmth of the building."

"Wait. Give me a minute or two. You stirred things up. I need to let things dissipate. I do not need to be embarrassed before a long flight."

Charlotte smiled and giggled, again. "I'm sorry we cannot take care of it in a more enjoyable manner."

"That is not helping, Charlotte."

"I'm sorry. I just wanted to give you a send off you would remember."

"You have accomplished your objective, my dear."

"Excellent."

People, men and women, left the building and walked toward the pier. Chief Steward Haggler stepped out of the building, looked to Brian and motioned for him to come. Brian turned and led Charlotte back to the office building.

"It is time to board, sir."

"Certainly."

Brian turned and embraced Charlotte. They kissed one last time. "Good-bye, Charlotte. I'll return as quickly as I can."

"I know you will. Thank you for tolerating my playfulness."

"I love you, Charlotte."

"I love you very much, Brian."

Brian kissed her one last time, and then joined the small line at the pier. He counted roughly two, dozen passengers, mostly men with only three women. Mister Haggler went to the front of the line with his clipboard and pen in hand. The first launch would carry half the passengers. The other launch cast off from the flying boat's port sponson for the return to the pier and the remainder of the passengers, including RAF Flying Officer Brian Drummond. Haggler ticked off Brian's name and motioned for him to board the launch. Brian looked one last time. Charlotte remained where he left her. She was waving to him. He waved back and flew her a kiss. Charlotte returned the gesture of affection. He hesitated to enjoy the magnificent sight of her, and then descended into the covered launch and his journey home began.

Brian helped several other passengers onto the launch. He was the last passenger to disembark from the launch onto a small floating platform, and then onto the aircraft's large, left sponson. Brian had to duck as he stepped through the main entry hatchway. A steward checked his ticket and showed him to his seat – a comfortable, spacious, lounge chair compared to the aircraft seats he was accustomed to using.

The stewards gave their instructions for the flight to all of the passengers. Their route would take them to: Lisbon, Portugal; Horta, Azores; Hamilton, Bermuda; and finally New York City and the Marine Terminal. Brian watched and listened. Out the port side portals, he watched the last launch towed the boarding platform slowly back to the pier. He heard and felt the first engine start – the No.1, left most of the four engines. The engine remained at fast idle for several minutes, and then the other three engines were started in quick sequence. With all four propellers turning, the aircraft moved slowly away from its mooring. The pilot maneuvered the behemoth seaplane away from the shore, toward the southeast, presumably to give himself plenty of takeoff room, and then turned into the light breeze from the southwest. All four engines advanced smoothly to takeoff power. Speed built up slowly. He could see spray off the hull chine, and they began to feel the thumps from the swells against the hull. The frequency of the hull thumps increased rapidly, and then disappeared entirely. They were airborne. When they cleared the Swanage salient, they turned due west along the coastline as they continued to gain altitude.

The hum of the engines on top of the restless night with Charlotte induced a slumber for Brian.

—

Sunday, 9.February.1941
Pan American Airways Yankee Clipper
49° 03' North; 10° 03' West
13:45 hours

Brian felt a hand shake his left shoulder. He returned to consciousness with Chief Steward Haggler bent over toward him.

"Excuse me, sir. Captain Jennings has requested your presence on the flight deck."

"Is there a problem?"

"No sir. I believe he just wants to meet you."

Brian nodded his head, unbuckled his seat belt and followed Haggler forward to the Galley. A small, circular ladder occupied the forward, starboard corner of the galley compartment.

"Up the ladder is the flight deck, sir."

"Thank you."

Brian climbed the circular ladder and stood on the upper deck, just aft of the co-pilot seat of a long flight deck. The young-looking man in the forward, left, captain's seat, rose and stepped toward him. He extended his right hand to Brian. "First, may I offer my sincerest, heartfelt condolences on behalf of myself and the crew, for your loss. We are happy to be of service for your return home."

"Thank you."

"And, I must say, it is a distinct honor to meet you, Mister Drummond. I'm Captain Harold 'Harry' Jennings in command of the Yankee Clipper."

"Brian Drummond . . . Captain. This is quite a machine."

"First time?"

"Yes sir. I'm just a fighter pilot."

Jennings laughed hard. "Gentleman," he shouted, "just a fighter pilot. May I introduce Flying Officer Brian Arthur Drummond, goes by the call sign Hunter, appropriately so I must say. He's from Wichita, Kansas, and volunteered for the Royal Air Force before the war started. He is also three times an ace, holder of the Military Cross and Distinguish Flying Cross, and last year was awarded a Commander of the British Empire by King George the Sixth himself." He turned back to Brian. "Your humility is refreshing, Mister Drummond; but, you are way beyond just a fighter pilot."

"Thank you, Captain. My machines are toys compared to this," Brian said, as he waved his hand across the compartment.

"Toys with teeth."

"Yes, they do have a bite."

"Please allow me to give you the cook's tour of the flight deck." Brian nodded his consent. Pointing toward a large panel to the aft of the long compartment on the starboard side, he said, "This is the flight engineer's station. Steve Ramsey is our chief engineer." Ramsey stood, saluted and extended his hand. Brian shook his hand. "Steve manages the engines and the auxiliary systems. Forward of the engineer's station is our radio operator. John Jones is manning that station." Brian shook his hand. "Sam Armstrong is my co-pilot." Brian leaned forward to shake the co-pilot's hand as he twisted in his seat. "The passage way forward goes to the mooring station and some of our support systems. Over here," Jennings said, gesturing to the long table on the port side of the flight deck, "is the Navigator's station. Jerry Harrison is our navigator for this flight." Brian shook Harrison's hand.

Brian looked out the port side portals over the navigator's table. "We're headed south, now . . . not west."

"Well done," said Harrison. "We headed west after takeoff to this point," he said, pointing to a spot on the large map, "before we turned south. We needed to be well off the Normandy coast. We don't need the Germans getting interested in us. We have no protection. We'll maintain our due south course until we turn east to head into Lisbon."

"Do you get fighter escort in the war zone?"

"Interesting that you should ask that," responded Captain Jennings. "Normally, no, we are a commercial flight and technically fly at risk when we are close to France, Ireland or England. On this particular flight, we had a section of Spitfires, high and behind us, watching over us at Prime Minister Churchill's insistence, until we were beyond RADAR range."

Brian felt strange. "Certainly not because of me."

Jennings laughed. "It should be, but no. We have another distinguished passenger on board."

"Who?"

"I am not at liberty to say. I'm sorry. Would you care to take the controls to get a feel for the aircraft?"

This time Brian laughed. "I doubt highly that the passengers would appreciate my feeling the aircraft, but thank you for the offer . . . perhaps another day when we don't have passengers to worry about, I would love to see how this monster flies."

"Very well. If you should change your mind, please let me know. I know you will not fly this big seaplane like one of your Spitfires."

"Thank you."

"Now, if you will excuse me, I should return to my duties."

"Yes, certainly."

"It has been a genuine honor to meet you, Brian."

"The honor is mine, sir." Brian waved to the crew, left the flight deck and returned to his seat. He missed the lunch service, but the stewards fed him separately, while they tended to their other duties.

—

Sunday, 9.February.1941
Pan American Airways Yankee Clipper
38° 39' North; 12° 18' West
20:50 hours

The sun set several hours ago, which meant the first leg was taking longer than expected or planned. The flight had been surprisingly smooth and uneventful. The size of the aircraft allowed all of them the space and opportunity to stand, stretch and even walk, which in turn, made the flight even more comfortable.

A middle-aged, thin, rather frail-looking man appeared beside his seat and extended his right hand. "Mister Drummond, I presume. I'm Harry Hopkins." Brian stood to face Hopkins. "Would you care to join me in my compartment?"

That's a rather odd question. Who is this guy? Why is he asking me to join him? Where is this compartment he claims to possess? The puzzled expression must have been noticeable to Hopkins. "What do you want with me?" asked Brian.

"Excuse me for being so direct," he answered. "I will explain, if you will come with me."

Brian did just that, followed this fellow Hopkins aft, through another passenger compartment and into a compartment he did not know existed. Hopkins shut the door behind Brian.

"My apologies for all the mystery, but I am not supposed to advertise my presence. I am the special assistant to President Roosevelt. I am returning from a presidential mission to England. I will ask you not to discuss any of this with anyone else." Brian nodded his consent. "I was informed you were on board and I wanted to meet you. I will explain later, but first, the crew has made special arrangements for me to listen to Prime Minister Churchill's radio broadcast that is scheduled to begin shortly, and I thought you might be interested in listening as well."

"I do enjoy his speeches, so thank you for your consideration."

"You are most welcome. Let's see if this will work."

"Mister Hopkins, this is Jones," the radio operator announced over the aircraft's intercom system. "Our HF radio is not cooperating at the moment. I will keep trying to pick up the broadcast for you."

"Thank you," Harry responded. "While we are waiting, I am also informed that you are returning to the United States on bereavement leave."

"Yes sir. Both my parents were killed in an automobile accident in the early morning of New Year's Day."

"I am so sorry to hear that. You have my sympathy."

"Thank you."

"When I was informed of your presence, I thought I remembered your name. As I recall, the President issued a full pardon for you last year, for your violation of the Neutrality Act."

"Yes sir, he did. I have it with me, if you would like to see it."

"That is not necessary. I remember, now, recommending your pardon to the President."

"Thank you for that, Mister Hopkins, and please thank President Roosevelt. I did not want to offend anyone, or violate any law. I just wanted to fly, to defend freedom."

"We know, and we appreciate your sacrifice and service, even if it is for the British at the moment."

"Thank you."

"How is it flying that new Spitfire airplane?

"I'm flying Hurricanes for Seventy-One Squadron at present."

"Ah, yes, the all-American Eagle Squadron."

"Yes, precisely, but to answer your question, it was a dream come true – best damn machine I've ever flown."

"Excellent."

Scratchy static came from the speaker on the small table in his compartment. They could hear an occasional word or two of Churchill's distinctive voice. The signal would come and go. The radio operator was clearly struggling to gain a clear signal. Brian noticed the engine sound change. He guessed they were beginning their descent for landing. They listened to the annoying, scratchy static overwhelming the occasional audible words, and then the speaker went silent.

"I'm sorry we cannot get a clear signal," Hopkins said.

"I'm just amazed they can pick up any signal at all. The radios in our fighters are line of sight only."

"Now, there is that. I'm not sure I understand the magic of radio, but I know they have picked up broadcast radio before, so maybe we are just in the wrong spot."

"Perhaps. We have begun our descent. We are late."

"Yes. I was informed earlier that the captain had to deviate west when they received a warning signal of unusual German air activity out of Brest."

"Well, then, good to deviate . . . better safe than sorry, as we say."

Harry looked at his watch. "The captain estimated a new landing time in about 20 minutes."

Chief Steward Haggler knocked, opened the door, and told them to buckle their seat belts for landing. The scratchy static returned, and then miraculously Churchill's voice came through crisp and clear. Haggler smiled and departed, closing the door behind him.

"I must again emphasize what General Dill has said, and what I pointed out myself last year. In order to win the war Hitler must destroy Great Britain. He may carry havoc . . ."

Static again overwhelmed the signal. It was frustrating, but both men sat patiently. The clear signal returned and Churchill's distinctive voice was easily identifiable.

"The other day, President Roosevelt gave his opponent in the late presidential election a letter of introduction to me, and in it he wrote out a verse, in his own handwriting, from Longfellow, which he said, 'applies to your people as it does to us.' Here is the verse:

"'. . .Sail on, O Ship of State!

Sail on, O Union, strong and great!

Humanity with all its fears,

With all the hopes of future years,

Is hanging breathless on thy fate!'

"What is the answer that I shall give, in your name, to this great man, the thrice-chosen head of a nation of a hundred and thirty millions? Here is the answer, which I will give to President Roosevelt: Put your confidence in us. Give us your faith and your blessing, and, under Providence, all will be well.

"We shall not fail or falter; we shall not weaken or tire. Neither the sudden shock of battle, nor the long-drawn trials of vigilance and exertion will wear us down. Give us the tools, and we will finish the job."

The broadcast ended. Jones said, "That is the end of the broadcast, Mister Hopkins. I apologize for the earlier problems with reception. It happens from time to time with high frequency radio signals."

"Thank you, Mister Jones. I know you did the best you could."

"Thank you, sir. We are on approach to Lisbon. We will be landing shortly."

Hopkins chuckled. "It was worth the attempt. We did not get to hear his whole speech, but those last few sentences were classic Churchill."

"He is a most impressive speaker."

"A bit of an understatement, I should think. I have always admired President Roosevelt, but even Franklin admits that Prime Minister Churchill is in a league of his own. Have I been informed correct . . ."

Hopkins stopped mid-sentence when they felt the thud and rapid slapping of small swells on the aircraft hull. They seemed to bounce a couple more times before the aircraft settled into the water and the engines were slowly pulled to idle. It was dark outside. They should see lights along the shoreline. There was no blackout in Portugal. Various engine sounds accompanied the pilot's maneuvering of the large seaplane to its assigned mooring.

"I guess we are here," Harry said.

"So it would seem."

"As I was going to ask, I understand you have met Mister Churchill."

"Yes sir. Several times."

"Charming fellow, don't you think?"

"Very much so."

Chief Steward Haggler knocked and opened the compartment door. "We have arrived in Lisbon harbor. We shall be moored in another five minutes or so. If you have no objection, Mister Hopkins, we would like to deplane you last. We have a separate launch for you. The ambassador has asked for a separate meeting with you for some official business."

"No problem."

"We will refuel and re-provision the aircraft. We expect to take off in two hours time." Haggler turned to Brian. "Mister Drummond, as a uniformed military combatant of a belligerent country, the Portuguese authorities have asked that you remain aboard, so as not to jeopardize their neutrality."

Brian was a bit taken aback by Haggler's statement, but he quickly understood. He nodded his head in acknowledgment and acceptance.

The chief steward continued, "Captain Jennings suggests you could avail yourself of a bunk in the crew bunk room, aft of the flight deck. That way, our housekeeping crew can tend to the passenger compartments."

"That is very generous of you. Since I am confined to the aircraft, I think I will take you up on his offer."

By the time Haggler came to retrieve Harry Hopkins for his shore meeting with the U.S. Ambassador to Portugal, all of the passengers except them had disembarked for a short respite at the airline's shore lounge while the aircraft was serviced. Haggler informed them that everything was going according to schedule, so the departure time would remain the same. One passenger left, as Lisbon was his destination. Three additional passengers would be joining them for the remainder of the flights to New York City. Haggler showed Brian the small, efficient, crew rest compartment that contained six narrow bunks complete with light curtains for each bunk. Brian wasted no time in hanging up his uniform tunic, loosening his shirt collar and necktie, choosing an unused bunk and falling into a hard sleep.

—

Monday, 10.February.1941
Marine Air Terminal
New York Municipal Airport
East Elmhurst, Queens, New York City, New York
United States of America
07:55 hours

Morning twilight opened as they had been eating breakfast. Brian had been served in the first sitting, allowing him to return to his compartment and find an open seat by a portal. He was awe-struck by the expanse and enormity of New York City as the morning sun illuminated the tall buildings. The contrast between New York City and wartime, bomb-damaged London was far beyond dramatic, verging upon tragic. The view of the city was magnificent as they descended on approach and landed smoothly just beyond Rikers Island. They taxied to and moored at the dock for the Marine Air Terminal. The flight had taken nearly 26 hours clock time, across five time zones, to complete. The trans-Atlantic flight was dramatically better than the 10 days transit by freighter Brian had taken to England in the spring of 1939, and surprisingly comfortable, rather elegant from what he was accustomed to flying.

As Brian waited for the other passengers to disembark, Harry Hopkins stopped to say good-bye. "Again, my condolences for your loss, Brian. I trust you will make quick work of handling your parents' estate."

"Thank you, sir."

"I would like you to stop by the White House on your return to Great Britain. I would be honored to introduce you to President Roosevelt, and I know he would cherish the opportunity to meet a genuine American hero."

"I am no hero, Mister Hopkins. I am just a guy who loves to fly."

"Your humility is admirable, Brian. Yet, the facts speak volumes beyond that. Please let me know when you can stop in Washington. I will make all the arrangements from there."

"Thank you very much, Mister Hopkins. I would be honored."

The two men shook hands. Hopkins departed. Brian thanked and said good-bye to the cabin and flight crews, and then he deplaned. He walked up the pier and into the impressive art deco, Marine Air Terminal building. Several uniformed officers watched and guided them into a separate closed room with more uniformed officers. Brian recognized the uniform . . . the same as the immigration inspectors of the Immigration and Naturalization Service at the border check point in Detroit two years ago, when he had crossed into Canada.

Brian was the last in line and the last passenger to reach the stand with another uniformed officer behind it.

"Passport," the man said in a very non-caring, distant tone.

Brian produced his passport. *Oh damn, I forgot all about this part. Are they going to arrest me? Thank goodness I have my presidential pardon letter inside my uniform tunic. Look calm, you idiot. You've done nothing wrong . . . well, other than break the law. Calm, be calm! I need to look like I don't care either.*

"Well, well, well," he said, and looked over his shoulder. "Sergeant, we've got one of those violators they told us about."

A man in the same uniform with three chevrons on his sleeves came over, took Brian's passport, looked at the document and scanned Brian several times, and then motioned for Brian to follow him. The sergeant led Brian into a small side room and closed the door. "Stand here," he commanded. Brian did as he was instructed. The supervisor went behind a small desk, sat down, retrieved a clipboard of papers, leafed through several pages, placed Brian's passport on the selected page, and compared information. "It seems, Mister Drummond, that you have violated the federal Neutrality Act of 1937 and 1939. Are you aware of this fact?"

"Yes sir, but . . ."

"No, buts; just yes or no, and since you have just admitted to violating the Neutrality Acts, you are under arrest." He must have hit a hidden buzzer. Two other uniformed border officers entered behind Brian.

"Wait!" Brian protested.

"What?"

"I have a presidential pardon."

"You have a what?" shouted the sergeant.

Brian reached to his left inside pocket and pulled out his letter. He opened it and handed it to the sergeant. The man read the letter, and then held it up, as if to show the two other officers.

"Signed by Franklin Roosevelt himself," the sergeant said. All three of them laughed. "How am I supposed to know whether this letter is genuine, or just another well done forgery?"

"Call the White House."

"Oh yes, you smart ass, I'll get right on that. Cuff him and take him away, guys."

"Wait," Brian said in a more subdued voice. "Please, the letter is genuine. Mister Hopkins, the president's assistant, just went through. Perhaps you can ask him. He remembers this letter." The sergeant did not move. "I am on my way home on leave. Both my parents died in a car accident. Please, sergeant, have a heart."

"Have a heart, he says," the sergeant sneered. He stared at Brian. After what seemed like several minutes, but was actually just a few seconds, he lifted the desk telephone. He explained the facts, as he knew them, to someone else, and then hung up. They waited for 20 minutes without a single word. The telephone ring startled Brian. "Sergeant Ferguson," he said, and then listened. His expression changed dramatically from smug righteousness to what appeared to Brian as fear. The sergeant's eyes began darting back and forth between Brian's eyes and the papers on the desk. "Yes sir. Right away, sir." Sergeant Ferguson made a handwritten notation in Brian's passport, stamped over it, folded Brian's letter and placed it in his passport. He stood, came around the desk and handed the documents back to Brian. "On behalf of the Immigration and Naturalization Service, Mister Drummond, I am terribly sorry for the confusion this morning. Your documents are all proper." *I wonder what the hell they told him, but I am sure not going to look a gift horse in the mouth.* "I have noted in your passport that you possess a proper presidential pardon. You are free to go. I am terribly sorry for your loss and for this delay. Have a safe journey."

Brian nodded his head, took the documents, and returned them to his left, inside, tunic pocket. He took the sergeant's proffered right hand and shook it. He left the room, which by now contained only a couple of the inspection officers.

Just inside the main lobby, an Army captain with air corps insignia and pilot's wings approached him. He appeared to be older than Brian. He was a good four inches shorter with a trim build and rather longish, dark brown hair underneath his crushed rim, Army officer's green cover with brown bill and stowed chin strap.

"Flying Officer Drummond?" he asked. Brian saluted him. The man sloppily returned Brian's salute.

"Yes sir."

He extended his right hand to Brian, which Brian shook. "I'm Captain Yardley, John Yardley, of the 14th Transport Squadron. I have orders to fly you directly to Wichita, Kansas."

"Just me?"

"Those are my orders. Let's retrieve your baggage and let's blow this pop stand."

Brian laughed and nodded his head. His bag was waiting for him when they got to the baggage claim area. An Army olive drab, 1939, Chevrolet sedan, with a large white, five-pointed star on the door, waited for them outside the terminal building. An Army private first class soldier drove them to an olive drab, medium size, tail-wheel-configured, twin radial engine aircraft with big white, five-pointed stars on the empennage and wings.

"What is this?" Brian asked.

Yardley laughed. "Not quite the Spitfires you fly, but she's a dependable bird. This," he said, waving his left hand toward the transport aircraft, "is a Douglas C-39. The civilian, commercial version is the DC-2."

"I've never seen one, let alone ridden in or flown one."

"Well, we can fix that. It will take us about six hours to get to Wichita. Weather should be near perfect, so no problems there. Once we are airborne and out of the New York City airspace, I'll kick my butter bar co-pilot out of his seat and send him back to trade places with you. I'd love to hear about what you've been doing over there and let you fly the machine as much as you wish." Brian nodded his head in agreement. "Great! Then, let's kick this pig. Climb aboard. My crew chief will brief you on our procedures. I'll give the bird a good look-see, and we'll be off."

Captain Yardley was a rather effervescent, out-going man, although he seemed rather loose and cavalier from the RAF officers he was used to working with in England. Yardley and his co-pilot made quick, professional work of their take-off and departure. Brian got to enjoy the scenic view of the New York City skyline, again. The Empire State Building was incredible in its size and dominance of the skyline. *Yardley said six hours, plus another time zone, that would put us in Wichita at early afternoon. What the heck am I going to do when I get there? I've not seen the place in nearly two years. Damn, I wish Charlotte was with me. It would have been a great way to introduce her to flight.* About 40 minutes into the flight, they had leveled off and the terrain gave way from cityscape to green conifer forest with snow covering the ground. It was still wintertime. The second lieutenant appeared and motioned for Brian to go forward. Brian left his cover on his seat and joined Yardley in the cockpit, taking the open right seat.

—

Monday, 10.February.1941
Wichita Municipal Airport
Wichita, Kansas
United States of America
14:35 hours

Six hours of near continuous chat had been quite tiresome for Brian. Captain Yardley turned out to be a curious, ambitious and inquisitive man, and more out-going than Brian had originally thought. He had grown up in Lincoln, Nebraska. His father was a professor of history at the University of Nebraska. John graduated from the university in 1937, with a bachelor's degree in mechanical engineering. He had acquired the flying bug early in his teenage years, and managed to gain a commission in the Army and a ticket to flight school. Yardley had wanted to fly fighters, but the only seats open for his flight school class were in transports. He continued to toy with the idea of resigning his commission, so he could volunteer for the Royal Air Force and Fighter Command, as Brian had done.

Brian learned from John for the first time about an organization he referred to as the Central American Manufacturing Company, or CAMCo., that was recruiting military pilots for what they called the American Volunteer Group, or AVG, under the command of a guy named Chennault, for service in China. According to John, they were looking for fighter pilots, but he had put his name in as a stand-by, in case they could not find a sufficient number of qualified fighter pilots. John admitted the attraction of flying an unspecified fighter aircraft appealed to him more than China or the adventure of the AVG.

They also discussed the return procedures. Yardley gave Brian two telephone numbers and a Western Union address. As soon as his business was complete and he was ready to return to New York City, he was to notify John's squadron one to two days in advance. Yardley did not know if he would get the assignment, but he was going to ask for the task.

Captain Yardley allowed Brian to fly most of the way and to land the big transport airplane. Brian's landing was not perfect, but was pretty damn good for his first effort, and he did not break anything. The concrete runway at the Municipal Airport had been under construction when he left in the spring of 1939, for Canada and England, and was less forgiving than the grass he was used to landing on. Taxiing the big aircraft proved a little more difficult, but he quickly adapted.

As they approached the terminal building, both pilots noticed several automobiles, a small throng of people and a six-person band. Yardley was the first to speak. "Looks like you have quite a welcoming committee there, Ace."

"Not for me."

"We're the only airplane moving on this whole airfield."

"Maybe there is someone on approach after us."

"Perhaps, but I doubt it. I suspect you are more of a hero than you let on."

"Nonsense."

"I'd better take the controls. This bird can be a little tricky in parking and securing the engines."

"You have the controls."

Captain Yardley adjusted their direction. Instead of turning into the wind, he was going to pull up in front of the terminal and the welcoming committee, as if Brian was the celebrity they were waiting for, so that the passenger door faced the building. "While I shutdown things up here, you'd better go back, straighten up your uniform, look pretty and gather your stuff. Don't forget to give us a couple of days advance notice for your return flight."

"Yes sir."

"Just John is good enough for me, Brian. It was a pleasure and an honor to fly you home." They shook hands. "Hopefully, we shall meet again, soon."

"Yes sir. Thank you, John."

Brian straightened his uniform, retrieved his cover and his bag. Brian thanked the lieutenant for giving up his seat, so Brian could fly the machine. The crew chief waited for the engines to shutdown, and then he opened the passenger door and lowered the folding ladder. Brian waved good-bye to the faces watching him. As he stepped down to the concrete, the small band began to play John Philip Sousa's "Stars and Stripes Forever." Camera flash bulbs began to fire away. Two gentlemen in suits, one more distinguished looking than the other, began walking toward him. A dozen others, who appeared to be reporters and photographers, ran past them toward Brian. He could only catch odd words – home, pilot, hero, famous – as they shouted over reach other.

"Please, please, gentlemen, give the man some space," shouted the distinguished looking man and held up both arms high. As the cacophony calmed somewhat, he turned to Brian, extended his right hand, and said, "Mister Drummond, I am Jonas Braddock, your parents' attorney."

"Nice to meet you, sir."

"May I introduce Wichita Mayor Elmer Corn."

Brian shook his hand. "Welcome home, Son. It is an honor to meet you. I am terribly sorry for your loss. I knew your Mom and Dad quite well . . . good people they were . . . such a tragic loss. On behalf of the people of Wichita, I offer the city's assistance in any way we are able to help you in this difficult time."

"Thank you, sir."

The Press began shouting questions at Brian, again. It was rather overwhelming and intimidating. Again, Braddock raised his arms. "Quiet, please!" The reporters ignored him. He waited for even a slight subsidence. "Mister Drummond has suffered a grievous loss and just arrived after a very long journey. Please give him a few days to catch his breath. With his permission, my office will arrange a press conference for him to answer your questions, if he wishes to do so." They ignored Braddock and started shouting questions, again. Braddock turned to Brian and leaned toward his ear. "I have a car. Let us seek refuge there." Brian nodded his head and followed Braddock to a large, shiny black, 1940, Cadillac Series 72 limousine. To Brian's surprise, Mayor Corn joined them. The driver shut the door, which offered some very welcome, near quiet. "I am sorry for all this. It has to be a bit overwhelming."

"A bit . . ."

Braddock waved for the driver to go. They soon left the reporters and photographers behind. "I assumed you would like to go home, first. We have straightened things up and cleaned the house for you. If you wish to stay somewhere else, I would be happy to make those arrangements for you."

"That won't be necessary. I grew up in that house. It is the only home I have ever known. I shall be just fine."

"If you should change your mind, please do not hesitate to ask. Please take whatever time you need to rest up. When you are ready, simply call my office," he said and handed Brian his business card, "and make an appointment at your convenience. We need to go over your parents' will. There will be some papers for you to sign, and then, if you wish, we can make whatever arrangements you decide to implement regarding the disposition of your parents' estate. You are the sole heir, so any subsequent action will be entirely up to you."

"I'm not sure what all that means, but let's shoot for Wednesday."

"As you wish."

Mayor Corn finally spoke. "If it is not too much trouble, Mister Drummond, I would urge you to make yourself available to the Press. Many Wichitans, many you have never met, I'm sure, have been following your accomplishments with considerable interest. Those reporters can be so aggressive sometimes, but it is a sign of their eagerness to get the story. You have become rather famous, I must say. Your parents were very, oh so very, proud of you." *Except when they tried to get me deported back home.* "Mister Braddock has offered to make the arrangements, but I would urge you to not wait very long to meet with the Press."

"Why don't we try to do that on Thursday or Friday," answered Brian, and then turned to Braddock, "if that is OK with you."

"As you wish, Brian. It is totally up to you."

Brian nodded his head. "Would you mind if we stopped by the cemetery where my parents are, before we go home?"

"Certainly." Braddock told the driver what to do.

Brian had no idea how long or even what was involved, but he did know he had to take advantage of the time he had. He needed to go see and pay his respects to Gertrude Bainbridge. He even thought of Rebecca Seward. She was probably away at college, but he could say hello to her parents and find out how she was doing. There would be plenty of time for all that. Brian missed Charlotte the most . . . more than flying. *Damn, what a send off she gave me. Now, that is a helluva woman.* He wanted to get this business done and get back to her, even though he knew that he would have to return to the war before he was ready. *First things first! Don't get ahead of yourself, hoss.* All of a sudden, Brian felt very tired, exhausted in fact.

—

Chapter 13

A fool knows more in his own house
than a wise man in another's.

- George Herbert (1640)

Monday, 10.February.1941
349 North Parkwood Lane
Wichita, Sedgwick County, Kansas
United States of America
16:10 hours

The visit to Maple Grove Cemetery to see his parents' final resting place had been more emotional than he expected. Braddock had done a good job with their interment. Brian appreciated Braddock's initiative. Even the headstone had been quite tastefully done. Brian felt no urge to change a thing.

Mister Braddock accompanied Brian back to the empty house of his childhood. Brian had hesitated on the front porch. Braddock waited patiently behind Brian, leaving him to his private thoughts. *What am I going to do? The last time I saw Mom and Dad was when I went to bed the night before I left for Canada. This was their house – the house I was born in, the only home I have ever known.* After several minutes, Brian extended his left hand. Jonas placed the house key in Brian's open hand. Brian opened the screen door, put the key in the door lock and opened the door.

Brian stepped inside. The house was in pristine condition and smelled fresh, like his parents were home in another room. Brian stood in the living room and absorbed every detail. His mind was numb. *I've had five days to reckon with this. I knew it was coming, but this is too much.* Brian dropped to his knees. Braddock stepped toward Brian and placed his right hand on Brian's left shoulder.

"Is there anything I can do for you?" the attorney asked.

Brian shook his head in the negative. Tears descended his cheeks. He instinctively knew he could not speak coherently. They remained as they were for several minutes.

"Well, then, I shall leave you to it. Take a day to . . . to . . . to reorient yourself. It has been nearly two years since you were home." Brian nodded his head in agreement. "We have an appointment Wednesday morning to conduct the official reading of your parents' wills. It is pretty much a *pro forma* exercise, since you are the only beneficiary." Once the official business is done, I would like to discuss the future with you."

"Certainly. That should be no problem."

"If you would permit me to be rather direct, how long will you be with us?" asked Braddock.

"A couple of weeks, and then I have to get back to my duty."

Braddock cleared his throat and shifted his weight from foot to foot. "If I may be so bold, do you really have to go back? After all, you are a volunteer."

"Mister Braddock . . ."

"Please," Braddock interrupted, "Jonas. I prefer the familiar, if you don't mind."

This feels quite odd. Braddock is at least 30 years older than me and older than my father was. "Very well, Jonas it is. So . . . I appreciate your thoughts and sentiment, however, I need to be precise and clear on this point. I left home two years ago, against my parents' implied wishes, and I joined the Royal Air Force to fly fighter airplanes in defense of freedom."

"I have no intention of arguing the wisdom of war, and especially this war. It is just that, as you will soon learn, you are a wealthy man with a lot to manage and deal with in life, now."

"OK," Brian responded in a hesitating and halting manner.

"We can discuss all this on Wednesday. For now, I need to give you some time. You must be very tired from your journey."

"Thank you, Jonas, and thank you for all your efforts today. I will see you Wednesday, then."

"Very well. Please get some rest. If there is anything you need, please do not hesitate to call my office, or me, anytime day or night." Braddock handed a business card to Brian. The card had his office telephone number and a private number, presumably for after-hours calls. Braddock nodded his head and extended his hand. The two men shook hands, and then Braddock departed.

Brian waited and stared out the etched glass insert in the front door. The blurred image of Braddock's car disappeared. He looked around the house. Brian felt the presence of his parents. This was their house, their photographs, their knickknacks and their memories. Brian took a deep breath and walked through the house. The kitchen . . . well, every room . . . was pristine. Nothing was even dusty. No dishes left at the last minute. His parents' bedroom was perfect . . . untouched. Even his room looked like a showroom display. Nothing was out of place. Brian was surprised, even his bedroom looked like a picture. This house was not alive. It was not lived in. The basic housekeeping had to be Braddock's doing . . . to make sure the house was clean and presentable, but his parents were missing. *I will never see them, again.*

Brian went to the kitchen and opened the refrigerator. It was fully stocked . . . sliced meats, bread, boiled eggs, and two six-packs of beer. The refrigerator must have been freshly stocked, probably this very morning. Brian popped the top on a cold beer bottle and sat down at the kitchen table. *Damn, that beer sure does taste good.* He had not finished that one beer, when his eyelids became quite heavy. The turmoil of the day claimed the last of his awareness. Brian finished the beer, left the empty bottle on the table and went to his bedroom. Sleep claimed him before he could even get undressed.

—

Tuesday, 11.February.1941
315 North Ridgewood Drive
Wichita, Sedgwick County, Kansas
United States of America
16:30 hours

Brian made the appointment yesterday evening with Mrs. Seward. The plan agreed to with 'Becky's Mom called for him to arrive a little early, before Mister Seward returned home after work. Brian knew that was a good suggestion. Mrs. Seward had always been more on his side than her husband. With everything going on in his life and especially in the next few days, Brian knew he had to talk to Rebecca's parents . . . perhaps as a means of closure to that part of his life. He did not expect 'Becky' to be home from her university studies.

The Sewards lived on the next street over from his childhood home. A light snow was falling with essentially no wind to make it bite more. Brian chose to walk the short distance in the chilly air. He wore his Levis, heavy flannel shirt, and sheepskin fleece jacket and gloves along with a heavy knit cap given to him by his now deceased maternal grandparents.

The walk in the quiet and darkening afternoon took just a few minutes and felt good. The familiar house stood in fine form as he turned off the sidewalk to the dry front porch. Brian knocked on the door.

Mrs. Seward answered the door and immediately embraced him. "So good to see you again, Brian. Please come in out of the cold." Brian stepped inside and Mrs. Seward closed the door behind him. "May I take your jacket?"

Brian removed his gloves, put them in a jacket pocket, removed his jacket and hung it himself on an open hook of the wall mounted coat rack, as he had done many times before. He placed his cap on the hook over his jacket.

"Thank you for taking time to come see us. I am so sorry about your parents," she said, gesturing toward the living room couch. Brian moved to the far side and waited for Mrs. Seward to sit on the other end of the couch before he sat.

"Thank you. It was quite a shock."

"Of that I am certain. Would you care for some fresh coffee?" she asked, motioning the pot and cups on the table.

"No thank you. I'm good."

"Rebecca is in Lawrence at KU."

"I suspected so. I hope she is doing well."

"Yes, she is doing quite well. We see her two or three times a year. She was home for Christmas and the New Year."

"Excellent. This is my first trip home since I left in June of '39."

"Are you home for good, now?"

"No. I have a few weeks to get things in order before I have to head back. There is still a war on."

"Not for us," she responded with a muted voice.

"Well, Mrs. Seward, it is only a matter of time, I suspect."

"I hope not." Mrs. Seward paused, and Brian chose not to fill the silence. "Brian, I must tell you, Rebecca has a boyfriend."

"I know. She sent me a letter a year ago and told me so. I hope she is very happy."

"She seems to be. He's a nice boy . . . a sophomore at KU as well. They both intend to declare for pre-med next year . . . to become doctors." Mrs. Seward paused and looked down. "I'm sorry, Brian."

"Don't be. It hurt when I received her letter, but I'm happy, now. I'm married to an English woman and we have a baby on the way."

"Well, congratulations, Brian. I am so happy for you."

"Thank you, Mrs. Seward. I wanted to stop by to pay my respects to you and Mister Seward . . . and, to ask you to update 'Becky' when you are able. Please convey my appreciation to 'Becky' for writing to me and explaining her feelings. I fully understand. I truly regret that I had to leave as I did, but I saw no other choice. I just had to go over there to fly those machines. Mister Bainbridge tried to convince me not to go, but I just knew I had to go."

"We have seen several articles about you in the Eagle."

"So I hear."

"I saved the articles, Brian, if you would like to read them."

Brian held up his left hand, palm out. "That is not necessary, but thank you, Mrs. Seward. I just wanted to stop by and say hi, and perhaps if I got lucky, thank 'Becky' for our friendship. I fully understand why she had to dump me, running off like I did. She is very special."

"That is so sweet, Brian. I will make sure to pass your kind words on to her."

"Thank you, Mrs. Seward. Now, I'm afraid I must be . . . ," the door opening interrupted his sentence.

Mister Seward appeared and removed his hat and overcoat. Brian stood. Mister Seward turned, saw Brian, and said, "Look what the cat dragged in."

"Good afternoon, Mister Seward." Brian walked to 'Becky's father and extended his hand. The two men shook hands. "I really must be going. I have another appointment this afternoon," he said, offering a little white lie to disengage.

"You don't need to run off on my account," Mister Seward said. "I kinda wanted to hear about your adventure in England."

"Really not much to tell, Mister Seward. I'm just a pilot in the Royal Air Force."

"As you wish then, I will catch up with mother."

Brian said good-bye to the Sewards, hugged Mrs. Seward and shook Mister Seward's hand, again. Brian donned his coat, gloves and hat. He stepped out into the cold evening air and descended the porch steps to the walkway. Brian turned back and waved as he reached the sidewalk. The brisk air felt good and invigorated his soul. *Well, I'm glad I did that, but I'm also glad it is done. I can close the book on that part of my life.*

———

Wednesday, 12.February.1941
Law Offices of Bender, Braddock and Sloan
221 South Broadway, Suite 400
Wichita, Sedgwick County, Kansas
United States of America
09:30 hours

"**W**elcome to Bender, Braddock and Sloan, Mister Drummond," the receptionist said, as Brian entered the lobby. She was all smiles and acted as though she had known Brian for years.

"Thank you. I have an appointment . . ."

"Yes. Mister Braddock is here and ready for you. Please follow me." The young, modest looking woman rose from her small desk behind the counter and led Brian through a set of double doors. She walked several paces ahead of him and stopped at an open door. "Mister Braddock, Mister Drummond is here."

"Thank you, Alice. Show him in," came the muffled, distant response.

Brian entered Braddock's spacious and rather opulent office. One wall was floor to ceiling law books.

Braddock came around his large, nearly bare, polished desk. They shook hands. "Good morning, Mister Drummond," Braddock said.

"Good morning to you, Jonas."

"Please," he said, motioning to one of a couple of chairs opposite his chair, across his desk. "I trust you are rested and settled."

"I don't know about settled, but yes, I am rested."

"Excellent. Would you care for a cup of coffee . . . or something stronger?"

"No thank you."

Brian sat in the expensive leather chair. Braddock walked around the desk, sat in his chair, and opened the only folder on this desk. "These are never simple times. On behalf of our firm and myself, please accept our condolences for the loss of your parents." Brian simply nodded his head in acknowledgment.

Jonas Braddock read both last wills and testaments for Susan and George Drummond. The reading took 20 minutes, according to the clock on the wall opposite his bookshelves. Brian could not believe what he had just heard. His thoughts repeatedly returned to one single thought – *why had they kept all this from me?*

Between Braddock's reading of the rather generalized and broad description of the transfer of ownership and his recounting of the supporting facts he had been directly involved with, Brian understood he was the sole owner of ten sections of land in Sedgwick and Butler Counties. They had been extraordinarily lucky to own 15 acres of farm land that his parents had purchased before he was born. An exploratory well on their property had struck oil, and not just struck oil but the well had been producing at an annual average rate of 2,200 Stock Tank Barrels per Day. His parents had invested the income from the first oil well into buying land, which in turn made possible additional productive oil wells. Six of the ten sections of land were contiguous. All in all, nearly 7,000 acres of prime farm land, most of which were leased and actively farmed by neighbors or other operators. The land leases provided their own income streams. The most shocking of his parents' assets were the half dozen bank accounts totaling well into mid-eight figures. The small bakery that had been the only business his parents operated was a mere blip on the scale of his parents' assets.

"Your parents were very humble, quiet, frugal people," Braddock said. "But, they were also wise and forward-thinking. Early on in the process, they established a trust of which you are the sole designated beneficiary, so the transfer of ownership is fairly simple in legal terms."

"I had no idea . . . not even a hint of any of this," responded Brian. "The only thing I can recall from my childhood, my school years, was the bakery. I worked in the bakery occasionally, but my interests were with machines that fly."

"I know. They knew about your flying with Mister Bainbridge . . . may God rest his soul. They did not like your fascination with airplanes, but they accepted it. They wanted you to follow them in the bakery. They were devastated when you left home with only a note."

"Yes, well, I knew they would not agree with my plan and I did what I had to do." *Damn, he's a lawyer. I wonder if he helped my parents with their efforts to achieve my extradition during the Phony War.* "Did you provide them legal counsel for my return from England?"

Jonas Braddock shifted in his chair and averted Brian's gaze. He clearly was not comfortable with the question, or more properly the answer he was framing in his mind. Jonas looked back to Brian. "Simply and directly, yes. I have been under retainer twenty-five-plus years. Understandably, they sought my counsel. I know Senator Capper, Arthur Capper, personally, as a friend of decades. I do not know what happened in England, but I can imagine it was not pleasant; but, I must tell you, it was Senator Capper, at the behest of your parents through me, who approached the White House and the President for the pardon you eventually received."

Well . . . so that is how it happened, or at least part of it. I am finally beginning to see what has been unseen for nearly a year. "Thank you, Jonas. I hold no animosity. You did your job. You did what you had to do." Brian studied Braddock's face. Jonas remained transfixed and emotionless. "I had no intention of violating the law, but I had to fly Spitfires. I had to do what I had to do . . . just like you."

"I will never feel that passion, Brian . . . that . . . that drive to defy the law." The room remained stone cold quiet, except for the ticking of the clock – tick-tock, tick-tock. "I am honored that we were able to obtain the presidential pardon for you. You deserve no less. The medals on your RAF uniform are testament to the courage of what you did and the wisdom of what we did to support you. Thank you for doing what you do . . . and do with *élan* and *panache*." Brian nodded his head in acknowledgment. "Now, if I may, I would like to discuss the future."

"By all means," Brian answered.

"Let it suffice to say, there are more details to your parents' holdings – investments, projects and plans. The bakery appears to be operating well under the control of your chief baker Rodrigo Rodriquez. Your father hired a manager and several accountants to keep track of everything. His name is Travis Atherton. He is the one that has kept operations running smoothly before and after that fateful night. I would urge you to meet with Mister Atherton at your earliest convenience. Especially with your intention to return to England and military service, I would strongly urge you to prepare a last will and testament. With assets like you are now the present sole owner of, I do not believe it to be wise to relegate your holdings to intestacy succession laws in Kansas. You have no siblings I am aware of, and no living parents or grandparents. I assume you are not married."

"No. I am married. I married an Englishwoman – Charlotte Tamerlin. She is also pregnant and due to deliver our first child in June."

Braddock noticeably raised his eyebrows, as if to say, are you out of your mind? "Yes, well, all the more reason you need a will. Frankly, you should have had a will before you left for England, or even before you started flying, but that is water under the bridge. Now that you are sole property owner, we really should modify the Drummond Trust documents to reflect you as sole Trustee. Further, I would also recommend you formally designate secondary trustees such as your property manager and a trusted attorney to ensure the provisions of the Trust are maintained properly, especially given your current occupation. At an absolute minimum, I would strongly recommend you file a will with designated beneficiaries before you leave Wichita. The last will and testament can be included with the modified Trust account, when or if you so choose. I can assist you with that, if you wish to retain my legal services. I do not presume to inject myself into your affairs and whether you wish to retain the services of Mister Atherton, I also strongly urge you to retain a trusted manager to maintain your day-to-day operations of your properties in your absence. If you will permit me," Braddock paused for Brian's gestured acknowledgment, "take a few days to absorb everything. You have no obligation to me . . . or this law firm, for that matter. However, given your holdings, you really must stabilize your situation before you leave."

"Wise counsel, it seems to me. Yes, I have an awful lot to wrap my mind around. I will take the rest of the week to sort things out in my mind. I will let you know what I am thinking later this week, or early next week, and we can proceed from there."

"One more topic before we close . . . As Mayor Corn indicated on your arrival, the Press has been very dogged in seeking to interview you. Have any journalists contacted you, as yet?"

"No."

"If they do, I would strongly urge you to avoid talking to any of them, as it will only create a feeding frenzy, and refer them to me. With your permission, I would like to arrange a press conference . . . probably in our main conference room, so that we can control attendance . . . in perhaps a week's time or so. I will coordinate with Mayor Corn. I believe the City Council wanted to give you the key to the city to recognize the contributions of your parents and your connection with the city."

"OK by me, but let's make it a fortnight."

"Two weeks?"

"Yes. Once I get a handle on things, I need to make arrangements for my return to England. I'm currently thinking about departing on the 10th of March, and I do not want to crowd that date."

"Very well. This law firm and I stand ready to assist you in any manner you choose. We will await your decision."

"Thank you, Jonas. I appreciate everything you have done for me . . . and for my family. Thank you for your time."

The two men stood, shook hands, and Braddock escorted his wealthiest client to the elevator. They said good-bye. Brian left to consider his future.

—

Friday, 14.February.1941
Cabinet War Rooms
New Public Offices
Whitehall, London, England
United Kingdom

Churchill had never liked the underground bunker complex and still did not like being in the facility. The perpetual light, constant din of activity and lack of even one window remained a continuous irritant to the Prime Minister. He had not realized how important a spot of sunshine or the distortion of rain drops were to a man's psyche . . . well, at least his, until those simple pleasures were denied him by this damnable war. His head acknowledged and understood why His Majesty's Government had to hold important meetings in the War Rooms, but his heart yearned for the pastoral scenery and peace of the Kentish weald of Chartwell. The Blitz was still on. The nightly insult continued through the foul weather of winter, although the intensity had diminished somewhat after the Second Great Fire of London, six weeks ago.

Churchill had reluctantly agreed to the afternoon combined meeting of the War Cabinet and the Defense Committee, in order to dispatch the government's business as quickly as possible, so he could make the journey to Chequers for the weekend. Clementine and Diana, their daughter and oldest child at 31 years of age, already married, divorced and married again, were already there. Diana would spend the weekend with her parents and without her second husband Edwin Duncan Sandys, who was a Member of Parliament and serving on active duty with the Royal Artillery,

The conference was crowded, as it always was for these combined meetings. Several staff members could not even fit in a loose chair and had to stand.

As Prime Minister Churchill took his seat at the head of the table, he looked to Cabinet Secretary Sir Edward Bridges, "Let us proceed, Sir Edward."

"The first order of business is the situation in North Africa . . . Mister Margesson."

Secretary of State for War Henry David Reginald Margesson, MC, PC, Member of Parliament for Rugby cleared his throat and grasped a single sheet of paper. "Intelligence analysis produced this morning clearly indicates the Germans have decided to reinforce the Italians in Libya, and they intend to take up the offensive probably in the spring. A most secret source," most but not all of the people in the room knew that phrase meant ULTRA and the Enigma decrypts, "confirmed the arrival of General Rommel in Tripoli two days ago."

"I presume," Churchill interrupted, "this new information has been passed to Dalton and the SOE?"

Minister of Economic Warfare Edward Hugh John Neale Dalton, PC, Member of Parliament for Bishop Auckland formed the Special Operations Executive (SOE) in July 1940, under the mandate of the War Cabinet and the personal instructions of Prime Minister Churchill. They began with a singular mission to set German occupied Europe ablaze. That simple directive evolved to mean attacking German infrastructure and logistics facilities, and encouraging and supporting indigenous resistance movements in the occupied territories.

"Yes sir."

"Who knows, those rogues might be able to strap something together."

"Quite so, sir. General Dill has confirmed by message traffic with General Wavell that the Army of the Nile is already aware of this intelligence. The Germans are building up their ground, armor and air forces in Libya. They intend to fight."

Churchill looked around the room to find Chief of the Imperial General Staff General Sir John Dill. "General Dill, have you received Wavell's latest plans for the desert offensive? We need to get ahead of Rommel, to keep him off balance and from taking the initiative."

"The Plans staff is digesting the information as we speak."

"Fine. I want to see those plans as soon as you have completed your review and assessment. Now, my question, why would that foul dictator send one of his premier generals to the desert?"

"He must feel an obligation to his partner," answered Margesson, "after Wavell pushed the Italians well back into Libya last fall."

"Is this their next big offensive, despite what we learned last December?" Winston could not say it directly, but he was referring to their intercept and decryption of the German High Command's reference to Hitler's Directive 21, and the apparent planning for offensive operations against the Soviet Union in the spring. *Why would he put one of his best armor generals in the desert, when he is planning what would have to be a massive armor offensive in the east?*

"We don't think so, Prime Minister," Sir John answered. "We suspect he is trying to put sufficient forces in Libya and using Rommel's reputation to reassure Mussolini that he is serious about supporting the Italians. Further, we cannot ignore the potential they will continue to add forces in an effort to take Cairo, Egypt and the Suez, and perhaps press on to the oil fields of the Gulf."

"That makes sense. We cannot allow that to happen. Pray tell Sir Archibald he must renew his offensive before Rommel's Africa Corps can gain strength."

"Prime Minister," said Margesson, "we stripped out several divisions from Wavell's army for redeployment to Greece, and the Greeks are demanding more ground and air forces. Sir Archibald believes he no longer has the forces necessary for an offensive, and in fact, he feels he now has barely sufficient forces to defend the ground he has already taken."

"Nonsense. His job is to find a way, to use the forces he has to carry out his orders."

"We will work with General Wavell to see what we can do," General Dill added.

"Do more than that, General," said the Prime Minister with a stern voice. "If we wait for Rommel, he will have the initiative and momentum. He will be harder to stop and beat back. When we have the initiative, we control the fight. We are all aware that the War Cabinet thinned the Army of the Nile, to meet other requirements and obligations. He has enough men, enough armor, to take the fight to Gerry. He has a powerful air force at his command, and a navy that controls Gibraltar, Malta, the Suez and the seaward approaches to the battlefield."

"More or less," mumbled someone, barely audible.

"If you have something to say, something to add, speak up and be recognized." He waited. No one spoke or twitched, and a few might not even be breathing at the moment. "Very well, then, Minister Margesson, General Dill, please assist General Wavell in finding the path to the offensive, to disrupt Rommel's plans before he gets to execute those plans."

"Yes sir," Margesson and Dill responded in unison.

Churchill nodded his head, more in acquiescence than approval. "Very well, then, let's move to the naval situation. A.V., if you would be so kind, pray update the War Cabinet."

First Lord of the Admiralty A.V. Alexander placed his left fist before his mouth and cleared his throat – a common gesture for him when he did not have good news. "I'm afraid I must report and confess our shipping losses remain well above sustainable levels."

"We are bleeding to death," interjected Winston.

Again, the First Lord gave his usual mannerism. "Yes sir, to be blunt, we have spurts of success when we . . . ," he hesitated to scan the room. Those with access knew he wanted to refer to the productivity of ULTRA. Fortunately, he recognized he could not. ". . . when we are able to locate the U-boats before they can attack a convoy. The difficulty we face remains the location of their U-boats before they can attack. The research lads are making progress on detection technology, but not fast enough for the fight we are in. The Tizard Mission lads in America have identified a number of promising improvements from the Americans in millimeter wave RDF and active underwater detection. Recent experiments demonstrated the ability of the new equipment to detect just a periscope above water. The Americans call their underwater detection equipment Sonar, an acronym that stands for SOund Navigation And Ranging. The basic physics and mechanics are not significantly different from our ASDIC; however, the major difference lies in the electronic processing and presentation of the signal return. Our engineers are apparently very excited about the potential for the combination of their technology and ours."

"And yet, we continue to bleed," the Prime Minister again interjected, this time rather grumpily. "Will our destroyers and corvettes deploy this new wizard gear in time . . . before we bleed to death?"

"We have our best collective minds working that part of the task. We have agreed, together, to take enormous risk in starting up production in the United States before the development work is complete. To answer your query, Prime Minister, I pray every day that we will. I can assure you, the Americans feel the same urgency we do. We expect to begin refitting our escorts later this year or early next year. Our operational personnel are also deeply involved as development continues, to work out procedures, tactics, training and mutually supportive operations with the Americans."

"Presumably, the United States will produce these SONAR sets faster than we can retrofit them. If so, His Majesty's Government will order every available, capable and compatible shipyard and dock facility in the Kingdom to make the retrofit of this equipment their highest and preemptive priority. A.V., I want to see you plan for managing the retrofit process as fast as humanly possible, while you maintain the convoy escort coverage, next week – a fortnight at the latest." The First Lord nodded his head in agreement. "As I read the shipping reports from the Admiralty, no day can be spared. You simply must find the means to get ahead of this damnable U-boat threat. And, I must say, I use the term U-boat in the broader sense as the collective threat to our shipping lifeline. It truly is a matter of life and death. We are not winning the Battle of the Atlantic. They continue to sink far more of our ships than we sink of theirs. In the generalized threat, I include the *Luftwaffe*'s contribution with those long range Condor missions and the surface raiders, which in turn brings me to . . . the *Bismarck* was declared operational last August. We could see her on the high seas any day, now. Those 15-inch main battery rifles will be formidable. Pray provide me your plans for dealing with that behemoth, when she does finally set sail for combat." Again, the First Lord nodded his head. "Now, pray tell us why we have not been able to stop *Scharnhorst* and *Gneisenau*? The 11-inch guns of that pair have dispatched more of our shipping tonnage than any other surface ship in this war."

"As you know well, Prime Minister, Admiral Günther Lütjens is an extraordinarily capable tactician. He has commanded that task force–*Scharnhorst*, *Gneisenau*, the cruiser *Köln*, and nine destroyers – with exceptional skill, using their speed to evade our capital ships. Admiral Tovey has deployed three battleships, eight cruisers and 11 destroyers to engage the Germans. We have come close several times, but we have been unable to finish the job."

Admiral John Cronyn 'Jack' Tovey, CB, DSO, had been appointed Commander-in-Chief Home Fleet and served in that capacity since November.

"And," Churchill again interjected, "they continue to sortie against our commercial shipping. Where are the bastards now?"

"Admiral Pike's lads and Colonel Menzies's agents are trying to confirm their locations as we speak. We believe *Scharnhorst* is at Trondheim and *Gneisenau* is at Kiel. The escorts were divvied up equally, but we do not have confirmation, as yet."

"The U-boats are bad enough. These big gun warships are something altogether different. We must find the means to stop them. If we are unable to sink them, then we must confine them to harbor somehow."

"Admiral Tovey understands his orders and the importance of his task."

"I am certain he does." The Prime Minister lapsed into thought. The War Cabinet Conference Room remained silent – no rustling of paper or coughs, not a peep. "We shall skip the Air Force this afternoon. Is there anything else that should be brought before the War Cabinet or the Defense Committee?" Those who did reply responded in the negative. "Very well, then, you have your orders. I am off to Chequers in short order. You know how to reach me, should the need arise. Have a good and hopefully peaceful weekend." The room waited for the Prime Minister to depart before they dispersed.

—

Wednesday, 19.February.1941
Port of Bristol
Avonmouth, Bristol, England
United Kingdom
10:35 hours

It had been a dark and stormy night.

The large, four-engine, Boeing Model 314, Pan American Airways Yankee Clipper landed smoothly in the River Avon Estuary and taxied to its designated mooring. This particular trans-Atlantic crossing flight carried, among its nearly full capacity of passengers, the new U.S. Ambassador to the Court of St James's Gil Winant.

As soon as the aircraft was secure to its mooring and a platform attached, the ground crew began off-loading baggage and passengers.

The U.S. Embassy's *Chargé d'Affaires* Herschel Johnson stood on the dock, watching the arrival process. Microphone stands had been set up for the assembled Press. Perhaps a dozen, if not a score, of reporters and photographers were on the dock, behind the microphones, for the arrival of someone important, although no one seemed to be talking about who the celebrity was in this instance.

The covered launch maneuvered smartly and expertly to the dock and tied up. Johnson recognized Ambassador Winant as the first passenger to disembark. The photographs sent ahead had been current and quite illuminating.

"Mister Ambassador, a few words, if you please," shouted several journalists. "Please, Mister Ambassador."

Johnson was surprised they recognized him and he was the apparent celebrity they were waiting for. The *Chargé* glanced at the reporters, who were visibly excited and agitated, as they jostled for position. Photographers' flash bulbs bursting and popping marked images being taken. Johnson stepped forward and extended his hand to the new ambassador. "Ambassador Winant, I'm *Chargé d'Affaires* Johnson from the embassy in London." They shook hands. "Welcome to England, sir."

"Thank you very much, Mister Johnson. I did not expect such an enthusiastic welcoming party."

"Me neither, I must say. It does reflect the importance of the connection between our country and theirs, I do believe. His Majesty's Government is certainly keen on the relationship."

"So I gather. I suppose I should make a statement for the Press."

"That would be most appropriate, sir."

Winant nodded his head and stepped to the microphones. "Thank you for the welcome, gentlemen. I'm very glad to be here. There is no place I would rather be at this time of trial and sacrifice than in England with the British people. We are will you at least in spirit."

"There's The Blitz going on, you know," one of the reporters shouted.

"Yes, and as the United States Ambassador to the Court of St. James's, I shall stand with the British people."

"What does that mean?" shouted another reporter.

"It means precisely what the words convey. I am here to represent the President and the United States of America for as long as I may be of service. We have and will continue to support the United Kingdom in the present struggle with the fascist dictatorships on the Continent. Freedom is too precious to stand idly by on the sidelines, while our brethren are under siege by evil forces."

"Is America going to join us in this fight?"

"One step at a time, gentlemen. I have not yet presented my credentials to the King. I have much work ahead to be formally accepted as the ambassador. Please allow me to get settled before I take on your meaty questions. Thank you, again, for your welcome." Winant turned away from the microphones and the Press, despite their protestations. He stepped closer to Johnson. "Let's go."

"Yes sir. I have a couple of men who will tend to your baggage. I have a car to take us to the Bristol Railway Station. The journey into London should take a few hours. I have a private compartment reserved and held with a security officer from the embassy. We can safely talk during the journey."

"Very well. Excellent. Thank you for making all the appropriate arrangements. I look forward to working with you in the coming days, months and years, until our service is done."

Johnson nodded his head and gestured toward the waiting limousine and driver. He then gestured to his men to collect up the ambassador's baggage. A few reporters tried to follow and continued pressing the ambassador, but they were stopped by two unidentified, serious looking, large, fit men.

—

Wednesday, 19.February.1941
Bainbridge Ranch
Rural Route 14
Wichita, Sedgwick County, Kansas
United States of America
14:00 hours

The bicycle journey brought back memories of so many similar trips he had made in his youth. Mister Braddock had offered an automobile and driver.

The ride even in the winter cold meant more to Brian than his comfort. He had considered wearing his RAF uniform for Mrs. Bainbridge. The awkwardness of his uniform overcoat made riding a bicycle an unacceptable challenge. His Levi's, winter boots and sheepskin fleece jacket and gloves made the winter ride rather pleasant and invigorating. The bike ride had been everything he had hoped it would be . . . thankfully the roads, both paved and unpaved, had been free of snow or ice.

Mrs. Gertrude 'Gerty' Bainbridge must have been watching for him to appear on their long driveway. She was standing on the porch, dressed in a long, ankle-length, black dress with a full apron with flower prints. Her arms were crossed below her bosom against the chill. As Brian leaned his bicycle against the bush adjacent to the short, front porch steps, Mrs. Bainbridge descend the four steps and extended her arms to Brian. They embraced as mother and son. She pulled back just enough to kiss Brian on the left cheek, and then released him.

"It is so good to see you, again, Brian, my dear one," she said.

"It's great to see you, Mrs. Bainbridge."

"Come," she said, motioning to the front door, "I have a nice fire going. It's warm inside. You must be chilled riding your bicycle out here."

"It wasn't bad. I enjoyed the ride like I used to do when I was younger."

"Let me take your coat and gloves." Brian removed his heavy jacket and gloves. She lay the jacket over the back of the living room couch and put the gloves on top. Gerty led him into the kitchen. She motioned for him to sit at the four-place, kitchen table, as he had done many times as a teenage visitor. Brian sat in one of the wooden chairs. "I'm sure you could use something warm. Would you care for some coffee, or tea perhaps?"

"A spot of tea would be nice," Brian answered with his best British accent.

Gertrude laughed softly. "Tea it is, then." She must have anticipated his drink of choice, since she simply lifted the kettle off the stove, poured the steaming water into a pot and placed a knit tea-cozy over the pot. Gertrude also placed a plate of undoubtedly freshly backed chocolate chip cookies on the table.

"You didn't have to do all this. It's just me."

Gertrude stopped her preparations, turned and stared at Brian for several seconds. "Mister Drummond."

She's never called me that before.

"Even without your uniform, I know what you have accomplished. I know how many times you have been wounded and even how many times you have been shot down."

How the hell can she possibly know all that?

Gerty placed a cup and saucer before Brian and another cup in the adjacent place. She poured two cups of tea and sat across the table corner from Brian. The puzzled and shocked expression on Brian's face must have been obvious to Gerty Bainbridge. "John and Mary Spencer have been most gracious in keeping me informed of your . . . your . . . your service over there. Plus, the Eagle carried at least two stories . . . that I'm aware of . . . about your exploits. I also heard the Edward R. Murrow report on the radio about you last summer. Enough of that. Thank you so much, Brian, for your letters to me, calling me and especially for taking your precious time at home to come see me."

"I could not come home and not see you. I have not seen you since Malcolm's passing. I offer you my deepest and most heartfelt condolences for your loss, Mrs. Bainbridge."

"It has been nearly a year, but it is I who must offer my condolences to you. That was such a tragic accident."

"Thank you. Can I ask, what do you know about Mister Bainbridge's accident?"

"We don't know for sure, Brian. I've asked several of his pilot buddies. The best anyone could determine is icing. He made a special delivery to Denver and was apparently trying to make it home before sunset. They say it appears that he was attempting to land in an open field and the airplane stopped flying before he could get it on the ground."

Stall! That is very uncharacteristic of Malcolm's flying, which would be consistent with icing adversely affecting the aerodynamic performance of the wings and forcing him down. I need to get off this subject. "How are you doing, Mrs. Bainbridge?" Brian asked rather awkwardly.

Gertrude waved her hand dismissively. "You can talk to the fellows that found him and examined what was left of the Jenny. I can give you their names and contact information." Brian nodded his head. "But, before you have to leave, I have something I must tell you." Again, Brian nodded his head. "Malcolm and I had discussed his airplanes even before you left. Brian, he wanted you to have them."

"What!"

Gertrude smiled. "Don't be so shocked. You know he loved you . . . as the son he never had. I cannot fly them. He arranged for a Beech mechanic to maintain them and run the engines once a week, but they need to be flown, as Malcolm had intended."

"I don't know what to say, Mrs. Bainbridge."

Gerty giggled and said, "A simple yes and thank you would be sufficient."

"Thank you so much. I'm not prepared to fly them today, but I will . . ." Brian paused to think about his rapidly filling appointment schedule. "I have a lot to get done before I must return to England. I will try to arrange to fly each of Malcolm's aircraft on Saturday. I will call you tomorrow to confirm."

"They are your aircraft now, Brian."

"Yes, certainly. I will need to make arrangements to store them somewhere."

"No, no, you can leave them here. I can do nothing with his hangar or barn."

"OK, then I will need to talk to the mechanic you have maintaining them."

"I'll give you his name. I would suggest you might wish to meet with Mister Beech, if you are able to do so. It was the relationship Malcolm had with Walter Beech that was the key element to the maintenance support."

"I've met Mister Beech a few times, when Mister Bainbridge was arranging for the Mystery 'S' modifications. I will go visit Beech Aircraft to make sure the aircraft are maintained. Now, you successfully avoided my earlier question, Mrs. Bainbridge. How are you getting along?"

Gertrude stared at Brian. She lifted her teacup and took several sips without breaking eye contact. "You do not need my burdens, Brian."

"Nonsense," he interrupted. "I asked because I care. I found out a week ago that I am a very wealthy man. I am able to help in any manner I can, in anyway you need."

"Well, against my better judgment, I will confess . . . not well. Malcolm's airmail and delivery business was the only income we had, and now that has stopped. I have not been able to pay Charlie's wages . . . he's the Beech mechanic who continues to maintain the aircraft. Walter Beech has been covering that for me, but that is not fair to his generosity. I have the land and that is about it."

Damn, it is worse than I imagined. She was honest with me. I must be honest with her. "That is not acceptable to me." *Should I be aggressive with her?* "First, I will make arrangements with Mister Beech to repay him and maintain the wages for Charlie the mechanic, until I can make more permanent arrangements. I will make sure he has whatever he needs to keep Malcolm's aircraft in fine fashion. Second, I can offer you two options that I can think of at the moment. 'A': I can establish a bank account for you and ensure you receive a monthly stipend, so that you can live comfortably. Or, 'B': I can buy your land at a better than market price and lease it back to you for one dollar per year. You would be able to live here as long as you wish without worries."

Tears were flowing down her cheeks. Gertrude Bainbridge choked out her words. "I . . . I . . . I don't . . . I don't . . . what can I say?"

Brian smiled, "As you told me a while back, yes would be sufficient." Gertrude laughed and cried at the same time. "Take whatever time you need to consider what is best for you. If you think of any other options, please just tell me what best suits your needs. We can talk about this anytime you wish, or when I come back to fly Malcolm's aircraft."

Gertrude's sobbing diminished sufficient for her to speak. "You are a sweet boy . . . sorry . . . young man." She paused to study Brian's eyes. He did not even blink. "Please pardon me for being so crass, but they must pay you very well in the Royal Air Force these days . . . much better than they paid Malcolm."

Brian laughed. "Just one word . . . inheritance."

"Oh. I cannot do that."

"First, I can assure you . . . I am more than able to help. Second, you have but to tell me how best to help you. Third, as my parents' lawyer informed me, I must do a will before I return to duty. We are in the process of doing just that. I will ensure you are respected in whatever form you wish, if, God forbid, something happens to me."

"As it nearly has four times that I know of," Gertrude added.

"Yes, there is that. Nonetheless, I am here now. Are we agreed?"

"Could you give me a few days to think about what you said?"

"Yes, of course. Take as much time as you need, Mrs. Bainbridge. I plan to return to England in the second week of March, so I have a couple of weeks before I must go. Even if you need more time, I am certain we can handle the arrangements with me over there. Now, I am terribly sorry, but I must be off."

"Please take the Ford pickup," Gerty offered. "It will be warmer and quicker than your bicycle, and you can put the bike in the back."

Brian remembered the blue 1938 Ford pickup truck Malcolm purchased new, six months before he left for England. *She is right. But, the bike ride will be good for me, in more ways than one.* "No thanks, Mrs. Bainbridge. I enjoyed the ride out, and I dare say, I will enjoy the ride back into town. Thank you so much for the delicious cookies and tea. I hope to see you in a few days." Brian stood. "Good day, Mrs. Bainbridge."

Brian retrieved and donned his jacket and gloves. Mrs. Bainbridge kissed him on the cheek. He mounted his bicycle and headed down the driveway. He turned to look back and to see her standing on the porch. He waved. She returned the gesture. *Wow! Will wonders ever cease?*

—

Saturday, 22.February.1941
Bainbridge Ranch
Rural Route 14
Wichita, Sedgwick County, Kansas
United States of America
13:00 hours

Fortunately, the air temperature on this particular mid-winter day was unusually mild by comparison to last Wednesday's bicycle ride to the Bainbridge homestead.

Several meetings with Walter Beech had helped solidify arrangements he would discuss later with Mrs. Bainbridge. He also met with Beech senior aircraft mechanic Charles 'Charlie' Rogers, previously known as Charlie the mechanic. Charlie indicated he needed half a day to get Malcolm's aircraft ready for flight and said he would be ready by mid-day this Saturday.

The moderated temperature would make the flights in the open cockpit aircraft slightly more tolerable. Brian had accumulated sufficient odd clothing from his childhood closet and his father's hunting and fishing attire.

Once again, Mrs. Bainbridge was outside in the cool air as he pedaled up the drive to the main house. "Good afternoon, Mrs. Bainbridge."

"Good afternoon to you, Brian. This cold air cannot be helpful to you. I must insist upon you taking the Ford pickup."

"Well, as much moving around as I have done since I've been home, I think I will take you up on your offer."

"Come on in and get warm before you go fly."

Brian leaned his bike against one of the porch awning support posts and followed Mrs. Bainbridge into the house. It was indeed warm inside and the scrumptious aroma of fresh baked cookies added to the pleasurable sensations he felt.

"I've made some nice hot tea for you," she said, facing the stove with her back to Brian. "Take a seat. Let's get you warmed up. Charlie has been out there since early this morning. I took him some hot coffee a couple of hours ago. I think he is ready for you."

"Good . . . and thank you for the tea and cookies. I can never refuse your cookies. In England they call them biscuits."

"So Malcolm told me."

Gerty returned to the table with a pot of tea under a full knit cozy. She poured each of them a cup and sat down.

"Brian, perhaps we should wait until you are finished flying, but let me just mention that I have thought about your most generous offer." Brian raised his right hand gesturing for her to stop. "No, I need to say, thank you very much, but it is not fair to you." Gerty took a sip of her tea. Brian did the same and did not want to interrupt her thought. "I will find a better way."

Brian waited to ensure she had completed her thought. "I have some other ideas, and I need more time to present them to you. Allow me to get this flying done, so we don't tie up Charlie even more than I have already."

"Yes, yes, certainly. I'm not going anywhere."

"Excellent. This should take me an hour or so. I've not flown several of the types, so I'll be a little slower than I will be with the other aircraft."

"Take your time, Brian. Don't rush. Just be safe. I'll have fresh tea and coffee for both of you when you're done."

"Thank you." Brian polished off his tea and second chocolate-chip cookie. "I'd better get on with it."

Gerty stood with Brian. She went around the table and hugged him. "Be careful."

"I will."

Brian donned his makeshift cold weather flying attire and walked out to the barn/hangar. Two newer buildings had been built since he left for England in '39, presumably for Malcolm's additional aircraft. The first hangar protected Malcolm's prized Sopwith F.1 Camel, the modified Beech Mystery S he had flown at the St. Louis Air Meet with then Group Captain Spencer observing, and the remaining Stearman C-3R Speedster. Brian remembered hitting a neighbor's dog on landing and cartwheeling the other Stearman. That accident led to Malcolm turning him loose with the Camel. The Speedster was in front of the other two aircraft, so that would probably be the first aircraft he would take to the air. Brian needed to talk to Charlie first. The next building hangared two, identical, Curtiss JN-4 Jenny biplanes. The extra space had probably been for the third Jenny—the aircraft Malcolm had been flying when he crashed. Brian had not yet flown the Jenny. The third hangar had only one aircraft, a bright red, brand new, Beech Model D17S Staggerwing. That is where he found Charlie, who was working on the engine.

"Hey, Charlie," Brian called as he approached.

"Hiya Brian." He stopped his work and turned to Brian. "All the other aircraft are ready, except for this bird." He patted the leading edge of the lower wing. "I need to change the seal on the generator drive pad. I should be finished in 20 to 30 minutes. What do you want to start with?"

"The Stearman is in front. Let's start with her."

"No problem. What order do you want to do them in?"

"No matter to me. I need to give each aircraft a good warm-up. I'm not going to go anywhere . . . just around the field for 15-20 minutes."

"Excellent. I'll get the Stearman outside for you. While you're flying, I'll pull the other machines out. They'll be waiting for you. I'll have the Staggerwing finished and ready before you get to her."

"Sounds like a plan," Brian confirmed.

Brian helped Charlie push the Stearman out of the first hangar turn it into the light southern breeze and to avoid the prop wash disturbing the other aircraft. Brian did a quick walk-around to make sure he had all the required parts, climbed up and into the aft cockpit, and strapped himself in. Charlie inserted the hand crank and waited for Brian's start signal. The mechanic cranked the handle several times. Brian could hear the whirr of the flywheel, intertia starter. He cracked the throttle open and yelled, "Clear!" He engaged the starter clutch and switched the magneto to both. The engine fired off promptly. *He must've started the engines earlier. That was too easy for this ambient temperature.* Brian kept the engine at a fast idle to let the engine warm up. When he was ready, he instinctively signaled for the chocks to be removed. Charlie smiled and shrugged his shoulder empty-handed. Brian felt a twinge of embarrassment that he did not remember there were no wheel chocks. He saluted. Charlie returned the salute and motioned for Brian to go.

Brian advanced the throttle slightly to move the aircraft away from the hangars, and then turned and headed to the downwind end of Malcolm's nice, grass strip runway. Brian performed his engine and control checks to make sure everything was as it should be for flight. He advanced the throttle to begin his takeoff roll. Gaining speed, he adjusted the control stick to raise the tail, and smoothly pressed the throttle full forward. The aircraft literally flew off the grass.

The area around the Bainbridge Ranch and airfield appeared the same as he remembered in the drab, shades of gray, winter scenery. Brian made several low passes down the runway. He noticed and waved to Gerty Bainbridge. She waved back, and then went back inside to the warmth of the interior.

After making several circuits of the surrounding area, Brian performed a handful of touch-and-go landings, before landing and taxiing back to the spot he had started from. He shutdown the engine, locked his flight controls, and extracted himself from the cockpit.

The Mystery S was next in line. The remainder of the aircraft, except for the Staggerwing, required Charlie to pull the propeller through a turn or two before the engines fired off and came to life. The modified Mystery S brought back great memories of those grand old days before the war. The Camel was just as much fun as ever, and now he could imagine what it must have been like for Malcolm and John Spencer flying similar machines in the dangerous skies of Eastern France a little over two decades ago. Brian spent a little more time with the Camel, finding a fair-weather cumulus cloud to flirt with in the sky. The Jennys appeared to be military surplus aircraft Malcolm acquired after Brian had departed for England. He had rigged a net enclosure in the front cockpit to retain the delivery packages for his air service work. All of the aircraft performed flawlessly.

The Staggerwing intrigued him. It was the only enclosed cockpit, the only one of Malcolm's aircraft with an electric starter, and it had a decent heater once the engine warmed up. It was also the only one of Malcolm's aircraft to have a radio, although he never switched it on since there was no one to talk to in the countryside around the Bainbridge Ranch. Brian took some extra time to assess the handling qualities of the Model 17 in the clean and landing configurations. He performed several stalls to validate the speeds and characteristics. The beautiful machine was the fastest of Malcolm's aircraft and certainly had far better creature comforts than the other open cockpit machines. After completing several touch-and-go landings, Brian cleaned up the aircraft, climbed in a wide circuit, and then pushed the throttle full forward and dove the aircraft to red line airspeed to make a high speed pass down the length of the runway just above the grass and well below treetop height. As he approached the tree-line at the upwind end of the grass strip, Brian pulled the nose up to 20 degrees and rolled the aircraft twice in his own victory roll. He set up a nice circuit, and lowered the landing gear and flaps for a full stop, final landing.

"Well, what is your determination?" asked Charlie.

"Perfect, I say. You've done a magnificent job maintaining these machines. Now, I must ask, will you be able to keep up this routine? If so, do you need anything from me?"

"Well . . . yes, I suppose so . . . but . . ."

"But what?"

"To be frank, Brian, this situation is rather unstable."

Brian smiled. He recognized the same reality. "I have a proposal for Mrs. Bainbridge to fix the problem. Give me a day or so. I expected to have a solid offer for everyone. Please hang in there with me. We'll get this sorted out. I want you to feel you can depend upon his job." Charlie nodded his head in agreement. "Excellent. I expect to have a satisfactory solution in place for everyone before the next engine run in a week. If I can available, I'll fly 'em again next Saturday."

"OK. I'll stick with the plan and wait for your proposal."

"Excellent. Thank you, Charlie. Now, let's get these flying machines put away," Brian said.

Charlie had already returned the two Jenny's to their hangar and closed the door. They stored and secured all the aircraft with the Staggerwing last. With everyone settled in place, Brian checked his wristwatch.

"Seven and a half hours today?"

"Yeah." Brian paid Charlie for 10 hours. "That's not necessary, Brian."

"Sure it is. Call it a bonus for a job well done, or just good will." Charlie shook his head, smiled and took the proffered cash. "I'll be in touch one way or another next week."

"Thank you, Brian."

"Mrs. Bainbridge has hot coffee and tea before you go."

"I'll pass. Please thank her for me, but I'd like to get home to my family."

"Understood. Have a great weekend, and again, thank you very much for your expertise, Charlie."

"You are most welcome. Good day."

Brian watched Rogers drive away in his faded blue, '34 Ford. When his car disappeared through the far tree-line, Brian turned and walked to the house. He explained what they had done this afternoon and Charlie's early departure. Again, they sat down at the kitchen table with a fresh pot of tea. Brian availed himself of two delicious cookies.

"Malcolm's aircraft are in great shape . . . well maintained, thanks to Charlie," Brian said.

"They are your aircraft."

"Well, that is the basis of my alternative proposal. I will need to confer with my attorney, Jonas Braddock, regarding the transfer of title based on Malcolm's last will and testament. I know what you told me regarding Mister Bainbridge's wishes, but I am not aware of any legal transfer of title. We'll get that part sorted in short order, I suspect. Did Mister Bainbridge engage a lawyer for his air delivery business?"

"No . . . not that I'm aware of."

"Did he set up a legal entity—a company or corporation?"

"Again, not that I'm aware of. He just did the delivery business because he loved flying."

"Did he employ other pilots?"

"I think so, not consistently or regularly, just when the demand needed them."

"OK. Those are details that will need to be sorted out. What I am proposing, Mrs. Bainbridge, is the formation of a proper company. For now, let's call it the Bainbridge Air Service to operate the aircraft for deliveries, and perhaps even passenger transportation. I would like you to be president of the company with a proper salary."

"Brian, I can't," Gerty protested.

He held up his right hand to gesture for her to hear him out. "If you approve, I intend to hire an operational manager to run the day-to-day activity. You can be involved as much as you wish to be, and more importantly, not worry about your income."

Tears descended her cheeks. "Do you really think that will work?"

Brian smiled and nodded his head. "I'll make sure it does."

"But, you are away fighting a war," she said, as she wiped away her tears and dealt with her sniffle.

"True. However, as I learned a week ago, my father employed a man to watch over their holdings. His name is Travis Atherton. I've met with him nearly every day since I learned all this. He has done a masterful job and he will continue to do so, while I am away. Jonas has helped me arrange for permanency should something happen to me. I ran my idea past Travis and Jonas since I was here last Wednesday. Both of them think it is workable, not without risk of course, but workable.'

Gerty stared at Brian as she considered his words. She stood and went to the kitchen window. Brian gave her the quiet time, resisting his urge to press home his argument. He enjoyed another cookie, finished his tea, and poured another cup. Gerty turned back to face Brian and leaned back against the counter.

"What do I need to do?" Gerty asked.

"First, Mister Bainbridge built some nice hangars to protect the aircraft. With your permission, I would like to operate out of these existing facilities. That means you will have daily traffic. We'll have to build a small office to provide workspace for the necessary employees to operate the company. Travis or I will introduce you to the operating manager, once we have him hired. We can work out the details as we go. You will be welcome to be involved however you wish to be. I will not likely be available when issues come up, so I would like you to build a relationship with Travis and trust him with handling whatever matters might arise. I need to give you my post address as well as Charlotte's. She is stable and has a very nice, productive ranch. She will know how to get ahold of me as this war progresses."

Again, Mrs. Bainbridge stared at Brian. "OK. That should be alright."

"Excellent. We'll get to work setting things up. I'll try to get this settled out before I need to head back to England. I'll keep you posted," Brian said, as he stood.

Gerty Bainbridge went to a kitchen drawer, retrieved a set of keys, and handed them to Brian. "Here are the keys to the pickup, the house, should it ever be locked, and to the barn."

Brian took the keys. Gerty hugged Brian.

They said their good-byes. Brian loaded his bicycle in the back of the pickup. He drove away and noticed Mrs. Bainbridge in the rear-view mirror, standing on the porch watching his departure. Blessedly, the truck heater worked and made his journey back into town far more comfortable.

—

Tuesday, 25.February.1941
Bainbridge Ranch
Rural Route 14
Wichita, Sedgwick County, Kansas
United States of America
12:30 hours

The cold of the winter day made Brian appreciate the heater in the borrowed Ford pickup truck. The drive to the ranch had been easy and uneventful. He parked on the far side of the loop driveway terminus at the ranch. Gerty greeted him at the door.

"Thank you for hosting this meeting," Brian said, as he stepped inside the warm home, "on such short notice."

"There was no problem for me, Brian. I am honored that you are including me. Malcolm has talked about Mister Sales more than a few times, so I am familiar with the name. He has even flown in here to meet with Malcolm a few times, but I never met him."

"We'll see that changes shortly."

"I have prepared some ham sandwiches, since it is noon time, and I imagine Mister Sales will be hungry, as I knew Malcolm was at this time of day after flying. I made some fresh cookies this morning, and I have milk, or fresh coffee or tea."

"You are most generous, Mrs. Bainbridge," added Brian.

"I should have said this much sooner, Brian. I am embarrassed that I did not. If we are going to be working together, I must insist upon you using my nickname."

"As you wish, Gerty. My lawyer is working on the proper paperwork to form the company and that should be ready later this week. I think Bobby may be the correct person to run the day-to-day business. We shall see. I wanted to come out early to answer any questions you might have before the others arrive."

"I am curious to see how this idea evolves, but no, I don't have questions. I am just grateful, as I said earlier, that you included me."

The sound of an automobile engine and the crunching of gravel signaled the arrival of Travis Atherton, prior to Bobby's arrival, as planned. Gerty and Brian went to the door. Brian stood behind Gerty. She opened the front door as Travis ascended the front porch steps.

"You must be Mrs. Bainbridge," Travis said, as he approached.

"Welcome to my home," she answered. "Yes, I'm Gerty Bainbridge, and you know Mister Drummond."

"Yes, I do," Atherton responded and extended his hand to Brian. "Great to see you, again, Brian. Thank you for including me."

They retreated to the warm interior. They had not reached the kitchen when the distinctive combination of sounds—full-throated engine, whistling of speed, and the sharp beat of a propeller—announced the arrival of Bobby Joe Sales.

Brian bent down slightly to look out the living room window to see the flash of a Grumman FF-I pursuit plane making a low level, high-speed pass down the runway. He went outside, off the porch, and acquired the odd, almost teardrop-shaped biplane beyond the tree-line in a climbing, near vertical banked turn. *Nice way to announce your arrival, Bobby.* The aircraft rolled level on the downwind leg. Brian watched the wheels come out of their fuselage wells, as Bobby manually cranked them to the down and locked position. Next, the forward canopy slid back.

Before Bobby turned to his descending base leg, Brian walked toward the hangars. Bobby landed on the grass strip with one slight bounce. Once Sales slowed the aircraft to taxiing speed, he turned back toward the hangars. Brian watched as his guest turned the aircraft with his tail toward the first hangar and shutdown the engine. Brian walked to the aircraft and waited at the left wing root for Bobby to extricate himself.

"Welcome to Wichita," Brian said, as Sales removed his headgear and jumped off the lower wing.

"Thanks for inviting me," Sales responded and shook Brian's hand. "Great to see you, again, Brian. Welcome back from the war."

"Thanks."

"Perhaps after we've done our business, we can chat. I've thousands of questions about what you've done over there."

"Sure, if there's time. If you want to get back to St. Louis before sunset, we don't have a lot of extra time."

". . . a few hours perhaps," Bobby added.

"Then, let's get to it," Brian said and began walking slowly toward the house, and Bobby walked beside him. "I'll save my description for the group. Besides me, Malcolm's widow . . ."

"Gerty?"

"Yes, Gerty Bainbridge and my foreman, Trevor Atherton, will be sitting in."

"Fine."

"I'll describe in general what I'm looking for. From that, we'd like to know how you feel you can help achieve the results we want."

"If I may ask, why is Gerty involved, and what is Atherton's position in all this?"

Brian stopped short of the front porch and turned to face Bobby. "Gerty will be the president of the new company. I've told her she can be involved as much as she wished to be part of the operation. I do not expect her to be more than a figurehead, but that is her choice entirely. She understood and knew about Malcolm's operations. I want special care and attention to her wishes . . . unless they become excessive, at which time, they will become my problem. Trevor's primary job is managing the operations of my parents' properties."

"Which are?"

"We can get into that later. There is no reason for your not to know. I am just mindful of the time. Let it suffice to say, they acquired more than a little land and that land produced several oil wells."

"So, you are a rich man?"

"I would not say that, but I will not argue the point. Let's go inside and get this interview done."

Sales nodded his head. They went inside. Brian introduced everyone. Gerty placed lunch on the table and they each helped themselves.

"Let me begin," Brian said, "by describing what we are trying to do. I am proposing the formation of an air transport business called Bainbridge Air Services, Incorporated. My lawyer, Mister Braddock, is producing the necessary legal paperwork to create the company. It will take some footwork to regain Malcolm's original business. Gerty might be able to help with that." She nodded her head. "Malcolm has several aircraft . . ."

"You have," interrupted Gerty.

Brian smiled at Gerty. "Braddock is still working out the details, but Gerty has indicated that Malcolm transferred the aircraft to me upon his passing. This discussion is based on the execution of that transfer. So, for now, let us assume I am sole owner of the subject aircraft. My point is, we have multiple aircraft that are in fine shape . . . I flew them all last Saturday . . . and can be put to productive use." Looking directly at Sales, Brian continued, "We have discussed the future of air transport."

"Yes, we have."

"Well, the bottom line is, this is your chance, our chance, to make air transport an effective business."

Gerty and Travis remained mostly quiet listeners and engaged when they felt appropriate. Bobby demonstrated his preparation for this opportunity and this moment. He had clearly thought through the difficulties as well as the possibilities. They discussed future growth potential and how they might realize that potential. Bobby painted a bright and attractive future. He felt he had the skills to run the business. They also talked about financial budgets including advertising and marketing expenditures, as well as capital investments to upgrade aircraft as the business grew. Lastly, they discussed compensation for Bobby as well as future employees in operations.

Brian had discussed with Travis the establishment of an operating budget that assumed net losses for two to five years as well as the constraints on those losses. Travis recognized his lack of experience in aviation, but felt he could contribute from a business perspective.

"Any questions?" Brian asked Bobby.

"Tons."

"Shoot."

"You are going back to war as you mentioned on the telephone the other day. How will you be involved?"

"Distantly to not much. I have discussed with Travis and he will provide the necessary supervision. As I mentioned earlier, Gerty, Travis and I will serve as the company's board of directors. I don't know how much I will manage to be involved, but I shall try. Travis has managed my parents' assets for more than a decade. I have confidence in his ability to assist you with the business. While you must manage the business, we will rely on your aviation knowledge, expertise and passion to make this enterprise successful."

"What about after the war?"

"That is a way off." Brian glanced at Gerty and back to Bobby. "I have to survive the war, first. If the company is running well, I see no reason to interfere. Heck, if I no longer have a stick to waggle, perhaps I will just become one of your line pilots."

"That would be interesting."

"Anyway, the point is, you can have this job as long as you wish, as long as you are enjoying it and make it successful. I like the idea of an air transportation company for the future, but I also want a living tribute to Malcolm."

"I can do that."

"I am convinced you can. What other questions?"

"That should suffice for now. I think I can operate successfully within the boundaries you have established. I look forward to contributing to the realization of your vision, Brian."

Brian looked first to Gerty, and then to Travis. "Do either of you have any questions." Both shook their heads in the negative. "Then, we are concluded. You have the job."

"Excellent."

"You can expect to hear from Jonas Braddock in the next day or so. Oh, I forgot, one more thing. As we discussed on the telephone last week, you intend to move here and live here once all the arrangements have been made. Is that correct?"

"Yes. That is my intention . . . as quickly as possible . . . and with my aircraft."

"Jonas will make the arrangements."

"Perfect."

"Now, I am very mindful of the time. Let's get you saddled up and on your way, to get you home before sunset." Brian stood, followed by the others. They shook hands with each other. Brian said good-bye to Travis, thanked him for participating, and told Gerty he would be right back after he got Bobby into the air and on his way. Travis departed. Brian walked with Bobby back to his aircraft.

Brian pushed the handcart fuel bowser to the aircraft and began pumping fuel into Bobby's machine.

"So, is it true . . . what the papers say . . . that you're an ace three times over?"

"Apparently so."

"I knew you were a magician when we flew those encounters two years ago with Malcolm and Group Captain Spencer."

"Now Air Commodore Spencer."

"What is that?" Bobby took his turn on the handpump.

"The RAF equivalent of a brigadier general."

"Wow, good for him. What is your rank?"

"Flying officer . . . equivalent to a first lieutenant."

"Are you going to stay in the military after the war?"

"Hard to say at this stage. I do love the flying, although I'm not so keen on the getting shot at part." They both laughed. "Stop!" Bobby stopped pumping immediately. "You're full." Brian returned the nozzle to its holster on the bowser and wheeled the cart back to its spot, while Bobby closed the fuel cap and did a quick check of his aircraft. "You should be ready to go."

"Yep." Bobby extended his hand to Brian. They shook hands. "Thank you for thinking of me for this company, Brian. We're going to do a great job. You just stay safe and come home when you're done."

"Thanks, Bobby. Fly safe. Talk to you soon."

Sales climbed into the cockpit and strapped himself into the seat. Brian backed away and forward to be abreast of the cockpit. Bobby started the engine easily. When he was ready, he looked over to Brian and saluted. Brian returned his salute in fine British fashion. Sales took off, did a circuit around the grass strip and made a nice low pass before heading east.

Once Bobby was out of sight, Brian headed back to the house. Gerty was in the kitchen, finishing up the dishes from lunch. "What did you think?"

Gerty finished washing, dried her hands, turned and leaned against the counter. "He seems nice enough. Are you sure you can trust him?"

Brian thought for a moment. "Do you know something I don't? Did Malcolm say something about him that does not sit well with you?"

"No, no, nothing like that. Malcolm had nothing but good things to say about Mister Sales, but Malcolm was not in business with him."

"Good point. I would say, yes, I do; however, I will make arrangements for both Atherton and Braddock to keep a close eye on things. Plus, you will be here to watch. You will know if something is not right. You watched Malcolm fly. You know."

"OK. I suppose you're correct."

"Thank you, again, for hosting this meeting, Gerty. I'm excited about getting this operation going. Now, I'd better be going. I've another appointment and need to get back into town."

"Thank you for including me. Have a great day." Gerty gave Brian a hug and a kiss on the cheek. Again, he watched her watching him as he drove away.

—

Thursday, 27.February.1941
Law Offices of Bender, Braddock and Sloan
221 South Broadway, Suite 400
Wichita, Sedgwick County, Kansas
United States of America
09:30 hours

"**W**elcome back to Bender, Braddock and Sloan, Mister Drummond," Alice the receptionist said, as Brian entered the law office lobby, dressed in an ill-fitting, medium gray suit he found in his father's closet. He felt even more ill at ease standing before the attractive, auburn-haired woman a few years older than himself with no ring on her left ring finger.

"Thank you," Brian responded. He walked up to the counter and extended his hand to her. "I am embarrassed to admit to not properly introducing myself. "My name is Brian."

Alice shook his hand and answered, "Nice to meet you properly, Mister Drummond. I'm Alice White."

"Great to finally meet you, Alice. Now that we are properly introduced, I prefer the familiar."

"As you wish, Brian. Mister Braddock is waiting for you."

"Thank you, Alice."

Brian knew the way and made his way to the office of Jonas Braddock. Jonas was standing in front of his desk as Brian knocked on the open door. *Alice must have buzzed him.* They shook hands. Braddock gestured for Brian to sit in one of the spacious leather over-stuffed chairs, as he closed the office door. Jonas then sat in an identical chair facing Brian.

"Thank you for meeting with me before the press conference. I expect the journalists and photograph to arrive soon. Our large conference should be sufficient. I understand you have done these press conference events, so I won't bore you with my guidelines. Let if suffice to say, I will be ready to intervene should any question exceed your tolerance threshold. American journalists tend to be a little more aggressive and raucous than the international variety. I would also suggest you avoid answering questions regarding legal or personal matters, and any answers that might place you in a position of speaking for the U.S. or British government."

"Understood. Where are we on Bainbridge Air Service?"

Braddock smiled. "May I suggest we focus on this press conference? I will gladly bring you up to date with our progress after the press conference. I am trying to be a good attorney for you."

"Very well. I'll wait."

"Thank you. Do you have any questions regarding the impending event?"

"What is the mood? What are the likely questions? I imagine you have received some of those questions since our connection became known on my arrival."

"Hard to say. Questions they ask me may not be the same as they ask you. I suspect there will be questions about your decision to defy U.S. law and go to England before the war? Some of them may be aware of your parents' assets and might well ask you about your plans for those assets. Those, to me, are legal questions and should be referred to me to handle for you. Whatever personal information, like your marriage and such, you wish to share with the public is your choice entirely. I will only remind you that I will be ready to jump in wherever you wish me to run interference for you. We should agree on a signal for you to indicate you want me to handle any particular question."

"A signal?"

"Yes, like tapping the table two or three times with your finger or scratching your cheek. I'm sure you recognize that you have no obligation to answer any of their questions whatsoever. However, I think you can appreciate the public interest in your exploits that the press interest represents."

"Yes, I do. I may not like it, but as several wise men have taught me, public relations is an ancillary but important part of what I do. I may have said this before, but that is some of the frustration my brothers-in-arms and I feel."

"How so?"

"We feel like we have become a show squadron rather than a fighter squadron. Since we were collected up in Seventy-One Squadron, we have done far more press events, displays and such than we have actual combat."

"Perhaps that will change."

"So they keep telling us. We were declared operational early last month, we have only flown convoy escort patrols and back up to the back up patrols. My old squadron has flown more than a few attack missions into France. We have flown none."

"Perhaps that is a good thing."

"No, Jonas, it is not. All of us volunteered to fight. It is what we do. We cannot help win the war by flying benign, safe missions."

A knock on the door broke their discussion. Braddock's legal secretary, Mrs. Betty Carrington, a silver-haired, matronly woman, opened the door and announced, "The media people have gathered in the large conference room, Mister Braddock."

"Thank you, Betty." Jonas turned to Brian. "Are you ready?"

"Sure. Let's get this done, so we can get back to real business."

"There should be water on the table. Keep your throat wet. I'll say: one more question, when the allotted 30 minutes has expired." Brian nodded his acknowledgment. Jonas stood, followed by Brian, and gestured to the door. Braddock led the way to the conference room.

Brian followed Jonas into the packed room. The cacophony hushed immediately. The room was overflowing with journalists and photographers with others outside in the hallway, straining to see. Light bulbs flashed as shudders clicked. Braddock gestured for Brian to take the farther of two chairs remaining on the long side of the table. All of the other chairs had been removed to make room for the crowd.

Braddock held up both hands, presumably to signal for the photographers to stop their picture taking for his introduction. "Thank you, gentlemen. I am Jonas Braddock, a principal partner in this law firm. May I introduce native-son Brian Drummond."

"Why aren't you in uniform?" immediately came the first question.

"I am on leave from my duties to allow me time to tend to my parents' affairs."

"We are so sorry for your loss," several of them said in unison.

"Can we see you in uniform and get some photographs?"

"Sure . . . when I leave here in a few weeks."

"Not before then?"

"Nope. I think not."

"Why did you defy federal law and run off to Canada right after you turned 18?"

Brian glanced at Jonas. "Mister Drummond had no intention of violating any law. He was simply fulfilling his perception of duty to defend freedom."

"But, the war had not started, yet."

"Yes, well," Braddock continued, "he felt it was inevitable after the Munich Agreement."

"How long will you be home?"

"I think I already provided that information."

"How does it feel to be home from the war?"

"I wish my visit was for better or more joyous reasons, and I wish it was summer rather than winter."

Most everyone in the room laughed.

"What's it like over there?"

"Deadly serious. People are dying on both sides.

"Have you experienced The Blitz?"

"Yes, on several occasions; however, we are not based in London or near any other city, so we don't get the worst of it. But, we certainly see the results."

"What's it like?"

"That is hard to explain. During the air battle of last summer, our airfields were bombed a lot. It is very rattling, fearsome and unnerving when bombs start exploding around you. Hopefully, none of you will ever have to experience that rather horrific activity."

"Are you winning?"

"That is hard to say as well. I'm only a line pilot. But, I think it safe to say we stopped the Germans from invading England last summer. That does not mean they will not try again when the weather improves, but they told us the Germans came very close to that invasion."

"They said you were nearly beaten when Hitler turned on London. Is that so?"

"Again, that is hard for me to judge. I am just a pilot."

"Just a pilot!" someone interjected.

"Yes, just a pilot. We had been flying combat sorties three, four, sometime five times a day, seven days a week, for nearly six weeks. We were all exhausted and our numbers were being rapidly depleted by the Germans' aerial onslaught. I think all of us who participated would agree with that statement—we were nearly beaten. There is no question the turning point came on the evening of the 7th of September, when the Germans turned their sights on London rather than Fighter Command."

"We understand that you are an ace with 19 kills."

"I use the term victories . . . yes, that is what they tell me."

"How many Americans are over there?"

"I have no idea, frankly. I know there are 11 in my squadron, including me. I know Fighter Command is in the process of forming other American volunteer squadrons. I imagine there are other Americans serving in other branches of the British armed forces, but my attention has been and will remain on those who fly with me."

"Are you saying you are eager to return to the war?"

"I am eager to return to my . . . ," Brian stopped himself. *I don't want to bring Charlotte and the baby into this.* ". . . to my buddies."

"You mean you like war?"

Brian stared at the middle-aged man who asked the question. *What a stupid damn question.* Brian raised his finger to tap out, but changed his mind. "Have you ever been in combat, sir?"

"No," the man answered promptly.

"Then, you have no ability to comprehend what you just asked me."

"Do you?" he persisted.

"I will not dignify such a foolish question with any answer."

"OK, gentlemen," Braddock injected, "one last question. Our allotted time is up."

"Do you agree with or support President Roosevelt's 'Arsenal of Democracy' premise?"

Brian tapped his right index finger three times as he stared at his new inquisitor.

Braddock received the signal. "As Mister Drummond indicated previously, he is just a pilot serving in the defense of freedom. It is not his place to judge the President's actions or words. Thank you very much for your interest in Mister Drummond. We are done here. Have a great day." Braddock grasped Brian's elbow signaling for him to stand. They departed the room to a barrage of additional questions—some antagonistic, some personal, some quite inappropriate. Brian felt the urge to respond, but Braddock squeezed his elbow to press him to leave.

Back in Braddock's office, Jonas gestured to the same leather chairs as he closed the door. Before he was fully seated, Jonas said, "That went quite well, Brian. You handled their questions with skill far beyond your years, especially that 'like war' nonsense."

"Thank you. I've had to do these press things more times than I can count. I will never like them, but I guess they must be done."

"Yes, well . . . well done nonetheless. Now, let me jump to your earlier query, tabled for the press conference. We are nearly done with the preparation of the founding documents for incorporation of Bainbridge Air Service, Inc. with Mrs. Gertrude Bainbridge as president with the salary you indicated, Travis Atherton as managing director, and as you indicated yesterday, Bobby Joe Sales will be the operating manager. Mister Sales will be in residence by the end of the month, by the way. He has already signed the employment contract, for your information."

"Good."

"Also, Gertrude, Travis and you comprise the board of directors."

"When will the documents be ready to sign?"

"Tomorrow. I'll have Betty make an appointment for us tomorrow afternoon."

"I would like to have Travis and Mrs. Bainbridge in attendance, as witnesses, and to sign the founding documents as founding directors."

"It shall be so arranged. If I may ask, Brian, how do you know this Mister Sales?"

"He is a friend of Malcolm's, and I flew against him several times at various air meets in '38 and '39, but most notably, during my evaluation flight with then Group Captain John Spencer. He is an aviation believer." Brian smiled. "He is also one year short of being beyond draft age."

"Interesting. Small world."

"Indeed."

"Was there anything else you needed today?"

"Bobby will report to Travis during my absence. I would like both you and Travis to review the books on a monthly basis until we can all gain confidence in Bobby's ability to manage the business."

"As you wish."

As Brian departed the downtown office building, he reminded himself that Travis already knew of the arrangements, but Mrs. Bainbridge did not. *I'll drive out to the ranch to inform Gerty, and perhaps enjoy another one of her magnificent cookies.*

—

Chapter 14

Intelligence is quickness to apprehend as distinct from ability,
which is capacity to act wisely on the thing apprehended.
- Alfred North Whitehead

Sunday, 2.March.1941
Chequers Court
Ellesborough, Buckinghamshire, England
United Kingdom
12:30 hours

"Thank you for making the journey to the country," the Prime Minister said and extended his right hand to Bill Donovan. "I know you just arrived back in Mother England and you are not yet complete with your assessment tour, but this opportunity opened. I wanted to take advantage of this window for a private, personal discussion. We are still scheduled for a welcome home dinner party a week from today, and I trust it will not interfere with your plans. Let us retire to the study."

The Prime Minister led the way to the well-appointed, book-lined study. Winston closed the door and gestured to two, facing, spacious, over-stuffed, brown leather chairs.

"My apologies for all the covert arrangements, but I thought this meeting between us should be off the diary, so to speak. We will discuss the official stuff next week. I want to convey my feelings at a personal level."

"Understood and accepted. It is always a pleasure to chat with you, Winston," Bill Donovan responded.

"I cannot and will not attempt to predict the future. Franklin has not shared his precise thinking with me and I do not know what he intends to do relative to your contributions to the war effort. That said, let it suffice to say, I see your latest mission as well as your shorter previous visit last July in comparatively clear terms. I think so much of our collaboration will depend upon our personal, private, and intimate relationship—you and me, Franklin and me, and directly between you and Franklin. In thinking through his particular exchange, I felt the need to convey my feelings to you, and I shall refrain from probing your findings until your inquiries and fact-finding are complete. While I cannot dictate your feelings or approach, I wanted to look you in the eyes and tell you a genuine friendship and faith in each other is and will be essential as the basis for our professional relationship. To that end, I want you to hear it from me, to feel it from me, that you will have access to me anytime—day or night—wherever I may be.

Winston continued, "As you know, my opinion remains entry of the United States toward the ultimate defeat of Germany is inevitable. Congress is nearly the final floor votes for passage of the President's Lend-Lease program that is vital to our sustainment of the war effort and avoidance of financial collapse. The joint military staff conversations that began in January are nearing completion, and it is my understanding they have made substantial progress in laying out the military strategic approach to the ultimate defeat of Germany. I also believe we will create a joint development program for atomic munitions, once the MAUD Committee completes its assessment for our collective review. We . . . our two, English-speaking countries . . . are engaged. The same engagement is evolving for our critical intelligence apparatus. That is where you come in. I believe Franklin is headed as quickly as he feels possible toward a strategic intelligence agency to advise him above the current, parochial, departmental level. I also believe he is preparing you to be the chief of that new organization."

"That may be, Winston, but Franklin has made no commitment, in fact, not even indicated to me his plans or intentions."

Churchill smiled at his guest. "Bill, you are an intelligent man with worldly experience. You are also an accomplished attorney, quite accustomed to evaluating people and situations. Furthermore, your international business over the last two decades has provided you incalculable contacts across the globe. I accept your underplay, but I want you to know from me that I appreciate the skills you bring to the table, and I am certain Franklin does as well. In no small measure, I believe you are uniquely qualified to be Franklin's strategic intelligence chief."

"I will not argue the point," Donovan said. "At the bottom line, it is Franklin's decision alone what he is going to do to solve his perception of the void in strategic intelligence and who he chooses to run the organization however it should be configured."

"Agreed . . . *in toto*. My only point is, regardless of Franklin's pending choices, I would like to build and maintain a close personal relationship with you."

"I am honored, Winston . . . and, I see no obstacles to that end. I have always appreciated your incisive insight and means of expressing those views. We can help each other."

"Yes, we can. I am mindful of your time and busy schedule . . . ."

"Thank you. Yes. I must get back to London to pick up Bill and one of Ambassador Winant's attachés for my visit to Scapa Flow next week. We leave tonight by overnight train. We should be back in London by Thursday.

Thank you, again, for your frankness and candor with me. I shall endeavor to be worthy of your trust and confidence in me, however this plays out."

"I can ask for no more," Churchill added, and then stood. The two men shook hands. "Now, I must be a proper host and send you along your way. I hope you enjoy your visit and find everything you seek at the main anchorage of the Home Fleet."

"I'm sure I will. I will see you again next Sunday."

Churchill walked Donovan back out of the manor house to the American's waiting embassy staff car.

"*Bon voyage*," Churchill said. Donovan waved his acknowledgment as he entered the back of the sedan and closed the door.

—

Wednesday, 5.March.1941
Munitions Building
Constitution Avenue & 20th Street
Washington, District of Columbia
United States of America
09:30 hours

The gold lettering on the half frosted glass door stated:

Chief, Army Air Corps
Maj. Gen. H. H. Arnold

Air Chief Marshal Sir Hugh Dowding, attired in a well-tailored, medium gray, business suit, thanked his Army captain escort, and then entered his intended, destination location. He was promptly announced for his scheduled meeting with the roughly equivalent chief of U.S. air staff.

The two men introduced themselves to the other, as it was their first face-to-face meeting, although both men were well aware of the respective positions and contributions of the other. They sat across at small conference table from each other.

"Thank you for taking some time from your busy schedule to see me, Sir Hugh."

"You are and will be always on my list of essential destinations, 'Hap.'"

Arnold nodded. "As I am certain you are aware, the President's Lend-Lease Program has passed the House and is expected to be passed by the Senate on Friday or Saturday. If reconciliation is necessary between the two versions, that process should be completed in short order, perhaps even as simple as the House affirming the Senate's version. I am told the President will sign the bill within a day or so of passage by Congress."

"I cannot claim definitive understanding of the process, but I am generally aware of the status."

"Excellent. I asked for this meeting with you as the chief air liaison officer for His Majesty's Government to inform you, the RAF and the government that I have already ordered 260 primary and 285 advanced trainer aircraft be dedicated exclusively to pilot training for the RAF. Those aircraft seats will be immediately available for your use upon the President's signing of the bill into law."

"Excellent. We genuinely appreciate your initiative on this matter."

"I expect the bill to pass the last few hurdles by next week. Based on that assumption, I would suggest we start to fill the pipeline. You have candidates en route to Canada already. Perhaps a portion of those can be diverted to prime our training capacity devoted to your supply. Also, initially, I expected to staff these training assets with American instructors, but I suspect you may well wish to use British instructors and use your own curriculum."

"We have discussed all that. The position of His Majesty's Government is to accept your instructors and your curriculum of instruction until such time as we can safely say the invasion threat has sufficiently diminished, or we have sufficient pilots to fill all of our operational seats. Once we have reached that point, we would appreciate the opportunity to adjust the curriculum and assign some of our more experienced and seasoned pilots to the instructor role at your bases."

"That sounds reasonable. I will issue instructions to our Training Command to that end, and I will use the term indefinite for the duration of my orders.

"That is quite reasonable," answered Sir Hugh. "Now, if I may," he waited for Arnold's confirmatory head nod, "I would like to discuss pilot recruitment at least for this interim period until our collective training capacity can be increased to meet our joint needs."

"What do you have in mind?"

"We have heard that orders have been issued to allow direct recruitment from your active duty pursuit squadrons."

Arnold's grin disappeared and was replaced from stone cold stare that last several long moments. "I must ask, where have you heard this rumor?"

"I was not told the source." Arnold's expression did not change. "If the topic is too sensitive, we can move on."

Arnold considered his response. "If it was anyone other than you inquiring on this matter, I would end our discussion without acknowledgment." He paused. Dowding did not react. "In strictest confidence, I will inform you that the President issued a secret order a month ago allowing volunteer recruitment of qualified military pilots from active duty squadrons for service with the 1st American Volunteer Group in China to bolster the defenses of the Nationalist Chinese forces against the Japanese."

This time, it was Sir Hugh Dowding's turn to stare. "So, it is true?"

"Yes," Arnold responded. "As you have probably deduced by now, the President has tacitly accepted the recruitment efforts of Colonel Sweeny, Clayton Knight, and Marshal Bishop from our civilian pilot population. The presidential order I mentioned earlier confines recruitment by Colonel Chennault for the AVG to military pilots and prohibits his recruitment from civilian pilots. Conversely, we must ask that British recruitment stay within the de facto system as it has evolved. We do not want competition between the two groups."

Dowding thought about Arnold's revelation. "Recruitment of qualified pilots significantly reduces the necessary training time to make a pilot operational within our system."

"True. However, I'm afraid we must insist. The U.S. Government, and the President specifically, is walking a very thin line regarding current law. Competing for pilots would seriously complicate the government's position with respect to Congress and the American people. I trust you will appreciate and understand the position we are in here. The Clayton Knight Committee recruitment efforts have been established and underway for almost two years. For better or worse, that process is supplying several squadrons worth of pilots. This seems like the best solution to the dilemma we face. Depending upon how the Lend-Lease Program is implemented and accepted by the American people, we may be able to make adjustments by summer or fall. For now, however, I'm afraid we must insist."

"Do Knight, Sweeny, Bishop and the others know these rules?" asked Dowding.

"Yes, as a matter of fact, Knight has been briefed in general . . . not with the details I have given you. He . . . they do not know why, as you do, but they have agreed to operate within the expressed guidelines."

"*Prima facie*, I think these guidelines are acceptable and workable. It would be appropriate to inform the Chief of the Air Staff, and to that end, I shall request your consent to inform Sir Charles."

Arnold briefly considered the request. "I agree. It would be appropriate. Please ensure Marshal Portal is clearly aware of our sensitivity. I am scheduled to visit the United Kingdom next month. I would be happy to brief Sir Charles and Marshal Douglass myself during my visit."

"Very well. I will ensure he appreciates the situation."

The two senior aviators concluded their meeting. Arnold walked Sir Hugh to the lobby. They wished each other well. Arnold saluted Sir Hugh before he turned to exit the building.

—

Sunday, 9.March.1941
Chequers Court
Ellesborough, Buckinghamshire, England
United Kingdom
19:15 hours

"Thank you for joining me before dinner, Bill," announced Prime Minister Churchill, as he extended his right hand to Colonel Bill Donovan. They shook hands, and then Churchill extended his hand to Donovan's companion. "Always a pleasure to see you, again, Bill," he said to Bill Stephenson. The door to the library study closed behind the two men.

"Great to see you, as well, Prime Minister," Donovan responded, with no reference to their private meeting one week prior.

"Welcome back from your extended journey. I am pressing the limits of my protectors by hosting this meeting and dinner at Chequers rather than Ditchley, as the full moon is just three days away."

"Thank you, sir. Hopefully, there is no risk realized for the convenience of the closer location. At the outset, I must thank you profoundly for your direct support of my mission and especially for assigning Colonel Dykes as my escort and ramrod."

"Ramrod? . . . as in cannon charging ram?"

"Well, that metaphor would work, but actually, I was thinking of the Old West in the United States and the individual on cattle drives or wagon trains who made things happen."

"Ah yes, the Old West . . . very rowdy period in American history. I learned something more, today. Thank you for that, 'Big Bill.'"

"You are most welcome, sir."

"Please, 'Bill,' Winston is sufficient in our private conversations, which is precisely what this is. Now, pray tell me about your journey, and if you are permitted, about your findings. We have a little over an hour to dinner time and joining the remainder of my guests."

"As you wish, Winston, and President Roosevelt encouraged me to be frank with you."

"Excellent. Please continue."

"I believe you are well aware of my itinerary, which we followed precisely, thanks in no small measure to Colonel Dykes in resolving the inevitable hiccups that occur on such missions." Churchill nodded his head in acknowledgment. "I also appreciate your personal tolerance with respect to my detour to Vichy. The President specifically asked me to visit Admiral Leahy and explore intelligence options in Vichy, France."

"That is perhaps the most critical element of your entire journey. What did you learn, if I may ask?"

"Have you met Admiral Leahy?"

"Not as yet, I must say, but I do look forward to the day."

"He is a good man. I think you will like him. He is also a realist. He knows he is under constant surveillance by the French and probably the Germans. He holds no illusions regarding Vichy French and German suspicions of him and the Americans at the embassy. He had some worthy ideas on how we might infiltrate agents. It was my private conversation with Ambassador Leahy that helped bring into sharp focus my view of strategic intelligence."

"How so?"

"I had a fairly clear view after my visit last July with enormous thanks to Colonel Menzies, Admiral Pike, Brigadier Harker, David Petrie, Commissioner Game and so many others, but the realities of Ambassador Leahy's situation helped bring the image into focus."

Brigadier Oswald Allen 'Jasper' Harker, CBE, had served as Director-General, Security Service (MI5), since the Prime Minister and Home Secretary had agreed it was time for the Service's founder to retire in June of the previous year. By that agreement, Harker served as interim director to allow the chosen successor to be free in his conduct of a thorough examination of MI5 operations and personnel. David Petrie, CIE, CVO, CBE, KPM, was nearly complete with his assessment and would soon receive his appointment to reform and lead the Security Service.

Commissioner of Police of the Metropolis Air Vice-Marshal Sir Philip Woolcott Game, GCVO, GBE, KCB, KCMG, DSO, had been the chief policeman of London since 1935. In addition to the normal law enforcement operations, the Met, or Scotland Yard as it was popularly known, also worked closely with MI5, as the execution agency for the Security Service.

Donovan continued, "The first question the President asked me was the survivability of Great Britain. My observations toward that answer will be no surprise to you. Your forces are stretched incredibly thin. The Germans and Italians have the advantage in the lines of communications and their logistics are comparatively consolidated. Yours are directly dependent upon the Royal Navy and extraordinarily vulnerable control points – Gibraltar, Malta and the Suez – and, of course, the Atlantic approaches that are the vital supply line to sustain Great Britain. While merchant losses remain a net positive, the loss rate remains quite negative. I must report to the President the bleeding remains profuse."

"Yes, well, as you stated, we are quite aware of our vulnerabilities, Bill. The President deserves your independent and candid assessment. I shall not insult him or you by any attempt to sugarcoat the reality we face. The *Luftwaffe* continues to bomb our cities, although I must note the intensity has subsided from what we faced last fall. Did Colonel Menzies share with you our assessment of German intelligence and strategy?"

"Yes, although he was unable to share your sources."

"In time, 'Bill, in time, but we have strong indications that the mad corporal has turned his attention eastward. He has moved significant ground and air forces from France for rest and refit in Germany, and then into Poland. We believe the Soviet Union is next, although he might strike south into the Balkans and Greece to strengthen the Italian position in North Africa."

"Certainly. I think I understand why you have that assessment, which in turn further relieves the pressure of invasion from your immediate concerns."

"Yes, but it does not remove that threat."

"Agreed. As long as England remains free, you remain an inescapable threat to his holdings and his objectives. Hitler may have turned his eyes elsewhere, but that is a temporary respite. He simply must subdue, or at least marginalize, Great Britain, if he is to have any hope of holding what he has taken."

"I assume you have also conferred with Hugh Dalton."

"Yes sir. He has been most generous with his mission and plans. Those discussions bring me to the President's second question to me . . . how to construct our strategic intelligence apparatus and clandestine operations?"

"And, your answer is?"

"We are clearly and obviously behind what you already have in place in Europe. I would like to think we could build a comparable strategic intelligence organization that will complement your capabilities. My recommendation to the President will be an intelligence service modeled after SIS and a clandestine service similar to SOE. The cooperation between us must come from you and the President."

"Excellent and agreed. That very question is paramount on my list when the United States joins the war effort."

"We are already in the war effort, Winston."

"Yes, yes, and in a very important manner, but I am referring to the far greater involvement that I believe is inevitable. I think Franklin shares my view, but he is constrained, and I acknowledge those constraints, by the isolationist movement in your country and more specifically in Congress. I would like to support and assist where possible in your efforts to satisfy President Roosevelt and the needs for your country. Hopefully, if you will guide me in that process, we can rapidly expand our cooperation, as you refer. What of counter-intelligence? Director Hoover has not been so eager or willing to cooperate with MI5."

"Yes, well, that is a different kettle of fish. My discussions with Brigadier Harker and David Petrie have been most useful. I do not know how the President is leaning on this question, but I am perceptive enough to recognize the advantages of engagement with MI5. Hoover is not easily swayed, and he has been and will likely remain a tenacious protector of his dominion. Our vulnerabilities have been rather public in the last few years, with the various networks exposed."

"Interesting word choice – dominion – and quite apropos from my knowledge. Unfortunately, we can only assure you . . . this is but the tip of the iceberg. I wish Director Hoover was more willing to cooperate with MI5. We need each other." Churchill paused and held Donovan's eyes, clearly cogitating over what or how much to say next. Donovan remained silent. "I shall trust your discretion with what I am about to say." Winston waited for an affirmative nod. "A serious and perhaps fatal apprehension, on the part of many around me and in His Majesty's Government has been and remains the security of the United States . . . the ability of the United States to keep secrets, to be blunt. That one concern nearly stopped our technical exchange mission last year and keeps our intelligence services reserved regarding how much to share. That issue is vital and will be high on my list of topics to discuss with President Roosevelt whenever we meet. I say this, partly to be candid with you and the President, but more importantly, to urge you, in whatever new organization evolves, and in your military and governmental apparatus, to find the means to protect highly sensitive information that we might share. We must gain confidence in that ability, if I am to convince my ministers that sharing our most vital secrets with the United States will remain safe."

"I understand and appreciate your candor, Winston. I can assure you that our handling of classified material, especially of a highly sensitive nature, is on my findings list for my report to the President. People's lives will depend upon secrecy, especially when we start placing agents into enemy territory, or operatives for offensive action like SOE is doing, now."

"Precisely . . ." A knock at the door interrupted the Prime Minister. All three men looked to the door. Frank Sawyers, Winston Churchill's long-time valet, stood in the partially open door.

"Sir, your other guests have arrived, and Mrs. Landemare is ready to serve the evening meal."

"Thank you, Sawyers. Give us a few more minutes, we shall join the party."

"Yes sir." The door closed.

Churchill turned back to Donovan. "When do you plan to return to the States?"

"I'm scheduled to fly out of Bristol on Tuesday, the 11th."

"Perhaps, we can chat more later tonight or tomorrow. I presume Little Bill is returning to his post with you?"

"That is correct, Winston," answered Stephenson.

"Excellent. Now, we shall join my other guests momentarily, and being a proper host, you should know that joining us tonight will be my science advisor Professor Lindemann, along with your new ambassador Gil Winant and Doctor 'Jim' Conant, both of whom arrived a couple of weeks ago. I know the ambassador is aware of who you are and what your mission has been, but I doubt Doctor Conant is aware. Have you met either man?"

"No."

"I have no intention of illuminating who you are other than to introduce you as Colonel Bill Donovan on special assignment from Secretary of the Navy Knox, as we did last year."

"That should be sufficient, Winston. Thank you. Who is Conant and why is he here, if I may ask?'

"Certainly. James Conant is president of Harvard University. He holds a doctorate in chemistry also from Harvard, and like you, he is on special assignment from President Roosevelt. 'Jim' is leading a small scientific team from 'Van' Bush's National Defense Research Committee, and specifically the S-1 Uranium Sub-Committee, in talks with our scientific community regarding nuclear explosives."

"Ah yes, your MAUD Committee."

"Yes, precisely. Doctor George Thompson's so-called MAUD Committee is due to report their assessment of the science and engineering involved in this endeavor, next month. I expect the outcome of this collaboration will be a joint development program in the United States."

"MAUD?" asked Stephenson.

"Military Application of Uranium Detonation . . . the near instantaneous releasing of the enormous energy of nuclear fission. It shall be a reality, I just know it, and we must beat the Germans to such a device. We can discuss this more at dinner, and we really should not keep our guests waiting any longer."

"Thank you for your time, Winston, and thank you also for inviting us to your dinner party."

"Nonsense. We are honored to have you. And, I believe Gil Winant is going to inform us the Senate passed the long-awaited Lend-Lease Bill, last Friday, and hopefully, he will tell us when the President will sign the bill into law." Winston paused, and then motioned toward the door. "Shall we?"

—

Monday, 10.March.1941
1600 Pennsylvania Avenue, Northwest
Washington, District of Columbia
United States of America
11:00 hours

Brian had seen pictures of the White House in books, but the real building seemed far more majestic than the pictures appeared.

Brian had arrived yesterday afternoon. It had been the first time Brian had worn his RAF uniform in a month. None other than Captain Yardley with a different co-pilot and another C-39 had picked Brian up in Wichita and delivered him to Bolling Field, across the Anacostia River from the federal city. An Army sedan and driver had deposited him at the Mayflower Hotel on Connecticut Avenue, where he had enjoyed an exceptionally good meal and excellent night's sleep. The steady morning rain convinced him to take a taxi rather than walk, as he had hoped. The cab driver asked him twice where he wanted to go, as if he had misunderstood or misheard his passenger's request. The short drive took just a few minutes.

The uniformed guards at the perimeter gate had checked his identification against the approved visitor's list on a clipboard. They graciously offered him an umbrella, or brolly as the Brits call a hand-held canopy for rain cover. He was pointed toward the main entrance double doors for the West Wing.

Harry Hopkins was waiting for Brian inside the Lobby with a broad smile on his face. The interior guard performed exactly the same identification check and ticked Brian's arrival off on his clipboard list. Another guard took the courtesy umbrella before Brian could shake it off and collapse it. Brian removed his brimmed service cover and placed it under his left arm.

"Great to see you, again, Flying Officer Drummond," Hopkins nearly shouted.

Brian saluted the President's Special Assistant in proper British manner. "Thank you for the invitation, Mister Hopkins."

The two men shook hands. With his entrance procedure completed, Brian followed Hopkins out the door on the right of the large Lobby Room, and then left down the corridor. Hopkins turned left again at the end of the corridor and proceeded down a wider hallway. He stopped at an open door on the right, halfway down the hallway to a curved wall at the end. Hopkins gestured for Brian to enter the office. Once inside the comparatively large office, Hopkins closed the door behind him, motioned for Brian to sit at the wall couch with a modest coffee table, adjacent similarly upholstered chairs, and a combined coffee and tea service. Harry asked his guest if he wanted anything to drink, but Brian declined. Harry sat in the single chair to Brian's left.

"Again, I offer my sincerest condolences for your dreadful loss. I trust you were able to satisfactorily complete your estate business," Harry said.

"Thank you, sir. Yes, as best I could in the few weeks I had."

"Good. Never a pleasant task. I wanted to reconnect and have a quick chat before I take you into the Oval Office to meet the President." Brian smiled and nodded his head. This is surreal, Brian thought. "The President has eagerly awaited this opportunity. To my knowledge, you have never met President Roosevelt."

"Correct. I've only seen photographs in the Wichita Eagle, our local newspaper."

"Very well. In the interest of avoiding any awkwardness, I would like you to be aware that President Roosevelt contracted polio two decades ago and he is confined to a wheelchair. Understandably, he will not stand, but he will extend his hand to you. I tell you this to avoid your being surprised by his disability and treat him as you would anyone in a similar condition."

"I did not know."

"Most people do not, which is why I thought it best to inform you and prepare you. So, you are on your way back to the war."

"Yes sir. I have an Air Corps transport to New York this afternoon, and then fortunately, I have a seat on the Pan Am Yankee Clipper back to England."

"A very gentlemanly mode of trans-Atlantic transportation."

"Indeed."

Hopkins glanced at his office wall clock. "It is time for the President," he announced.

Both men stood. Brian tugged at the bottom on his service tunic to smooth and straighten his jacket. They left Hopkins' office, turned right and entered another door on the right, just beyond the curved wall. Harry introduced Brian to the President's Private Secretary 'Missy' LeHand. She indicated the President was free and ready for them.

Brian followed Harry into the Oval Office. The President was sitting in his chair between two long, facing couches. Brian stepped inside and immediately snapped to attention and saluted the President.

Roosevelt returned the salute and extended his right hand to Brian. "Come here, young man. It is an honor to finally meet you."

Brian stepped smartly to Roosevelt and shook his hand. "The honor is mine, Mister President."

Roosevelt motioned for Brian to sit to his right. Harry sat opposite Brian. "I have so many questions for you . . . may I call you Brian."

"Yes sir."

"Before I jump to my questions, please allow me to offer my sincerest and most heartfelt condolences for the tragic loss of your parents earlier this year. I understand that was the catalyst for your return to the States."

"Thank you, sir. Yes, it was."

"I lost my father some years ago . . . and my mother is quite ailing and I fear near death's door. I cannot imagine the grief of losing both of your parents together and at such a young age. I trust you have completed all of your necessary arrangements. Is there is anything we can do for you, please do not hesitate to let us know," the President said and nodded to Hopkins.

"Thank you, sir. I think we have things well in hand."

"Very good. I am informed that you were the first American to join the British . . . or the French, for that matter, before the war in Europe began."

"That is what I am told, sir."

"You went through the worst of the Battle of Britain."

"Yes sir."

"And, The Blitz as the Press call that horrific bombing of London."

"We see the results when we go into London, but they stopped bombing our airfields late last summer. During the winter, most, if not all, of our squadrons were refitted and replenished. We are a whole lot stronger today than we were last summer. And, some of the squadrons have started flying offensive operations into Northern France and Belgium."

"A good sign, it seems to me."

"Yes sir, most definitely."

"Have you flown into France, yet."

"No sir."

"You've flown the Spitfire fighter airplane?"

"Yes sir, although we are flying the Hawker Hurricane Mark Two at the present time."

"Are those airplanes as good as they say they are?"

"Without question, sir. They are not perfect, but they are very capable machines and a dream to fly."

"In what sense are they not perfect?"

"We need more fuel for more endurance in combat and we need bigger guns. We have three oh three machine guns. The Germans have 20-millimeter cannons . . . better impact power."

"I see," the President answered. "I understand you are with Seventy-One Squadron, now."

"Yes sir."

"The all American volunteer squadron the Press call the Eagle Squadron."

"Yes sir, but not just the Press." Brian pointed to the silver on blue embroidered patch on the left shoulder of his uniform tunic. "The 'E' 'S' stands for Eagle Squadron. The RAF leadership coined the term."

"Very good. Now I know. What are your breast ribbons, if I may ask?"

Brian pointed to each one from left to right. "This is the Distinguished Flying Cross, the Military Cross, and the ribbon for a Commander of the British Empire."

"If I recall, the CBE is one step short of knighthood."

"That is my understanding, and yes, I know as Americans we cannot become knights of the realm, but it is nice to be recognized by The King for the work we do."

"You have every right to be proud, my boy," Roosevelt said and nodded to Brian. "Now, I'm afraid I must conclude our visit. I have a rather busy schedule today."

Brian stood. "If I may, sir, before I go, I wanted to thank you personally for the presidential pardon you issued for me last spring."

"You are most welcome, my boy. You really must thank Senator Capper of Kansas. Your mother was a very persuasive woman I must say Brian. May God rest her soul."

"I had no idea. When I received your letter, it was a total shock . . . but a very welcome surprise. I had no intention of violating any laws, but I just had to fly those machines."

"We are glad you did, Brian. We are very proud of you. We stand in awe of your courage, your commitment, your sacrifice and your accomplishments. Once Senator Capper presented his case, I was all too eager to assist and lessen your burden. I shall pray that God keeps you safe and you can return home to peace and quiet when this dreadful affair is done."

"Thank you, sir." Brian saluted, again. "By your leave, sir."

"Granted. Safe journey, Brian," the President said, returned his salute, and shook hands with Brian.

Harry Hopkins led Brian out of the Oval Office and back to the Lobby. Brian noticed the rain had thankfully stopped, even if temporarily. Someone had arranged for an Army staff car to be waiting for Brian and to take him back to Bolling Field. Brian thanked Hopkins for arranging everything. Both Hopkins and Roosevelt had been most gracious with their precious time. It was time for him to return to duty.

—

Tuesday, 11.March.1941
Oval Office
The White House
Washington, District of Columbia
United States of America
16:30 hours

President Roosevelt sat in his special, low profile, wheel chair behind his large oak desk. The signing ceremony would be short and sweet, but incalculably important. His long-term, loyal, private secretary, Marguerite Alice 'Missy' LeHand opened the door. "Mister President, Secretary Hull and British Ambassador Lord Halifax are here with your other guests for the signing ceremony. The President nodded his head and waved his hand for them to enter.

Secretary of State Cordell Hull led the group into the Oval Office, followed by Ambassador Lord Halifax, Edward Reilly Stettinius Jr. and William Averell Harriman, with Harry Hopkins bringing up the rear and closing the door behind. The staff photographer entered from the side, interior door.

"I trust everyone has been introduced," said Roosevelt.

"Yes, Mister President," answered Hull.

"Excellent. Then, let's make this official." President Roosevelt picked up, uncapped his fountain pen, and promptly signed the legislation approval page before him. "The Lend-Lease Bill is now law," he announced. "Lord Halifax, I invite you to officially inform His Majesty's Government of this momentous event."

"I am honored to do so, Mister President."

"Ed, I asked Ed Stettinius and Averell Harriman to join us. I have asked Ed to lead the Lend-Lease Administration here in the States. He will run the program for all of us. I have also asked Averell to take up his assignment in London, as my special representative, envoy to Europe and principal in situ agent for Lend-Lease activities. To put it perhaps crudely, Averell will take your orders and 'Ed' will deliver your orders as swiftly as possible."

"On behalf of the His Majesty King George the Sixth and his first minister, I thank you, Mister President, and the American people for bringing this vital legislation to fruition in such a comparatively short time."

"Thank Harry for that. He spent more than a few hours and days on Capitol Hill arm twisting, cajoling and coaxing this bill along. Considering the magnitude of what this bill represents, it was indeed a very short time for passage. Thank goodness we have it now. 'Ed' will work with your office and Bill Stephenson in New York to get the pump primed. With this bill in hand, my principal concern shifts from producing the material you need to protecting all those ships moving the material across the Atlantic."

"That concern remains valid and appropriate, Mister President. I should note the relevant committees of the technical exchange program have already begun to deliver on many of the scientific means we collectively need to beat the Germans."

"Excellent. Let us pose for a picture to commemorate this occasion, and then I will leave you to get on with the details. Do good work!"

The attendees stood behind the President. The photographer took several additional pictures, including one with the President pretending to sign the bill. When the photographer had enough, Secretary Hull led the men out of the Oval Office, except for Harry Hopkins, who remained at the President's side.

"Well done, Harry."

"Thank you, Mister President."

———

Tuesday, 18.March.1941
RAF Kirton-in-Lindsey
Kirton-in-Lindsey, Lincolnshire, England
United Kingdom

Flying Officer Brian Drummond noticed the squadron's 'XR' fighters were not present, as he walked to the Dispersal Hut. It was a good, weather day for flying. The sky was clear. The air temperature was cool but not cold, especially for late winter. *I wonder what their mission is? Ah, we'll know soon enough.* Brian opened the Dispersal door and entered the warm interior.

"Good morning, Mister Drummond," said Corporal Harris. "Welcome back."

"Thank you, James. Great to be back. Where's the squadron?"

"Another training mission, sir."

"Oh my, the guys will not be happy with that."

"We have had a few shipping patrols while you were gone, but no enemy engagements. Mostly training sorties like before you left."

"The Air Ministry or Fighter Command must be concerned about something."

"I have no idea, sir."

"Me either, James . . . just thinking out loud."

"Very good, sir. The lads have been complaining a lot about the near constant stream of visitors and newspaper reporters wanting their attention."

Well, that certainly has not changed. "When did they take off?"

Harris checked his logbook and the wall clock. "Thirty-five minutes ago."

"OK. I think I heard them take off as I arrived, but I could not see them. They'll probably be out for another hour or so. I think I'll go for a walk about until the Skipper returns."

"Very well, sir. With your permission, I will record your arrival for the log. I will inform Squadron Leader Taylor, as soon as he returns."

"By all means. See'ya shortly."

Brian walked out into the bright, warm sunshine and cool air. He walked toward the central aerodrome operations building and air traffic control tower. The squadrons assigned to the airfield had not changed – two Spitfire squadrons and two Hurricane squadrons – one of each airborne, during his stroll. The fighter base did not have the intensity of operations they experienced at RAF Middle Wallop during the peak of air combat last summer. The three hangars seemed to be the preponderance of unseen activity with their main doors closed to retain some warmth for the ground crews. The distinct rattle of aluminum being pounded into the desired shape or position could be heard from inside the hangars. By the time he returned to the squadron area, Brian saw his 'XR-G' Hurricane all closed up. Two additional Hurricane fighters sat in similar fashion beyond his aircraft. He considered grabbing his flying kit from Dispersal and taking his aircraft up to get back in the saddle . . . at least to do something other than waiting.

With the idle time, Brian's thoughts returned to his reunion with Charlotte. It had been everything he had imagined and perhaps dreamed about during his month-long absence. Fortunately for both of them, Squadron Leader Taylor gave Brian an extra three days of leave after his arrival early last Friday morning. He marveled at her vitality and energy. Pregnancy had made her even more attractive than she already was. She had now been pregnant more than half of the entire time he had known her. Pregnancy, six plus months along, had not slowed her down in the slightest – one of many attributes he truly loved in her. Charlotte had also matter-of-factly reported a short visit by Rosemary Kensington and a telephone call from Mary Spencer, who was due to deliver her child early next month. Charlotte spoke of them and their interaction in rather glowing and friendly terms – another of Charlotte's attractive attributes. The farm was also doing quite well. Her milk and cheeses were quite popular and in high demand with rationing so prevalent, expansive and frankly oppressive. Some new government program enabled her to acquire three additional cows and a bull to help produce additional milk producers. She also received governmental dispensation to hire a teenage boy, who conveniently lived near Horace Morgan in Winchester. Jacob Holden was barely past puberty at 13 years of age, but he was an eager learner and energetic worker. Jacob's youthful energy had enabled Charlotte to reduce the amount of work she was performing and prepare for the birth of their first child. The timing of his return to Charlotte had been near perfect, since he was introduced to Mrs. Barbara Grey – the middle-aged woman who would serve as Charlotte's midwife for the birth. Mrs. Grey was an effervescent woman, who was apparently highly regarded in the community and took her profession very seriously, although perhaps a little too conservative and traditional. Charlotte was happy and content with her preparations. She enthusiastically devoured Brian, making his return even more rewarding. Life was good, but now, he waited to return to the war . . . at least he would soon have the controls of an agile fighter in his hands.

Brian checked his wristwatch – approaching lunchtime. The squadron must have diverted for some reason. Brian stepped back into the squadron Dispersal Hut.

Before Brian could ask his question, Corporal Harris announced, "The squadron diverted to RAF Cottishall in Norfolk."

"What happened?"

"I was only told that information, sir. Well, and, they have been assigned another mission once they have refueled and rearmed."

"Rearmed, you say?"

"That is what Group told me."

"This should be interesting. So, they will not likely return until mid to late afternoon."

"Probably not, would be my guess, sir."

"Very well, then, it is nearly lunchtime. Can I watch things here for you, while you grab a bite?"

"Oh no sir. That would not be proper. The flight sergeant will send a relief, when it is my time."

"OK. I guess I'll walk to the Mess for a bite myself, then."

"Very well, sir. Enjoy."

"I doubt it, but things are usually edible."

They both laughed, and then Brian departed for the Officer's Mess.

Brian saw several pilots he knew previously. None appeared to know why he had been missing for a month, and if they were curious, they did not ask. He sat at one of the large tables alone, and ate his cheese sandwich and bowl of noodle soup with a few vegetables. The tea was exquisite, as usual. He had missed English tea, whatever variety it was. He was certainly no expert or aficionado of varietal teas, but he did enjoy a couple of mugs. Most of the pilots did not dilly-dally. They finished their meal and left, as the operational day for the day-fighters was still very much active. A couple of new pilots from the other squadrons stopped to introduce themselves. Apparently, 19 aerial combat victories resulted in some celebrity status. Brian politely accommodated the new pilots, two of whom appeared to be older than him. His 20th birthday was next month. The Mess stewards went about their work cleaning up, while Brian leisurely finished his tea and humble meal.

Brian stopped by the Kirton Sector Control Station on his way back to Dispersal. Armed guards challenged him, scrutinized his credentials, and then allowed him to enter. Several sector squadrons were airborne, as indicated on the wall tote board opposite the sector controllers; however, there were no red blocks on the map board laid out before them. Like No.71 Squadron, those active squadrons were outside Kirton Sector control. Several senior officers nodded to him, but no one talked to him. He did not stay long.

By the time Brian returned to the Dispersal Hut, Corporal Harris had taken his lunch. He still did not have an inbound on the squadron. Brian grabbed one of the folding, garden chairs and set it up outside. The sun felt good. He dozed off in the warmth of the Sun.

The distinctive, melodious sound of Merlin engines brought Brian back to consciousness. Hurricanes landing. All 11 aircraft were on the ground and taxing when he could finally see the 'XR' tail marking. This was his squadron returning. Brian folded the garden chair and returned it to the interior. Squadron Leader Taylor's 'XR-A' Hurricane was the first to shutdown. He jumped out, waved off his crew chief, and strode smartly toward Brian.

Brian crisply saluted his commander. "Flying Officer Drummond returning to duty," he announced.

Taylor returned Brian's salute in a more casual manner. "We could have used you, today, Hunter. Let's talk, and then you can say hi to the guys."

Brian followed 'Billy' to his office.

Taylor closed the door. "Have a seat," he said, patting the back of the straight back, wooden chair opposite his desk and chair. He doffed his flight gear and hung it on the peg in his office. "Welcome back."

"Thank you, sir. It's great to be back."

"I think not. War is not fun, but I take your sentiment."

"What happened today, if I may ask?"

Taylor coughed what was supposed to be a laugh. "We went up for what was supposed to be another training mission, but got diverted to cover a small convoy. Damn Krauts brought in a squadron of One Ten's, apparently configured for high speed, low level operations with bombs. The RDF guys did not pick 'em up until it was too late, and we were the only armed fighters airborne and close enough to help – first shots for most of the guys. We did not down any, but managed to chase them off without serious damage to any of the ships, but they came dreadfully close to success. We passed Bingo fuel, so Cottishall Sector diverted us to RAF Cottishall for refueling and rearming. Then, we went back up to protect that convoy before being released to come home."

"It's been a while since we've had a tangle."

"Indeed. Now, to the serious part, I trust you were able to handle your affairs in Wichita?"

"Yes sir, as much as could be handled . . . at least the important stuff, according to my parents' attorney. Thank you for your support and assistance."

"I wish it could have been for a more pleasant reason, but you are most welcome. To be frank, I was not sure we would see you again." The statement surprised Brian. He had not even considered not returning. "Don't look so shocked, Hunter. There's not much anyone could do, if you had decided you were done with combat, and I imagine there was plenty to deal with at home, especially after losing both parents and having no siblings."

"There was not much reason for me to stay. I'm flying machines I dreamed of flying. I'm married and my wife owns a serious farm, and we are expecting our first child in a few months. I had every reason to return. I'm eager to get back in the cockpit. In fact, once I realized that you had been diverted and extended, I thought about taking my bird up to get back in the saddle."

Taylor smiled and stared at Brian. "I'm glad you did not succumb to temptation. That would've gotten both of us in trouble. Not a lot of sunshine left today, so your return to flight status shall have to wait until tomorrow morning. The Met guys say we should have fair weather at least until tomorrow afternoon. I'll go up with you for a little playtime."

"Works for me, sir."

"Is there anything else I need to know?"

"Charlotte is due around the first of June, so the doctor and midwife say. If at all possible, I would like to be there for the birth."

"I can make no promises. The mission comes first. The best I can say is, I'll see what I can do, but there is no way to predict what our situation will be until we get there. Anything else?"

"No sir."

"Fine. Now, we'll be released shortly, and I'm sure the lads want to welcome you back properly. Just don't over-do things tonight. Everyone needs to be ready to fly at dawn."

"Yes sir. Thank you again for allowing me to take care of my family business, and especially for your support in helping me get there as quickly as possible."

"My pleasure. Now, get out of here."

Brian rose to a position of attention, saluted his commander, executed a proper about-face and left Taylor's office, closing the door behind him. The guys were waiting; most were standing and the rest stood. They shook his hand, slugged him in the shoulder, a few hugged him, and they all offered words of welcome and greetings to him. As things began to settle out, the squadron was released. They walked together to the Officer's Mess. They asked questions around his journey, offered condolences and words of envy that he flew both ways in a Pan Am flying boat, even more so when Brian told them he got to fly the machine for a while on the return flight. He left out his chat with President Roosevelt and Harry Hopkins, as well as the resistance of the immigration officer on his return and the real purpose of his journey. He saw no need to complicate his relationship with the other pilots or disclose his newfound wealth.

They would eat their evening meal in the Mess, and then they all planned to gather at The Sprite pub in the village beyond the gates. Brian knew it would most likely be a raucous night, but he knew it was also necessary. His life was returning to normal, and it felt good.

—

Wednesday, 19.March.1941
Oval Office
The White House
Washington, District of Columbia
United States of America
09:45 hours

Executive Secretary to the President of the United States Missy LeHand opened the main door, stepped inside and closed the door behind her. "Mister President, Mister Donovan is here early."

"Thank you, Missy. Fetch Harry, if you would, and then show Bill in. I'll take him early."

"Yes sir."

LeHand left and closed the door. Franklin eagerly anticipated this meeting. Donovan had returned from his three plus month inspection tour of British field operations. His findings would clearly be the best, most comprehensive assessment yet presented to him. The State Department intelligence branch gave him a slice of diplomatic intelligence. The Army's G-2 intelligence chief gave him the Army's perspective, and the Navy's Office of Naval Intelligence offered the Navy's view of events the Navy was concerned about. No one gave him the complete, independent, broad, strategic intelligence assessment he needed, especially in these tumultuous times. Roosevelt had such high hopes that a smart, tough warrior like Donovan would see the big picture, resist the political turf battles of inter-departmental parochialism, and give him accurate, sound intelligence – good, bad, or ugly.

Harry's characteristic quick double knock on the door to the private study and dining room was immediately followed by his entry. "I understand 'Wild Bill' Donovan is here early," Hopkins said.

"So it seems. I'd like you to listen to this conversation. I suspect there will be some secret agreements, and you should witness whatever is discussed and agreed. Have you read his trip report?"

"As you wish, Franklin. My pleasure, as always, and yes, I have read it."

"What are your thoughts?"

"Very thorough, I must say. Based on our discussions, I'd say he hit the head squarely and drove the nail home in one stroke."

"My impression, as well. The problem is, the intelligence folks will not be happy with his recommendations, especially if I decide to implement them."

"Those same folks have largely failed you, Franklin. They are far more concerned about protecting their territory than filling in the gaps in our intelligence."

Roosevelt nodded his head in agreement. "Let's get him in here and get started."

Hopkins acknowledged the direction and went to the main door to the secretary's office and waiting room. Roosevelt wheeled his chair to his usual place between the facing couches and opposite the small fireplace. Donovan entered first, followed by Hopkins, who closed the door behind him.

"Good morning, Mister President," Donovan said and accepted Roosevelt's proffered right hand. The two men sat on opposite couches, nearest the President."

"Welcome home, Bill. I trust all is well with Ruth and family."

"Yes sir. Thank you for asking."

"Would you care for some coffee or tea?"

"No, thank you, sir."

"I have waited none too patiently for this conversation. I have read your report, several times I must say. Well done, Bill. It is everything I expected and more. You touched on more than a few things I had not thought of, frankly. I will send Winston a personal note of gratitude for his support," Roosevelt said and nodded to Harry, who would take care of that item for his signature. "Your vision for the strategic intelligence organization is exactly as I see the need. I could accept your recommendation directly, if not for one significant problem." The President paused to give Donovan an opportunity to respond, but he did not. Donovan remained motionless, unblinking and focused on the President. "While I like your recommendations, I am sure you recognize that none of this will go down well with the G-2, ONI or State for that matter. I would like to hear how you propose to deal with those damnable jealousies."

"Certainly sir." Donovan did not hesitate. He had clearly thought of this aspect. "The present organizations have solidified and been tempered by the Great War. They are not likely to amend their mindset spontaneously, and they are equally likely to resist, at least passively, if not actively through Congress, any attempt to envelop or supersede their domains, even if it comes from this office."

"A rather sobering assessment, don't you think, Bill?"

"I understood you asked me for an unvarnished evaluation of strategic intelligence in the country. This is your choice entirely, Mister President, but I know you are also a politically savvy, realist and skilled politician. It is my opinion you are not likely to gain their consent for a strategic intelligence organization, and whomever has that job will not have an easy go of it."

Roosevelt laughed heartily and started to cough. "Water, please, Harry," he said, as his laughed transitioned to a persistent cough and struggled to regain control. Hopkins handed a glass of water to the President, which in turn calmed his cough. "It seems my throat is still irritated from a recent cold." The President took another few swallows and placed the glass on the end table beside him. "Now that I have regained control, please continue, Bill."

"My apologies for causing you any discomfort, Mister President."

"Nonsense . . . nothing to apologize for. I was simply struck by your understatement of reality in this matter. Continue," he commanded.

"The only means I can see to overcoming the status quo with our existing intelligence agencies is to have the new director report directly to you, either within or as an adjunct to the Office of the President."

"If we were to do that, what functions would you include in that organization and under that aegis?"

"The new organization must avoid infringing upon tactical intelligence functions. The existing organizations appear to perform that function for their respective services fairly well, from my perspective. The focus must be on strategic intelligence . . . the policies of other governments and the strategic direction of other governments, both friend and foe."

"So, you would advocate we spy on our friends, like Great Britain?"

"Short answer, yes sir. We cannot afford to exempt anyone."

"Interesting . . . quite a contrast with Henry Stimson's 'Gentlemen do not read each other's mail' of a mere decade ago."

"I would have disagreed with Henry, then, if I had been asked, and I do not believe Henry retains that opinion, today."

The President chuckled, trying to avoid laughing and irritating his throat, again. "He does not. Both Henry and Frank Knox share my views toward strategic intelligence, but they also represent the parochial forces within their departments. Now, I distracted you from your answer to my query." He gestured for Donovan to continue with his response.

"To be direct, I think the new organization should fill the voids in what is not being done today, so that would include strategic intelligence, strategic counter-intelligence and more importantly special operations."

"Tell me more about that latter element."

"I have been and remain most impressed with Prime Minister Churchill's vision for and his selection of Hugh Dalton to lead their Special Operations Executive, SOE for short. Churchill's direction to Dalton is to set the occupied continent on fire. That is a pretty liberal mandate. SOE works in conjunction with MI6 regularly on intelligence matters, but occasionally with MI5, when their field agents acquire applicable leads or information. By the way, you may not be aware that the British government is nearly complete with its transition from General Kell, MI5's founder, to the man who will become the next Director General, David Petrie. Brigadier Harker has done quite well filling Kell's famous shoes."

"I knew Winston was working on a replacement for Kell, but I had not heard Petrie's name before. I also know Winston has not been particularly pleased with or complimentary to J. Edgar Hoover's running of the FBI, and I must say, in all candor, I share Winston's perspective and assessment. Edgar would not be pleased if he sensed you were dabbling in his pond."

This time Donovan chuckled, "Now, you have succumbed to understatement."

They all laughed, but Franklin tried to suppress his reaction.

"Yes, well . . . for the time being, let us keep everything on the table. I know and acknowledge that Hoover could use the help of MI5, even if he refuses to see reality. I have heard about Dalton's SOE, and I do agree, we need that capability and it does not now exist." Roosevelt glanced at the wall clock. "Time is getting on, and I have a full calendar today. Again, well done, Bill. You have done yeoman's work here. I would like you to transform your working hypothesis into a draft charter document. Please work closely with Harry. This initiative will have to remain between the three of us, for now. I cannot afford any premature turf battles. I trust you can do this work alone, with Harry's assistance."

"Yes sir. How soon do you need this draft document, Mister President?"

"How about a month. Let's start there."

"That should be sufficient, Mister President. I will keep Mister Hopkins informed of my progress. I shall give you my best shot."

"Of that I am quite confident, Bill. Thanks for taking on this daunting task. Now, if you will excuse me, I am already late to my next appointment."

"Thank you, Mister President. Good day."

Hopkins left the Oval Office with Donovan, and then returned a few minutes later. Roosevelt moved along to the next subject, trusting his lieutenant to handle Donovan's project.

—

Chapter 15

Freedom's just another word for nothin' left to lose.

- Kris Kristofferson & Fred Foster

Wednesday, 19.March.1941
Munitions Building
Constitution Avenue & 20th Street
Washington, District of Columbia
United States of America
09:30 hours

The Secretary of War intercepted the Chief of the Army Air Corps in the latter's outer office. "I thought I'd catch you before your press conference, and as such, I'll make you a few minutes late." Arnold did not respond to the pause. Stimson continued, "I would suggest we steer clear of press questions regarding Lend-Lease. We have a lot of details to work out before we can answer appropriate inquiries." Arnold nodded his head in agreement. "Also, this announcement is crucial to modernizing the military. You may encounter some hostile questions. The President and the Cabinet are quite sensitive to the mood of the nation and the inherent resistance to such changes by a portion of the citizenry. Try to avoid antagonizing that portion. We want this move to be successful. Frankly, we need this action to be successful. You know quite well how under strength our air arm is."

"Yes, Mister Secretary, I am keenly aware of the potential resistance. I shall do my best to hold the line."

"We know you will, 'Hap.' Good luck. Now, best be on your way."

The two men departed Arnold's office together and went opposite directions—Stimson headed back to his office, Arnold to the department press conference room.

The usual cacophony of intermingled, disassociated conversations died down to silence before General Arnold reached the podium.

"Good morning everyone. I have a short important announcement to make, and then I will take a few questions. As you may recall from our public announcement two months ago, the War Department activated the 99th Pursuit Squadron at Maxwell Field near Montgomery. This activation was pursuant to the national defense act of 1939. Contract orders have been issued for the construction of an airfield at Tuskegee, Alabama, for a regular flight training school as part of the Army Air Forces Training Command. We expect the airfield, provisionally designated Sharpe Field, to be ready for operations later

this year, at which time the 99th Pursuit Squadron and other associated training
assets will be transferred to Sharpe Field. Now, are there any questions?"

"This is a rather unusual announcement, General, for the activation of
a single squadron."

"Is there a question?"

"What is special about the 99th Pursuit Squadron?"

"The 1939 federal law I referred to, established a flight training program
for negro pilots. The 99th Pursuit Squadron will be manned by negro pilots
and ground crews."

"Is that a wise idea?"

Arnold smiled and waited a few seconds for effect. "Clearly, we did or
we would not have issued these orders."

"Don't you think you are asking for trouble with this?"

"No."

"Could you expand that answer a little?"

"I always thought no is fairly precise."

"Why is the Army challenging Southern society?" the man asked with a
discernible drawl.

"We have no intention of challenging anything. We are simply taking
appropriate steps to increase the number of qualified pilots available for service
with the Army Air Forces."

"General, trying to be as delicate as I can, what if these . . . pilot candidates
do not perform up to standard?"

"Then, they will not be pilots and will revert to some other assignment."

"Will the standards for these . . . pilots . . . be the same as for white pilots?"

Arnold stared at this particular inquisitor as sternly as he could. "Are you
serious?"

"Yes, General," he responded without hesitation, "I am."

"I am reluctant," General Arnold paused for emphasis, "to dignify such
a question with an answer. Yet, as a servant of the people, I am compelled to
respond. So, allow me to be as precise as I am able. There is only one set of
standards in the Army. Candidates either meet those standards, or they move
onto other assignments more appropriate to their skills. Pilots require a very
special skill set to perform properly, to accomplish the missions they are assigned,
and to survive the rigors of combat. The pilots who will man the 99th Pursuit
Squadron will be just as qualified, just as capable, as any other pilot in any other
squadron. Is that precise enough an answer?"

"I understand your words, but I . . . perhaps we, more than a few of us . . .
wonder whether you . . . or the Army . . . have thought this through to the end?"

General Arnold was unable to mask his irritation and urge to confront the antagonistic bigotry just under the surface of the question. "And, what end might that be?"

It was now the turn of his journalist inquisitor to fidget in his seat. "Well . . . I doubt a white bomber crew would appreciate the risk to their lives with nig . . . negro fighter pilots charged with protecting them."

"You are wrong," Arnold said more sharply than he should have responded.

"How so?" the man persisted.

"The bomber crew of any color will only care about the skills and performance of the escort fighter pilots of any color, period."

"Is that an order?"

"You have had more than enough questions. Are there any other questions from anyone else?

"Yes sir," another man interjected. "Why Tuskegee, Alabama?"

"There were several factors involved in the decision to select Tuskegee. One, Maxwell Field is already over capacity. Two, in accordance with the laws recently enacted, we must expand the capacity of our pilot training system. Three, survey results from numerous sites indicate the location selected for Sharpe Field was appropriate and comparatively close to Maxwell, thus making expansion quicker and less expensive. I will also say Tuskegee is not the only expansion site being developed."

"Why Alabama? Why not some northern site, like New York, or Massachusetts, perhaps, for a squadron of this type?"

"Weather . . . for one. I want to emphatically state we have soldiers in the Army. We are not interested in colors."

Another journalist asked, "Aren't you actually contributing to segregation by moving the 99th Pursuit Squadron and the associated training assets to Tuskegee?"

"No. Most definitely not. Pilots, instructors, commanders, maintenance crews . . . all of the necessary personnel to support air operations will be assigned to these various bases regardless of the color of their skin."

"Then, why are only negro pilots being assigned to the 99th Pursuit Squadron?"

"We are realists, not idealists. We need pilots. We will embrace them from any source and train them as well as test them. Only those who pass muster will be awarded their wings and ordered to operational assignments."

"Will those pilots be officers?"

"Yes, of course, as long as they meet all the requirements. One last question. I really must get back to work."

"Would you fly with them?"

"Yes, absolutely. All I care about . . . all any of us should care about . . . is whether they are good pilots. Initial reports from early training exercises indicate they are very capable pilots . . . some are even exceptional . . . as with other pilot candidates. Let's give them a chance to show their mettle. Thank you for your time, gentlemen. Good day," General Arnold said and walked smartly out of the conference room, ignoring the bombardment of additional questions shouted at him.

—

Wednesday, 19.March.1941
No.10 Downing Street
Whitehall, London, England
United Kingdom
20:30 hours

By Winston Churchill's standards, or at least his usual practice, this was a small, more intimate dinner party . . . well, not a dinner party but rather a private dinner. He chose to take this particular meal in the small dining room rather than the larger state dining room. The prime minister's office and residential apartment in Whitehall was still being restored after the bomb damage of last fall. As a consequence, they had a minimal staff on hand. Mrs. Landemare remained at Chequers with Clementine and one or more of their children, as they happened to be in the vicinity. This week, it was only Mary, their youngest child, who was 18 years of age, finishing her secondary education, and hopefully headed off to a university in the fall.

His dinner guests this particular evening were U.S. Ambassador Gil Winant and the newly arrived and credentialed U.S. Ambassador to the governments-in-exile in London – Anthony Joseph Drexel 'Tony' Biddle, Jr. Winston expected this to be more of a working meal, as he sought to measure up Tony and continue the process of strengthening his relationship with Gil. He had met with Winant at least a dozen times since the ambassador's well-publicized arrival a month ago. Winston understood in a short order why Franklin privately referred to him as 'Utopian John,' and for that he was immensely grateful as Gil Winant stood in such graphic contrast to the defeatist Irish-American Joe Kennedy.

As Winston entered the room, both men stood. "Welcome to London, Ambassador Biddle. You will have to pardon the mess our fair city happens to be in at the moment. We seem to be plagued by nightly vandals, who are not particularly respectful of our noble capital city."

"It is an honor to join you, Mister Prime Minister."

"Fine. Formalities concluded. I prefer the more personal among friends, of which I trust you will be one, as Gil is," Winston said and shook hands with both men. "If I may, I understand you prefer the familiar Tony, if you don't mind."

"By all means, Mister Prime Minister."

"Likewise, I prefer Winston, among friends."

"Certainly."

Churchill nodded to a formally dressed man, who was their chief server this evening. "If you both will pardon my crass manners, but we do not have much time before our nightly visitors arrive, so I will apologize and dispense with our cocktail hour. Let's get you fed."

"No problem for us," responded Winant.

Churchill motioned for the two ambassadors to take their seats at the table on either side of him – Winant to the right and Biddle to the left. They began with a nice, simple but rather elegant onion soup.

Winston turned to Tony. "I understand you have enjoyed a rather eventful and exciting diplomatic career in the last few years. Pray tell . . . share what you can."

They continued their meal as they talked. The soup was followed by lamb chops, green beans and scalloped potatoes . . . not an elegant meal but passable.

"I suppose that is one way to put my experience. I had been ambassador to Poland for two years when the Germans invaded. We did not quite know what to make of the German intentions and objectives in those first few days. It was perhaps the fourth or fifth day when the Germans bombed Warsaw, hitting our embassy. I happened to be in the office at the time, and fortunately, my wife and children were unharmed, while eating breakfast at our residence when a bomb exploded nearby and riddled the building. We fled with what we could carry along with staff and some members of the Polish government. We made our way to Paris, where the Poles re-constituted their government in exile. The President retained me as the ambassador to the Polish government in exile. That lasted for not even six months, when the Germans invaded France and the Low Countries. We did not wait to be bombed, again. We made our way out of France through Saint-Nazaire. I was recalled, got my family safely home and settled, and then Secretary Hull asked me to return in this capacity, to represent the United States for the exiled governments of the occupied countries here in England."

"No small task, I must say. We shall do our best to assist you."

"Thank you, Winston. You are most kind."

"Nonsense, it is what friends do. Together, we are going to beat that vile corporal. We will not travel a smooth and unobstructed road. The journey will be, as it has been, tortuous and fraught with danger. I must confess that President Roosevelt asked me if your experience might be useful to our situation, and I believe your experience will be of exceptional assistance to Gil in his capacity as ambassador to the Crown, and me and Anthony Eden. As you both know, we are the temporary home for exiled governments from each of the occupied countries . . . well, except for the Baltic States, I should say. The Poles are particularly problematic having suffered the assault of both the *Wehrmacht* and the Red Army. My intuition tells me the plight of the Poles will likely be the lasting problem in the post-war era."

"I have yet to reconnect with colleagues from my time in Poland."

"Everything in due course. I dare say you have more contacts than the rest of us. I shall ask Eden to facilitate your reunion with those Poles who escaped and landed here."

"Excellent."

The chief steward re-entered the small dining room. "Excuse me, Prime Minister. The Air Ministry has informed us there is an inbound enemy raid, and they expect to sound the alarm shortly."

"And so it begins. Please secure the kitchen and instruct the staff to proceed to their shelter." The man nodded his head and departed. Winston turned back and looked to both of his guests. "I would like you to join me in observing tonight's event."

"Observe?" asked Gil Winant.

"Yes. I make no claim that it is not without risk, but that is part of war. I find it instructive and informative to witness what these raiders do. If they get too close, we will seek shelter, as well. However, my experience is they rarely hit Whitehall."

"Is this risk really necessary?" Tony Biddle asked.

"I think so. I have watched their attacks more than a few times since The Blitz began. Once you get past the imagery, I think you will see what I mean." The air raid siren began to wail. "Shall we go? We have but to walk across Whitehall and enter the Richmond Terrace entrance to the Air Ministry building and proceed to the top floor. "You should see the guns that will open this episode."

As Churchill led them out of the small dining room, Detective-Inspector Thompson was waiting at the door. Churchill turned to his two guests. "Gil, I know you remember Detective-Inspector Walter Thompson, but I know Tony has not been properly introduced. Walter is my guardian angel." The men shook hands and exchanged greetings. They all followed Winston through the corridors, through the blackout curtain, and out onto darkened Downing

Street, turning east toward Whitehall. Winston continued his explanation as they walked. "He would be joining us in protest, but Walter has accepted reality. While my roof-top, air raid observations are not carried out every night, I have done this more than a few times."

———

Wednesday, 19.March.1941
Air Ministry
Whitehall, London, England
United Kingdom
21:25 hours

The normally bustling streets of London were dark, devoid of any other human or vehicular traffic. A high overcast blotted out any illumination from the waning, near quarter moon. Winston knew the way. The two Americans shuffled quickly to keep sight of their leader. Churchill was careful to call the curbing as they approached. The four men walked the comparatively short distance without incident to the Richmond Terrace entrance across Whitehall from Downing Street, took the salute of the armed guards at the entrance, and ascended the interior in a selected elevator. Within minutes, they were standing on the south edge of the roof between the first and second of four, two-story extensions to the building. Fortunately, a waist high railing marked the actual edge of the roof.

The warning sirens could be heard from various directions and distances, with a diminishing number, as their purpose had been served. They could see the River Thames beyond The Embankment's surviving trees. The overcast denied them even starlight, which made it difficult to see any details.

"We arrived before the show is to begin," announced Churchill. No one answered. Several minutes passed. Their eyes continued to adjust to the deep darkness. Slowly, a few buildings on the south bank became discernible. Ever so faintly, an intermittent, pulsating drone was detectable, as long as they remained very still . . . even the soft rustling of their clothing or footsteps would over-power the pulsating sound. Churchill had clearly been through this process. As the pulsating sound of the unsynchronized engines of the enemy bombers became constant and louder, Winston announced, "The cannons and searchlights will open up soon." Perhaps ten seconds later, a half dozen, bright white, focused beams of light stabbed into the darkness south of the city and probed for their targets.

The first muzzle flashes could be readily seen south of the city. The muffled sound reached them 15-20 seconds later. Barrage balloons could be seen, anchored at various heights above the city. The short, sharp flash of artillery shell detonations could be seen at altitude. The combination of light and sounds moved progressively closer to them. No one on the Air Ministry roof spoke. There were only the four of them, at least as far as they could see. No one else sought the thrill of the spectacle unfolding before them.

Large caliber, anti-aircraft artillery cannons behind them fired, startling the two ambassadors. They saw the beams intersect with a German, twin-engined, medium bomber clearly illuminated. Shells burst near the hapless aircraft, causing fires in both engines. The searchlight beams sought another target, leaving the burning and now spiraling aircraft descending like a flaming leaf toward the ground. Bombs began to explode on and among the buildings to the south and east of the Air Ministry building. The flashes of the bomb explosions momentarily silhouetted buildings in the vicinity. Intermixed with the high explosive bombs, they saw bright, white, hemispherical blooms of phosphorous, incendiary bombs exploding and quickly starting fires with virtually everything the burning chunks of phosphorous touched.

"They are getting closer," Winant observed amid the rumbling thuds of the bombs and the sharp reports on the cannons all around them now.

"We are not the target with this raid," Churchill responded matter-of-factly.

"Some comfort," Gil added.

Dust and smoke began to obscure the following detonations and offered an eerie secondary illumination of the Bromley, Southend, Blackheath and Greenwich districts. Fresh bomb explosions flashed to their east.

"The docks and Canning Town," Churchill said.

The bomb explosions stopped. The anti-aircraft artillery continued, occasionally finding success, but the number of shells fired and exploding at altitude vastly exceeded the handful of successes. The cannon muzzle flashes receded in reverse of how they began. Soon, the flashes stopped.

"Is it over?" asked Tony Biddle.

"For this raid wave, yes, but there will likely be one, two or three more tonight," answered Churchill. "Let's wait a little longer. We witness a treat."

They waited. Several of the fires southeast of them grew rapidly. The faint combination of bells and sirens announced the Fire Brigade response to the evening's attack. The All-Clear siren signal marked the conclusion of this particular raid.

"There," shouted the Prime Minister, as he pointed toward the south and intermittent flames of another enemy aircraft hit. "The night fighters got another one. We should see several more before they are too far away." Sure enough, three more night successes could be seen. "The night fighters have improved every night. They attack the enemy before the anti-aircraft artillery, and they continue their night intercepts until they reach the Channel."

"How on earth do they see anything up there at night?" Tony asked."

"They are special aircraft fitted with a rather crude radio detection kit. We continue to improve it. Our combined team of engineers and scientists are working on a new system in Massachusetts, we expect will prove even more effective."

"Amazing," Gil added.

They witnessed several more, silent, night victories before this episode was done.

"That will do it for an hour or so . . . perhaps for the night," Churchill observed. "The raids have been diminishing in magnitude and frequency since the Great Fire just before New Year . . . dreadful event. Anyway, the fireworks are over, for now."

"Incredible, Winston," Tony said. "Thank you for insisting we witness The Blitz as few have been able to, I'm sure."

Churchill moved on. "What say you, shall we retire to Number Ten for dessert, brandy and a delightful Cuban cigar? I just received a fresh box from the Duke of Windsor, our ambassador in the Bahamas."

"How could we say no," Gil answered.

The four reversed their path in similar fashion as The Blitz bombers. The Prime Minister returned the salutes of the entrance guards and said, "Thank you for the use of your building, gentlemen."

"Anytime, Prime Minister," one of them said.

The four visitors chuckled audibly. People began to appear and pick up their affairs.

"Life goes on," Winston offered as they crossed Whitehall. They were back onto Downing Street and re-entered No.10. The two ambassadors would remain with the Prime Minister until after midnight.

———

Saturday, 22.March.1941
RAF Kirton-in-Lindsey
Kirton-in-Lindsey, Lincolnshire, England
United Kingdom
16:15 hours

"**W**hat are y'all doing with your 48-hour pass?" asked Rocket Downing, to Red Burns and Rusty Bateman, who both sat in garden chairs on the other side of Hunter Drummond.

The comparatively rare, late afternoon sunshine on the second day of astronomical spring in the northern hemisphere made the cool but dry air temperature seem far less important than the warmth of the sun. Half were lounging outside the Dispersal Hut.

"A bunch of us are going into London," Rusty eventually answered. "Going to see if we can turn up some 'dolly-birds,' as the Brits say. Lord knows it's too quiet up here."

"If you make it to Shepherd's, say hello to the lads for us," Brian added with his eyes closed.

"Will do, Hunter, although I have no idea what any of us are going to do," Red acknowledged.

A lone Merlin sputtered and coughed on final approach. Brian did not look up until he heard Red say, "Hey, Hunter, that's a 'PR' Spit from our old squadron." Brian immediately sat up and watched. The battered Spitfire landed perfectly, slowed, and turned off the grass landing strip and toward them. The Spitfire appeared from behind parked Hurricanes and Brian could see the tail designator – 'PR-K.' "That's Harness," Brian observed and stood. He looked around. One of the crewmen ran down the line to direct the Spitfire to his parking spot. Brian began walking toward the intended parking spot. The 'PR-K' Spitfire expertly swung his tail into the directed spot. The canopy slid back. The pilot shut down his engine and secured his aircraft. He unstrapped, disconnected his helmet and oxygen mask, removed his flight gloves, and pulled off his helmet, mask and goggles. It was indeed Jonathan Kensington, who looked over his right shoulder at Brian and waved.

Brian came around the tail as Jonathan completed his instructions to the ground crewman. The two men embraced as brothers and old friends.

Jonathan kissed Brian on the cheek. "Great to have you back, mate."

"Great to see you, again, my friend," Brian responded. They walked toward the Dispersal Hut. "To what do we owe the pleasure of your visit?"

"I need a maintenance check flight on my aircraft, so I asked the Skipper if I could take the aircraft for an overnight to catch up with you. I called down here a few weeks ago, only to learn that you had gone back to Wichita, after your parents' passing. I . . . my whole family . . . offer our condolences for your loss, Brian."

"Thank you, my friend. It was a freak traffic accident. A truck lost a wheel and careened into them on the way home from a New Year's party."

"Tragic, Brian, simply tragic."

As they reached the squadron Dispersal Hut, Corporal Harris stood outside the closed door. "Sir, the squadron was released. 'A' Flight must report for duty at dawn."

"I'm sorry to hold you up, James. This is my best mate, Flying Officer Kensington. Jonathan, Corporal Harris is our squadron Operations Clerk."

"We pronounce it 'clark,' mate, but you know that."

They laughed. "We shall forgive the Yank," said Harris. "Great to meet you, sir. By your leave, sir," he paused. Brian nodded his consent. "Have a good evening. Don't get in too much. I will see you bright and early tomorrow morning."

"Have a good night, James."

Corporal Harris saluted smartly. Both officers returned his salute. As Corporal Harris turned the corner of the building, Brian checked his watch. "They will be serving evening meal at the Mess," Brian said.

"If you don't mind, why don't we go to your favorite pub in the village, so we can toss back a few pints and grab a bite there? I would like to talk, to catch up with your life. I've missed you in our squadron."

"Sounds like a plan. My favorite here in Kirton is The George, a 17th century carriage house inn, restaurant and bar – great beer, good food, wonderful setting and fantastic people."

"Then, we have a date."

—

Saturday, 22.March.1941
The George Public House
Kirton-in-Lindsey, Lincolnshire, England
United Kingdom
19:20 hours

Brian and Jonathan stood outside The George. Even in the dark of the blackout, they could see the historic building.

"If the beer and food are as good as the appearance of this pub, we shall have a grand ol' time tonight," Jonathan announced.

"Then, let's get to it."

They went directly to the bar, ordered two pints of bitter, and found a corner table out of the way. The large, dark, oak beams that supported the first floor were set low enough to catch Brian low on the forehead. He ducked under each beam as they made their way. The pub appeared to be roughly half full, with mostly local men and women, with a smattering of RAF officers.

"Here's to your health, Brian," Jonathan said, holding his pint glass toward Brian.

"And, to yours, Jonathan."

They took a good swallow each.

"My sister sends her regards," Jonathan began.

"Thank you."

"She still cares for you a great deal."

"She is an incredible woman, but I am married, now."

"She is not offering to bed you, mate."

"Isn't she?"

"You nasty boy. She vowed to me that she would respect your marriage, but I know her. She is a very headstrong woman."

Brian felt the urge to change the subject. "How's Linda?"

"Well done, mate." Jonathan smiled, took another good swallow, and said, "She is a fine woman, Brian. I think she would get married like you and Charlotte, but I struggle with what we do. How, or more importantly why, did you do it?"

"Charlotte changed her mind . . . perhaps it was the pregnancy, I don't know. All I do know is, she said she was ready to marry when I was with her on my Christmas break."

"Are you happy?"

"Yes, I certainly am, and I think she would say she is as well. Yet, there should be no doubt she is not happy about what we do. I mean she is proud that we are defending the country, but she does not like the risks we take. That day I landed in her pond still haunts her."

"Yeah, that event for which the King awarded her the George Cross." Jonathan smiled briefly. "Linda seems to be more tolerant of that aspect."

"Not many people have suffered the losses that Charlotte has."

"True. I know Linda hasn't. For her, our flying is more romantic, like knights defending the virtue of maidens."

Brian laughed. "I doubt Charlotte ever had that thought."

"Maybe we should just get married."

"Your choice, my friend, well, you and Linda."

An attractive, young waitress with a large apron covering her simple, floral print dress approached them. "Would you gentlemen care for menus?"

"Yes," responded Jonathan, "and, another round of bitter for me and my mate."

"What label?"

"Surprise us. We are not particular."

In a few minutes, she returned with two pints of dark beer, two menus and collected their empty glasses. They both quickly scanned the menu. Brian knew what he wanted. The waitress returned and looked to Brian.

"I'll have a full serving of shepherd's pie."

"Likewise," Jonathan added.

The waitress did not write the order down and left without another word.

"When is Charlotte due?" Jonathan asked.

"The end of May, beginning of June, the midwife says."

"Not much longer. She must be really showing by now."

"You got that right. I love it. Her round belly adds to her beauty, and I'll be damned if this hasn't made her more horny than ever."

Jonathan laughed hard. "Then, you must be in heaven when you see her."

"Always."

"If I may ask, how is your other pregnant woman?"

Brian sneered at his friend. "You would bring that up, wouldn't you?"

"Well?"

"She is due in a couple of weeks. The last time I talked to Air Commodore Spencer, she was doing fairly well. They are excited to have their first child."

"And, you must be so proud that you could help them with their excitement."

"Jonathan, stop!"

"Does the Air Commodore know what you have done to his wife?"

"Sometimes, I think so . . . little gestures, expressions and choices of words, but neither he nor Mary has told me directly."

The waitress returned with their meals and placed them in front of each man.

"Thank you," Brian said. She looked a bit surprised, as if she did not receive words of gratitude often.

They each took a few bites of their meals.

"Very good," Jonathan said.

"One of my favorite dishes, although this is not quite as good as Charlotte's version."

"Of course you would say that. She has meat. The rest of us usually aren't so blessed, which makes this particular helping a rather pleasant surprise. So, tell me about your adventure."

As they ate, Brian recounted the high points of his experience on the flying boat, his encounter with Harry Hopkins, the misunderstanding with the immigration officers in New York, the special flight from New York to Wichita, as well as his return flight by the same means in reverse, and as fate would have it with the same flight crews for each segment of his return. Brian also recounted his unplanned, additional, brief stop in Washington to meet President Roosevelt, as requested by Harry Hopkins.

"You are a most fortunate man, I must say," Jonathan noted. "It was a terrible reason to make that journey, but I am so glad that arrangements could be made for you. Not to pry, Brian, but did you manage to get everything settled with your parents' estate?"

"Yeah . . . at least for now. The lawyer said it will take several months, perhaps a year, to complete all the paperwork for the state. Much to my shock, my parents did rather well for themselves. We lived simply during my childhood. I had absolutely no clue how much they owned. According to the lawyer, they were in a perfect position when the Great Crash came in 1929. I am their only heir. I will soon be the owner of quite a bit of land and several businesses."

"Are you going to return to manage your newfound assets?"

"No, of course not. Why would you think I would?"

"Brian, seriously? There is no reason for you to be here, taking the risks you do, especially when you now have much more to be home for."

"Well, except for Charlotte, and my soon to be born first child, and you and Rosemary, John and Mary, and this glorious struggle we must win."

"All noble motives, my friend."

"You could be doing other, safer things as well, Jonathan."

"Well, now, that is true, too, I suppose."

"We fly because we love flight and the machines that enable our flight. I would rather be flying Spits, but these Hurris will do in a pinch."

"True, but I fight because my country is threatened."

"So is mine, even if most Americans do not yet realize the reality of this war."

"Well said. So, you are going to stay and fight?"

"Yes, as long as I am able."

"You are a good man, Brian Drummond . . . even if you are foolish and naively patriotic."

"No less than you."

"*Touché!*"

The waitress returned with two additional pints, unordered by them and apparently purchased by local appreciative patrons. She collected their plates and empty glasses.

"By the way, I meant to ask you, did you get to see Malcolm's widow?"

"Mrs. Bainbridge, Gertrude, yes, I did . . . several times while I was there. I took her to dinner, and she invited me to dinner at their place before I left. To my shock and surprise frankly, she asked me to check on Malcolm's aircraft and to fly them for her. She had an aircraft mechanic from Beech Aircraft Company to handle and maintain the aircraft for her. He still had the

Sopwith Camel, a Stearman like the one I crashed, and two remaining Curtiss JN-4 Jennies, like the one he crashed. He also still had the modified Beech Mystery S he built up for me to fly at air meets. To my surprise, he had a brand new Beech Model 17 Staggerwing—one of the first retractable undercarriage aircraft of its type—with five-passenger seats, all enclosed and heated. I was even more shocked when she told me the aircraft were mine, and that she and Malcolm had agreed to bequest their land, property, and whatever remains of their assets upon her passing. They had no children, and they both thought of me as their son."

"Your cup runneth over, my friend. Now, you have your own air force."

"Not quite."

"Close enough, I should think . . . more than any of the rest of us. You said she asked you to fly them. Did you?"

"Yes, every one. She stood outside watching every flight. She said it did her heart good, to bring back Malcolm in that way."

"A Sopwith Camel?"

"Yes, helluva machine for its day."

"So, they say. You want another round?"

"Maybe one more, and then I gotta go."

Jonathan raised his right hand, caught the waitress's attention, and extended two fingers. "Out of curiosity, did you ever find out what happened to Malcolm?"

The waitress returned with two more pints of bitter.

"A year ago, almost to the day. I doubt we will ever know precisely what happened. I talked to a couple of his pilot buddies and got the best view I could. Apparently, he was on his way home from delivering a special package in Denver and got caught in an icing event that caused him to stall before he could get the aircraft on the ground. They found him the next day in a farm field, north of Garden City, Kansas. The aircraft was broken up pretty good, crushed, apparently, near flat impact and no fire . . . thank goodness."

"Most unfortunate."

"Yeah. It could have happened to any of us. The JN-4 Jenny is far less tolerant of ice than our aircraft, but still ice can get any of us."

"To be avoided."

"Indeed."

Jonathan took a good swallow of beer. "You have had to deal with so much in the last six weeks. What are you going to do with your newfound aircraft assets?"

"We formed a new company with those aircraft. We called it the Bainbridge Air Service. I hired a former competitor of mine and friend of Malcolm's to run the operations. He's the same guy that brought two surplus, Grumman FF-1 pursuit planes to the St. Louis air meet where I flew against him and John Spencer."

"How does this fellow obtain military fighter aircraft?" Jonathan asked somewhat surprised.

"The Navy declared the aircraft obsolete and thus surplus. Apparently, they considered them scrap. They were built in 1933 . . . biplanes, kind of like the Gladiators we flew, except they had a retractable undercarriage. At least it had an enclosed cockpit and a rear seat for a tail gunner that he turned around. In service, the aircraft had only two three-oh-three Browning machine guns. The aircraft he bought were barely six years old with virtually no flight time on them. So the story goes, he bought them for scrap, but decided to keep them flying."

"Who is this fellow?"

"Bobby Joe Sales is his name. Malcolm said his family was fairly wealthy . . . river transport, or railroad, or something. He also brought his aircraft to the new company, not that they will be of much use, but he happens to have a Jenny as well, so that one can contribute. Initially, we'll try to pick up Malcolm's package delivery business, maybe some air mail contract work for the Postal Service, and we might even try some passenger transport with the Staggerwing. We'll see where this goes, but we'll make a good go of it."

"Interesting," was Jonathan's simple response.

"Yeah . . . quite a menagerie. We'll see how the business develops. If it is going to work, we'll need to acquire more capable aircraft."

"Perhaps this new company will give you something to do when this whole dreadful war affair is concluded."

"There is that."

"How has your return to flight duty been?"

"The perfect medicine. Flying is the best thing for me. Although somebody above us . . . whether it's Group, Fighter Command, or even the Air Ministry itself . . . don't know . . . they keep us back here. We train and fly shipping patrols, while you are going across the Channel and into France, taking the fight to the Germans. We do more photographs, interviews and visits than we do anything else. We're more like circus animals than fighter pilots."

Jonathan laughed. "I guess a squadron of Yanks in the RAF is a bit of a novelty."

"Or, they are trying to protect us from getting hurt, killed or captured."

"Now, there is that, I suppose."

"We are a fighter squadron, or at least we are supposed to be . . . not a display squadron." They finished their beers. "I've talked enough. Tell me what the old squadron has been doing."

"We are rotated south every week or so to fly a RODEO or RHUBARB mission into France or Belgium."

"What's the difference?"

"RODEOs are usually combined fighter sweeps, one squadron to shoot things up on the ground, to stir things up, and one or more squadrons high, waiting for the German fighters to come up. RHUBARBs are a squadron or a flight to go in low, often when there is a low overcast. We have been going after fighter bases, sometimes bomber bases, and at least once a building they told us was a *Luftwaffe* headquarters. We've heard of another mission they call a CIRCUS – fighter escort for a bombing mission. We've not flown one of those, yet."

"Heck, we've not flown any of them."

"You will. I'm sure."

"I sure hope so. I didn't come over here two years ago, to be a circus dog." They both laughed.

"You came here to be a fighter pilot, but you are now a husband and in a few months a father."

The waitress arrived, this time without beers. "Would either of you care for another round?" she asked.

"No, I think not. I'm on duty tomorrow," Brian said. Jonathan shook his head in the negative and the waitress left. "I have had too many blurry mornings."

"At your youthful age . . ."

"Yes, at my young age, but enough, nonetheless, as you well know."

"Indeed. I remember more than a few of 'Spike's counseling sessions, and I was not even the object of his dissatisfaction."

"Exactly. So, I think I will head back to base. Do you want to stay?"

"I think not. I came here to see you, to catch up with my best friend. I'll go with you."

"Are you up for a bit of a walk?"

"Sure. Why not."

They paid their bill and headed out into the chill of the night. They needed their overcoats, which neither of them had. The blacked-out streets made the journey back a little more difficult, despite the fact that Brian had made the walk a handful of times. The two friends continued their chat as they walked – with more familial topics rather than their profession or current events subjects. Only two vehicles passed them, both military trucks with the headlights covered with mere slits allowing very dim lighting. They were inherently cautious, when they heard motors in the still of the night, as they knew the drivers would not likely see them with the minimal blackout lights. Once back at the Mess, Brian found Jonathan a spare room, fortunately furnished, and they retired for the night.

—

Thursday, 27.March.1941
10,000 feet altitude
42° 14' North – 69° 31' West
Off Cape Cod, Massachusetts
United States of America
15:15 hours

The Army Air Corps Douglas B-18 Bolo, twin-engine, medium bomber cruised in level flight, in a long racetrack pattern oriented in an east-west direction. This particular aircraft and crew had been consigned to the Radiation Laboratory, Massachusetts Institute of Technology, Cambridge, Massachusetts, from the Material Division, Wright Field, Dayton, Ohio, operating out of Hanscom Field, northwest of Boston. This particular aircraft had little outward appearance difference with the standard Air Corps Bolo aircraft, except a bulbous protuberance on the belly of the aircraft, where the bomb bay doors were normally located. The interior resembled virtually nothing of the bomber configuration with panels of indicators, dials, knobs, crude cathode ray tubes, wire bundles and two, small, makeshift desks. The normal aircraft crew of six had been reduced by two. Four Rad Lab engineers, two American, two British, operated the electronic equipment filling the interior and replaced the two gunners. The pilot, co-pilot, bombardier-navigator and radio operator were retained and supplied by the Army.

The on-board equipment was an engineering prototype conglomeration with the British cavity magnetron for high, transmitted power and the American duplexer switch that allowed a single antenna to be used as a transmitter and receiver. The ground testing of this breadboard unit proved quite encouraging, and this day was the first airborne testing of the full capability.

After some initial tuning problems, the engineers quickly picked up ships going into and out of Boston Harbor, but that was not the purpose or objective of this particular mission. The engineers modified their equipment settings to begin their objective. When they were ready, a blackout curtain was pulled across and fastened, isolating the engineers from any outside reference. Unbeknownst to the sequestered engineers, Army supervisors had selected a Lockheed A-29 Hudson medium bomber and a Curtiss P-40 Hawk fighter to be the target aircraft for this test.

The prototype airborne intercept radar equipment detected the Hudson at four miles distance, established the altitude, direction of flight and speed of the bomber, and then directed the Bolo's pilots to a position in trail, directly behind the target aircraft. They repeated the detection / intercept test a half dozen times from different engagement aspects.

Without informing the engineers, they changed to the smaller fighter aircraft target. While the detection range was roughly half that against the larger Hudson, the engineers were able to duplicate their performance against the small fighter.

One last surprise target had been inserted to the test – USS *Thresher* (SS-200), a submerged submarine moving at seven knots at periscope depth and its periscope extended. The engineering team was instructed to look for a surface target and not told what they were looking for. Again, they easily spotted ships, but they missed the moving periscope. The flight crew descended to 5,000 feet . . . same results. They descended to 2,000 feet. They detected a suspicious target on their equipment. They vectored the flight crew to approach the moving target from astern and marked it precisely overhead. They descended again to 500 feet altitude. The radar crew located and tracked the periscope at triple the range.

All the test objectives had been met. The pilot terminated the test and headed back to Hanscom. The Rad Lab scientists and engineers would take several days to study the data collected on the test flight. Yet, they did not need an official report to know that the new equipment had achieved enormous success against airborne, surface and subsurface targets. A new era had dawned. They would continue testing the prototype units. However, the joint leaders of the Rad Lab team agreed to the initial production start-up for an airborne intercept radar unit that both British and American night interceptors and anti-submarine aircraft would utilize effectively against their enemies.

—

Sunday, 30.March.1941
Cabinet War Rooms
New Public Offices
Whitehall, London, England
United Kingdom
18:30 hours

The Prime Minister had departed Chequers early on Sunday afternoon, to make it back to London in time for a special weekend meeting of the War Cabinet and Defense Committee without staff support and specifically without anyone not cleared for ULTRA, or 'Boniface' as they often referred to the special intelligence material.

The reports from the Mediterranean region illuminated a major fleet action between the Royal Navy and *Regia Marina*, the Italian Navy. Churchill wanted the latest information from the battle off Cape Matapan, Greece.

Churchill preempted the Cabinet Secretary, Sir Edward Bridges, with his impatience. "Let's see the intelligence first."

Chief of Naval Intelligence Admiral Sir Geoffrey 'Jumper' Pike passed a red folder to the Prime Minister. "The first message is the one that gave us the decisive clue."

Churchill read the top message.

MOST SECRET - ULTRA

```
SECRET
DATE: 25 MARCH 1941
TO: HEADQUARTERS ITALIAN NAVY ROME
FROM: COMMANDER MAIN BATTLE FORCE
BREAK
TODAY IS THE DAY MINUS THREE
END
SECRET
```

MOST SECRET - ULTRA

"Why was that significant?" asked Churchill.

"We knew from field agents that activities at Taranto indicated something big was in the works. Bletchley decoded that message within minutes of receipt. Between Bletchley, MI6 and the Admiralty, we all agreed it was a backhanded way of telling the fleet and naval staff that Vice Admiral Angelo Iachino planned to sortie the fleet, probably to relieve pressure on Axis forces in North Africa. We did not know precisely what the objectives were for the Italian fleet action. What we did not know was when."

The First Sea Lord jumped in. "Admiral Pike immediately passed the information to Admiral Cunningham. He had general plans for such an eventuality. We quickly agreed to flesh out the specifics. He dispatched a Sunderland flying boat reconnaissance aircraft to provide cover for subsequent action, and he would make a rather theatrical performance to suggest to Italian agents in Alexandria that he would be in port for several days. Then, during the night of the 27th, he sortied nearly the entire Mediterranean fleet, leaving a cruiser and destroyer flotilla to cover the approaches to Alexandria and the Suez." Sir Dudley nodded to Sir Geoffrey.

"In no small measure, the first message enabled the near real-time decryption of the second message that confirmed our interpretation of the original message."

MOST SECRET - ULTRA

```
SECRET
DATE: 28 MARCH 1941
TO: HEADQUARTERS ITALIAN NAVY ROME
FROM: COMMANDER MAIN BATTLE FORCE
BREAK
FLAGSHIP SAILED TO PLAN BREAK JOINED BY SIX
HEAVY CRUISERS TWO LIGHT CRUISERS AND THIRTEEN
DESTROYERS BREAK EXPECT ENGAGEMENT TOMORROW
BREAK PRAISE ITALY BREAK
END
SECRET
```

MOST SECRET - ULTRA

Pike continued, "We confirmed Iachino's flagship was the battleship *Vittorio Veneto*, a formidable warship, under the command of an able seaman. The Sunderland located the Italian force and in turn was detected. The Intelligence Branch had done its part. The rest was up to ABC."

"ABC?" asked War Minister David Margesson.

"Admiral Cunningham's initials and nickname," answered Admiral Pound. Margesson nodded his acknowledgment. "Cunningham brought a superior force to the fight, including three battleships and a fresh aircraft carrier – *Formidable* replaced the damaged *Illustrious*. He had one other significant advantage – radar, as the Americans call it. Two of the three battleships and the aircraft carrier were equipped with search and gun-laying radar units. With his flag aboard *Warsprite*, Admiral Cunningham expertly maneuvered his force to maximum advantage. At 06:00 hours, Friday, a division of light cruisers led by Vice Admiral Pridham-Wippell made contact with the main Italian force. A running gun battle ensued, the Italians gave chase, and the cruisers drew the Italians toward Admiral Cunningham's battleships. Radar made the vital difference, as Cunningham brought his main battery fire to bear with devastating results. The Italians must have realized the trap they had entered, turned hard and attempted to withdraw. The best we have determined so far, the Italians had been surprised by the appearance of three battleships against them and even more so by an aircraft carrier."

"Well done!" exclaimed the Prime Minister. "What was the tally?"

"We had four light cruisers slightly damaged and two torpedo aeroplanes were lost along with their crews."

"And, the Italians?"

"We do not as yet know precisely their losses," responded the First Sea Lord. "We know we sunk three heavy cruisers and two destroyers. We believe we seriously damaged the *Veneto* and one or two additional destroyers. Our sailors recovered over a thousand survivors, who are now prisoners of war. We estimate perhaps two thousand perished. We expect to transfer the survivors for interrogation by the Combined Services Detailed Interrogation Center. We may gain more intelligence. Admiral Pike's lads will participate and amplify any valuable information."

"Dear God . . . a rather lopsided victory. Pray tell us," said Winston, "did Admiral Cunningham press home his advantage?"

"His fleet certainly made a valiant effort. He used his carrier aircraft to maintain contact as well as slow down the fleeing Italians. In the chase, they came within range of enemy, land-based aircraft. They shot down several German bombers before they had to abandon the chase."

"Between Taranto and now Cape Matapan, we are not likely to see the Italian Navy any time soon," the Prime Minister observed.

Attlee added, "On behalf of the War Cabinet, please pass along our sincerest congratulations to Admirals Cunningham and Pridham-Wippell, and the fleet."

"And, from the Defense Committee," Churchill contributed. "I will send a personal note to Sir Andrew. I will also inform The King as soon as possible." The Prime Minister stood, leaning forward and placing his fists on the table.

"I must say, and emphasize to all, this victory at sea is yet another example of why we must so zealously guard the secrecy of ULTRA. Sir Andrew must also be complimented for his ingenuity in protecting the information he was given. We must not lose the advantage ULTRA gives us in the current war."

"Hear, hear," said Attlee and several others. Numerous attendees clapped in appreciation.

"Does Wavell and the Army of the Nile know of this victory?" asked Churchill.

"If he does not, he soon will," answered Margesson.

"Please ensure that he does. Now is the time to strike . . . when the enemy is stunned." Minister Margesson and General Dill both nodded their heads in agreement. "Are there any further matters to discuss this Sunday evening?" Churchill waited and heard no response. "Very well, gentlemen. We are adjourned. Have a good evening."

The Prime Minister went to his underground study to provide the appropriate directions to his duty private secretary and to dictate his congratulatory letter to Sir Andrew. He wanted an audience with The King tomorrow, but if he was unavailable Monday, he should be able to inform him at their weekly luncheon on Tuesday.

—

Cap Parlier

Author

—

Cap and his wife, Jeanne, live in Fountain Hills, Arizona, along with their precious dogs. Their four children have begun their families, raising seven exceptional grandchildren. He is a graduate of the U.S. Naval Academy, a retired Marine aviator, Vietnam veteran and experimental test pilot, and has finally retired from the corporate world to devote his time to his passion for writing a good story. Cap has numerous other projects completed and in the works including screenplays, historical novels and a couple of history books.

—

Interested readers may wish to visit his website at http://www.Parlier.com for his essays and other items, or subscribe to his weekly Blog: "Update from the Sunland." Cap can be reached at: Cap@SaintGaudensPress.com

—

Printed in the United States of America

CPSIA information can be obtained
at www.ICGtesting.com
Printed in the USA
FSHW022109291218
54489FS

9 780943 039459